Sign up for our newsletter to hear
about new and upcoming releases.

www.ylva-publishing.com

Other Books by Lee Winter

On The Record Series
The Red Files

Standalone
The Brutal Truth
Shattered
Requiem for Immortals

Under Your Skin

Lee Winter

Dedication

For the woman I have loved for two decades. You may not like ice queens, but I appreciate how much time and effort you put into my books anyway, to make them the best they can be. No greater love...

Acknowledgments

This book could not be possible without my good mate and beta reader Lisa. She was my Iowan insider who showered me with her own videos of the State Fair, fried monstrosities on sticks, the jacked-up, sleek Chevy the brothers drive, gorgeous willow trees, and butter cows. All so I could experience exactly what Ayers would on her trip to Lauren's home state.

Aside from making Iowa burst into life for me, I'm also grateful for Lisa's endless patience at all my Iowa questions.

My other longstanding beta, Charlotte, earns my eternal thanks, especially for (sweetly) holding my feet to the fire until I got a particular scene right…at a certain bed and breakfast.

Thanks go to my softball-loving guru Amy, for explaining the thrill of being in a pickle when facing a rundown, plus other quirky rules I never knew existed.

To my editors at Ylva and beyond, I offer massive dollops of gratitude for making me look good.

Lastly, there's my friend, occasional editor, boss, and publisher, Astrid. I love how much she adores Ayers. Her enthusiasm helped me through my I-Hate-Every-Word days. Thanks for the ongoing encouragement and support.

Chapter 1
The Idiot from Iowa

SENATOR FREDERICK T. HICKORY WAS practically dead—not that he seemed to know it.

His brown suit had all the fashion savvy of a corpse, and his craggy sixty-three-year-old face indicated early-onset rigor mortis. But it was more than that.

Catherine Ayers had been reading the man's autobiography of late. Never had a shallower book crossed her news desk. Somewhere between asides on fly fishing, pie baking, and cow tipping lay an ambitious politician desperate to be taken seriously but who didn't have a clue how.

She gazed at the senator from Iowa, who was holding forth with a monotonous nasal drone.

This was *not* how.

Catherine glanced around at her media colleagues squinting under the sun's midday glare lancing off the water pool at the Memorial for American Veterans Disabled for Life.

A pair of veterans in wheelchairs bookended the senator at the lectern. The one on the right had nodded off ten minutes ago. The one on the left looked envious.

She could relate.

Most of the gathered journalists appeared semi-comatose. They hadn't so much as twitched for five minutes.

"Christ, Ayers," muttered Pete, beside her, as he adjusted his TV camera. "Can you do something to resurrect this boring clusterfuck? I don't often beg, but hell, if anyone can put a rocket up ole Hicks, it's you."

"Pete, here's a shocking thought—why don't you get your own reporter to ask a relevant question? Or any question?"

Both their gazes travelled to a young, lantern-jawed blond man with a smart suit and vacant expression. He was fiddling with his hair—and had been for some time.

The cameraman gave Catherine a pained look.

"I see." Catherine sighed. "Would it be too much to expect the rest of DC's media to actually do their jobs?"

"But that's what our Caustic Queen's for." He grinned at her, apparently sensing victory. "If you're going to slum it with us lowly media rabble today, you gotta expect we'll call you in as the big guns."

She rolled her eyes, already regretting her interest in a story outside her usual White House beat. Curse her curiosity over the bizarre topic, and the fact she'd been stuck for a column idea all week. Catherine took a few steps closer to the front, drawing the eye of the senator.

Hickory blanched in recognition. Not surprising, really, since she'd already obliterated his career once, years ago. Back then he'd come up with the *genius* suggestion of using "quantitative easing" to solve his state's budgetary woes.

When she'd asked him, in a live press conference, why he thought Iowa somehow had the power to simply print more federal money, Hickory's gaping, shocked moment of realization about what his bold idea actually meant had become a viral sensation. The only surprise was that he'd bounced back at all after that humiliation.

But here he was, once again attempting political relevance and promoting the stupidest idea she'd ever heard in her life. And that was saying something.

At least he was consistent.

She cleared her throat and about a dozen half-lidded eyes popped wide open and looked suddenly interested. The reporters around Catherine all shifted slightly away from her, as though afraid any impending fallout from her questions might spatter in their direction. Even so, their tape recorders and microphones swayed toward her, like spokes on a wheel.

Figures. *Now* they were awake.

"Senator Hickory, Catherine Ayers, from the *LA Daily Sentinel.*"

Despite the six lanes of traffic crawling along Washington Avenue beside them, it suddenly seemed silent as a church.

"Yes, the *Sentinel*'s infamous DC bureau chief. Should I be honored you've deemed my little press conference worthy?"

His snark needed work.

"Senator, as I understand it, your idea for solving the veterans' health-care claim backlog is to implant each person with a data chip in the left hand, between their thumb and index finger—"

"It's so small! The size of a grain of rice—"

"—so, when they seek assistance, they have to wave their hand across a scanner for their medical data to appear on screen."

"It's entirely voluntary," he said, nodding furiously, "not to mention fast, and it will streamline a complicated process. Even the worst bureaucrat or computer system can't lose a veteran's files or confuse them with someone else's. MediCache is revolutionary. Vets are lining up to volunteer for the trial."

"No doubt because the people who sign on get fast-tracked for treatment over the rest. Are you really suggesting that because our government's systems are so awful, we should outsource medical records to a patient's *own anatomy*?"

"Lost medical histories could cost lives. And if this fixes it, why not?"

"What about privacy laws?" Catherine countered. "And how the current technology is so unsecured that any veteran walking past any radio frequency ID scanner would have their medical results pop up instantly?"

The reporters tittered.

There was an indignant sound from Hickory. "Did you forget the part about it being *voluntary*, Ms. Ayers? Want me to look that up in a dictionary for you?"

Catherine's smile turned dangerous. "I really don't think you, of all people, should be lecturing me on misunderstood definitions. Do you?"

At his momentary silence, satisfaction flooded through her.

The surrounding snickers made the redness rise up his neck. Hickory's jaw worked. He turned to the rest of the gathering. "Are there any other questions?" His tone was faintly desperate now.

"I have just one more," Catherine said.

"*Anyone?*" His gaze roamed the crowd.

Catherine glimpsed a familiar profile out of the corner of her eye. Her heart did its usual pleased flip at the sight of her fiancée. She kept her professional mask firmly affixed and tried not to react when Lauren quietly stepped up beside her.

The senator sagged at the absence of other questions. "Well, if that's all," he said, shuffling his papers and turning to leave.

"One more," Catherine tried again. "If this is such a brilliant idea, Senator, when are you getting your own data chip embedded? For solidarity with the vets?"

The group burst into laughter.

The slumbering vet suddenly jerked awake. "The hell?" he grumbled.

"It'd make a great photo op, too," Catherine continued, her tone droll. "Just name the day and time. You'd have plenty of volunteers to capture the moment." She gestured to the other reporters who called out a few cheers of approval and suggestions.

"We can do it right now!"

"Say yes, Senator!"

"You'll make history."

"Even better! You'll lead the news!"

Hickory coughed sharply, remembered an important engagement, and declared the press conference over. He strode off.

Pete wheezed with laughter. "Thanks, Ayers, that was perfect." He flicked off his camera. "Christ, you're always good for a bloodless evisceration. Did you see that choking expression he made? My boss will love you. Thanks again." He gave an admiring mock-salute and started packing up.

Catherine turned to Lauren. "Hello. You're a welcome sight after the world's most idiotic press conference. Are you just passing by?"

"Nope, I saw your calendar at breakfast and knew you'd be here, so I wondered if you've got time for lunch?"

"Sure." Catherine glanced around. "Where?"

"Not far. Walk with me. I have a surprise."

As they walked, Catherine shot an appreciative gaze over Lauren's rear-hugging khaki pants, pale blue button-up shirt, and smart brown boots. The sight of her in any outfit, though, never failed to improve her mood. Such a shame Lauren's newspaper had moved ten blocks from Catherine's office building. Their lunches together had been sporadic ever since.

"Did you have fun demanding my state's senator get microchipped like a stray puppy?" Lauren gave Catherine's sleeve a teasing flick.

"Probably," Catherine admitted with a smile. "But he has a knack for endorsing atrocious ideas."

Lauren nodded and then beamed at her.

"All right, spill. What has you in such a good mood?"

"You'll see." Lauren grinned even wider.

They crossed Washington Avenue and made their way into a small, immaculate triangle of garden.

"Bartholdi Park?" Catherine examined the sign. "There aren't any food outlets here."

"Nope. Not yet."

"I don't follow."

"Patience." Lauren led them to one of several heavy wooden tables dotted around a paved area that surrounded an enormous, ornate fountain.

They settled into the chairs, and Catherine's gaze scanned the area with interest. The centerpiece featured lamps, cherubs, turtles, fish, and... "Nymphs?" Catherine's eyebrows rose. "While I appreciate the admiration of statuesque women, can't we just find a nice corner table at Mastro's?"

"You missed the frogs." Lauren pointed them out. "And it'll be here soon."

"What will?"

Lauren gave her a small smile and then turned to watch the park's entrance. "Wait and see."

A few minutes later, a low whirring noise reached her ears. A small, six-wheeled white robot appeared and rolled along the path. A long rubbery antenna was at the back of the unit, with a round camera on top, like the pouf on a poodle's tail.

Catherine stared at it as it trundled around the far side of the fountain and then made a beeline for them. "What...?"

Lauren grinned as it stopped five feet away. "Not bad. Pretty accurate. I supplied the Google Maps coordinates of where we'd be." She walked over and lifted the curved lid on top, tapped a code, and then flipped up a smaller inner lid. "Our lunch is served."

"What *is* that thing?"

Lauren lifted some Italian-smelling dishes to the table. "This is an autonomous delivery unit. Cutting-edge, temperature-controlled, cheaper than hiring a driver, and it can shoot all around the streets delivering takeout. Customers just stand outside their home or office to wait for it when it's due to arrive. The owner ordered a pair of them from Estonia. This is their first day in service for Antonio's Pizzeria. It's part of a story I'm working on."

There was a rustle of plastic as Lauren tugged more bags out of the machine and sorted through their lunch. The moment she slapped both of the robot's lids closed, the machine beeped, made a tight about-face, and whirred out of the area.

The feast involved several pasta dishes and one small pizza box. Delicious scents of garlic and tomato filled the air.

"So, a new delivery robot is your story?" Catherine asked in surprise. "Doesn't sound like something for the *Washington Post*'s metro desk. Nothing crime-related about robo-takeout."

"Ordinarily true." Lauren handed her some plastic utensils. "Here's what I know: Both robots each have a camera onboard which snaps 360-degree images of their journey and beams the photos back to the restaurant in real time. So, if anyone interferes with them, the owner, Antonio, knows pretty much immediately the where and the who."

"Ah." Catherine snared a foil container and peeled back its cardboard lid. Tomato penne with mozzarella. *Promising.* She eyed her fiancée. "Now, why do I think this is about to end badly? Since you're on the case and all."

"Nothing escapes you." Lauren's eyes twinkled. "And yes, despite all Antonio's security efforts, one of his two robots was stolen. Simply disappeared. The thief might be any of the witnesses it filmed just before that. Which is where I come in. I'm on the case of the missing pizzeria bot."

"How exciting," Catherine drawled.

"Not exciting, but surprisingly funny." She pulled out her phone and scrolled. "And here's why. These are all the screen snaps from the footage sent back to the restaurant just before the robot vanished." She laid her phone on the table.

Catherine swiped through the photos between bites, watching as image after image of curious people stopped, stared, waved, did bunny ears, and even mooned the passing robot's camera. "I see it attracts a high class of tourists."

"Yup. But this lady's my favorite." Lauren scrolled to a picture of a forty-something woman in a bright orange top peering into the camera as if it were a creature from outer space. In six of the photos, her long, painted-green fingernail was tapping the camera as though convinced it might start talking back.

"I take it she never did figure out what she was poking?" Catherine asked.

"Doubt it. But her *what-is-this-demon?* expression is an Internet meme just waiting to happen."

"I suppose so."

"Oh yep, she's about to be famous. See, Antonio says he's already sent all these pics to the cops for them to follow up, so I get to keep these copies and run any I want with my story."

"Well that's nice." Catherine paused. "But so far I'm seeing not much more than click bait. Where's the story?"

"The story is what happened to New York's first automated food-delivery unit. The mystery. The theft."

"Are you sure? Isn't it the implications of a less personalized society? What if everyone uses robots and drones for everything? What's next? What will we become in even five years?"

"Catherine, my paper doesn't want me to write intellectual commentaries on society. They want me to do light, fun, factual, and engaging. I'm expected to stick to the basics of my beat and not drill too deep unless I somehow unearth a major scandal. But *this* is my job." She tapped her phone screen. "They'd laugh me out of the bullpen if I turned in an analytical think piece on society's woes based on a stolen food robot. My job is chasing..." She waved at the photos.

"People doing bunny ears," Catherine finished.

Lauren nodded. "Yeah. And it's not *that* tragic. We're not all at the top of the mountain like you are. We don't all cover the White House and get to write deep philosophical columns every week."

"True." Catherine dabbed her lips with a paper napkin she'd found in the food bag. "Sorry. I don't mean to judge. I'm just used to looking for the layers in stories. It doesn't help that the senator from Iowa is ruining my famously friendly disposition with this absurd campaign to shove tech into people's bodies."

"Well, hopefully, lunch is helping your mood."

"It's pretty good. Thank you."

"High praise." Lauren grinned. She pulled a small pizza box toward herself and thunked her feet up on a low wall beside them. "By the way, the pizza's totally lousy, so I won't foist it on you," she joked. "But I better have another piece, to be sure."

Catherine eyed the elevated boots. "Ground…now. Or I call security about a wild animal loose in the gardens."

Lauren's boots plopped to the ground. "You don't mind me being a wild animal sometimes. Last night ring a bell?"

Catherine packed the empty containers into one of the bags as she smirked. "That's different. Liberties are allowed in certain situations."

"Like when we're naked in bed?" Lauren's lips curled.

A flash of desire shot through Catherine. Her skin still felt heated from the memory of the many and varied places those taunting lips had been last night. She refused to blush. Clearing her throat, she quickly cast around for something else to discuss. "Are you feeling any better?"

"About?"

"Our trip to Iowa next week? To plan a certain wedding?"

"Oh. That." Lauren hesitated and shot her a bright smile. "So, we're getting married in three months. And I'm taking you home next week to meet the family. No big deal." Her laugh was weak. Her gaze shifted away from Catherine.

"And yet you change the subject whenever I so much as mention the weather in Cedar Rapids."

"Oh," Lauren said again. "Actually, I think maybe work's been on my mind. Distracting me."

"Why? You can write lost robot stories in your sleep."

"Well, yeah. It's not that. Sometimes my boss looks at me like he can't believe I'm the same reporter who helped get a world-famous scoop. The thing is, I only pulled off the first big story with you. But he hired *me*, not both of us. Besides, as long as I'm assigned to write metro briefs and puff pieces, where's my opportunity for pulling another rabbit out of the hat anyway?"

Catherine stopped. "You really think I'm the only reason we got the SmartPay story? We each independently worked out something odd was going on at their business launch."

"Yes, but we worked out what it all meant together. I haven't had any major scoops since, and I'm wondering if I've already had my biggest story. Like, is this as good as it gets for me? What if it's all downhill from here? So maybe that's why I'm a little checked out."

Catherine bit back her smile. "You're not even thirty-five, and think you've peaked?"

Lauren gave a miserable shrug.

"Mm. Well, all right, let's review: Together we won a national award for our exclusive. And then I oh-so cleverly lost my head and outed us to the world in my thank-you speech last year. Then, mystifyingly, given how much I loathe virtually everyone in DC, I invited the whole room to attend our wedding. In Iowa."

Lauren exhaled. "Yeah." She bit her lip. "That was unexpected. Especially for President Taylor."

"You know, he did tell me later he was sorely tempted to say yes just to annoy his party's conservatives." Catherine still appreciated the devilish look he'd had in his eyes.

Lauren stared mournfully at her pizza. "Please just tell me the White House press corps isn't going to invade our wedding? You know what reporters are like with the offer of free food and booze."

"Is that's what's been stressing you? Lauren, our nation's finest media would sooner drink bleach than voluntarily go to the Midwest."

"Now you're just trying to make me feel better." Lauren's attempt at humor morphed into a wan smile. "Hey? I'm sorry my fears are leaking all over you."

"As is your pizza."

The slice Lauren had set aside was starting to droop off the table. Her arm flashed out and she plucked it from thin air as it began to fall.

"Trust your softballer's reflexes to kick in to save a pizza."

"No better cause," Lauren said earnestly.

9

Catherine laughed. "Now, although I'd love to admire your athletic skills some more, I have to turn Senator Hickory's weird addiction for terrible ideas into a news column."

"No probs." Lauren began packing up their leftovers.

"And I somehow have to do it without resorting to citing *Brave New World* about the destruction of humanity as we know it. For some reason my editor doesn't appreciate my end-is-nigh societal autopsies nearly as much as I do. He thinks it's a downer."

"Shocker. I'm with Neil."

Catherine huffed out a breath. "Even so, it's important. This is an invasion of our bodily integrity. I don't understand why everyone's asleep on the implications." She paused. "What will you do with the rest of your day?"

"I'm backgrounding food-delivery robots around the world for a sidebar. You should see the freaky-cool shit Japan does."

"*Fascinating.*"

"Well, smarty-Ayers, it *will* be to my readers. Never underestimate people's interest in new ways to get food."

"I suppose there is that. And on that note, I definitely appreciated my food delivery today."

"Good." Lauren leaned forward to give her a quick kiss. "See you at home tonight. Oh, and the best part is, I'm cooking." She waggled the bag of leftovers. "And by cooking, I mean reheating." She offered Catherine a stunning smile, then spun on her heel and walked away.

Catherine inhaled deeply. She still wasn't used to the sight of all that love directed at her. She let out the breath and marveled at how so much had changed for her in such little time.

With a final glance at Lauren, Catherine rose and turned in the opposite direction. She had to get back to her office. She still had a story to write about the idiot from Iowa. And he most definitely wouldn't like it.

Chapter 2
Evil Twins

TWO DAYS LATER, LAUREN PUT down the phone and dropped her pen to her notepad. She glanced at her work calendar. Damn. Still Thursday. Only one more day and they were officially on vacation. A week and a bit in Iowa. Lauren exhaled. Her usual insecurities floated up and marched a circuit around her brain.

Dying for a distraction, she peered at the surly bear of a man working at the desk facing her. Bob Grimes was stuffed into an old brown suit and typing up his usual two-fingered storm. She could see only his forehead and furry eyebrows above the frosted-glass divider.

"Has it happened?" she asked. "Has the judgment been handed down in the Charlton case?"

He didn't answer immediately, so she glanced up to one of the twenty-one monitors that encircled the walls above the news hub inside One Franklin Square's east tower. She paused when she spotted her story on the food-robot abduction. It was still trending strongly, according to the live analytics.

She got a pleased jolt every time she saw it doing well. Even so, Lauren was pretty sure that the hilarious photos of all the curious onlookers had a lot more to do with the story's viral success than her reporting. Especially Orange Shirt Lady, as she'd come to think of the most hilarious witness.

Her smile faded. Catherine wasn't entirely wrong. This was barely news. Not exactly the White House beat she'd always dreamed of doing.

Bob Grimes grunted a belated affirmation to her question.

Lauren looked at him. He wasn't the most talkative colleague, although he wasn't that much worse than the others.

The truth Catherine didn't know was that her outing of them had cost Lauren a lot of respect. Catherine had been so delighted that she'd overcome her fear of revealing their relationship that Lauren didn't have the heart to reveal the downside.

Lauren had returned to work after the awards night to a much chillier newsroom. Not because her colleagues were homophobic—far from it— but they'd looked at Lauren with fresh eyes. And they'd seen someone with a limited news background, whose most immediate reporting beat had been the LA party circuit. Put alongside Catherine's exhaustive, in-depth CV that stretched back two decades, despite a brief fall from grace, they'd reached a certain conclusion. They clearly assumed Catherine had given Lauren credit on their scoop because she was sleeping with her.

One photographer had even elbowed her the day after her national outing, winked, and said, "It's not what you know, but who, am I right?"

The fact Lauren hadn't been pulling out huge scoops since starting at *The Washington Post* just convinced colleagues like Grimes that their assumptions were right. She glanced back to the analytics monitor. Stories about stolen food robots, no matter how viral or funny, wouldn't change their view, either. Lauren still had to prove herself.

A familiar despondency settled over her. It had been building for a while. It wasn't just work. Not just next week's Iowa trip, either. It was everything.

She chewed her lip and thought back to the call she'd just finished to select an Iowan wedding planner. Time would be tight. They only had ten days in Iowa to book the venue, catering, and order outfits, so it made sense to use a professional. Even just choosing a planner, though, made it all feel so immediate.

Her work phone jangled, and she recognized the internal number.

"King."

"Front desk security here. I have a Fiona Fisher demanding to speak to you. She appears...agitated."

"Oh?"

"Something about a story you wrote?"

Lauren grimaced. "I'll be right down."

She hung up, grabbed her notebook, and headed down to the foyer. She passed through the low glass security barriers and looked around. A large, dark-skinned woman was pacing the front area. She was in her forties, with piercing brown eyes, and seemed sort of familiar.

Oh. Orange Shirt Lady.

The security guard cleared his throat and pointed the woman in Lauren's direction.

The stranger turned her head sharply, meeting Lauren's eye with a furious expression.

Uh-oh.

"You King? Lauren King?"

"Yes." Lauren pointed her over to a seat.

"Fiona Fisher. You put me in the paper." Her lips turned into a snarl as she dropped into the seat.

"The missing-food-delivery robot story." Lauren nodded, sitting beside her. "You were one of the witnesses who interacted with it as it passed."

"Witness, my ass. I just stuck my face in for a look, and next thing I know you run my picture with your story. People think I stole that damn thing."

Lauren frowned. She'd made sure she hadn't worded it that way. So had the *Post*'s lawyers. "Sorry," she said, "but I didn't say that. I mentioned how dozens of people stopped and engaged it in funny ways before it disappeared. We ran photos of ten people, not just you. And in none of them did we say the people had anything to do with stealing it."

"Bull. Lady, you out and out called me a thief."

"No, ma'am, I'm sorry you see it that way, but I really didn't."

"Then how do you explain this?" Fiona pulled out a cell phone and scrolled to an app button that had the initials "MET" over a picture of a balaclava. "My daughter's friends were playing with this stupid thing at school. It's called My Evil Twin.

"Okay." Lauren hadn't heard of it. "What's it do?"

"You give it a photo of a person and it matches it with a criminal—the criminal who looks most like you. Now look right here who my Sadie's picture was matched with." Fiona spun the phone around with a soft growl.

Lauren examined it. A teenage girl's photo was next to one of Fiona. Except the photo of Fiona had prison bars running down the picture,

"Evil Twin" stamped on her forehead, and the words: "Suspected Thief" underneath. She frowned. "But what's that got to do with…" Lauren suddenly noticed the orange top in the photo. It was the photo taken by the robot's camera. The same photo her paper had run.

"See? Now tell me, why are you giving my photo to those app people to tell lies about me? I'm no evil criminal. Worst I ever had was a parking ticket. My girl's a laughing stock and so am I."

Lauren shook her head. "I'm really sorry this has happened, Ms. Fisher, but it has nothing to do with me or my paper. Now, Antonio's Pizzeria gave a copy of those photos to police. And, I mean, it's just a guess, but it looks to me like the police have uploaded the witness photos into their database, probably looking for a match with a criminal, and somehow that Evil Twin app has found your photo from that."

Fiona Fisher blinked at her and then rose to her full height, towering over Lauren.

"That sounds like ass-covering bull to me. How could some stupid free app like this be able to get into a police database?"

Now *that* was a really good question. Lauren thought hard. "I really don't know. Look, I think you're right; it's something to investigate. I will do my best to get to the bottom of this. Can you leave me your contact details?" She held out her notepad and a pen. "I'll let you know what I find, okay?"

"This better not be some brush-off. 'Cause I'm mad enough to sue someone." She reached for the pen and notepad and began to scribble. "Sue someone real hard."

"I can understand why. I'd be mad as hell, too."

The woman shoved the notepad back at Lauren, turned, and stomped out of the foyer, muttering under her breath, "This ain't damned right."

No. It really wasn't.

Lauren felt a familiar sensation creep along her skin. It was similar to how she'd felt at a business launch party two years ago when something seemed very wrong indeed. Curiosity mingled with excitement. If her hunch had been right once…

Returning to the seventh floor, Lauren sat at her desk and typed *My Evil Twin* into her search engine. *Ouch.* 527,000 results.

"Okay." Lauren hitched up her sleeves, rolled her shoulders, and got to work.

She started with her half a dozen contacts at the Metropolitan Police Department. They seemed mystified, and each confirmed no one had been supplying photos to anyone beyond their own police databases. No security incursions, either. No hack attempts. She knew these officers well. They were straight shooters, and she believed them.

She phoned Antonio, who denied passing his photos to anyone but her and the police. Then he cheerfully offered her a lifetime pizza discount if she found his robot-napper.

Next, she did a series of corporate searches. Far from being shady, My Evil Twin belonged to a regular brick-and-mortar DC company, Lesser Security. It offered a suite of respectable protection and security software programs and hardly seemed the sort of business to offer such a lowbrow app at all.

She downloaded My Evil Twin onto her phone and emailed the ten photos from the robot-napping story to her device. It was the easiest way she could think of to find if they were all in the app's criminal database or just Fiona. She presumed the program would just match each person to themselves.

One by one, she loaded up each of the witnesses' faces. One by one, they were paired with other "evil" people, but not themselves.

Lastly, she put Fiona's photo in. Sure enough, she was matched with her own picture. Lauren studied the image of Fiona behind cartoon jail bars and *Suspected Thief* stamped underneath it. What was it about Fiona that made her different from the others caught on camera? All ten witnessed the same thing that day. All ten had had their photos given to police by Antonio. But only Fiona was now in My Evil Twin.

Two hours later, Lauren decided to simply ask Lesser Security. The company CEO insisted on handling her call himself for some reason. He agreed immediately to an interview but insisted it happen face to face. How unusual.

She stared at the company website on her phone as she waited in the foyer to be admitted up to his office. The business's other apps were mostly run-of-the-mill, such as My Security Hours, a staff-management tracker for security companies. Another one, My Suspect Customer, tracked "problem" customers in real-time and flagged them to a mall or store owner's on-site security guards to keep an eye on. She wondered how the app decided who was a problem or not.

She added it to the growing list of questions for the founder and CEO of Lesser Security.

Douglas Lesser was thin, tall, and pale, with a smile that was only just on the polite side of condescending. He was not the sort of man you'd expect to be running security apps at all, Lauren decided as she eyed him over his enormous power desk.

She'd been surprised to find his office, in a prime real estate location, was lavishly furnished in dark woods. Was security really *this* profitable?

Lauren showed him Fiona Fisher's photo on her phone. "So, as I explained during our call, I was wondering how this woman ended up in your My Evil Twin database? She has no criminal past. Police tell me they have no particular reason to suspect that she's the one who stole the food-delivery robot this photo was taken from."

"I'm sorry," Lesser said. "I can't discuss proprietary information."

Lauren gritted her teeth. He'd made her come out to visit him for a *no comment*? "Your app is free. You're not exactly going to be losing money if you tell me."

"Retaining confidentiality gives us our competitive edge."

"What competitive edge? There are no other criminal-matching apps out there."

Another almost-mocking smile was his answer.

"Okay, well, can you at least tell me if the database info comes from DC's Metropolitan Police Department?"

"It doesn't."

Lauren shifted in her chair. "If it's not sourced from the local police, and only they and I have a copy, how do you explain this?" She waved at Fiona's photo.

"All my data is obtained legally, Ms. King. That's all you need to know."

"Fiona could sue you. You've plastered her face as a suspect all over America's most-downloaded app."

"Who, *her*?" He peered at the photo, studying Fiona's bright outfit in detail. "She won't."

"You sound so sure."

"I am sure." He leaned back, putting his hands behind his head. "She's wearing a ten-dollar Walmart top and three-dollar plastic earrings. She'd hardly be a compelling witness, either."

"How can you say that?"

"She's too stupid. It's clear from the photo she can't even work out what an autonomous delivery unit is."

"Come on, these robots are brand new. Not something you see every day. That actually makes her intellectually curious, not stupid."

He laughed. "I know people. I study people. She won't sue. Next question."

So smug. She looked about his office, thinking hard. "Why are there so many number twelves in here?"

For the first time, he seemed surprised. "No one usually notices. Twelve's my favorite number. By the way, you seem familiar and I'm good with faces. Hell, look at my apps. They're all about faces, aren't they?"

It was creepy when he said it like that. She shifted in her seat. "Why are you based in DC and not, say, Silicon Valley?"

"This is where the real power is. No, really, how do I know you?" He squinted at her.

Lauren ignored the question, well aware she'd never seen him before in her life. "What's the deal with My Suspect Customer? How does it work out who's a threat or not?"

"All customers are possible threats. Doesn't matter how innocent they appear." He leaned forward and put his palms on the desk. "But I wrote an amazing algorithm that takes into account many factors. Those factors are proprietary information, too."

"An algorithm." She gave a disbelieving laugh. "So, it just…guesses."

"Educated guesses."

"I'm sure the lucky customers getting side-eyed by security guards love that. 'Don't be offended, ma'am, I'm watching you because of the algorithm.'"

He shrugged, but it was too practiced to be casual. "Simply put, my software isn't designed with human sensitivities. If there's a potential problem, it highlights it, no matter how unpalatable that truth may be for some. That's it. Tell me, Ms. King, are my clever little algorithms what really interest you?"

She glanced around his office to avoid his intense gaze. On the walls were photos of him with various politicians—none at the top of the food chain—a framed photo of a bulldog, and a few odd symbols on paperwork on his desk that seemed meaningless.

"I take it by your silence that you've run out of questions?" Lesser's voice contained just the barest politeness. "Was there anything else?"

Lauren shook her head and stood. "Thanks for your time, Mr. Lesser." She held out her hand. When she met his eye again, there was a shift in his expression. It now contained recognition.

His eyes gleamed, hands unmoving. "Enjoy Iowa."

She froze. "Why do you say that?"

"This is DC, Ms. King." Lesser stretched back in his chair. "I told you: I'm good with faces."

He laughed as she strode quickly out of his office. She could still see his smirk the whole time she hailed a cab and raced back to her office.

Lauren's work phone rang just as she was settling into her chair, her nerves thoroughly jangled.

"*Washington Post* Metro desk, Lauren King speaking."

"Mmm, I do so love your professional voice. It's why I call your work phone so often."

A warmth filled her. "Catherine," she breathed.

"How did it go?"

Lauren blinked in confusion. *How did what go?*

"Is Mrs. Potts officially our wedding planner?" Catherine continued when Lauren didn't reply. "Or will we have to employ the spirited and opinionated services of your Meemaw?"

Wincing at that frightening mental picture, Lauren said, "Mrs. Potts says she can do it. She'll come by Dad's place on Monday at nine."

"First thing? Good."

"Mm." Lauren fiddled with her cell phone and stared at the picture of Fiona again. She puzzled at the mystery before her.

"What are you up to? You sound distracted."

"I just had the weirdest meeting with an app company's CEO. He was creepy as hell. As I was leaving, he called out 'Enjoy Iowa.' I hadn't even mentioned Iowa."

Catherine went silent. Then her words were small. "I'm sorry."

"For what?"

"My spontaneous outing of us. I should have thought it through better. By inviting everyone to Iowa for it, I informed the whole world where you were from. I took away your privacy. And then the video of my proposal went viral, so now complete strangers recognize us." Catherine's disapproving tut would have been funny if Lauren wasn't so disconcerted.

"Yes, but he said 'Enjoy Iowa' like he knew I was going back there next week."

"He was just fishing, Lauren. Trying to get a reaction. Chances are you'd have to return home sooner or later, given our wedding's there in three months. Besides, everyone knows everyone's business in DC."

"I guess so." Her tension eased a little. "That's true. You'd think they'd have something better to talk about than us."

"Oh, they talk about that, too. Look, try and relax. You'll have forgotten him by tomorrow."

"Probably. He was just so annoying."

"Sounds like it. Meanwhile, I've been researching Iowa. It's frankly alarming the things I'm turning up."

"Is this about Hickory? God, what's he up to now?"

"No, it's about me. I thought I should have at least some idea of local culture before I landed in it. Did you know there's this thing called a Combine Demolition Derby?" Catherine's voice rose to incredulous. "Combine harvesters collide into each other for fun. What will they think of next?"

"You're adorable."

"Mmph. *Lies.*"

Lauren laughed and glanced at the time. "Hey, I gotta go. I have the crime briefs to file now."

"Until tonight, then," Catherine said. "I'll present you with the rest of my disturbing findings then."

"Can't wait."

Chapter 3
Baggage Handling

THE NEXT EVENING, CATHERINE LOWERED her book as the front door to her DC apartment unlocked. It closed again with a loud snap. A backpack-sized clunk sounded on the floor. Then came two smaller, matching, boot-weighted thuds. She glanced at the clock. Almost ten.

A blur of girlfriend flew past in a sea of brown hair, shedding shirt, and flushed skin.

She cocked an eyebrow. *Well*. This was getting interesting.

"Oh, hey!" Lauren hopped back into view with one leg out of her jeans.

Catherine regarded her in amusement. "Hello."

Lauren toppled back toward the bathroom. There came a bang, an "oops," and one final thud.

Catherine didn't ask. Shower time for Lauren could be a loud and uncoordinated affair when she was home this late and this exhausted.

She contemplated returning to her book, but Senator Hickory's butter-dish-shallow worldviews were not holding her attention.

A head reappeared around the corner. "How late am I?" Lauren asked, yanking her hair from its ponytail. "Did I miss dinner?" Her look of hopefulness warred with her tone of sorrow that she'd maybe missed out.

"That depends on your definition of 'missed.'" Catherine slid a bookmark in between the pages and placed it on her bedside stand. "I left you some. It's in the oven."

"Ooh!" Lauren beamed. "Thanks. I'd kiss you, but I still smell of that factory fire today. My hair reeks of smoke and something weird. I think my notebook may have to be put into one of those bunkers for nuclear waste."

"Well, by all means," Catherine said with a wave, "get decontaminated. Try not to leave a glowing towel."

Lauren laughed and disappeared. There was another familiar crash as Lauren skidded into the bathroom cabinet, courtesy of socked feet on shiny tiles. The teeth-rattling noise was accompanied by a pitiful "Crap! Sorry!"

Catherine picked up her book again. She glanced at the next page and dropped it with a sigh. Did Hickory really think people cared that his wife grew the neighborhood's best pickles? Catherine was still having a hard time reconciling that the senator waxing lyrical about vegetables was also spearheading revolutionary new technology. It was like two different people.

She was tempted to ask him about it, but her column on his veterans' data chip program had already come out, and she was definitely on Hickory's black list. Again.

The hiss of the shower stopped.

Moments later, Lauren, in a white robe, stumbled into the bedroom, her hands furiously working a towel through her hair. She slung it over the back of a chair and flopped onto the bed with a hearty huff of air.

With a long look at Lauren's wild hair and exhausted blue eyes, Catherine reached across, combed a stray tendril from her eyes, and smiled. Even when Lauren was too tired to see straight, she looked adorable. Well, adorably rumpled. "A late one tonight. Feeling better now?"

"You know, I think I do. Got my second wind. Whatever you've done in the kitchen smells amazing."

"It's seared tuna with scallops cooked in a reduction of lime butter, bok choy, and yellow pepper, and a corn salad with turmeric dressing—plus basmati risotto, of course."

"Of course." Lauren gave a tired laugh.

"Just something I threw together. I put the fish and scallops on when you texted me that you were on your way. There's *nothing* worse than overdone fish."

"Nothing." Lauren broke into a smile. "My God, I live with someone who sears sesame tuna." She sat up, rummaging under her pillow, and dragged out a pair of pajama bottoms and a tank top. Flinging off her robe, she slid on her clothes and rolled over toward Catherine. She planted a kiss on her cheek. "You spoil me."

Catherine shrugged, but she was warmed by her lover's reaction. She'd always liked to cook as a solo pursuit, but when you had someone to cook for, it was surprisingly gratifying. Even eating her own portion alone at a more reasonable hour, all Catherine had thought of was what Lauren would think of it. Of course, the salad was something she assumed any Iowan girl would appreciate. It had corn in it, after all.

Lauren kissed Catherine again, on the lips this time, and whispered in her ear, "Love you."

It made Catherine's heart quicken. "Mm. That's possibly your stomach talking."

Crawling back to her feet, Lauren nodded. "Oh yep, that, too." She plodded toward the kitchen.

Catherine smiled, rose, and followed.

With a yawn, Lauren rummaged around for cutlery. Catherine took the warmed meal from the oven to the square wooden kitchen table. After pouring herself a wine, she joined Lauren at the table.

"Thank God we're on vacation next week," Lauren said, digging into the meal with enthusiasm. "I know, I know. We have to pack tonight and ask the neighbors to collect the mail and *blah blah blah*, but I can't wait to just finally *stop*. Relax. Unwind and suck in the fresh air back home." She paused and chewed more slowly. "God. This is fantastic. You should write down the recipe. Hell, sell it."

Pleased, Catherine sipped her wine and allowed the conversation to flow on to light topics as Lauren finished the rest of her food with a series of excited murmurs.

"So," Catherine finally said when Lauren pushed the plate away, "can we talk about why you're still changing the topic within a minute every time Iowa comes up?"

The haste with which Lauren swallowed down her wine was probably an insult to the vintage. She scooped up the empty glass and plate and headed for the sink. "I don't think I am. Hey, did I mention how much we have to do? The planning? The packing? I really hate the packing. I truly lack that gene."

The whoosh of water and clanking filled the air as she rinsed off her dishes in a whirlwind of elbows. Lauren finished up, offered a tight grin, and bolted from the kitchen.

Catherine watched her go with a small frown.

Lauren threw things into her bag in a frenzy, glad to have something to focus on. Well, something else. Underwear, socks, and jeans were pummeled into place. T-shirts were poked into corners as if with a jackhammer.

"What did that shirt ever do to you?" Catherine neatly prepped her own bag on the bed beside her.

Lauren glanced at it. Of course. It was like something from a magazine spread. *How to Pack—The Ultimate Traveler's Guide.*

"It existed," Lauren grunted. She hadn't properly slept in two days. And one thought kept niggling its way into her head and torturing her. What if they got there and everyone hated Catherine? Yes, Catherine could be pleasant when she wanted. But Lauren had never seen her be forgiving when she was pushed. Lauren knew that better than anyone. So, what if her family pushed a little, then Catherine pushed back, and her family told Lauren to take sides? If her dad took Lauren to one side and said...

"Choose."

Lauren's head whipped around. "Huh?"

Catherine jangled two different boots. One, a black pair of designer footwear that would look stylish anywhere but would last all of three seconds in a rural setting.

"The brown ones." Lauren pointed.

"But they look like I should be on a horse. Which is fair since I last wore them on one. When I was twenty."

"Which means they'll cope with a bit of wear and tear. We're not off to a fashion expo."

Catherine slid the brown boots into her bag. "All right, what's wrong?"

"Why are weddings such a big deal?" Lauren whined. "I thought Mrs. Potts was nuts when she said the earliest bookings left for most wedding venues were in November. And how can December and January be already gone? It's *Iowa.* How much demand can there be?"

"Iowans do get married in as vast numbers as anywhere else, I imagine."

23

"But she made such a big deal out of it. It's a wedding, not an inauguration." She glared at her T-shirts that were stubbornly refusing to stay tucked at the suitcase corners. "I'm not ready for this!" She rammed her T-shirts again.

"Not ready to get married?" Catherine asked quietly, turning to look at her.

"Not ready for Iowa," Lauren whispered. "Not ready to have everyone…"

"Have everyone what? Judge you? Lauren, you're a successful, award-winning journalist. You have nothing to be…"

"Not me." Her words were a bare whisper.

Catherine inhaled sharply. "Ah. You think they'll judge me?"

She looked away.

"Lauren, I know what my reputation is, but you know very well I can be nice when I want to be."

"Like that senator you dared to microchip himself?" Lauren's voice was tinged with skepticism.

"Well, to be fair, I didn't *want* to be nice to him."

Lauren appreciated the attempt at humor but couldn't find it funny right now. She rammed more things into her bag.

"I see. Is it the me being from Boston thing, the lesbian thing, or the White House media thing that you think might be a problem?"

"It's not really any one thing. I mean, you're just different from what they're used to. More…complicated."

Even as she thought about it, Catherine meeting her family filled Lauren with dread. She loved Catherine, for all her protective walls and acerbic tongue. She was beautiful, brilliant, and every kind of fascinating. The Kings were nothing like Catherine and had almost certainly never met anyone like her before, either.

"*Complicated.*" Catherine tasted the word. "You're worried I won't play well with your family? We've just been over this. I can do nice."

"What if they're being idiots to you? I have the worst nightmares about this…you all not getting on."

"You know what my job is. I am well used to dealing with big personalities." She gave her a reassuring smile. "But I get it. There's me with all my elite, liberal, media baggage. And there's you with your five mechanic brothers and father. Who you're terribly afraid will embarrass you

24

somehow. And who will judge me. And I them. And as a result, I'll possibly judge you."

Lauren froze. Sickness filled her. "Is that what you think will happen?"

"No. I think it's what you're afraid of, though, and it's what's keeping you up at night. Now that the meet-the-family date is upon us, you're suddenly panicking."

"I am not panicking. And if you knew my brothers, you would so, um, not-panic, too."

"Mm." Catherine looked amused. "That was convincing."

Lauren's lips twitched.

"But if it makes you feel better," Catherine continued, "*my* nightmares involve my sister, who thinks she's as liberal as the next woman…well, the next rich, elite, white Boston woman with dressage as a hobby. Phoebe believes, in her usual oblivious way, that she's as down to earth as anyone, but she's never even met anyone from the flyover states. Her clueless entitlement is a thing to behold and will in no way endear her to anyone in the Midwest."

Lauren swallowed. "Oh, crap."

"But in my waking hours I remember something I think you've forgotten. Your family and I have something in common: we both wish you to be happy." Her serious look turned teasing. "But me especially. So… come here." Catherine's voice dared her to obey.

After a small pause as Lauren debated whether to comply or not, she swayed toward her. There was something about that exact tone of voice that always did funny things to Lauren's insides.

Catherine gave Lauren a kiss so reassuring that she lost herself for a moment.

"Trust me, Lauren," she murmured, "it will be fine." Catherine leaned back. "So, is that everything you're worried about?"

Lauren offered a wan look. "I guess. I'm sorry. I'm losing my mind and driving us both crazy."

"Yes, you are," Catherine agreed. "Fortunately, I am somewhat fond of you."

Lauren shifted her ball of socks to a roomier corner in her suitcase. "So funny," she muttered. She had to stop pre-disastering their trip. Catherine would be nice. Her brothers would behave. Meemaw and Dad would like her. It'd be fine. "It's just a wedding-organizing trip, anyway."

25

"It's also so we'll get the family introductions out of the way now so that all we will be thinking about on our wedding day is each other."

"You are wise, Obi-Wan." Lauren glanced at Catherine's suitcase as her lover resumed packing. "Although I might revise my opinion if I see you in that in Iowa."

"Too much?"

"Overkill."

Catherine removed her designer mohair sweater from the suitcase.

"Pity," Lauren added. "I really like you in that. Always makes me want to stroke it."

"I know." Catherine suddenly sounded much huskier. "Why do you think I was packing it?"

"Oh no, none of that!" Lauren looked askance. "We are not getting up to any funny business while we're there. Not with Dad, Meemaw, and two of my brothers all just down the hall from the guest room."

Catherine gave her a skeptical look, and her eyes became half-lidded at the challenge.

"I know that look. I'm not changing my mind, either." Lauren shook a warning finger at her.

"Sure you are." Catherine's sexiest, ivory-colored satin briefs were pointedly tucked into her bag.

"I'm really not," Lauren whispered as the matching bra went in, too.

"Ten long days and you'll keep your hands off me the whole time?" Catherine's suggestive voice was doing thrilling things to the pit of Lauren's stomach. *"Really."*

"Y-yes. Really."

Catherine's throaty laugh at Lauren's fading willpower was the final straw.

She pounced. Catherine was flat on her back, pinned to their bed in seconds, two suitcases flying to the floor with a crash.

"That does mean I will need to store up a lot of memories to last me for the next ten days." Lauren gazed down at her, memorizing her face. Her excited fingers undid Catherine's shirt buttons and slid inside, dusting her bra. "So, get ready."

The bright smile on Catherine's face was far too knowing.

Until Lauren covered it with her lips.

Chapter 4
Brave New World

A BELLOWED "LAUREN!" REVERBERATED THROUGH the arrivals area as they plucked their bag off the conveyor belt. It sent a shiver down Catherine's spine.

"Matthew!" Lauren cried out.

Catherine turned and glanced up—and up. Matthew, she knew from Lauren's many stories, was Lauren's oldest brother at age twenty-nine. He wore a tattered red cap with a beer logo, and a broad grin that added to his handsome looks. The hulk of a man engulfed his sister in a hug that lifted her off the ground.

He turned to Catherine. "So, this is the one?" he asked Lauren, giving Catherine a wink.

"I am," Catherine replied with a small smile. She gave his tree-trunk-wide arms a nervous glance, well aware she was a lot less robust than her athletic girlfriend at withstanding stuffing-squeezings.

"Okay, then." He swept her up in a hug, too, but mercifully kept her feet on the ground. "Welcome to the land of the Kings, Cat. I'm Matthew."

She nodded, praying the circulation would return to her upper body. Anacondas probably had a less brutal PSI. "Good to meet you. And it's Catherine," she said, injecting a tight smile. She had promised to be nice, after all.

"Sure thing. Boys are waiting in the truck." His shaggy brown hair bounced vigorously before he turned to Lauren. "Tommy's a no-show 'cause he's met some hot new girl. Dad's still working', but he can't wait to see you. Meemaw's put on some lunch and says we can't hang around here or the pork tenderloin sandwiches'll get cold."

He smiled at Catherine. "You're in for a treat. Meemaw makes the best. Pork's crumbed, deep-fried, and it's big—like, gotta hang over the bun." He held his hands a foot apart. "She won prizes at the fair and all back in the day."

Catherine smiled hard until it hurt. "I can't wait."

Lauren, who had been subject multiple times to Catherine's views on an oil-dipped lunch, shot her a long glance.

After grabbing Catherine's bags without even asking permission— apparently, gallantry didn't need such social lubrication—Matthew spun around and began to wheel her Louis Vuittons out of the airport. "Follow me before the boys get bored and start tipping cars." He strode out at a fierce pace, no doubt fueled by the alluring power of Meemaw's pork.

Catherine turned to Lauren. "Is he joking?" she asked, gazing after him. "About tipping cars?"

"Probably." Lauren slid a nervous look her way. "Last chance to back out."

Catherine idly wondered how bad it would be if she suggested staying at a hotel. "I'm still trying to work out how four of your brothers, plus the two of us, are going to fit in one car."

"Well, I'm sure they've brought the Beast Senior. That's Matthew's Silverado 1500." There was a slight pause as Lauren clearly remembered to translate. "It's a pickup truck." She gave Catherine's slight frame the once-over. "Although load distribution could be a problem."

"Will I be expected to sit in the back with the chickens?"

Lauren laughed. "Nope. Won't come to that. I don't think. Come on."

They headed through the exit doors and looked around. Matthew had disappeared. Catherine slid on her sunglasses against the harsh sunlight and scanned the parking lot. Where on earth had the man gone? The oldest King boy wasn't exactly hard to miss. "It appears your brother has many skills."

"Don't ask me where he got to. He's got legs like a lumberjack's. He's probably halfway across the lot by now." Lauren folded her arms and squinted.

A flash of red caught Catherine's eye, and a Chevy swung around a corner, then roared up, screeching to a halt in front of them. Two men in the rear bed started yahooing the moment they clapped eyes on Lauren.

A shudder passed through Catherine. It was like a John Wayne convention.

"Laur!" one King shouted. He thumped the side of the truck.

The other brother hurdled easily over the side of the truck, his muscled right arm acting as a pivot point. He gave Lauren her second crushing hug of the day.

Catherine leaned away, not anxious for a repeat anaconda experience.

He glanced at her and stepped back.

Catherine eyed him curiously as his cheeks reddened.

He scratched his neck and his head dropped, eyes darting away.

Lauren smiled. "That's John." She laughed at some inside joke. "You'll find he doesn't say much."

"Hello," she said. "I'm Catherine."

He nodded, then looked down, the tips of his ears glowing like a lava pit. *A mute King. What a welcome change.* She smiled to herself.

Another brother leaped out, making an alarming beeline straight for Catherine, bypassing Lauren, arms outstretched in open challenge. "Well, hey there, pretty lady! You must be Cat!"

"Catherine," she murmured and took a wary step back. "It's Catherine."

Lauren flung herself between them before he made contact. "Nope, leave her stuffing intact, Lucas," she told him. "She's not used to monster hugs from you big bruisers."

One of the back passenger doors flung open, and a third male stuck his head out, laughing. "She's not used to their smell, either!"

This King brother unfolded to the same cloud-poking heights of the others and looked much the same as the rest did. Dear God, it was like a cloning program. Some experiment in muscle-bound Iowan swizzle sticks. Which reminded her—she could *really* use a drink.

"I'm Mark." He ambled over and politely held out his hand to Catherine. "I'm glad to finally meet the famous Catherine Ayers."

She shook it, pleased one of the brothers embraced basic etiquette. "My reputation precedes me."

"And how. You actually won over Lauren, who's picky as all hell. Bonus points for not dumping her the first time you heard her do karaoke."

"Oh?" Catherine felt a perverse surge of devilry at this interesting fact. She slid her gaze to Lauren. "I don't believe I've yet had the pleasure."

"Nothing pleasurable about it, trust me." Mark chuckled.

Lauren slapped his arm and laughed. She swallowed him up in a hug, hanging onto him much longer than the others.

Ah. So, Lauren had a favorite.

The horn sounded. "Sorry!" Matthew called cheerfully from the driver's window. "It was my knee."

Lucas scoffed. "You just want to get home to Meemaw's pork."

"That, too. So, get your asses on board, okay? Oh, Cat. Sorry 'bout the language."

"I've heard worse. And it's Catherine."

"Oh, right. Sure thing. Sorry. I'll try and remember." He actually sounded sincere, so Catherine chose not to think evil thoughts.

"I dunno. *Cat* seems like a great name to me." Lucas leaned back against the truck. "Kitty Cat. I like it."

Catherine fixed him with a look that could turn hardened senators into puddles.

His eyebrows lifted at the challenge. He folded his arms and opened his mouth, no doubt to unleash his next comeback.

Lauren's gaze darted between them. With sudden haste, she flung open the front passenger door and gestured for Catherine to get in. "Guest privileges mean you get the front seat. More leg room. I'll brave the back with my brothers."

Catherine's head snapped around. "You're not riding in the truck bed, are you? Is that safe?"

Snickering at her, Lucas cut in, "Best way to ride. Well, if you're not afraid to break a nail. Although Matthew won't go around corners on two wheels, if that's what you're asking."

"I'm riding in the back, *inside*," Lauren said. She flicked a glance at John and Lucas. "But don't let me stop you two from bouncing around the rear bed."

Matthew started the engine, presumably as a hurry up. The radio came on.

Catherine climbed into the front seat, which required some mountain goat skills, and stabbed the button to roll the window down. As it lowered, she heard Lauren hiss at Lucas, "Stop being an ass! That's my fiancée you're poking a stick at."

Lucas's voice was muffled but Catherine made it out nonetheless. "Hey, I'm just getting to know her, Sis. Seeing what she's made of."

Catherine couldn't hear Lauren's low, irritated retort.

"Come on, man," another brother called out. "Give the shit-stirring a rest. I want lunch." She guessed it was John, given the voice came from near Lucas.

So, not mute after all.

There was a powerful thud that shook the truck as Lucas, presumably, jumped into the bed. "Food first," he agreed, a smile evident in his voice. "DC Queen autopsy second."

Catherine sighed. Why would anything ever be easy? Still, she could do this. She would endure the gauntlet of misplaced brotherly affection and a whole side of Meemaw's deep-fried pork if that was what would make Lauren happy.

The back door groaned open, and Lauren climbed in beside Mark. Lauren caught Catherine's eye in the mirror. "Everything okay up there?" she asked.

"Peachy."

"Great." Her wide smile was far too bright to be real.

The truck rumbled off, and Matthew turned up the radio. They pulled out of the Eastern Iowa Airport and turned north.

Lauren had told her the King home was fifteen minutes away. That was endurable. She settled back and took stock. Actually, the vehicle was extremely comfortable. It had a great deal of leg room, which made sense since the passengers all had a great deal of legs.

They roared along and, after a few miles, the radio station, which had been talking about sports results and something about the upcoming Iowa State Fair, suddenly switched to a country song with a thudding bass beat.

The lyrics kicked in. The singer sounded awfully proud of his large, black, jacked-up truck.

There was a low moan, and Catherine glanced at the rear mirror in alarm. Lauren's head was in her hands.

Her brothers began belting out the song, loudly, with varying degrees of competence. *Well.* This was different.

The next verse was about the joys of corn rows, floating boats down the Flint River, and catching catfish for dinner.

Catfish dinner? Catherine paused.

And for the lyrical pièce de résistance, was a verse about being a winner for laying his lady down and loving her right.

The man was a poet.

The song eventually ended, and the full-throated, chesty yowlings of the King boys finally abated. The tension in her shoulders slowly eased.

"Sorry," Lauren called to her. "That's their song. Luke Bryan's *That's My Kind of Night*."

"Ah." She had never heard of this Bryan man, with his black jacked-up truck and exotic catfish dinners. Her ears were still ringing from the throaty macho accompaniment.

"We all got tickets," Matthew announced, drumming his thumbs on the steering wheel. "He's touring here soon. Shame you're here so early and all. Damn. You'll miss out."

"Oh, that's all right," Catherine drawled. "Next time."

It was going to be a long ten days.

The truck continued to bounce along the road, and Catherine closed her eyes to gather her thoughts. A strange aroma greeted her, and she frowned. She darted a look at the driver, but Matthew did not react. She looked back at Lauren, whose expression was wistful.

"What is that smell?"

"Pretty sure it's Captain Crunch day." Lauren smiled. "A whole bunch of food manufacturers have their factories in Cedar Rapids. It's the cereal capital of the world for a reason. And today..." She paused and sniffed. "Yep, fairly sure they're running Captain Crunch on the factory line."

"I see."

"Hey, be glad it's not the dog food day," Matthew chimed in. "That stuff's potent." He slapped his steering wheel with a laugh.

Yes, Catherine was extremely glad.

The houses began thinning out as properties grew larger. The landscape, occasionally dotted with corn and soybean fields, was flat and green as far as the eye could see. They turned off onto a narrow road signposted as *Old River Rd SW*. Their vehicle hurtled along at speed.

"Almost there," Matthew told her. He licked his lips. "Can taste lunch already."

Catherine tried to look interested.

Their truck passed an RV park on the left and moments later turned right into a long driveway. A sign at the front said *King and Sons Car Repair—drive on thru to the back.*

Catherine winced at the deliberate mangling of *through*.

In front of her was a gray, two-story, wooden Colorado-style ranch house. Its peaked roof was a matching color, and a giant stone chimney ran up the front of the house. Five cars were parked around the house; two looked like they hadn't moved in months. The noses of more still, around the back, were just visible, reflecting in the sun.

They pulled under a carport. Just behind it squatted an enormous green steel shed.

What could possibly be in something so huge? A plane? A flotilla?

"Home sweet home," Matthew said. He followed her gaze. "You're looking at the garage. Dad's workshop. Wait'll you see it."

She climbed out of the truck—well, *freefell* might be a better word. Beyond the carport, flat, open grassed land greeted her. It seemed to go on for some distance. A sound of barking came from inside the house.

Lauren hadn't said there would be dogs. She hoped they were not the leaping, horse-sized varieties. But given everything else in this family of giants, they'd probably be excitable, hairy T-Rexes.

Lauren's arm slid around her waist. "Boomer and Daisy, our Lab retrievers," she said, nodding toward the house. "They're harmless. Big, furry, friendly lugs. Plus, there's our haughty cat, Miss Chesterfield. She's less harmless or friendly."

"You have a cat named Miss Chesterfield?" *What an odd name.*

"No, my grandmother does. So, no dissing the cat or the name in Meemaw's earshot, or it will end badly. Meemaw protects her own."

"Noted." Catherine paused. "Can I ask why she's called Meemaw? I thought that was a Southern thing."

"Well, there's a story. After I was born, she and Grandpa were in their favorite diner, showing off my baby pictures, when their waitress, who was from Georgia, said, 'Oh, bless your heart, you're a meemaw now!' Apparently Grandpa thought that was hilarious and used it every chance he could. It stuck after that."

"Ah." Catherine nodded.

Lauren's arm swept over the view in front of them. "Right, sightseeing time. It's a couple of acres. Come on, I'll give you the tour while the boys take our bags inside."

"You know, I could have stayed in a hotel nearby," Catherine said quietly. "Would be more room for you, and your brothers could catch up with you without me underfoot."

"And have everyone mad and feeling snubbed? Nope. Besides, I promise it's only chaos if you stop and look at it. Rest of the time it's just fun. Now, come on, let's stretch our legs."

They strolled around the back of the house. The backyard was a field dotted with trees, including one enormous weeping willow in the distance.

Markings on the ground in front of Catherine indicated a long-forgotten softball diamond. Lauren's fond expression would have answered who loved to play on it even if Catherine didn't know her future wife had been a college softball star.

A rustic graying wooden shack was nearby, open on two sides. An old picnic table sat inside, and assorted weather-worn sport and beer memorabilia was tacked up on the wall.

"Our tiki bar," Lauren said. "The boys threw it together in high school. They've had some great parties out here. They'd get the grill out and have all this space to themselves."

"There is a lot of it." Catherine glanced around. "I'm still getting used to how quiet it is."

"Wait till night, and then you're in for a treat. You'll see. Stars that go on forever. It's beautiful."

They'd walked on for a bit when Catherine felt the vibration of her phone. She pulled it out and had a quick read.

"Anything important?"

"Depends. Does a high-ranking senator with a weed stash found in his gym locker count?"

Lauren made a strangled half groan, half laugh. "Phone away. You can survive ten days without work."

"I may quote you on that. I saw you checking your work emails at the airport."

"Okay, yeah, but technically we hadn't left DC yet."

Catherine tucked her phone into her pocket and suddenly let out a short burst of laughter as she worked out what had been niggling her all day. "Your brothers… They're Matthew, Mark, Lucas, and John, in that order?"

"And Tommy."

"The four Gospels: Matthew, Mark, Luke, and John? And, if I recall, Thomas was an Apostle."

Lauren gave a long-suffering sigh. "Yeah, yeah, I know. Meemaw laughs every time Dad calls them out in order. But then, she did help Mom name the boys."

"So, your grandmother is religious?"

"Oh yeah. Big time. Proud Methodist. Church every Sunday. She also loves a good joke. Like those names? She thinks she's hilarious."

"No doubt. So, is your whole family religious?"

"Nah, we're not *that* Biblically observant. Dad's rule was, 'Follow the Commandments and don't argue back when Meemaw's quoting scripture.' But how did you notice my brothers' names? You're not religious." She squinted at her.

"My mother ensured that Phoebe and I had a good grounding in religion, etiquette, home skills, and anything else she thought would raise our social standing. It's the reason I can play piano, perform an excellent dressage serpentine, and bake a bracing flan."

"A bracing flan?" Lauren laughed. "What is that?"

"A flan that can withstand even my mother's staunch criticism."

"Ah. So, she's a bit harsh, then? It's funny how you never talk about them."

"I prefer not to dwell on things best left buried." Catherine inhaled. "Everything was about appearances for my mother. The worst sin I could commit was to embarrass her."

"Was it the same for your sister?"

"Yes, although Phoebe found it harder. She did everything she could to please our mother." Catherine set her mouth to a grim line. "She even married Dad's business associate to please our parents, and never a blander male ever shuffled across this earth than Miles Sutherland. It was never enough to earn Mom's approval, though. I was fortunate to have an insight quite young that satisfying her wasn't actually achievable. That whenever you got close, the goal posts moved. Best not to work yourself into knots trying for the impossible."

"What about your dad? Was he the same?"

"I never saw that much of him. He was so involved in the family business. He tried to lure me into the company at various times from about age eighteen, but I didn't want to be a secretary."

"What a waste of talent that'd have been. All those scoops unscooped."

"True." Catherine smirked. "And I doubt anyone would be mourning my loss to the secretarial pool."

"Then they're idiots. You'd rule that pool by now."

"I suppose so." Catherine couldn't quite picture it. "Well, I know what my father thought of my scandalous career move into journalism. What about yours?"

"Dad was behind me all the way in anything I chose."

"Anything?" Her lips quirked up. "So, he'll approve of me, then?"

"Once he gets to know you, he'll really like you. Oh, and, um, with my brothers, don't be alarmed if they want to haul you off to a tractor pull or something. They'll just be doing it for a reaction. New sister to haze and all."

"A tractor what?"

Lauren laughed. "Oh boy, are you in for a treat."

"You and tractors. Why am I not shocked it runs in the family?"

"I thought you liked my tractor cap."

"Possibly I'm just partial to who wears it."

"That sounds about right. By the way, my brothers *are* decent guys."

Catherine noted the slight hint of desperation in Lauren's voice. "Mm," she said noncommittally.

"They'll just want to see if you're cool before you inherit us as a family," Lauren continued. "But once they accept someone, they are loyal and fierce as hell in protecting their own."

What a disconcerting thought. She was at a loss over the idea of any family wanting to protect her.

They continued in silence before they came to the huge willow tree. The branches facing the house side wept so low they dragged across the ground like a grand dame's enormous hoop skirt. On the other side, facing the back of the property, the branches were a little higher, allowing them to stoop, then walk under it.

Lauren gazed up at the wide canopy—a brilliant fusion of green and yellow leaves—with a rapt expression on her face. "It's a golden weeping willow. Lucas and I measured it three years ago. It's almost thirty feet now. It was Mom's favorite. She called it her dreaming tree."

"It's beautiful."

"I inherited it from her. When I was a girl and wanted to escape brother craziness or all that engine revving, I'd come down here and daydream. Or I'd read. I'd think about my dreams and whether I had the courage to follow them. Because I have to say, girls from Iowa wanting to become reporters in DC aren't that common."

"And yet you did it."

"Yeah." Lauren's smile became soft. She glanced at Catherine. "Okay, enough reminiscing. Time to meet Dad. He'll be wondering where we are. And Meemaw will be climbing the walls with curiosity, dying to check you out."

Catherine offered a serene look even as her stomach tightened in apprehension.

Lauren's hand settled on the wide chrome handle of the sliding door to the workshop. "Dad's fixing up some politician's car this week. The mayor's, I think. He's proud as punch over it."

"Oh, I can imagine," Catherine murmured.

Lauren slapped her arm. "Enough of that. The guy may be small potatoes to you, but Dad's excited."

"I'm glad for him. However, I'm curious as to how this mayor found your father's mechanic business all the way out here. How does anyone?"

"Oh, Dad used to be based in the center of town before he decided to run things from home. He took all his clients with him, and the new ones now come by word of mouth. That's how good he is. And he's done the mayor's cars for decades." She started sliding the door. "I can't wait to see Dad. It's been almost a year."

Catherine nodded, but it was yet another unsettling concept. She'd never had much family to miss, and vice versa. Only her nephew ever said he missed her. Although he probably had to say that since he was living rent-free in her LA home.

"So…" Lauren sucked in a big breath of air. "Please remember, Dad takes a little while to warm up. So, don't be put off if he's a little quiet."

"A quiet King? I like him already."

"Ha-ha." She gestured to Catherine, who stepped inside.

The sharp smell of grease, oil, rubber, and cleaning products assailed her. The room looked like a giant, well-organized car burial ground, with mechanical parts sitting on shelves around all the walls. In the middle of the room sat four cars, the most luxurious of which was on a low hoist. A pair of scuffed black boots was sticking out from under it.

"Dad?"

A wrench dropped. The boots rolled forward out from under the car. A man in dark blue, dirty overalls sat up on the low trolley. He had a lined, tanned face which creased into a warm smile.

It was so filled with love that Catherine was speechless. She couldn't help but stare. Never in her life had her father ever looked at her like that. She glanced at Lauren, who wore a matching expression.

"Honey!" He scrambled to his feet. The man was tall, over six feet, his short, curly, light-brown hair graying above his ears. "I lost track of time. I thought I had another half hour."

Lauren shrugged. "It's okay."

He wiped his hands on a rag he plucked from his back pocket, which seemed to do little, and opened his arms wide to her.

The source of the family tradition for bear hugs immediately became clear when Lauren flung herself into his arms. They hugged, cheek to cheek, eyes bright, voices excited.

Catherine shuffled backwards, feeling like an intruder.

Lauren caught her eye and waved her over. "Catherine! C'mere. Meet Dad…um, Owen. Dad, this is Catherine."

"Nice to put a face to the voice at last," he said, wiping his hands harder on his cloth again. His smile was cautious but genuine.

"Wait, have you guys talked before?" Lauren asked, head snapping back and forth between them. "When did that happen?"

Catherine plastered on her politest smile. She'd spoken to him during one hellish night in LA that she'd spent trying to find Lauren, who had vanished after they'd had a…small disagreement. Catherine also might not have sounded entirely sane by the time she'd gone through all Lauren's friends and resorted to tracking down her father. "Just once," she told Lauren, keeping her voice light. "Nothing major. You were out at the time."

Owen's eyes crinkled at that outrageous tweaking of the truth, and he coughed over a small laugh.

"It's a pleasure to meet you." Catherine offered him her hand.

"Oh, sorry, best not to." Owen showed her his dirty palm, unable to be salvaged by the cloth. "Bit too messy for company."

"It's fine, Mr. King." She shook his hand anyway. "I gather it's an occupational hazard."

"It is. And call me Owen." He extracted his hand.

Lauren glanced between them. "So, how are things, Dad?"

"Good." He faced her and brightened. "Still doing up the mayor's car. He wanted a total overhaul this time." He jerked his thumb behind him. "He's a good man and all, but he's done things to his exhaust that shouldn't be physically possible."

Owen glanced at Catherine. "Do you share my daughter's love of cars, too, Ms. Ayers?"

"Catherine," she corrected. "And I couldn't grease a ball-bearing to save my life. I'm more interested in who's greasing politicians' palms."

Lauren winced at the attempted joke.

Owen looked as if he was in physical pain.

"Oh dear. Was it that bad?" Catherine asked with an ample dollop of self-deprecation.

"Yep, 'fraid so." Owen's wide smile was warm and friendly. He rocked back on his heels. "That coyote's what we'd call dead on arrival. Even its fleas are flat-lining. But I appreciate the effort and all."

Catherine laughed at his unexpected comeback. "I'll work on my material. Get back to you."

"Good plan." Owen's gaze became curious. "Well now, we've got a whole bunch of fresh air out here in Iowa. Lots to do. I hope you'll find some time to see the place in between all your wedding fixing."

"I admit I'm fascinated to see where Lauren comes from."

"Good. Real good." Owen's smile was approving. "Right then, I think we should go in for lunch before the boys riot. They've been talking about Meemaw's pork all day. I'll wash up. Meet you both inside."

"Sure, Dad." Lauren gave him a quick peck on the cheek.

Once again, the affection on his face at the small gesture was heartwarming. He glowed.

Chapter 5
Meets and Eats

THE MOMENT LAUREN OPENED THE door to the house, a pair of familiar chocolate-brown whirlwinds descended on her in a flurry of barking and clacking of claws on the floorboards. She felt Catherine freeze behind her, so she blocked the dogs' path to stop them flinging themselves at the exciting new human. She certainly understood that impulse when it came to Catherine.

Boomer and Daisy knew not to jump on people; months of expensive training had drilled that into them, but they could barely contain themselves at the sight of their mistress after so long. Their tails were thumping, and their whole bodies heaved with excitement.

"Hey, kids. Miss me, huh?" She knelt and gave them both hugs around the neck and a scratch behind the ears.

Daisy dodged under her arm and shot past her toward Catherine.

Uh-oh.

"Daisy!" Lauren turned, and glanced up to see Catherine's resigned expression as she planted her feet and braced herself.

Daisy dipped, preparing to leap.

"Daisy! Down!"

The tone was low, sharp, biting, and the absolute last thing Lauren expected. Its crack of command almost made her drop to the ground herself. Daisy scrabbled to a stop in an ungainly mass of fur, muscle, and swishing tail at Catherine's feet. Even Boomer dropped instantly to the sitting position.

"Good girl." The tone was slightly higher now, and Catherine knelt on one knee and offered Daisy her hand to be inspected and smelt.

"How?" Lauren's mouth fell open. "How on earth did you do that?"

Catherine smiled. "When I started out in journalism, I once had to write a feature article on the art of a well-trained dog. I interviewed all the top experts in the field. Spent many hours on it. The secret is in the tone of voice, apparently, and letting them know you are the alpha in the pack. You have to believe it. But it only works if a dog has been trained. It seems these two are."

"Don't sound so surprised." Lauren grinned. "And trust you to think you're the alpha."

"When am I not?" Catherine's smile widened. She focused on Daisy, upon whom she bestowed a polite pat for a few moments. She leaned over to Boomer and repeated the gesture for exactly the same length of time.

Lauren watched this ordered routine, baffled.

"Husky pack rules apply," Catherine explained. "You cannot give affection to one dog without any others becoming jealous."

"Um…okay?"

"Did you never watch the Animal Planet channel?"

Lauren shrugged. "No cable for us. Dad doesn't even watch TV." She crouched in front of Daisy and gave her a proper hello, earning a lick on the cheek. She glanced up. "Well, I gotta say you are full of surprises. So, you learned all this stuff at work? No dogs of your own growing up?"

"Pets were definitely not allowed."

"None? Not even a goldfish?"

Catherine rose. "They might have been a distraction from my schoolwork," she said dryly.

"A shame. You'd have been a great fur-parent."

"I like to think so." Catherine studied the attentive dogs, still sitting firmly at attention. "It was a pleasure to meet you two," she told them in a serious tone. "I appreciate you both for not mauling my Donna Karan blouse."

"Well, the Donna Karan is still at risk from Miss Chesterfield's razor-sharp claws, so don't relax yet. Come on, I'll show you around."

Lauren led her through to the L-shaped, open-plan living room, and then around the corner to the kitchen, which boasted rustic timber floors and polished hardwood bench tops. Everything was the same as she remembered. A wall of windows on one side showed the backyard to best effect, and the old, brown leather sofa and comfy armchairs reminded Lauren of many a day flopped in one, trying to do her homework when she'd have rather been tossing a softball around with whichever brother wasn't elbow-deep in an engine. Usually that meant Lucas.

Her old home was well lived in but neat. Actually, a little too neat. Meemaw had obviously given the boys their cleaning orders in time for their visit.

Speaking of her grandmother, the fastidious woman was bent over the stove, stirring a pot. Her round shape hadn't changed much, although she seemed a little wider under her apron strings and shorter than Lauren remembered. Her hair had been dyed reddish-orange as usual, and it matched the bold red sweater she was squeezed into above her worn jeans. The smells drifting from the kitchen were just as she remembered them.

"Ahhh. Heaven." She exhaled, letting her entire teenage food years waft over her.

Meemaw spun around. Her creased face came alive. She flicked the cooktop setting to low and elbowed her way out of the kitchen with haste. "Lauren Annabelle King, let me take a look at you."

Smiling, Lauren waited for the enveloping hug every bit as solid as her brothers and father had delivered. Meemaw's was warm and soft and felt like comfort. The rotund woman added an extra waggle at the end, then stepped back to take Lauren in.

Lauren detected her faithful hairspray brand, which hadn't changed in decades, and the rose-scented cream she loved to lather on her beefy forearms.

"Well." Meemaw peered at her, appraising them both at what seemed to be a microscopic level. She gave Catherine a direct look. "You must be the infamous Caustic Queen I've heard so little about."

"So little?"

"Oh, yes. All those big, manly King boys are terrified to talk about you in front of me in case I hear something unseemly. Goodness me, it was like playing charades trying to get out of them that Lauren was marrying some woman." She pursed her lips. "To be specific, some woman I hadn't even met." She lowered her voice to a cool whisper. "From *Boston*." She tilted her head. "Well, you've got fashion sense, at least. More than I can say for my granddaughter."

Catherine's lips curled. "Well, she has her own tastes. I believe they run toward chic tractorwear."

"That they do," Meemaw said in a sage tone.

"Hey! I'm right here!" Lauren protested.

"Hush, now." Meemaw eyeballed Catherine again. "I vote Republican. Always have. I love Jesus, gin, and my old double-barrel Browning, in that order. I also don't like being told what to think by smart people who've only just learned how to pull their britches on. So how are we going to get along?"

Lauren winced. *Really? Meemaw wants to do this right now?* She gave Catherine a pleading look to play nice.

"If you're asking whether I appreciate someone who has their own opinions, I do, as long as they don't force them on anyone else," Catherine replied evenly. "Because there's a difference between being resolute and being a bully." She softened her words with a smile, but her eyes glinted at the challenge.

Meemaw silently regarded her.

Oh, crap. Well, that escalated fast. Lauren glanced between Meemaw's appraising expression and Catherine's wary one. Their eyes were locked. "Um, hey, how about I get us all a drink? Anyone thirsty?"

Meemaw tilted her head at Catherine. "I'll let that pass for now." She drew in a deep breath, her ample bosom rising with it. "I like cats. Do you?"

Christ, Meemaw's cat test. If Catherine said no, she'd have no hope of ever gaining her grandmother's favor. But Catherine never lied to make peace, so... Lauren held her breath.

"I don't know," Catherine said. "I haven't been around any cats."

Lauren blinked in surprise.

Meemaw looked at her with the same flummoxed expression she usually reserved for anyone adding pectin to their homemade jam. "Well." She peered at her some more as though not quite believing the answer. "That makes you rarer than hen's teeth for sure. I'll spare us both me asking about God."

"Come on, Meemaw," Lauren cut in. "I didn't bring her here for a Spanish Inquisition."

Meemaw shook off the interruption. "You're not a Mormon, are you? Or worse, a Lutheran?" Her eyes sharpened.

Lauren groaned inwardly. So much for sparing Catherine the theology test.

"I believe in living an ethical life," Catherine said. "If that aligns with what a person of any given faith does, fine. If not, fine."

"You don't care if you're liked then, not with an answer like that."

"I'm used to being disliked, Mrs. Haverson," Catherine said in an even tone. "Comes with the territory. And I won't change my position just to make others feel comfortable. Not on God, guns, or who I love. That's not who I am. And it's not right for others to expect me to."

Meemaw said nothing for a moment, but her face lost its pinched look. "Call me Meemaw." She turned. "Lauren, call the boys in. They're playing one of those Game Station thingies in the front room. Let's get lunch started." She looked back. "Catherine, you'll set the table. Utensils are in that drawer." She jabbed a plump finger at it. "Plates are over there."

A truce! Catherine had stared down Meemaw and wrung a truce out of her. That had never happened in…well, the history of ever. Most people just got worn down and told her what she wanted to hear or got into a rafter-shaking war of words with the woman.

Lauren stared at her fiancée in amazement.

I'm gonna marry her.

Lunch with all the fixings was spread across the white-clothed table like some feast in a medieval tableau. Buttered corn, potatoes, and beans sat in plain white bowls, big fat steel spoons sticking out proudly. The aroma of freshness was something Lauren never experienced anywhere else. The whole scene gave her heart a little flutter. She couldn't decide whether it was Meemaw's pork, cooked to perfection as always, or the familiarity of it—the feeling of family that came with it. She felt so at home. And yet it wasn't quite the same. Her brothers were a little louder, their father a little older and quieter. And Meemaw was far too watchful to be safe for anyone.

Catherine seemed quiet, too, eyes widening at the portion sizes on the boys' plates. She demurred on seconds, which earned her an appraising look from Meemaw, but frankly Lauren was relieved she'd gotten through firsts.

There was more fried food on their table than Catherine had probably seen in six months.

"So, girls, what are your plans?" her dad asked, reaching for his beer. "How much of this wedding business is sorted?"

"Well, we picked a wedding planner before we left," Lauren said. "She has some venues to show us on Monday. And depending on how that goes, and how solidly they're booked and stuff, it will pretty much tell us the exact date we can get married. Once we know that, we can work out everything else."

"A wedding planner?" Meemaw huffed. "Who?"

"Mrs. Potts. You remember Jennifer who I went to school with? Well, her mother-in-law has a planning business."

"I know that one," Meemaw said. "Of course, it's up to you, but you could save yourself a bunch of money and let me do the planning. I have time. And I know what my only granddaughter likes."

"We didn't want to bother you," Lauren said with haste. Last thing she needed was Meemaw taking over and insisting on what they needed. And her taste veered on eccentric.

"Oh, it's no bother. None at all. That's what family does." Meemaw's eyebrows rose in challenge.

"Mrs. Potts will be able to get us bookings on any number of venues at short notice," Catherine broke in quietly. "She has contacts within the industry. It's her profession, after all. That will widen our choices."

"She also can get us a good deal," Lauren added. "She's not charging like a wounded bull just because the word 'wedding' is attached to something. Her prices are really fair."

"Well, that's good," her dad said with an approving nod. "If you won't take my money for your wedding, I'm glad to hear you're not being taken for a ride."

Lucas made a strangled noise and looked at Catherine. "Come on, you're loaded. That watch you've got on is worth more than the mayor's car Dad's fixing. What do you guys care if you can get a planner who can swing a cheaper deal?"

Matthew clipped Lucas around the ear. "Rude, Bro."

"Lucas!" her dad snapped at the same time. "Apologize or leave the table."

Lauren stared in shock at her brother, her cheeks reddening in shame at the way he'd treated a guest. What must Catherine think?

"*Sor-ry*," he muttered, raising his hands in surrender. Her grabbed his fork and stabbed at his potato. "God, speak the truth 'round here and everyone shits on you."

Meemaw glowered. "Watch your language, too. You were not raised with a tongue like that." She gave Lauren and Catherine an arch look. "And I was only trying to be helpful."

"I know, and we appreciate it." Lauren could hear the placating in her own tone. "And if we get stuck, I hope we can ask your advice."

"Of course." Meemaw lifted her water glass but still frowned as she sipped.

Lauren exhaled.

"Lucas," Catherine murmured, "please pass the salt."

He did so, and as their fingers met, she locked his briefly between hers and the shaker. "I work long, stressful hours for my money. So, does your sister. Why would I or Lauren pay an inflated price for things with the money we work so hard for? You wouldn't."

Lucas stared, unblinking.

Mark laughed hard, breaking the awkward silence. "Ha. Lucas hasn't worked hard a day in his life."

The rest of the table burst into laughter except Lucas, whose cheeks turned scarlet. He shot them all an unfathomable look under his lashes, and Lauren felt a prickle shoot up her spine. It was odd. She didn't think she'd ever seen him look that way before.

As the main meal gave way to rhubarb pie drowning in oozing puddles of thick custard, she puzzled over it. Lucas had always been the smartest of her brothers. He had also been so empathetic as a boy, forever rescuing stray animals. He hid his soft spot with a lot of bravado, brashness, and playing the clown. So, what was he up to? Did he even realize how immature he was coming off?

Mark interrupted her musings when he nudged her and asked, "Hey, I'm the best man, right?"

"Well, that was fun." Catherine unpacked her suitcase, snapping her clothes onto hangers and lining them up in the guest room's closet.

"Sorry about that." Lauren was more embarrassed than anything. "I truly thought I'd told them I was asking Josh to be best man. I really did."

"I think Mark looked most hurt that it was some handbag designer from LA he'd never met who'd edged him out, as opposed to another brother," Catherine said.

"He'd have been more hurt if he knew Josh hasn't said yes yet. Something about checking his planner. He's gonna Skype me later today. I'll get him to confirm then."

"I see." Catherine stopped unpacking and turned to her. "Why do you want Joshua to be best man and not one of your brothers? Mark did make a good point."

"It's like…husky rules apply. It's so the rest of them don't get jealous or think I'm playing favorites."

"Yet it's fairly clear to me that you like Mark best. Your brothers must be aware of that, too."

"I know. I mean, I've tried to hide it, but I can't help it. After Mom died, for months every night Mark came to my room and curled up next to me in bed. He was five. He didn't say anything; he just gave me a cuddle for a little while. I thought he must have needed it. We never talked about it. Years later, when I finally brought it up, Mark told me he did it because he thought *I'd* needed it and he didn't know how else to help me when his big sister looked so sad."

Catherine drew in a quiet breath. "I can see why you like him."

"Yes. I also know what my brothers are like. They can get jealous and competitive. I didn't want to cause any resentment by picking him, so I went outside the family. And Josh was so good to me when I first arrived in LA. He'll be great. Ugh." She threw up her hands. "Why is everything so complicated? I just wanted to make it easier. Instead, my family's being weird."

"You mean Lucas? Is he unhappy with me for some reason?"

"Unhappy?" Lauren tossed her underwear and T-shirts into a drawer. "Oh no, don't read anything into his idiocy tonight. God, I'm so sorry about that. He's just… He plays the smart-ass sometimes, and not always at appropriate times. I doubt it's personal. He's blunt and still trying to figure you out. I promise he's a really nice guy underneath all that. You'll see for yourself when you get to know each other. And, hey, at least Meemaw went soft on you during her little pre-lunch interview. That makes for a change."

"Meemaw is a clever woman. She knows that she could fight me head-on if she has reservations about me, but if she did, then she'd be fighting you. And she's smart enough to know that that's a war she might lose. So, she has elected to choose her battles wisely. Now, that is someone I respect."

"Huh. Yeah, that makes sense." Lauren paused. "So, what are your views on steak?"

"Steak?"

"Yeah. There's this place… It's a rite of passage for Iowan college kids. A little out of town, but the steaks are to die for. It makes my knees go weak just thinking about it."

"Well, by all means, let me chase down lunch pork with dinner steak."

"Okay, so was that a yes?" Lauren's look was hopeful.

"If you book me a personal trainer on our return, it's a yes."

"*Please*, you never gain an ounce. Hey, is it true what you said about cats? You've never even met one?"

"Why would I lie about that?"

"That's a point. It's just strange. Not even school friends or—"

"No."

"Well, now's your chance."

"What?"

"In your suitcase. Miss Chesterfield's made herself at home."

Catherine spun around and eyeballed the pure-white animal with huge green eyes now kneading her finery. "Out!" She waved her arm.

Miss Chesterfield blinked. Yawned. Turned around and curled into a perfect circle, ignoring her. She began to purr.

Leaning forward, Catherine said, "Miss Chesterfield, anywhere but there, please."

The cat's purring stopped instantly. She whipped around, her paw lashing out, and latched onto Catherine's silky blouse, puncturing it before retracting.

Catherine looked down at her top and then glared at the animal. "I see," she said, eyes becoming slits. "It's war."

"Um, no, *no war!*" Lauren's eyes widened. "Remember what I said about Meemaw and her cat? And I did warn you. Miss C. is a special brand of evil."

"That's fine." Catherine straightened, her expression becoming grim and determined. "Lauren, could you please give *the feline* and I a moment alone to get acquainted?"

"What? Now, you know cats are nothing like dogs, right? You can't just order them to believe you're their alpha."

"You don't say. Well? I just need a few minutes."

Lauren left the room and headed down the hallway. She could hear voices in the kitchen below and started toward them. As she neared, she heard Lucas's voice.

When she entered the room, he startled and looked guilty. She glanced around at her brothers, who looked just as caught. "What's up?"

"Planning your bachelorette party," Matthew admitted. "Details are on a need-to-know basis."

"I don't need a bachelorette party."

"Too bad. 'Cause we took a vote. If one of us doesn't get to be your best man, we've decided the least we can do as a family is give you the party."

"Please?" Mark dished up his best boyish grin.

Damn it. The big guns.

"Where and when?" Lauren sighed.

Triumphant grins wreathed their faces. "Friday night," Mark said. "We're gonna have it in the workshop. Back all the cars out, make a big space, trick it up. The garage will never be the same again."

"You mean the gayrage," Lucas chimed in. "It'll be spectacular."

"The *gayrage?*"

"Yep." Lucas laughed.

"We'll make it cool," John promised. "It'll be a *Grease* theme."

"Hey!" Lucas complained. "No spoilers."

"Sorry." John stuck his head back down.

"I'm not sure what Catherine will think of this," Lauren said, trying to picture her classy fiancée and *Grease* props in the same universe.

"Well, she doesn't have to show up if she doesn't want." Lucas gave her an innocent look. "Maybe she and Meemaw can sit around discussing pickling or knitting together instead."

Lauren stared at him. Okay, there was no hiding it this time; that wasn't something she could just explain away. It was plain mean. "Was that supposed to be a dig about her age?" she asked, tone dangerous.

For an awkward, painful moment, no one said a word. The grin dropped from Lucas's face, and his gaze shot around to his brothers, looking for support.

"Come on, it was a joke," he tried. His chuckle sounded hollow. "You know? Talking about the elephant in the room? You're thirty-four, and she's, what, fifty?"

"She's only ten years older than me." Lauren glared at him. "As you all know damn well."

"Okay, fine, but she acts wayyy older than forty-four. That's what the joke was."

"For it to be a joke, it actually has to be funny." Lauren's voice was now so low it was almost a whisper. "Listen up. If anyone ever runs her down like that again, I will kick your damn ass. I mean it."

She turned to glower at Lucas. "And while we're on the topic, what was all that stuff at lunch about her money? You know that fancy watch of hers you mocked? It was a gift from her sister when she won her first national reporting award. But that doesn't even matter. What matters is your attitude. Where'd that come from? Why be such an ass?"

Lucas spread his hands in surrender. "Hey, hey, sorry. You know me, always saying the dumb thing!"

His hangdog look was familiar. It had been so effective when he was young. It wasn't going to work this time. She gritted her teeth. "Can you all stop acting like a bunch of immature kids? It's like you *want* to make a bad impression. You trying to drive her off or something?" Dismay filled her. "Oh my God, is *that* it?"

"Whoa," Matthew cut in. "Lauren, no! That's not it at all, I promise. It's just you're here, which is exciting, and you're also marrying someone kind of famous, who we're curious to know more about. And *some* of us are blunter and more interested at cutting to the chase than others in getting

51

answers. Sorry. We'll dial it back a bit, I promise." He gave Lucas an elbow to the ribs. "All of us."

Lucas nodded quickly, looking contrite.

She exhaled. Her hackles went down. "You'd better. Right?" She looked at all of them.

They muttered "yeps," nodded, and shuffled their feet.

"Okay, then." She rammed her hands in her pockets, trying to find her earlier equilibrium. "So, a bachelorette party on Friday? Is that when I'm going to finally see Tommy?"

"Actually, he was supposed to be back tonight," John said. "But don't hold your breath. His girlfriend is taking up all his time right now."

At his appalled look, she laughed. Lauren wondered when her shyest brother would ever pluck up the courage to talk to a woman. "Is she anyone I know?"

"Nope," Mark jumped in. "New to town. Only been here, oh, eight years, I guess."

She smiled. He *would* think eight years was "new." "Okay, then. I'll let you get back to your party planning."

Her brothers shared pleased grins.

"But whatever you have in mind, skip the nudity." Lauren wagged a finger at them. She paused as another thought hit. "And that means no boobs, either."

"Aww," Mark moaned.

They all laughed, breaking the tension.

"Okay, I better go see how Catherine's surviving Miss Chesterfield," Lauren said. "Damn cat had drawn first blood when I left."

"You left those two *alone*?" Mark's voice was hushed.

All her brothers' expressions turned to shock.

Hell. Yeah, good point. She raced from the room and bolted upstairs.

At the end of the hall, she knocked gently before pushing open the guest-room door and glancing around. Catherine's suitcase had been packed away.

In a chair in the corner, Catherine sat serenely, stroking Miss Chesterfield in her lap.

"She lives." Lauren suppressed a nervous laugh. "Do you have any idea how much you look like a Bond villain, Ms. Blofeld?"

Catherine offered her a serene look. "We made our peace. I've decided I like cats."

"How did you do that?" Lauren peered at Miss Chesterfield. "I mean, that creature hates everyone except Meemaw. Seriously."

"I guess one animal of like mind recognizes another," Catherine suggested.

Lauren studied the pair. Now she said it, Miss Chesterfield, beautiful and haughty, tetchy, and all class when she strutted about, owning every room she was in, was quite possibly Catherine in animal form. Especially when you factored in the rapier-sharp claws when provoked.

"God, I think you're right." She leaned forward and gingerly attempted to stroke between the cat's ears. "Maybe…"

Miss Chesterfield's head swung around, and she snapped at Lauren with a sharp hiss.

Lauren retracted her fingers just in time. She gulped. "Or not."

"First law of surviving man and animal," Catherine said, eyebrows lifting. "Never assume one party's reaction to someone is true for all."

"You're loving this, aren't you? Trust you two aloof ladies to be in cahoots with each other."

Catherine's smile was beatific.

Chapter 6
RSVP

Josh beamed at Lauren through the iPad screen and wiggled his fingers hello. "Well, if it isn't my favorite former neighbor," he said. "New haircut? And it's chic in a Portia De Rossi Ponytail of Impeccable Sassiness kind of way. Is the Caustic Queen rubbing off on you? And I mean that a lot less sexually than it sounded." He gave a naughty laugh.

Lauren rolled her eyes. "If it helps, I'm still the 'fashion-curdled cherub' you dubbed me long ago."

"Yes," he said, giving her a pitying look. "I can see that. But we can't all be blessed with brains *and* taste."

"You know I didn't actually agree to this call just to be insulted."

"Pshaw. Call it a bonus. Value adding." He grinned. "Let me show you something." He leaned away and then held up a blue-and-white zebra-patterned handbag. "From my upcoming line. I call it Bi-curvy Zebra." He laughed. "Remember? When my gaydar first pinged on Tad?"

"I do," Lauren said. "And how is your long-suffering boyfriend?"

"Still has abs to die for and excellent taste in boyfriends." He glanced behind him. "Tad's in the other room. He wants to talk to his Aunty Catherine in a minute, but first"—Joshua's expression fell—"I have something to tell you."

He drew in a deep breath and then said in a rush, "I can't work out any way around launching the Joshua Bennett Collection *and* being at your wedding." He bit his lip. "I am so, so sorry, Lauren, but I'd booked the media, the show, everything for the end of November long before you'd picked your wedding month. And I'll be flat out like a squirrel on Route 101 trying to get everything ready in the weeks leading up to it."

Lauren's heart sank. "Oh. I'm sorry to hear that."

"I'm sorry to say it. Especially since it is such a fabulous honor you gave me." He eyed her seriously. "I've never been a best man." He gave a tiny dramatic huff. "See, I'm always the funny guy who makes the silly speeches and ends up on the wedding highlight reel. But this, being front and center, I can't even tell you... It's a huge honor. And I'm devastated I can't say yes."

Lauren hoped she wouldn't get teary. She'd never actually pictured her wedding without Josh being a part of it. He'd pulled her out of more than a few dives of despair when she'd first landed in LA.

"If it was any other month, I promise, as Cher is my witness, I would move heaven and earth to be there."

"I believe you." She tried to affix a grin. "I appreciate you telling me face-to-face, so to speak."

He nodded and hesitated. "I hope you're not too mad with me?"

"How can I be mad? You've been planning your handbag collection for as long as I've known you. It's not like you're blowing me off so you can go to the movies."

"Well," he said earnestly, "if it were a Judy biopic..." He shook his head with a chuckle. "Even then, no, of course not." He leaned forward and added in a conspiratorial tone, "I still can't believe you and Catherine are sealing the deal."

Lauren smiled. Neither could she some days. "I know."

"So..." he continued, eyes bright with enthusiasm, "how is Our Goddess of the Acerbic Tongue? You know she's like every queer fashion boy's supreme leader. Gay, stylish, *and* bitchy. What's not to love?"

"She's a lot less bitchy now. I think I'm a civilizing influence."

"Just keep telling yourself that."

Lauren laughed. "Okay, true. I guess she probably *thinks* her usual caustic comebacks all the time but doesn't say them as often now. It's surprising the level of discipline she has. I mean she's in Iowa and she's yet to make one crack about corn fields, gun toters, or farm boys."

"It must be love." Josh's expression was warm. "So, how is it being home again? I couldn't imagine it myself. Ten years ago, in Trumbull, Connecticut, I packed my sewing machine, my skinny Levis, and my *Vogues* and never looked back. Home has no lure for me, but I know it does for you. So, spill."

"It feels…familiar. In a good way. And also weird. Like time has stood still. And yet it hasn't. Like, all my brothers are still mechanics. But now I find out that Mark is at night school, learning how to teach the next generation of grease monkeys. John, somehow, got his dream job. He works on the electric cars division at some new technology plant. And my youngest brother, Tommy, I haven't even seen him yet because he's apparently discovered girls. Not that I can blame him." She laughed. "So, see, they're all the same lugheads I grew up with, but they're moving on, too. It's a little weird to discover what they're like now."

"I bet they think the same of you," Josh said, resting his chin on his fist. "You're the sister they grew up with. They probably aren't quite sure how to react to this fabulously successful DC reporter with dire fashion sense that they see before them now. You're one of them…yet not."

"Oh." Lauren hadn't thought about it quite like that. She wondered if that was why her brothers were tapping into their Cro-Magnon sides so much lately. They were reverting to how they'd behaved when they were all young and growing up together. When in doubt, fall back on what's familiar? It would certainly explain a few things.

"So anyway," Josh said, straightening, "I want to say I'm sorry again about not being able to do the best man duties. I'd have been legendary, too. I have a dirt file on you bigger than your Internet search history. In fact, my dirt file actually *contains* your Internet search history, thanks to Snakepit and Duppy. What's the point of knowing a pair of world-class hackers if they can't crack your best friend's computer?"

Lauren's heart almost stopped. "What? Oh my God!" Her mind leaped to what she'd searched in the past few months. Nothing immediately incriminating sprang to mind, but still. Wait, there was that time a few months ago, she'd unwound by indulging in lesbian fanfiction. It was classy stuff, with a plot and everything, but still. Her cheeks reddened.

"God, you're so easy." Josh laughed, then paused. "But hell, now I'm really curious about what you've been Googling. I'll be disappointed if it's just porn like the rest of us."

Lauren screwed up her face. "Ugh! Too much information, Joshie."

"Well, on that note," he said, with a cheery wave, "Tad wants to say hello to his aunt. If you could scare her up for him, that'd be great."

Catherine eyed her nephew, taking in his blond hair, blue eyes, and rugged square jaw. She could see why he'd decided Hollywood would want him. But his big acting break hadn't materialized, unless you included fronting Orbit exercise equipment on the infomercial channel.

She still smiled every time he proudly emailed her links of him telling the world that he'd become "*buff—the Orbit Man way.*" Her oblivious nephew, who thought his acting skills meant no one in the industry would ever pick up on his closeted sexuality, had yet to realize the ad was dripping with homoerotic subtext in order to target the gay market.

"Hey, Aunty C!" Tad's teeth gleamed in a dazzling smile. He lifted his perfectly manscaped eyebrows. "Miss me?"

"I miss my beautiful LA house," she countered, tone teasing. "How is it? Are you looking after it?"

"Trashed it with another party." He offered a heavy sigh. "Had actors snorting coke off your antique coffee table until someone danced on it and broke it. Fairly sure models were doing *the deed* all over the house, including your bedroom. Couldn't see them myself. I was too busy cleaning up the Persian rug in your study." He lowered his eyes and whispered, "Don't ask."

An Oscar winner he'd never be. "Such a shame." Catherine gave a sad cluck. "Oh well, I'll bill you the cost of replacing the rug and the table."

"Yeah, don't do that," he said, and his easy grin was back. "Of *course* I'm looking after your place. It's a dream. I can't ever say thanks enough for letting me stay rent-free."

"Rent adjusted," she corrected with a twitch of a smile. "The deal was that if you actually get a paying role, you're supposed to pay rent."

"Semantics." He waved, and then dazzled the room with another grin. "I'd forgotten how funny you can be. I've missed going out to all the LA parties with you. They were awesome. Remember when you used to hate your wife-to-be?"

"I didn't hate her."

"Oh really? Well, nothing says love like threatening to clamp a girl's car."

Catherine gave him her best evil eye. Tad had never dared to joke about her love life before he'd met his boyfriend. "I see Joshua's been a bold influence on you."

His smile was replaced with a cautious look.

"And that's not such a bad thing," Catherine added quickly. "We both know too much about secrets and lies. Don't we?"

"It's the family way—don't ask, don't tell, never share a damn thing. God, I still can't even talk to Mom about Josh. She's just all… I mean, she makes comments about me not dating girls, but she never really *talks* about it. And sometimes she randomly says stuff like, 'Why do people have to put their private business out there? It's forcing others to think about unsavory things they don't want to.'"

Catherine felt her chest tighten. She'd always wondered what her sister really thought of her impulsive public outing of her and Lauren. How… disappointing. Tad was so right. Hiding things and never talking about them *was* the Ayers way.

Hell, her father had affairs, and they all knew it, including her mother, but it was decreed not so terrible as long as he was discreet. Catherine had only apparently brought great shame to her family the moment she was honest.

"Your mom must have worked you out by now, though," she suggested.

He shrugged. "Who knows? And Dad's so like Grandpa, only interested in the business and bottom lines, so what's the point?"

"I see. Look, I know we didn't discuss any of this before, and we should have. I'm sorry I didn't. But I want you to know you can always talk to me if you need to." She paused on unfamiliar words that stuck in her throat. "You…mean a great deal to me, Tad."

The moment she said it, she felt a surge of tenderness for her only nephew.

Tad visibly swallowed. "I appreciate that. I mean it. Thanks." He hesitated. "Which is why it's so hard to say what I'm about to." All the color seemed to drain from his cheeks.

Chapter 7
Rube's Awakening

IT HAD TAKEN AN HOUR to get to Rube's Steak House in Montour, Catherine noted with a scowl.

Lauren had borrowed one of her father's vehicles to drive them, some wrecking-yard rescue project that had limited suspension. Apparently, a sign of toughness was feeling every bump.

The blue classic Chevy looked exactly the same as Lauren's own tank-like red beast back in DC, which probably explained her fond sigh and the way she patted its dash, calling it "Kitten" when she first climbed in.

The eating establishment loomed in front of them—a monument to brown. Brown brick. Brown, lined, galvanized steel sides. Dark brown eaves with a sickly orange glow from a long column of downlights. Catherine supposed she could be in a more accepting mood, but her Skype call with Tad earlier had left a sour taste in her mouth. She bit back her first retort at the building. Then her second.

"I could lie and say it looks better inside." Lauren's tone was cheery as she parked and tumbled out. She hit the ground with much the same terminal velocity as the Chevy had afforded them. "But remember it's not about appearances. It's all about the taste. The food is amazing, I promise. And I'd crawl over broken glass for their bacon-wrapped rib eye."

"I am marrying a Flintstone," Catherine said with a wince. She slid out of the vehicle.

Laughing, Lauren came around to her side of the truck and looped her arm through Catherine's. "I appreciate your noble sacrifice. We'll hit all your favorite restaurants for a month when we get back to DC to make up for it."

Inside Rube's was like a butcher's shop had mated with a restaurant. Wall-to-wall fridges filled with raw meat selections were on display, beyond which sat tables and the smoky centerpiece—a giant grill which had a small crowd of diners standing around it.

"So, you select the piece of meat that you want from the fridge, then you throw it on the grill and cook it yourself." Lauren beamed from ear to ear as though this was the most incredible thing in human history.

"I see." Catherine shot her a cynical look. "Who needs to hire a cook when we do it ourselves?"

"At least you get it cooked exactly as you like it. And, of course, they have a cook. After all, you should see the dessert menu."

Catherine said nothing, eying those around them taking part in this primitive ritual. The food did smell good. And at least it wasn't deep-fried. Her stomach still hadn't entirely recovered from lunch. She supposed she could get in the spirit of things.

"What's the smallest thing they have?" she asked hopefully.

"Hey." Lauren nudged her as they were eating. "Earth to Catherine."

"Hm?" Catherine looked up. "Sorry. What?"

"Want to tell me what's bothering you? You've been in a world of your own since we got here."

"What makes you think I'm bothered?"

"The tiny little line between your brow is furrowed. That usually signals someone's about to meet a sticky end."

Exhaling, Catherine said, "I spoke to Tad." *It shouldn't hurt so much. It really shouldn't.* She reached for her glass of wine.

"And what did your nephew have to say for himself? Has he finally RSVP'd for our wedding?"

"Yes, actually."

Lauren's face brightened.

"He confirmed that he is *not* coming. He wants to support his boyfriend's big November launch. And Joshua cannot shift the date on it—a fact Tad felt the need to repeat about a dozen times. So, you need a new best man. And my nephew will not be in attendance."

Disappointment washed across Lauren's face. "Oh no."

Catherine nodded slowly. "I know you really wanted Joshua to be there."

Swallowing, Lauren reached for her beer and took a gulp. "Okay, true, but that's not why I'm so disappointed. I know how hard it is for you that Phoebe is your only family coming. And I'll be drowning in relatives, and you'll have only your sister, who you aren't that close to. So, I've been really, really hoping Tad would be there for you, too."

"Well, I'm used to family placing me second." Catherine froze, shocked she'd said such a vulnerable thing out loud. Her insecurities were usually much better buried. Her gaze darted to Lauren.

Lauren's hand covered hers on the table and gave it a squeeze. "I'm so sorry."

"Never mind." Catherine straightened. Pity she definitely did not need. "Let's consider the now. Has Mariella said yes to being matron of honor?"

"She has." Lauren's eyes were still soft with empathy.

Catherine extracted her hand from under Lauren's and let it slide to her glass stem. She watched as a laughing couple shared playful hip bumps at the grill.

With a vigorous head shake, Lauren said, "Look, I'll talk to Josh and explain he has to de-guilt Tad so he'll attend the wedding instead. I mean, Tad's only doing it to prove his loyalty to his boyfriend. So, I'll get Josh to make him see reason."

"No." Catherine's voice became cool. "Don't do that. It's Joshua's first designer line. It *is* a big deal. His boyfriend should be with him. Tad and I will catch up later. At Christmas, perhaps."

"Catherine, that's not the same, and you know it."

"Well, what do you suggest?" she snapped. "I force the only family member to whom I'm even a little close to choose me when he doesn't want to?"

Lauren winced. "Sorry."

Catherine pushed her plate away. "I can't eat anymore."

"Did you like it?"

"Yes." She regretted her outburst instantly—for taking her mood out on Lauren and for giving oxygen to her worst insecurities.

"I really am sorry," Lauren repeated. She frowned for a moment, then looked up. "Hey, we could just get married sooner."

"Mrs. Potts already said no one can book a wedding venue around here in less than three months. It's why we said November, remember?"

Lauren gave a reluctant nod. "Well then, we could get married much later. Next year?"

"You wish to delay our wedding?" Catherine schooled the hurt from her voice.

"No! Of course I don't *want* to delay it. It's just you clearly want Tad there. So, what's the alternative?"

"The alternative is not to worry so much about whether people like us as much as we do them." She felt the familiar ache at the reminder of how true this had been for her over the years. "I'm used to it. It's fine."

"No, it's not."

Catherine sighed. She should have known Lauren wouldn't let this go.

"I get it," Lauren continued. "You've felt let down by everyone—your parents, your ex, and those so-called friends in Washington who ditched you when that story destroyed you. It's also normal to want close family at your wedding. And you're allowed to be disappointed if that's not happening."

"I've learned to manage expectations." Her words were deliberately low and cold.

Lauren went very still, and her brow furrowed. Catherine knew that look. Her fiancée was getting ready to marshal another round of persuasive arguments. To what end, though? Tad had made his choice, and she would respect it. "You mentioned dessert." She grabbed blindly for the menu and stared at it. It took a few moments to even focus. "Well. I see why you were so enamored of it. Caramel or chocolate brownies? How will you choose? Or will you get both?"

The attempted playful edge to her voice deserted her, and the raggedness of it shredded the air between them.

"Catherine? Please don't shut me out."

"I'm only ordering dessert. And let me worry about my errant family members. You figure out yours." The words flew out, sharp and vicious. Oh, hell. She was doing it again—homing in on someone's sore point with the accuracy of a heat-seeking missile. All Lauren wanted was for Catherine and her family to get along. So, naturally, Catherine had hit that bruise.

Lauren pinned her with a dark look. "What do you mean, I should figure out my family?"

"Nothing."

"Come on, say it. Who's getting under your skin?" Lauren's voice dropped to a shaky whisper. "Or is it *all* of my family?"

"Don't be ridiculous."

"If not all of us, then who in particular?" Lauren shifted in her chair.

Us. Of course she saw it as an attack on her and her family. Catherine felt ashamed at her weaknesses. She'd already ruined their evening.

"Why do you want to know?" Catherine asked in her most reasonable tone. "No good could come of me answering that question. You'll feel defensive and want to take sides, and I don't want that. I promise I will deal with it if and when it becomes an issue. And it hasn't become an issue. Not at all."

Lauren stared at her.

"Trust me," Catherine added. "It's nothing." *Yet.* Although she'd be keeping a close eye on Lucas. He might fool the rest of Lauren's family, but he wasn't joking with his passive-aggressive barbs. His words had real venom behind them. "And I'm fine." *A complete lie.*

Lauren reached for her own dessert menu. "I'd think honesty's the best for two people about to get married." She paused. "But you're also probably right that I don't want to hear the answer. So, I'll trust you on this."

"Denial *is* preferable," Catherine confirmed, lips curving, willing the shadow around Lauren's eyes to leave. Regret filled her.

"Probably." Lauren glanced at her menu. "The cookie sundae." She plopped the laminated plastic rectangle to the table. "And I'm sorry if anyone in my family isn't treating you with the respect you deserve."

Catherine looked at her hands, discovering she was clutching her own menu too tightly. "It's nothing I can't handle." When she looked up again, it was with a reassuring smile.

"Even so," Lauren said, leaning closer. "You're an incredible woman. I wish everyone in your life made you feel that you really do matter."

The ache inside felt just a little bit less at her words. "I only need one person for that. And you do make me feel like I matter to you." She lifted her eyebrows. "Will I regret the brownie?"

"Definitely."

"Then that's what I'll have. Life's too short for regrets."

As Catherine changed for bed, she studied Lauren surreptitiously, wondering what she was thinking. Was it about seeing glimpses of Catherine's vulnerabilities? Even the thought made her want to close up and retreat. She'd never been one to wear her emotions on her sleeve at the best of times. But to reveal her secret fears made her feel naked.

Speaking of naked… Lauren turned, sliding on a long shirt as sleepwear. Her bare legs were an appealing sight, even if, for once, Catherine was in no mood to appreciate them.

"Hey." Lauren hesitated. "I've been thinking about it. I'm sure Tad's being eaten up inside having to choose."

"No doubt," Catherine said, quite certain her fickle nephew was not.

Lauren's hands slipped around Catherine's waist from behind. "He'd be crazy not to be."

"You're somewhat biased."

"True." Lauren kissed her temple. "But I think you'd be surprised how much Tad loves you, even if he's lousy at expressing it."

Catherine chose not to dignify that with a response.

Resting her head against Catherine's, Lauren whispered, "You're really upset, aren't you?"

She debated how to answer. Lauren didn't need to hear all the times she'd wondered, deep down, whether she wasn't worth caring about if so many people in her life had never fought for her. Was she really so unlovable? Catherine fixed a smile and prepared to lie.

"Don't," Lauren whispered. "There's no shame in any answer. It's just us. Okay?"

Catherine sighed. "Yes. I am upset. And no, I don't want to discuss it."

"Thank you for being honest. So, although the no-regrets brownie didn't seem to work, I have a better treatment to help out."

"Oh?"

"Mmm. Definitely. Get on the bed."

Catherine searched Lauren's face for some sign of her intentions. Failing to find any, she obeyed anyway.

The bed creaked as she climbed onto the thick downy spread.

"On your stomach," Lauren ordered with a grin.

Catherine rolled over and laced her fingers under her chin on the pillow. She felt the whisper of her shirt being slid up, so Catherine shifted, allowing it to be removed, exposing her bare back. Lauren's weight shifted onto the bed, and she slid a leg over Catherine's waist until she was straddling her. Catherine was suddenly reminded that *all* Lauren was wearing was that shirt.

Lifting her eyebrows, Catherine said, "I seem to recall you saying there would be no 'hanky panky' while under your father's roof."

"And there won't be," Lauren said, tone emphatic.

"Then you should probably put some underwear on."

Lauren gave a soft laugh. "Can't think straight?"

Catherine smiled into her pillow. "My thoughts are nothing of the sort."

"Well, put a cork in it, sweetie," Lauren replied, the smile evident in her voice. "This is one hundred percent therapeutic only."

There was a sound of oil being worked into hands—*where did that come from?*—and a faint, exotic, citrus-tinted aroma of bergamot. Catherine sighed in contentment.

The first touch on her back was electric. Tendrils of warmth shot across her nerve endings, and arousal filled her. Her body always reacted this way to Lauren. Even before they were dating, she'd had some intense dreams involving her colleague that were positively carnal. She'd awake aroused and shocked. She'd never meant to let her desire leak, either. Catherine had always thought she was the master of control…until the moment she suddenly wasn't. The moment she'd—

"What are you thinking about?"

"Our first kiss." Catherine smiled. "I'd just finished my pool laps, and you were on the stairs, looking at my family photos."

"Ah." A sensual smile was in her voice.

"Mmm. I recall you were a little annoyed with me at the time."

"You'd been pretending to date a certain hunky young man for weeks. You'd been lying to me. Of course I was pissed."

"I did no such thing. You simply assumed Tad was my boyfriend. Everyone did."

"Please." Her playful warm hands stopped moving. "We both know the truth. You wanted us to think that. So why did you kiss me out of the blue that day? I've always wondered."

Catherine's mind tasted the intoxicating memory. Lauren had been looking mussed and rumpled, as though she had only just fallen out of bed. Her guard was down. Her face was relaxed, soft, an inquisitive expression in her eyes. Those long, athletic legs were on display under her sleeping shorts and they were breathtaking. Something powerful stirred inside. She recognized it in a startling flash. She *wanted* Lauren. Not just the subconscious version of the woman who taunted her in her dreams. She wanted her in reality, too. And oh, how tempting all that vast expanse of flesh and muscle and attractiveness had been.

She remembered Lauren's irritation at the photos and what they meant. Who Tad really was. Or wasn't. Her narrowing eyes, the soft, full lips, pulling down.

"You were so very annoyed with me." Amusement leaked from Catherine's voice. "It was unexpectedly arousing. All that passion? All that electricity? I stepped up to you, inside your space. I thought about kissing the anger off your lips. Those beautiful lips that should be teased and tasted."

There was a soft gasp.

"I'm well aware I can be a closed book. But right then, I wanted you to know the truth. I wanted you to know I understood you way better than you realized. I was tired of having to pretend I didn't know how it felt to be gay and vulnerable. I admired that you wore who you were so bravely on your sleeve. No masks. I have so many. As I studied you, I had a brilliant idea to just…explain. Everything. And…well."

"You kissed me." The words were breathy.

"I did. And you kissed me back. I hadn't expected that. I mean, I'd perhaps hoped you found me attractive, too, but it was barely a conscious thought. Do you know how it felt when I realized my interest wasn't one-sided?"

"Probably about the same as me discovering that the woman I thought was hot as hell wasn't straight as an ironing board after all. You made my knees weak with that kiss." Lauren's fingers did a sexy little swirl across her back, slow and seductive.

Instantly, Catherine was back in that moment. As their lips and tongues had moved together, Lauren's breathing had grown ragged. Her arousal had fed Catherine's own, until the moment she'd realized two equal but opposite things: she wanted to keep on kissing this woman for a long, long time, and that was a very bad idea with her career in such a state of flux.

"So, our fighting was what turned you on?" Lauren teased her.

"Our chemistry did. The way you challenged me woke something up inside me. Well, a great deal of things." Catherine smirked.

"And look at us now." Lauren's fingers slid across her skin, swirling around her shoulder blades and then down to press the small of Catherine's back. Her thumbs skated up either side of her spine, pausing to dig in at intervals, until they reached Catherine's shoulders. Then her fingers slipped forward and over to brush her collarbone before gently pulling back on her shoulders, drawing all her tension out with it.

It was divine. Catherine moaned.

Lauren leaned forward and whispered in her ear. "Shush. We have to be quiet."

Her forward movement rubbed Lauren's bare center across Catherine's lower back. The heat of that motion made her flush and desire pool between her legs. "Do that again," Catherine said with a gasp.

"We can't." Lauren's voice was strained and regretful, but she obeyed anyway. She rocked against her, sliding over the small of Catherine's back.

Catherine forced herself not to react, not to say a single word that would stop the incredible sensations. Her breathing became deeper.

That appeared to set something off in Lauren who draped herself gently over Catherine and began to undulate against her, her coarse hairs pressed against the swell of Catherine's ass.

"Oh," Catherine groaned. She would kill to have something to purchase against. Her body was suddenly burning for release.

"Ssssh." Lauren's voice was strangled as she continued to rub against her.

"God." Catherine pushed back into the warmth. The bed squeaked loudly and thumped against the wall. She did it again, not caring. The sensation was amazing.

There was a muffled bang from somewhere down the hall, like something being dropped. It was probably unrelated, and Catherine was about to say as much when Lauren flung herself off her back with a muttered curse.

Catherine rolled over to protest but one look at Lauren silenced her.

Lauren's shirt was rucked up over her thighs, her arousal obvious, but the haunted expression on her face was anything but sexy.

"Hey," Catherine said gently. "You okay?"

Glancing at the door, Lauren tugged her shirt down with shaky fingers. "Damn it," she hissed. She shot Catherine a regretful look. "We can't. Not here. I just...I can't."

Catherine pulled Lauren into her arms, wondering what was causing such an extreme reaction. "Never mind," she said in her ear. She smiled. "It's not like we're all pent up and have to keep our hands to ourselves for an eternity."

Lauren's explosive giggle was muffled when she pressed her face into Catherine's neck. "God. I'm sorry I freaked out. I went straight back to being fifteen and caught."

"Caught?"

"You know. Um...stress relief."

"Ah. By whom?"

Lauren's cheeks flamed. "Meemaw. Who turned about as red as I did, then hauled me off to our local Methodist minister for this long, humiliating speech about worshipping my temple, not defiling it with lustful thoughts."

"Oh dear. You were defiling your temple?" Catherine whispered into her hair. "How terrible."

"Hey! It was awful. I was afraid this would happen. I just can't stay in the mood in the same house my family's in."

Catherine kissed Lauren's cheek. "That's a shame."

"Behave. No kissing me like that."

"I will be good," she promised. "No sex in the family home."

"No moaning, either," Lauren's muffled voice said as she burrowed deeper into her neck. "Or groaning. Or any of your sexy-as-hell glorious sighs."

"I see," Catherine confirmed. "Our bedroom will be like a temple."

"And no temple jokes," Lauren grumbled. "It will just make me want to defile it, and you, all over again."

"Okay." Catherine stroked her hair. "By the way, it was a lovely massage."

"Which part? Before or after the therapeutic aspects?"

"Yes."

Lauren gave a tiny snort. "We should get some sleep. Which will be hard since you have me so turned on I can't see straight."

"Sleep it is. And we just won't think about what almost happened." Her lips curved into a smile as she added sweetly, "Or how soft your skin felt, or the delicious, slippery, wet sounds of you sliding over my back." Desire shot through her again, and Catherine's breathing caught.

"Ohh. Stop it. You have to stop," Lauren begged. She slid around and spooned against Catherine's back, her rock-hard nipples pressing into her.

With a grimace at how aroused she was, Catherine clenched her eyes shut and resolved to sleep and not to think how very long ten days could be.

Chapter 8
Bases Loaded

"C'mon, Lauri!"

A banging on the door woke Catherine from her light sleep, and she rolled over blindly to nudge Lauren in the ribs. Unable to resist, her hand kept going and slid under Lauren's shirt to cup her breast. The sensation was delectable.

"One of your brothers is calling you," she mumbled, her eyes opening. "Probably should answer before he bursts in and finds you in a compromising position." She gave Lauren's breast a provocative squeeze.

Lauren inhaled sharply. She blinked a few times before her gaze fell to Catherine's bare shoulders. "I'm not the one who seems to think shirts are optional."

Catherine gave a languid stretch, allowing one breast to pop above the sheet. Lauren's conflicted expression made her laugh.

The door banged again. "Sis! Come on! We've cleaned up the diamond. It's Softball Sunday! Jace's crew's here. Meemaw's back from church. We're all waiting for you!"

"Softball Sunday?" Lauren moved in a flash, her torso suddenly vertical, taking the sheet with her. She stared at the door.

Catherine was now entirely bare down to her stomach. "Figures," she drawled. "*That's* what gets your attention."

The door knob gave a warning rattle.

Lauren's eyes went wide before her gaze shot to Catherine's state of nudity. "Matthew! Do *not* open that door!" She wrenched the sheet over Catherine, covering her head as well in her haste.

"As if!" The cackle from behind the door was far too suggestive. "Might scar me for life."

Tugging the sheet off her face, Catherine rolled her eyes. *If only we were doing something worthy of lifetime scarring.*

"Anyway, Laur, get your ass downstairs ASAP. If you can tear it away from your woman!" There was an even more raucous laugh followed by receding footsteps.

"Christ." Lauren hissed. "Matthew thinks we're going at it like rabbits." Her cheeks were red, which only increased Catherine's amusement. "And you're not helping."

"No? What did I do? I was just lying here."

"Topless. You were lying here topless. Reminding me of last night. And what I'm sorely missing." Lauren studied Catherine's naked torso with immense regret. "But it's softball," she whispered. "Do you know how long it's been?" Her voice lifted to a whine. "It's been forever."

"I see." Catherine dragged the sheet lower down her chest. "Softball."

Lauren's breath caught. "I mean, it used to be my life, you know?"

Catherine nudged the sheet lower, revealing her pale stomach and two tiny freckles. Then a little farther, hinting at the fact that she was indeed entirely nude. "I fully understand. By all means. Go...play...softball." She wrenched the sheet down to her thighs, revealing all.

Lauren's pupils became wide and dark. Then she shook her head. "I swear you went to bed with clothes on."

"Did I?" Catherine had in fact divested herself of her sleepwear after a bathroom break a few hours ago, hoping for some predawn intimacy while the house was asleep. She hadn't banked on falling back to sleep before she could wake Lauren.

"You're very beautiful," Lauren added in a reverent tone. She grinned at her and jumped to her feet. "But so's softball! Dibs on the shower."

Catherine pursed her lips. "Nice to know where I stand."

"Yup!" Lauren said cheerfully. "Besides, being pent up will help my game. I'm gonna thrash my brothers." She disappeared into the en suite.

As she heard the water turn on, Catherine huffed out a breath. Life was cruel. And she was definitely in the mood to see Lauren destroy the King boys now.

Catherine had never seen a full game of softball before. It hadn't particularly interested her. She did know enough about it to demur when the assembled players all tried to insist she "give it a go." Catherine had a policy in life that if one was going to embarrass oneself, doing it with witnesses was just foolish.

The players were comprised of Lauren and four of her brothers—God only knew where that missing one was yet—and a bunch of chunky redheaded neighborhood friends dubbed Jace's crew.

Meemaw was sitting on a beat-up wooden chair not too far from Owen, who was standing tall behind home plate, getting ready to play umpire. Catherine strolled closer, watching Lauren warming up in a white jersey with *Iowa* in yellow and black letters.

"It's her old Hawkeye team jersey," Meemaw said, catching her gaze. "One she wore when she helped her team win the Big Ten Championship in oh-three." She pointed to a nearby hay bale. "Draw that up. Sit. Watch and learn."

Catherine eyed the dusty hay bale and considered her expensive linen pants. Was there a dearth of actual seating around here for some reason? Or was she being tested?

"Well?" Meemaw's sharp eyes were challenging.

Catherine dragged the bale over, ignoring the itching of her fingers, and duly sat on it, crossing her legs at the ankles. She slid her sunglasses from her head to her nose.

Lauren was on the pitcher's circle and shouting to a redheaded girl guarding first.

"They're doing five-a-piece, girls versus boys," Meemaw said. "So, it'll be a pounding."

"Oh?" Catherine took in Lauren, who was now shaking out her right arm. "Whose?"

Meemaw smothered a snort. "You'll see."

Lauren turned back to face home, catching sight of Catherine. She straightened, grinned at her, then adjusted her black cap.

"Oh boy, fixing her cap like that." Meemaw cackled. "Sure sign there's gonna be trouble for someone."

The first pitch smashed into the catcher's well-worn glove with a thud. The catcher, a short and plump young woman, staggered backwards and gave a low whistle.

Catherine hadn't even seen the ball at all.

"Aw man, Laur, have some mercy!" the batter called. "You're not playing for the titles now."

Catherine squinted. From behind, all the King boys looked the same to her. But she was fairly sure from his sly tone that this one was Lucas. She leaned forward onto her elbows, savoring his upcoming humiliation already.

The second pitch was even faster, judging by the fact it landed the catcher flat on her back. Her ample belly went up and down as she sucked in a deep, gasping breath, then sat up.

"I was wrong," Meemaw said, delight evident in her voice. "She's got you to impress. Not gonna be a pounding but a massacre."

"You okay, Suze?" Lauren shouted.

The catcher nodded and crawled back into position, tossing the ball back.

"That was so fast," Catherine said. "I can't even follow the ball."

"Fast? That was nothing. In her heyday, Lauren was clocking just shy of eighty miles per hour. National team scout came and checked her out once. She wasn't too interested, though. Only ever wanted to be a reporter, that one."

The third pitch was a slightly slower ball that seemed an easy strike until it lifted suddenly to chest level. Lucas was already taking a wild swing, his bat clipping the barest edge of white leather. The ball spun and bounced almost at his feet, giving a drunken spin.

"Ha, it's her rise ball." Meemaw laughed. "That got him."

Lucas took off toward first base at a slow trot as Suze scrambled forward to pick it up.

"Hey, Laur," Lucas called as he jogged. "We heard about you and your girlfriend this morning." Innuendo dripped off his tongue.

Lauren bared her teeth at him before looking fearfully over to Meemaw and Catherine.

Meemaw stiffened. Catherine kept her eyes firmly on the game, refusing to be embarrassed. Not that they'd even done anything to warrant the innuendo.

Pointing at Matthew, Lauren threatened various dire injuries for his loose lips, causing the catcher to laugh hard, clutch her stomach, and add her own helpful suggestions for names to call him.

Suddenly, Lucas bolted like a hare past first base and on toward second. He was full pelt, his strong legs pounding the grass, arms pumping furiously.

"Crap! Suze!" Lauren shouted.

The catcher, cursing under her breath, sprang to her feet, and hurled the ball she'd scooped up earlier toward second. It was a deadly accurate throw, impressively so, but she was too late. Lucas bounced up and down on the base, shouting, "Suckers!"

"Was that legal?" Catherine frowned.

"Oh yes," Meemaw said. "It's also a mighty embarrassing thing to allow to happen. My competitive granddaughter will be dying of humiliation right about now for being tricked into getting distracted."

Lauren indeed had a pinched look on her face.

Lucas was doubled over laughing.

"Don't be a shit, Lucas." Lauren readjusted her cap, grim determination on her features. "No one likes a sore winner."

"Language!" Meemaw bellowed.

"Sorry!" Lauren threw her an apologetic look.

Catherine tried to hide her amusement at her hangdog expression.

With a scowl, Meemaw said, "Her mouth's been like a farmhand's since the day she moved to the big city."

"I can assure you she didn't learn those words from me."

Meemaw uttered a dissatisfied *harrumph*. Her gaze was drawn back to the game. There was a thwack and a cheer. "Oh dear."

Catherine returned her attention to the field to see Matthew diving at first base and almost taking out the legs of the woman guarding it. Fortunately, the fielder jumped in time. Lucas, meanwhile, ran on to third.

"This game seems a little dirtier than it first appears," Catherine noted.

"That's softball for you." Meemaw fixed her gaze on Catherine. "And a little dirt never hurt anyone. But I'm guessing you don't much get dirt on you, do you?" The challenging expression was back. "Funny that, given where you work. Our nation's capital's just a blackness on the soul, am I right?" Her expression demanded nothing less than absolute agreement.

Catherine eyed a redheaded teenager heading up to bat. He looked somewhat terrified. She wasn't surprised, given the speed at which Lauren pitched. "DC blackens many a person, true," she answered. "But take Lauren. She is the least power-hungry person I've ever met, so I'd say many people's souls survive there just fine."

"And how about yours?"

"I'm sorry?" Catherine's eyes narrowed, and she turned to look at Meemaw.

"If I recall, you printed a bunch of whopping lies about powerful folk. So, you're not afraid of getting dirty and printing a bit of fake news now and then."

Her expression was curious and her tone lacked any real bite. Nonetheless, fury sliced through Catherine at the unfair charge, even though it was hardly the first time she'd heard it. She'd been set up on that story. It had seen her demoted and sent packing to LA as a lowly gossip writer, humiliated, and worse. To have all of that categorized as "fake news," as though she was complicit? She stared morosely at the field, biting back an acidic retort as the fearful redheaded boy was struck out.

"Well?" Meemaw probed. "To think I heard you were a sharp thing, all angles and pointy bits." Her eyes gleamed with humor. "Not afraid to say her piece? What was that name? Caustic Queen? Where is she now? Or are you all crust and no pie?"

Her expression was keen, and once again Catherine couldn't see any malice, but she didn't appreciate the line of inquiry, either. She sighed. Why could her past not stay buried? Her thoughts darted into dark places as she considered her response.

John stepped up to home plate. He was windmilling his arm in ferocious circles while holding a bat, a determined look on his face.

"I smell vvvvictory!" Lucas taunted from third.

Catherine turned from his daring expression to Meemaw's matching one. *I can be nice*, she'd told Lauren. She studied Meemaw, a woman who believed herself impenetrable. She was the matriarch…queen of her domain and very sure her worldview was right and everyone else's dead wrong, or at best, mistaken.

One sentence. Catherine could bring her down in one, biting sentence. She could dismantle her lofty confidence, shake her to her core. She'd even had a vaguely polite invitation to show off her claws. A few years back, when she was at her lowest, she might have even been tempted. Instead, she met Meemaw's gaze evenly. And, in the briefest flicker of expressions, she saw it.

Worry. Those cool, appraising, ancient eyes said that no one was going to hurt someone in her family if she had anything to say about it.

Catherine drew in a breath and prepared to do the two things she hated most: explain herself and rehash the worst time of her life. "Believing in a source you trust and being betrayed by them is quite a different thing to deliberately printing a lie," she said quietly. "I was horrified to learn my story was all wrong. No one felt worse about it than I did, I can assure you."

"Must have been some source," Meemaw said, sounding curious. "To risk your whole career on it."

"Yes." Catherine squinted at the field. She forced her tone to neutral. "She was…some source."

Meemaw eyed her for a long moment. An uncomfortable silence followed, but Catherine wasn't about to elaborate. The woman hadn't earned that, no matter who she was in Lauren's life.

With a nod of finality, Meemaw turned back to the game. "I see."

For some odd reason, Catherine wondered if maybe she did.

John took the bait on one of Lauren's slower balls and misjudged its speed. The ball shot into the ground, then bounced straight back at Lauren, who caught it cleanly, spied Lucas on his homeward dash, and hurled it to the catcher.

Lucas scrabbled to stop in his tracks and sprinted back for third, with Suze, waving the ball, wheezing, and hot on his tail.

Shouting "rundown!" Lauren bolted toward home. The first base fielder called out "Huh?" and looked so baffled that Meemaw laughed.

By now, the catcher was huffing hard and not coming remotely close to tagging Lucas. She pitched the ball back to third with another superb throw and turned toward home again as fast as she could muster. About the speed of an asthmatic turtle, Catherine judged.

Lucas spun around again and headed for home as well. He gave a mocking wave to Suze as he dashed past her, gaze boring into Lauren who was now taking up position at home.

"What on earth is going on?" Catherine asked.

"Now, see, Lucas is in what they call a 'pickle,'" Meemaw said, sounding delighted.

Third base threw the ball back to Lauren at home, who shot a wide grin at Lucas. He was still pelting toward her, so she waggled her glove at him, containing the ball. He scrambled once more to slow himself, watching, with a wary look, as she burst forward toward him, still clenching the ball.

"This is insane," Catherine said. "It could go on forever."

"They'll get him sooner or later when he gets tired. That grandson of mine is not built for sprints."

It was true. Lucas had more a tractor-hurling look to him than that of an agile athlete.

Lauren had started closing the distance, putting on an impressive surge of speed.

Glancing over his shoulder again, Lucas spotted Lauren's hand come up to toss the ball back to third base, which was now just in front of him.

She drew her arm back. At the moment of her letting go of the ball, he spun suddenly around and sprinted toward home yet again. His grin became wide as he saw Lauren so close to him. Even Catherine now grasped the problem: Lauren was far from where she needed to be, protecting home plate. And Suze, still waddling slowly while bent over, was sucking in shaky lungsful of air, and nowhere near a threat.

Catherine felt a burst of disappointment. Lucas looked like he was mentally practicing his victory dance.

As Lucas thundered by Lauren, she simply leaned over and tapped him with her glove.

"Yer out!" Owen shouted.

"What!" Lucas spun around, eyes widening.

"Ha, foxed him." Meemaw cackled. "I was waiting for it. She never let go of the ball. Oh, and I'd keep my eye on Suze, too. She's Lauren's old softball teammate from college. They have a whole bunch of sneaky plays worked out between 'em to amuse each other."

Lauren snapped the ball back to third, getting Matthew out, too, as he slid into the base.

Suze immediately sprang upright and jogged easily over to Lauren, high-fiving her with a laugh. "Juilliard here I come."

"Fu-udge!" Lucas scowled at home plate. "Thought I was about to nail it."

Lauren laughed at his indignant expression.

"That girl is a star," Meemaw said with satisfaction. "The moment that bat slid into her hand, it was like she was made for it. She only took the game up after Margaret died."

"What was she like?" Catherine asked. "Lauren never talks about her mother."

"I s'pose I'm not too surprised. See Lauren adored her mom, and some days it feels like only last week, not twenty years ago. It broke her in half when she died. Breast cancer. Margaret didn't tell any of us she had it, either, only Owen. I figured it out myself and confronted her. She said she didn't want her last months spent being anybody's pity case. But by the time Tommy was born, there was little left of her to fight. She'd been hanging on for him. A week later, she was gone. Lauren had just turned twelve."

"I'm sorry. And twelve years isn't much time to have with your mother."

"No. Not near long enough. Especially given the close bond they had. Margaret always loved to read. She shared that joy with Lauren. Read to her all the time. I think she would have been so happy to know Lauren's job's all about words. That'd have pleased her no end." Meemaw stood, dusting off her floral yellow dress. She drew her light blue cardigan closer. "Well, I think I should get in and start prepping a feed. We've got quite the brood for lunch today."

Catherine frowned. Had she caused offense by touching on old wounds?

Straightening, Meemaw said, "Now, since we're on the topic, maybe you can promise me one thing."

"Oh?"

"Can you try and get my granddaughter to stop cursing? Last thing I promised my daughter was I'd try to help raise Lauren right. I don't like feeling that I've let my girl down. Either of them." Meemaw sounded aggrieved at the mere thought.

"I'll try." Catherine bit back a smile.

Meemaw studied her for a long moment, nodded, and bustled back to the house.

Lauren jogged over and pecked her cheek, ignoring an amused chorus of masculine catcalls from behind her. "Did you see that? Lucas's ass was mine. Toast. He always falls for a fake out."

"Toast," Catherine repeated, still watching Meemaw's disappearing form.

"The toastiest." Lauren glanced between Catherine and her grandmother's back. "Everything okay between you two?"

"I believe so." Catherine turned to face her.

"Seriously?"

"Yes. Although I'm apparently tasked with getting you to stop swearing. A matter of family honor."

Lauren laughed. "Boy, have you got your work cut out for you."

"I'm well aware."

"Um, is there some reason you're sitting on a hay bale when there's a perfectly good chair beside you?" Lauren pointed at Meemaw's vacated seat.

"I'm fine. I'm getting used to it." Strangely, she was. "So, what happens now? Is the game over?"

With a laugh, Lauren said, "Please. It's just begun. Soon you get to watch my fine ass bat."

"Ah." Catherine stretched out her legs again, feeling a surge of anticipation. "Well then, by all means, proceed."

Chapter 9
Finding Dreams

Mrs. Clarice Potts was a squat, no-nonsense woman with a round face, a shock of white-blonde hair, and large black glasses that made her brown eyes seem huge. She talked quickly, as though she had a million things to do and needed them all done this instant. Catherine wondered if this made her feel more efficient, because so far, the only thing she'd observed that was fast about her was her tongue.

Mrs. Potts seemed to know everywhere possible to get married within the bounds of Iowa generally, and Cedar Rapids particularly. And this also extended to...

"Barns?" Lauren repeated. "Those are possible venues?"

"Of course," Mrs. Potts said. "Done up real nice."

Lauren turned to Catherine, grinning. "You probably always wondered if I'd been raised in a barn." She nudged her. "So, Ayers, fancy getting married in one?"

Catherine didn't even bother with an eye roll. She heard a faint padding noise and glanced down to see a swish of white tail. Miss Chesterfield took one look at her and leaped into her lap, stalked around in a circle, piercing her designer jeans with her kneading claws, then curled up to go to sleep.

Lauren stared at Catherine in amazement before turning back to the wedding planner. "I'm not sure Catherine's a barn person, Mrs. Potts. She's from Boston. They don't do barns there. They probably don't even do cows. Too plebeian." Lauren's eyes sparkled.

"I'm quite certain even Bostonians do cows," Catherine retorted. "But we put the bovines in the barns and marry people in buildings. We're quaint like that."

Lauren laughed and reached out to pat Miss Chesterfield's head, only for a blurred paw to flash out, claws extended. Giving a startled yip, Lauren retracted her hand just before it made contact.

"Maybe we should scratch the barns for now." Mrs. Potts darted an exasperated look between the pair of them. "Although I could leave some brochures just in case."

"Oh, yes. You do that." Catherine gave the cat a thorough rub behind the ears.

"Having said all that," Mrs. Potts added, "we actually drive straight past the best barn on our way to Linn County to get your marriage license this morning, so I could point it out as we go by. You can see for yourself. They really are something else. Fancy even for the Boston cows."

Catherine paused, stroking Miss Chesterfield, wondering if the woman had just made a joke.

"Okay, have you sorted out wedding dresses?" Mrs. Potts gave them each a moment's consideration. "What exactly is your preference?"

Catherine slid a glance to Lauren, whose expression had lost all humor.

"We haven't discussed it," Catherine admitted.

Mrs. Potts studied Lauren, who now looked pained, before offering her a smile. "Tip Top Tux does some lovely suits, if that's your area of interest instead?"

Lauren exhaled. "Whatever I get, I just don't want to look like I'm off to my prom. That was traumatic enough."

"Oh yes, I saw the photos," Catherine said. "Hot pink. Ruffles, too."

Lauren groaned. "It was Meemaw's idea. And she made it herself, so I couldn't say no. I'm not wearing pink ever again."

"Good plan," Catherine said.

"No pink." Mrs. Potts wrote herself a note. "White?" She looked up.

Lauren shrugged helplessly.

"Why don't we talk about this and get back to you?" Catherine told Mrs. Potts. "What about reception venues?"

Mrs. Potts looked up from her notes. "That depends. Any thoughts on cuisine? And are we talking formal, casual, something in the middle...?"

Catherine hesitated. A lot of their media friends would be attending. Some from LA, some from DC. Her oldest friend, or frenemy—they never could decide exactly what they were to each other—Cynthia Redwell would almost certainly show. Anything with basic regional fare on the menu would see Catherine mocked for eternity. Besides, Meemaw's pork still sat heavily in her stomach—the ring of fat might never entirely dissolve from her throat.

Lauren turned to her. "Somewhere that has a showcase of local specialties? So everyone sees how awesome Iowan food is?"

Catherine steeled her jaw. Yes, Cynthia would dine out on this forever.

"With matching craft beer?" Lauren added.

For. Ever.

"Why not just hand out Hawkeyes hats at the door and be done with it?" Catherine suggested in a murmur.

"Perfect." Lauren laughed, then slid her a knowing look. "Mrs. Potts, could you give us a minute, please?"

The wedding planner glanced at them, nodded, and left the room.

"Catherine, if you can barely get through Meemaw's best dish—and don't think I didn't see how hard it was for you—I'm not going to insist we have more of the same at our wedding."

"It seems to matter a great deal to you to have the Iowa experience."

"Sure, but come on. You think I'm gonna insist we feed our uptown friends grits?" Lauren laughed. "Hey, you know we don't actually do grits in Iowa, right? Besides, deep-fried anything would make Cynthia gag."

"Very true."

"Although, you know, that would almost be worth it," Lauren said, looking positively evil. "Hey, why are you inviting her, again? Don't think I've forgotten how she mocked me in LA and everything about me. Hell, if you're the Caustic Queen, she's, like, the Acid Overlord."

"Well, yes, but she insists on coming." Catherine gave an aggrieved sigh. "I did try to talk her out of it, but she says she's already bought her 'Middle America galoshes.' The thing is Cynthia goes back to a time when we were both young and the only two women in a particular newsroom together. Our colleagues thought it hilarious to make inappropriate comments about us every day. Her comebacks kept me amused and sane. And not long afterwards, when my family disowned me, she fed me copious cocktails and told me I counted and to hell with anyone who couldn't see it. She was the first person who'd ever said that to me."

"Really? Cynthia did that?"

"Of course, she was trying to get into my pants at the time, but I still appreciated the sentiment."

Lauren glowered. "I knew there was a reason I didn't like her."

"She never had a chance."

"No?"

"Dating her would be like dating myself. I prefer someone not like me."

Lauren laughed. "Well, you took that to the extreme."

"So it seems." Catherine ran her fingers through Miss Chesterfield's fur.

"Which brings me back to our wedding menu. Are you really worried about our friends' opinions? Because if you are, we can pick somewhere classic and refined instead. It's okay. I'll understand."

Catherine thought about that. Actually, it seemed absurd one lifelong friend was making her second-guess how her own wedding should look. What did it matter how any of the guests might view their choices?

"I don't care what any of our friends think," Catherine said, reaching a decision. "It's our wedding, no one else's."

"Same goes for me. But insert family as well as friends. I don't have to have a wedding my family loves, just one that we do."

"Really?" Catherine found that hard to believe. She decided not to argue the point. "Let's get Mrs. Potts back in here so we can hear about the rest of Cedar Rapids' wedding hot spots. All I ask for is somewhere dignified for the actual vows."

"I'm sure we can manage that."

Wedding couture shops were scratched off the list by two o'clock. It turned out Cedar Rapids didn't have a large selection of ladies' wedding suits.

"Well, that sucked." Lauren's glare was grim as they stepped outside the last bridal store. Her mood had gone from somewhere north of optimistic to south of depressed. "So much for my grand plan to go local and support Iowa. I loved being called 'sir' and snickered at in that third place. Just because I don't ooze femininity doesn't make me a man. Or *the* man, which I suppose is what he was implying."

"It was appalling." Catherine's voice was icy. She appeared to be fighting not to say something more.

Lauren braced herself for a vicious serve about Iowa. Her shoulders slumped. She could hardly defend it right now.

Instead, Catherine said, "Look, we can pick up something back home sometime in the next three months. It would've been nice if Cedar Rapids had something we liked, but we'll figure it out. It's not a problem."

"Yeah," Lauren said, with little enthusiasm. "By the way, I texted Josh some pics of me in the outfits from the change room. You know, just to see if I was going crazy about how awful I looked in those suits. He agreed they all were terrible. Well, of course they were—they're made for broad-shouldered men with no hips or boobs. And I can't help I happen to have my fair share of both." The darkness of her mood was sinking its teeth into her. "I think what makes it worse is I'm so used to this...us...not being an issue."

"LA and DC are like living in a bubble, where familiarity often breeds acceptance," Catherine said. "I'd hoped it might be better here by now." She paused. "Actually it's obviously better, given how helpful some people were. Remember the manager in that second store? She was charming."

"Yeah. But it only takes one ass to ruin our day. Or in our case, two." Lauren sighed. "You know, I'm a little surprised you didn't go all Caustic Queen on their asses."

Catherine's eyebrows shot up in surprise. "I promised to be nice."

Lauren gave a wry huff. "Is that what it was? I've been wondering all afternoon whether you didn't think any of this was worth your breath. Like, their attitude didn't even bother you."

"Oh, it bothered me." Her voice dropped to dangerous. "Say the word, and it would be my pleasure to return to both those establishments and point out how their store's hick inbreeding program is yielding excellent results."

Lauren laughed. Being with Catherine Ayers was like having a pro wrestler in your corner, itching to be tagged in. "Thanks," she said. "I'll keep you in reserve for when it really counts. And these people? They don't even know us." She took Catherine's hand and ran her thumb over the knuckles. "They don't understand what we share. I love you."

Catherine smiled, eyes sparkling. "Now there's a coincidence."

Leaning into her, Lauren soaked in the warmth and solidness of the woman she could not imagine living without. "By the way, Josh says he's got an idea on how to help. He says he'll get back to us."

"I sense a colorful wedding outfit submission in our future."

"Probably rainbow pants for me." Lauren winced. "Great."

"That'd be cute. I always said we need more clashing primary colors in the wedding party." Catherine's lips quirked.

"I'm not sure we should let Josh solve this, because he's a handbag man not a dress designer."

"A valid point." Catherine's look was soft. "Lauren, I know the day hasn't been the greatest, but I may have a way to cheer you up. While you were trying on suits in the last store, I made a call."

"Who to?"

With a Cheshire Cat smile, Catherine simply said, "You'll see. Let's head home."

Meemaw headed them off at the front door when they reappeared with little to show for their day.

"Welcome back." She gave Lauren an appraising look. "Catherine tells me you had a hard time of outfit hunting'?"

Lauren grimaced. Wasn't that the understatement. "It was so bad."

"We met the full cross-section of Iowa today," Catherine explained. "Along with a few Biblically inaccurate quotes and other unimaginative insults."

Meemaw's expression turned fierce, and she sucked her breath in, her impressive bosom expanding with her anger. "Well now, there's always some fool out there giving nice Christian folk a bad name. One thing I know for sure is Jesus only had a mind for love, not hate. But they tend to gloss right over that part, don't they?"

Lauren's heart lifted. The day she'd come out to Meemaw, all she'd said was that God's children made a colorful and interesting family...and that she already knew. "Thanks, Meemaw."

"I only stated a fact." Her gaze shifted to Catherine. "Did it go any better with the wedding venues? Got your fancy 'I do' spot all picked out yet?"

"Not yet," Catherine said.

"Pretty sure Mrs. Potts thinks we're too picky," Lauren said. "She gave us a bunch of addresses and left us to our own devices after our tenth no."

"You want what you want, I expect."

"Exactly." Lauren's stomach rumbled, and she looked at her sheepishly. "And right now, all I want is a late lunch and to forget this morning ever happened."

"Ah, now on that score, I can help you." Meemaw reached behind her and pulled into sight a large picnic basket.

It smelled divine. Lauren's mouth fell open.

"Thank you," Catherine said sincerely, taking it. "I appreciate it."

"Happy to help."

Lauren glanced between Catherine, her grandmother, and the basket. Things were definitely looking up.

Meemaw smiled. "Catherine requested I scare up a couple of your favorite comfort foods, if I had any of them sitting around. Turns out I did."

"That was brave of you." Lauren turned to Catherine and beamed. "Since you'll be the one eating my comfort foods, too."

Catherine merely smiled and thanked Meemaw again.

"Anytime. Oh, and back on the wedding topic, if you need me to run you up something myself on my trusty Singer, I don't mind. Did Lauren tell you I made her prom dress?"

Lauren's smile became fixed.

"Oh, she did," Catherine murmured. "But it's fine, thanks. We'll work something out."

Meemaw took that as her cue to give them a wave and return inside.

After the door slapped shut, Lauren gasped out a breath. "Oh shit, I saw my life flash before my eyes. It involved a girly pink wedding dress with puffy prom-dress sleeves."

"Since I refuse to marry Anne of Green Gables, that will never happen."

"Thank God." Lauren looked around. "Okay, where are we going?"

"Where else?" Catherine pointed to the distant smudge of green at the far end of the property. "Your dreaming tree."

Lauren relaxed instantly. "Perfect," she said.

Damn if Catherine Ayers isn't romantic as hell sometimes.

Lauren sat on a blanket and pulled out packages from the basket. The deep-fried Southern chicken wings smelled spicy and looked golden and crispy. There was Meemaw's special-recipe potato salad. A tub containing fresh salad of greens…supplied in deference to Catherine's palate, no doubt. Warmth spread through her at her grandmother's thoughtfulness. Grapes, cheese balls, leftover rhubarb pie, and a bottle of homemade lemonade filled out the rest.

"Oh." Lauren gazed at it happily. "I think I'm in heaven. And you have to try this." She nudged a plate of fried chicken over and was delighted when Catherine took a piece.

"I think I'm going to have to do some high-octane exercise when I get back home." Catherine took a cautious bite and then swallowed. "One of those commando trainers who comes by at dawn, calls his clients a variety of unsavory names, and tells them to drop and give him fifty."

"Please, like you'd put up with that. First time he pissed you off, you'd shred him and he'd crawl out of there, crying like a baby."

"Perhaps." Catherine pulled the salad container over. "That might be amusing."

"You could take up softball," Lauren suggested. "That burns up a lot of calories. And I'd have someone to practice with."

"I don't think it's for me." Catherine speared tomato and lettuce on her fork. "Although I did appreciate getting to see you play. Feel free to wear that Hawkeye jersey to bed sometime." She paused. "Just that. Nothing else."

Lauren laughed, feeling her mood shift.

Catherine chewed slowly before her lips curled into a satisfied smile. "Meemaw makes an excellent salad." Her gaze roamed. "This is so serene. You can't even see the house from here. I can see why you come here. It's like being dropped off at the end of the world."

"I think my dreaming tree is symbolic of why I love Iowa. It's natural, back to basics, and so peaceful. It's a shame we have so little time, packing everything in. I'd love to show you around more."

"Speaking of our wedding planning, what did you think about the venues we looked at this morning? Did you like any?"

"I guess some of those halls were pretty elegant." Lauren jabbed at another piece of chicken.

"That's true. But they made me think of business meetings and seminars."

"What about the hotel ballrooms? The DoubleTree by Hilton was amazing. They do heaps of weddings."

Catherine finished her salad and put the lid back on the tub. "It seems odd to get married in a hotel that could be anywhere in the US. These places are elegant but generic." She glanced at her. "Which place grabbed you the most?"

"Quite liked that pink barn."

"Of course you did." Catherine smiled.

"It was very…festive. And you have to admit, even you weren't thinking about cows in there."

"No, I was thinking 'it is simply amazing how perfectly this barn matches my fiancée's prom dress.'"

"There is that. Anyway, I'm just teasing. I didn't really love anything. Nothing was really *us*. God, I had no idea weddings were this much work."

"Little wonder Mrs. Potts told us to come over sooner rather than later." She slid the salad container back in the picnic basket. "What is ridiculous is we're in such a beautiful part of the world, but there's nowhere suitable to get married."

"Beautiful part of the world? You wouldn't mind getting married outside?"

"Why would I mind?"

"Well, it'd be freezing in November."

"So, we could find a place that comes with an indoor option, too. We could have some nice scenery outdoors for the vows and photos and then head inside to warm up."

Lauren sat up straighter, eyes bright. "Then what about the river place? Do you remember? We drove past it on the way to the third place?" She recalled the quaint little restaurant by the water, a small jetty, and a stunning backdrop. It was a little off the beaten track, which meant it would be peaceful, too.

"You don't mean the Jumping Frog?"

"That's the one." Lauren grinned. "It has a lovely outlook. I went to a friend's wedding there when I was in college. It was gorgeous. Can you imagine it at sunset? The river sparkling, the trees swaying…"

"What was the food like?"

Lauren shrugged. "I don't remember throwing up later."

"There's a fine endorsement."

"The backdrop to the wedding photos was stunning."

"Well...the river vista does qualify as dignified," Catherine said after a pause. "And that's all I wanted."

"Yep." Lauren whipped out her phone and did a search for *Jumping Frog*. After a few moments, she said, "I'm emailing them now to see if they have any November dates free." She thumbed the *send* button.

"For some reason, I doubt the Jumping Frog has a line out the door of hopeful brides."

"Ha. You love saying the name, don't you? And I promise it's really beautiful inside, with restored riverboat memorabilia. Awesome for the reception." She flipped her phone around and showed Catherine the website photos.

"That does look...surprisingly refined."

"No higher praise." Lauren's phone pinged, and she checked her inbox. "Ooh. Someone was sitting on their emails. The manager says they only open for weddings twice a month. The first date's gone, but they're free on Saturday, November 18. They take parties up to eighty and require a twenty percent deposit."

"November 18..." Catherine exhaled. "Tad told me that's the date of Joshua's launch."

Lauren bit her lip. "Yeah, I guess that clinches it. They really won't be coming."

"No." She gave Lauren a curious look. "Were you holding out hope?"

"Perhaps a little. A thin sliver. Even though it was stupid," Lauren admitted. "Like maybe they'd fly in, fly out on the same day, and surprise us or something."

"Oh. I just assumed no meant definitely no."

"Well, it really does now. So, shall we do this? The little jetty where they marry people is gorgeous. See?" She pointed to the sunset photo.

"Why don't we book it now to ensure our spot and then visit tomorrow and make sure we love it before we pay the deposit?"

Lauren tapped out a reply quickly, accepting the date. "Done and done."

Catherine smiled. "Good, that's sorted. So it looks like today wasn't too terrible after all."

"Nope." Lauren's phone pinged in confirmation. She went to switch it off when a news flash caught her eye. "Hey, some senator just got caught with his sixth DUI."

"And we care about that because…?"

"He's on a road safety commission. And ooh, it's Davidson. He's one of my best contacts. I have his home number. Wow, this is gonna blow up so big." Lauren wondered if she could quickly write up the story and…

"Phone away," Catherine said, eyes half-lidded, looking greatly amused. "If I have to, then you do, too."

"What about the story always comes first?" Lauren said with a pout, quoting her fiancée's most famous line.

"Not when the reporter's having a romantic picnic."

"Ahh. I didn't realize there was a loophole." Lauren turned off her phone.

"There is. Just that one." Catherine's lips curled into a smile. "Although I do understand the temptation to stay in the loop. I've forced myself to stop checking in with Neil."

"You mean he told you to stop bugging him and to have a vacation?" Lauren guessed.

"Something like that. I may be useless at following his requests, however. But I'm trying."

Chuckling, Lauren flopped onto her back and looked up into the tree. It had an enormous canopy, and on three sides the branches hung down low, touching the ground. The fourth side, facing the rear of the property, was open and allowed in the warming sun.

Lauren had always loved that she could get lost out here, in her own world, far from loud engines or louder siblings. It had been her only place to find peace as a girl. Now, though, it felt wonderful having someone to share her secret spot with. She took in the softness of her lover's face. "Are you still hungry?"

"Yes. Very much so." Catherine's eyes became hooded.

Lauren swallowed. There was no mistaking the timbre of her voice. She shot a furtive glance around. Catherine's expression told Lauren she knew exactly what Lauren was calculating. They had distance, privacy, and a beautiful setting. But still…

"We can't…"

"Oh? Why?" Catherine moved the picnic basket off the rug and cleared a space. "We are miles from anywhere. Your father's in his workshop, under a car, along with your brothers, music blaring. And Meemaw's in the kitchen, probably figuring out what to feed everyone for dinner. I imagine even if she set her mind to it, she couldn't walk this far with her arthritis, even if she knew where we were."

"It's just…" Lauren swallowed. Her eyes widened as Catherine began to slowly unbutton her ivory blouse.

More and more soft skin began to be exposed, until Catherine finally slipped her shirt off.

"I…don't…"

"Was there an objection in there?" Catherine asked, voice dropping a register. "You said we couldn't make love under your father's roof. Well, we are not under his roof anymore. Are we?"

"No," she whispered.

Catherine reached around her back and undid her bra. "Remember two nights ago?" She dropped her bra to the ground, eyes challenging.

Lauren was soon transfixed by her swaying full breasts.

"You were so warm against my back," Catherine said. "Your skin was burning against mine. I knew how aroused you were. I could feel you. *All* of you."

Lauren gasped and tore her gaze away. She made herself look up.

"I wanted to flip you over and claim you until the bed shook. I wanted nothing more than to slide my fingers inside you and take you." Catherine's hand shifted to her belt. "But I didn't." She slid it out of its clasp. Undid it with a snick. Her voice dropped even lower. "Did I?"

Shaking her head, Lauren stared.

"So…" Catherine's voice was even, her eyes half-lidded. "Any objections now?"

Lauren's gaze darted around one last time, satisfying herself they were completely alone. "I… No. But we'd…have to be quick."

"We've been frustrated for three days." Catherine slid her zipper down and then lay on her side on the rug beside her, adopting a pose like a Rodin goddess. "I don't think being quick will be an issue."

"Oh." Lauren swallowed. "Good point."

The sun's dappled light caressed Catherine's skin. The gentle breeze, making a soft rustling noise through the branches, teased her nipples into hardness. With a knowing look, Catherine slid her fingers over them and sighed.

"Oh God."

Smiling, Catherine gathered Lauren's fingers in her own, then slipped both their hands into her unzipped pants and inside her silk briefs.

"I always said you'd get to enjoy these." The lingerie she'd teased Lauren with before they'd left home had turned damp.

"*God*," Lauren said softly.

"He can't help you." Catherine's heated gaze raked Lauren's. Her eyes crinkled. "I can." She slipped her own hand out of her lingerie, leaving Lauren's. Pivoting her hips, she leaned into her, offering a rough whisper. "Now have your wicked way with me."

Lauren slid into the wetness beneath her fingers. Catherine's soft groan hit her hard. Looking into her lover's blissful face, she began to slip her fingers in and out.

"Imagine," Lauren whispered, a taunting smile curling her lips, "that we're back in that bed, and I'm making love to you right now. We never stopped. I'm all over you. My fingers, my tongue, my touch. I'm still against your back. My bare skin's sliding against yours."

Her thumb nudged against Catherine's clit and rubbed. That earned a choked moan.

"You're helpless to stop thrusting up against me. You don't care how loud you are. Look at you, coming to pieces. You can't hide how much you need it. How badly you want it. How desperate you feel." Lauren's lips pressed against her ear. "Look at that. Refined, cool, beautiful Catherine Ayers, a writhing *mess*." Lauren pressed harder on her clit and thrust deeper into her. "It's delicious, isn't it? This feeling, on the edge. Like liquid and warmth and honey. It's so exquisite, and you're right *there*. Desperate for more. So desperate."

"Ah. Lauren... Oh."

"You're mine, Catherine. God, I love you so much."

Catherine's back arched off the blanket, and a flood of wetness coated Lauren's hand as she tumbled over the edge. Her face was so unguarded, so vulnerable and beautiful, that Lauren's breath hitched.

After a few moments, Catherine's breathing steadied. "Well," she said, and regarded Lauren with a slow-curling smile. "I can certainly see why you like this tree. I believe it's my favorite part of Iowa now."

Lauren's immediate laughter died slowly at her burning look.

Catherine ran the back of one elegant finger down Lauren's cheek, heat and desire rippling across her expression. "My turn."

Chapter 10
Butter Cows

Iowa's State Fair was a big, big deal. Catherine knew this because Lauren had told her so. Often. As had her brothers, father, and Meemaw over breakfast that morning, while pointing a gnarled finger at her as though daring her to disagree.

Catherine wouldn't dream of it. Well, not publicly.

She had agreed to go for two reasons: one, to take Lauren's mind off yesterday's suit-shopping debacle; and two, attendance appeared to be mandatory.

Catherine was sliding on her brown ankle boots when Lauren blew in like a hurricane, pulling her hair into a loose ponytail.

"Hey. You still getting ready?"

She rolled her eyes at the obviousness of the answer.

"Well, don't take too long. Can't you hear the boys? They're close to a riot."

It was hard to miss the honking from outside the window below, followed by booming masculine laughs.

"I may have noticed your brothers' impatience," Catherine said. "Aren't they working today?"

"No working when it's our family fair day. Although Dad has to stay home to finish off the mayor's car. Meemaw can't go anymore because it wipes her out. But I'm under instructions to take photos of the winning pickles, pork, apple pies, gourds, jams, corn, soybeans, and legumes." She checked them off on her fingers.

"Quite a list. I, for one, can't wait to see the winning legumes."

"That's what they all say. You know Meemaw used to win in some of those categories, so she's got a competitive interest."

"It all becomes clear." Catherine reached for her sweater, draping it over her shoulders.

Lauren took one look at her. "Man, they're gonna eat you alive."

"What is?" Catherine stood, tightened her belt, tucked her pale blue shirt into her jeans, then carefully turned up her sleeves.

"Not what, who. The entire population of Iowa. You're fancy even when you're trying not to be." She glanced up at her top. "If you want to blend in, it's shirt out and sweater in the bag. This isn't *America's Next Top Model*. Gotta look relaxed."

Catherine pulled the linen blouse from her belt and tried to straighten the newly formed creases. "I can do relaxed." She handed Lauren her pale blue sweater and winced as it was unceremoniously crammed into a backpack.

"If you say so. But I've yet to actually witness it outside our home."

Catherine resisted the urge to offer a snide rejoinder. There was relaxed, and there was *Iowa relaxed*.

"I dread to think what sarcastic little commentary is going on in your head right now, but I probably won't like it," Lauren said with a laugh.

"You know me so well."

The car horn sounded again.

"Oh boy," Lauren said. "They're sure desperate to be there."

"Why?" Catherine glanced at Lauren, who was stuffing her wallet into the navy-blue backpack. She looked spectacular even in old khaki shorts, a T-shirt, and a tractor cap. *The* tractor cap. She smiled when she recognized Lauren's paint-spattered old favorite.

"They've got some buddies they're meeting at the Cantina bar. I gather much beer consumption will be involved."

"Can't they do that anytime?"

"Yeah. But it's more fun there. It's the atmosphere. Besides, they like being a little buzzed and then doing the grape stomp. It's tradition."

"Tradition. Ah." Catherine slid her purse into a chic tan handbag.

"Nope. Leave the bag, take the purse. Or..." She pointed to her open backpack.

"Who knew fairs had so many rules." Catherine slipped the purse into her pocket and tossed the bag on the bed.

"That's the spirit." Lauren shouldered the pack. "We'll make a local out of you yet."

"No need for insults," Catherine teased, and led the way down the hall. "Now, the main thing is we get to see that butter cow. I recall you listed it as a highlight of your early journalism career in Iowa."

Lauren followed. "You just love to remind me of that."

"Mm. I'm picturing you on that hard-hitting dairy-produce beat. Tradition is important, is it not?" She headed down the stairs.

"You're really annoying. You know that, right?"

"I take my wins where I can. Especially since I'm going to a fair for the first time in my life."

"First time? Christ, what did you do all childhood long? Macramé? Chess?"

"Bracing flans, remember. And dressage on the beautiful Spanish Andalusians at our local equestrian center."

"Yikes. Well at least you're starting with the world's best fair."

"So I hear. It's not like any other one was turned into a musical."

"You butter believe it."

Catherine shot her a long-suffering look.

"Puns are language's lubricant." Lauren grinned.

"No, they're grounds for a trial separation. And Iowan puns will end it all."

The honking outside turned into a long, low moan.

"Do you think I could trial-separate from my brothers?" Lauren sounded wistful.

"Excellent question. Why don't you look into that?" Catherine suggested hopefully. She glanced around. "Are we ready? Apparently, I have a cow to meet."

Lauren groaned.

Lauren's excited brothers ditched them the moment they got through the gates. The price for that freedom was a promise to attend a tractor pull with them all later. Catherine gave an internal sigh of relief at their disappearing forms.

The King boys, she decided, were like a liberal-arts student's Starbucks order—tall, fat-free, slightly obnoxious, and best stomached in small doses. Catherine's favorite King brother, however, remained the eternally absent Tommy. That must be some girlfriend he'd found.

Lauren shook her head at the haste of her brothers' exits. "I swear they're not usually like this. They're actually fairly normal."

Catherine left that one well alone.

"Okay, what do you want to see first?" Lauren asked.

Catherine wondered whether saying beyond butter cows the State Fair held nothing of interest in her life. However, to be reasonable, she didn't know that for certain without a closer inspection. Those prize-winning legumes could amaze and delight her.

Her nose twitched at the smell of straw, livestock, and assorted frying foods. Catherine's stomach clenched in horror at the latter. "What's on offer?"

"Animals and exhibits that way," Lauren pointed. "Food over there. Thrill Ville that way."

"Thrill Ville?"

"Thrills and skill games. There's also a grandstand and speeches and stuff. A concert later."

"Speeches? As in politics?"

"Trust you to home in on that. The *Des Moines Register* has its Political Soapbox, which usually attracts someone quirky with a view or two."

"Anyone interesting this time?"

"Unlikely in a non-election year."

"Oh." Catherine deflated. She'd have quite enjoyed pricking the bloated ego of a local blowhard. That was always fun. Who needed Thrill Ville?

Lauren shook her head. "You're probably the only person in America disappointed by the lack of politics at a fair. Come on. Let's do a tour and see if anything else grabs you."

By late morning, they'd indulged in everything from a tractor pull and a chair lift to witnessing various prize-winning junior livestock. When they exited the Ag building, Catherine's mind was reeling from the sights, cacophony, and rustic smells of the fare inside.

"Well," she said, sliding her sunglasses back on. "That was illuminating. I particularly appreciated the 'How to Bootleg Your Own Bourbon and Whisky' stall."

"Don't forget rum," Lauren added cheerfully. "They cater to all tastes." She pocketed her cell phone with which she'd taken liberal snaps of winning vegetables for Meemaw.

The legumes had been about as entertaining as Catherine had envisioned. "God forbid I forget the bootleg rum. But at least I got to see a particular miracle of fats and sculpting."

"Seen one butter cow, seen them all." Lauren shrugged.

"Not for me. That was my first. So, did it bring back memories of the glory days of rural roundups?"

"You're loving this, aren't you?" Lauren folded her arms.

"Possibly. But this *is* how we met. Me teasing you, you drowning in embarrassment."

"Okay, first, you never teased me, you attempted to slice, dice, and julienne me with your vicious little tongue. But I like to think I gave as good as I got. Don't make me remind you of Craigslist."

Catherine's stomach fluttered at that heady night. "I did appreciate your originality of placing a fake ad for an assistant for me. I quite possibly fell for you that day—not that I was aware of it at the time. But hindsight has been quite a revelation."

"You are kidding me." Lauren's eyes went wide. "But you were so mad at me that night! The crappy things you said to me!"

"I was a little riled," Catherine conceded. "Some days I wonder how long I'd have spent wallowing around at rock bottom if you hadn't turned up to irritate me back into life."

"That's..." Lauren shook her head. "Actually, it's a little crazy."

"No, crazy is me at Iowa's State Fair, on a quest for so-called 'highlights.'" Catherine smiled but suddenly spun her head around, having the oddest prickling sensation, as if she were being watched. Her gaze shifted across the crowd, but she couldn't see anyone paying attention to them.

"Oh, please," Lauren announced. "This is a cultural experience, and you know it."

"Really?" Catherine turned back to her. "Well, the hard-boiled eggs on a stick were a nice touch. I'd never have thought to combine the two."

"Failure of imagination, Ayers. Wait till you see what else they put on sticks around here."

Five minutes later, Catherine was staring at the unholy temple of fat-soaked hell. "Deep-fried cheesecake? Deep-fried Twinkies? Golden-fried peanut butter and jelly on a stick?" She gasped. "Fried fruit kabobs? Frying fruit? *Fruit*? That is…unspeakable."

Lauren laughed. "I know, I know. It's part of the fun, okay? Not like we eat this way the rest of the year."

"Glad to hear it. Wait…" She squinted at a nearby stall. "Why are they frying *butter*? Oh, I get it—is this all part of some cunning anti-obesity initiative? Revolt the people into moderation? It could work."

"Sadly, no. But it's not all bad. Look—apple tacos!"

"Where's the 'not bad' part?"

"The apple part. It's healthy." Lauren laughed.

"Ah. That explains the lack of a line." Catherine's eye fell to a crowd spilling out the doors at the Steer 'N' Stein. "Whatever they're selling over there looks to be the most popular. I'm probably going to regret this, but I have to know what wins the hearts and stomachs of Iowans."

"There you go again, always getting to the bottom of all those hard-hitting mysteries."

"What sort of reporter would I be if I didn't?" Catherine teased. They drew closer until she could see the sign. "Oh God," she whispered. "Is that what I think it is?"

Lauren craned her neck. "Pretty sure, yep."

"The Pork-Almighty. People's Choice Award top-three finalist." Catherine looked at the photo of a bowl of beer-battered twister fries covered with cheese sauce, smoked shredded pork, sautéed onions, green peppers, barbecue sauce, and shredded cheese. *Cheese atop cheese.* The mind boggled. The calorific sticker shock was not the most alarming thing, however. The bowl was stuck to the top of a large soft-drink cup. A straw ran from the fizzy, liquid-filled cup, through the middle of the food bowl, and out the other side. One could hold their food and drink all in one hand.

"Wow." Lauren blinked. "That's design genius right there."

Catherine's mouth moved, but she couldn't find the words.

"Want one?" Lauren asked. "It's only twelve bucks. And on the plus side, you'd never have to eat for a month."

"To think I mocked the egg on a stick," Catherine said dryly.

"Okay, maybe it's not for you." Lauren drew her away from the crowd. "I can see you probably need a breather from all the exciting food on offer. So, let's hit Thrill Ville." She began to shake out her right arm. "It's either that or the weeds-identification competition."

"Now I know you're making things up. That can't be legal."

Lauren grinned. "Weeds, not weed. Hey, do you like pandas?"

Catherine's head spun at the abrupt shift. "Who doesn't like pandas?"

"Good answer. Let's go."

Lauren pushed her way through the packed food-and-drinks area, leading Catherine to a wide open space that contained a series of small, square, primary-colored tents, twirling rides, and screaming children. Machines spun, flung, then dropped people from a great height.

"I'm sure our washing machine could do the same for cheaper," Catherine said, aghast.

"Did you really never do any of this as a kid?"

Peering at the rides again, Catherine shook her head. "I think the difference between your family and mine is that we started out old and stayed that way, and you started out young and stayed that way."

Lauren's glance was startled. "Okay, I know how it probably looks, but just give my brothers a chance. I swear they're not normally this juvenile. I think you make them nervous. And they're really excited—their big sis is getting married to someone semi-famous. Actually, it's likely just the getting married part. They can be grown-ups when they have to be. Promise."

"Lauren, I'm not judging your family—just stating a fact. I was expected to be an adult very young. You weren't." Catherine pressed her lips together at the unsavory reminder. "Let me put it this way: I know which family has more enjoyment in life. And it's not the one that encourages little girls to perfect a dressage serpentine just because it sounds impressive to her mother's friends. It's the one that has a bunch of grown adults thrilled about Softball Sunday."

Lauren's smile blossomed. "Ah. You know, it's not too late to poke your inner kid into life. In fact, we're in exactly the right place for it."

"I think maybe all this is a little more than my inner kid could handle on short notice. I'm still not over car drifting." Catherine winced. "And you introduced me to that two years ago."

Laughing, Lauren said, "Good point. Okay, let me ease you into it. Wait right here." She headed to a kiosk and whipped out her wallet. She jogged back, waving a pair of gaudy wristbands. "Right, we're all set and loaded with credit. Now we have fun spending it."

She pointed to a bright yellow tent with rows and rows of stuffed toys. "And here's our prey."

Catherine glanced at the back of the stall to see half a dozen thick brown bottles, stacked in a pyramid, which had to be knocked over. Six of these pyramids were set up, side by side. Not much of a challenge to that.

As if reading her mind, Lauren nudged her and nodded toward a pair of boys at one side of the booth. "It's not so easy. Watch them."

The children were given balls that appeared squishy and insubstantial, like a stress ball. How could they knock even one of the bottles over, let alone all of them?

Each boy had a go at throwing the balls, but they bounced harmlessly off the bottles. The final attempt, done a little firmer, shifted a single bottle.

"Sorry, kids," the stall worker said. "Want another go?"

They mumbled no, looking disappointed, and stepped back.

Lauren moved forward and slapped a wrist band on the wooden counter. The man took one look at her and produced a long-suffering sigh. "Yes?"

"My friend would love to knock down those bottles," Lauren said.

"*She* would?" he asked, flicking a satisfied glance at Catherine.

Catherine frowned, trying to unravel the subtext between them.

"Yes. Let's start with her." Lauren grinned.

He nodded and pushed over a trio of balls. "G'luck, ma'am."

Catherine realized, as she picked the first one up, that Lauren hadn't actually asked if she wanted to do this, probably knowing she'd say no. With a quick look over her shoulder, she confirmed no one else was watching.

After an encouraging smile, Lauren leaned into her ear. "The games are rigged, of course. Those balls are hopeless without real force behind it. Remember, the aim is not for you to win—hell, I don't expect you to—but to have a crapload of fun doing it. It's about being a big kid." She stepped back and gave her a thumbs-up sign.

Winding her arm back, Catherine let the first ball fly. It landed with some impact, so that was good. Although, she noted ruefully, it had missed the bottles entirely. The two boys tittered. She resisted the urge to glare and remind them they couldn't afford to be so smug since they still had puberty ahead of them.

"So close!" the stall operator said, a hint of condescension dripping from his voice.

This was silly. *She* was silly. There was a reason she had a no-witnesses rule for things she wasn't good at or had never tried before. She turned. "Lauren, I don't think—"

"Good, that's it exactly. Don't think. Just focus." Lauren gave her a pat on the shoulder. "Think of your targets as some asshole senator denying you a story."

Well. That she could do. The second ball flew straighter and, to her secret pleasure, actually dropped the front bottle. The others all rattled.

"Ooh!" one of the boys said. "Good throw."

Smiling, Lauren said, "Now you've got the hang of it. Last ball." She handed it to her.

Catherine tossed the ball from hand to hand, briefly wondering how Lauren could ever pitch in front of crowds of thousands. The pressure would be crippling if it were her. And yet somehow, she just…did it. Catherine wound back her arm, sent the ball hurtling with everything she had, and two more bottles spun off the pyramid. Another pair gave a promising wobble.

"Whoa!" the same boy said. "That was awesome."

Well, it was only a few bottles, but for some reason she felt spectacular. She shared a smile with the kids.

"Wow. Nice shot. I've never seen a first-timer do that." Lauren sounded impressed. Her eyes were warm.

Catherine suddenly decided that fair games weren't entirely silly after all.

The stall vendor smiled at her, and this time he didn't sound the least bit sarcastic when he said, "Three down is pretty good, ma'am. Of course, you need four bottles down to win a mini prize. Five for the big one. All of them down for the grand prize." He pointed to the shelf behind him, which held an enormous panda.

Catherine blinked at it and slowly turned to look at Lauren. "This was the panda you were talking about? You've been here before."

"Wouldn't be a State Fair without me right here, gunning for a giant stuffed panda," Lauren said with a cheery grin. She slapped the other wristband on the counter, then stepped back and started rolling her shoulders. "My turn."

"Double credits or no play," the man said instantly.

Catherine looked at him in disbelief. "You can't do that. She pays the going rate."

"Double or don't bother," he repeated, and gave Lauren a sharp look. "And you can step back three more feet, too."

"Joe's just sore because of how things go with me playing his game."

"And how's that?"

"Double it is." Lauren turned to Catherine and said, "And you'll see."

The two boys were watching avidly now, as were their parents who'd joined them.

Lauren paced back three steps away from the booth, did a theatrical wind up, paused, winked at her small audience, and threw the ball with stunning force. Bottles flew in all directions. Only one remained—the one at the far right, on the end of the shelf. Two balls left. The children squealed in such delight that the crowd began to grow bigger.

"Two more steps back," the stall man said, pointing behind Lauren. "You moved forward last time."

"She did not!" Catherine protested.

"She did." He tapped a sign behind him. *No refunds. No arguing with management.*

Lauren laughed. "It's okay. He says that every year." She took another two steps back, then to Catherine's confusion, three steps to the left and wound back her arm.

Just as she was about to let go, Joe coughed loudly. It was a startling, hacking cough. Lauren's pitch shot wayward and padded uselessly into the rear canvas wall.

"Chest." The man tapped it a few times, looking anything but apologetic. "My bad."

Catherine gave him a lethal glare, one she was pleased to see was matched by the disgruntled crowd. The children were crying, "No fair!"

"Really should get that seen to," Lauren said, not sounding the least perturbed by his dirty tricks. Like she'd half expected something. "Okay, lucky last." She scooped up the third ball. "And if you feel the need to cough again, Joe, I can't guarantee this won't hit you between the eyes." Her smile was as charming as Joe's expression was sour.

She stepped even farther to the left, totally baffling Catherine, then turned and faced at right angles to the bottle. She wound back her arm again, let fly, and it was one of those fast balls Catherine remembered from the softball game. Too quick for her to even see.

The ball missed the last bottle, but it was clear she wasn't aiming for it, either. It hit the edge of the prizes shelf to the right of the pyramid with force, ricocheting off it and hitting the bottle on the side. It cartwheeled off to the left, taking out the second pyramid beside it as well in a loud crash.

Two pyramids down. Just one ball. A dozen bottles were tumbling all over the ground.

The kids screamed. The adults roared, whooped, and clapped. Lauren preened. And Catherine felt a wild surge of pride that was utterly ridiculous. Now she understood why these games were so popular.

"Christ," came the man's disgruntled sneer. "Ring in."

Lauren beamed and pointed. "The grand prize panda, please." She bounced on her feet, her grin as wide as a slice of watermelon.

The man grumbled as he handed the enormous stuffed animal to her. Lauren turned to give it to Catherine, who gave it an alarmed look.

"Oh no," she said hastily. "She who wins it, hauls it."

"But I won it for you." Lauren's expression dimmed. "You don't like it?"

"The panda has your big, innocent eyes. How could I not like it?"

Lauren chuckled and hoisted it on her hip.

"How did you do that?" Catherine gestured back at the stall they were walking away from.

"I worked out one year that the bottle on the bottom row, far right of each of the pyramids, has a little tab behind its base that stops it going backwards. You have to hit it side-on to win. I do it every year. Joe hates me for it. Although I've never flattened two pyramids before. He's lucky I didn't ask for two pandas."

As they headed closer to the grandstand, Catherine caught the sound of a microphone. She listened for a moment. "Is that what I think it is?"

"Are you asking is that a political speaker?" Lauren adjusted the panda on her hip. "Yes. All your dreams have come true. That's where the Political Soapbox is."

"No, I didn't mean that. It's just I swear it sounds like…" Catherine stopped and scowled. "Is he following me?"

"What? Who?"

She sighed. "Come on. Let's see."

Chapter 11
Past, Present, Piñatas

Catherine made a beeline for the sound of the speakers. As they rounded a corner, sure enough, there was Senator Frederick T. Hickory on a small elevated stage, surrounded by hay bales. A tiny cluster of people sat in chairs in front of him.

"What are the odds?" Catherine muttered.

"I'd say pretty good, given he's one of Iowa's senators. What's he rambling about?"

They listened for a few moments. Embedding microchips was good for efficiency. Cost-cutting. Safe. Won't someone think of the veterans?

Catherine eyed the crowd. They didn't seem terribly interested, but they hadn't left, either. Maybe the chairs were comfortable?

"See?" Lauren said. "He can't even enthuse his own supporter base, and you're worried the tech's gonna take off and be a thing."

"It doesn't matter if it doesn't take off. My issue is that it's a scandal having even one person who feels pressured to do this just to get their medical needs addressed. And to do it to the vets is the lowest."

"Hey, wanna heckle him?" Lauren's chuckle was pure evil.

Catherine smiled. "Want to? Yes. Should I?" She indicated with her head a local TV camera filming him. "Perhaps not."

"Yeah. Would have been fun, though."

"Technology is opening a whole new world for us right here," Senator Hickory continued. His bushy white eyebrows jiggled like dancing caterpillars.

Catherine's gaze slid down. His jeans looked new. Probably an attempt to look downhome. Although he maybe shouldn't have paired them with a silk shirt and thousand-dollar shoes.

"We have close to six hundred new jobs thanks to Ansom Digital Dynamics International opening its Iowa plant here a year ago, which I'm proud to say I fought to bring here. And they have the contract to create, right here in Iowa, the technology I'm talking about. So this isn't just about veterans. It's about jobs for Iowans. The cutting-edge…"

"Ansom?" Lauren nudged her. "Hey, that's John's company. He works in their cars division."

Catherine processed Hickory's words, dread filling her.

"What's wrong?" Lauren furrowed her brow.

"He just said he fought to bring that company to Iowa?"

"So?"

"Why? Hickory doesn't care about tech. I've read his book. The most high-tech thing in it is his fishing rod."

"Jobs are always good for winning elections."

"But he's talking up more than just the company. He's specifically touting their hand-chipping tech everywhere we turn. I mean he's virtually Ansom's PR man on Capitol Hill."

"It makes sense he'd want them to succeed," Lauren argued. "If they don't, he has egg on his face for championing a dud company. Plus, there'd be the job losses if it fails. So, wouldn't it be logical that he'd want their newest and most talked-about product to be a big success?"

"It's more than that." Catherine frowned. "Ansom's an enormous global company. It would hardly fold if Senator Hickory of Iowa doesn't get behind it. I smell a rat."

"You think maybe it's quid pro quo, then? What, they brought the plant here only if Hickory agreed to do all the hype and wave the banner for their most controversial product? He takes all the hits?"

"That will be the least of it. What I don't get is why him? He's sixty-three, has no power or authority, and couldn't possibly be able to wrap his brain around half their product lines. There had to be a dozen better-suited senators out there who'd be willing to take whatever deal Ansom offered. That company is not run by fools. Yet they chose him." She stared at Hickory. "Why?"

"You're making a lot of assumptions. It could be he approached them and offered to champion them. Now he's riding Ansom's coattails. Local jobs are a massive vote winner around here. And also, their fancy data chip has got him on the international news. Hell, he'd have paid *them* to do that for him. And, by the way, John raves about how great it is working there, so the company is actually decent."

Catherine had a hard time imagining silent John raving about anything. "It's not decent, though. It greases politicians' palms on a regular basis. Think: why would an international technology company bother with Iowa? They must be getting something really good out of the deal."

"What?" Lauren glared at her. "Iowa has cheap land, and last year we were number one nationally in infrastructure. We're not out in the damn sticks. We have top-class airports, too. Why *not* deal with Iowa?"

Catherine stopped, and her brain skidded back over what she'd just said. She exhaled. "Sorry. I didn't mean it that way. It's just that until now, Ansom's always set up near the major power hubs. Silicon Valley. Tsukuba in Japan. Guangdong in China. Silicon Allee in Germany. You can see why Iowa sounds a little odd on that list. I didn't mean to impugn your state's honor." She paused and offered a charming smile. "Well, this time."

Lauren rolled her eyes. "God, you're impossible. And I looked Ansom up back when John first told me he got a job there. It's one of America's biggest IT companies, a huge player on the world stage. No scandals. No dirt. So where are you getting this greased-palm stuff from? And how do you know where Ansom's plants are off the top of your head anyway?"

For a moment, Catherine said nothing. Well. She supposed she'd have to have faced this conversation eventually. She wished she could put it off for a little longer, though. She ran her hands down her pants. "My grandfather's name was Mason. Mason Ayers."

Peering at her, Lauren said, "Okay?"

Catherine sighed. "When he wanted to form a technology company, he came up with a name that was an anagram of his name. Mason became Ansom."

The silence was terrifyingly long as Lauren processed that. "Oh! Wait, so *that's* the family company you talk about? Your family... They have a stake in Ansom?"

"They *are* Ansom." Catherine bit her lip, not anxious to hear the part that always followed when she revealed that fact. It was why, after her middle school years, she'd stopped telling anyone at all. And apart from occasional vague, unspecific mentions of Lionel Ayers's family in financial publications, it wasn't widely known he even was a father. He almost never spoke of his daughters, and even his Wikipedia page didn't name them. No family photo had ever publicly surfaced. The result was that so far it had never been revealed, online or offline, that one of Lionel's daughters was actually a well-known DC bureau chief.

"Holy shit, Catherine." Lauren stared at her. "That's some high-powered family business. And talk about mega rich."

And there it was. Everyone got hung up on the money. She supposed she understood that; it was such a lot. But still.

Lauren frowned. "Why am I only finding about this now?"

"I don't see how it matters, since I was disowned after I became a journalist." *Well, not the whole truth. But near enough.*

"Yes, but—I mean—God. It's…" She shook her head. "I mean, you said your parents were well off, but you never said they were billionaires."

"What's the difference between somewhat rich and obscenely rich? Why does it even matter?"

"Why does…" Lauren sputtered. "It just does! Your family could buy all of Iowa if they wanted."

"Except they aren't interested in any part of Iowa, which is why even having one plant here is suspicious. But trust me on this—they didn't get to be a world leader in tech purely on their abilities. I met a lot of politicians over Sunday lunches growing up. I heard a lot of hypocrisy and lies and greed around that table. Deals were done, certain veiled rewards were promised. It was early training for me. I learned all about the way Washington really worked."

Lauren said nothing.

Taking her hand, Catherine said softly, "Please tell me this won't change anything between us. I couldn't bear that."

Swallowing, Lauren said, "I know you're not your parents, but even so, I think it'll take a little adjustment in my brain. I still can't quite grasp with the fact your dad's company's not just a Fortune 500 company, it's like a Fortune 10 company."

"More like number three these days." Catherine exhaled. "My father does have plans to be number one. He's not quite there. Yet."

"How is it no one knows who you really are?"

"Ah. That. Because, for starters, my birth certificate has me listed as Cathy. My parents usually don't mention me to anyone. They're not any fonder of the family connection between us than I am."

Lauren tilted her head. "Have no journalists ever dug this out? Asked where the missing Ayers daughter went?"

"I'm always 'overseas traveling,' apparently, if family friends or associates ask after me. Dad gives no interviews to reporters anyway, unless they're purely running business content."

"I don't get it. Why aren't your folks proud of you? You're so successful."

"Remember, they had other plans for me than journalism, and I was punished for not complying. Dad does love everyone to do exactly what he wants. No exceptions." Catherine's gaze flicked back to Hickory. "And I can see my father's been working on some new strategies. We'll have to reassess a few things now we know his company is behind the senator's groundbreaking data chips."

Glancing over at Hickory, Lauren said, "If Ansom's behind it, I doubt MediCache is intended for a small market or one isolated to just veterans."

"No," Catherine said. "It couldn't be. Ansom is a global operation."

Lauren drew in a deep breath. "Catherine? Your dad employs my brother."

"I know. However, I doubt my father's aware. King is not an unusual surname. And there are over a hundred Ansom plants worldwide, employing hundreds of thousands of people."

"This is so weird, though." Lauren kicked the ground. "Our lives, my family, my home—it must seem so small and poky compared with what you grew up in."

"It is," Catherine agreed.

Lauren's eyes tightened.

"But that's not a bad thing. Your family home is still far more welcoming than mine ever was. Phoebe and I each got our own wings of the mansion. It was…sterile at best. We never even saw that much of each other. We still don't."

"Wings. Of the mansion."

"Yes." Catherine really hoped they could get past this. Although suggesting to Lauren it was "only money" probably wouldn't work. It always bothered people when she said that as they assumed she was being entitled. That wasn't what she meant. It *was* only money. In its stripped-back form, it was a piece of colorful paper. Meaningless compared to what lay inside a person and what they did with their life. Who had the most stuffed in their wallet was hardly the measure of a man or woman. Still, she was aware that only someone who had been born with money would have the privilege to dismiss it so easily. It wasn't "only money" to a lot of people.

Lauren looked faintly ill.

"You all right?" Catherine asked quietly.

Shaking her head, Lauren said, "This is too much."

Doubt rocketed through Catherine. "Too much?" Her anxiety rose. "You mean—"

"I mean it's a lot, okay? But don't give me that look. I'm not walking away. Don't be an idiot. I just need to process. Right now, I need you to go back to being plain old Catherine again in my exploding head."

Hiding her relief, Catherine said with a small smile, "You think I'm plain? And old? Oh dear. How soon the gloss wears off."

"Ha." Lauren leaned into her. "I think you're neither. Never could be. My God, the things you do to me."

Her smile was teasing, if a little forced. But the fact she'd even made the effort to try and lighten the mood meant everything. Catherine felt her anxiety ebb away.

She attempted her own smile and nudged Lauren with her elbow. "No flirting in front of the senator. It would be far too effective aversion therapy. I'd never be able to have sex again without thinking of him."

Lauren laughed, and Catherine felt almost weak with relief at the sound. Good. They'd get through this. It was all perception anyway. She'd just have to make Lauren see that. Regardless of who Catherine's family were, she was still the same person. And it wasn't like she had any of that Ayers fortune. Nor did she want a dime of it. The price attached was far too high.

Shading her eyes, Lauren squinted into the middle distance. "Hey, you know all the jokes I made about getting you to fit in here? Wardrobe-wise, I mean. Well, there's a woman who keeps staring at you, and I swear she's cloned your DC look."

"My look?" Catherine turned and glanced behind her.

Oh God.

Even fifty feet away and wearing an improbable tailored pant suit at a State Fair, she was a woman Catherine would know anywhere.

Her world tilted sharply, and a shocked gasp left her lips.

The salon-teased, immaculate brown hair bob, oval face, and intelligent brown eyes were so familiar. This face had tormented her in her nightmares for four years. Seeing her in vivid color was overwhelming.

Her stomach dropped, and she felt the blood drain from her face.

"What's wrong?" Lauren's hand fell to the small of her back, circling it. The concern in her voice leaked out. "You've gone white."

The warmth of Lauren's hand was grounding. She drew in a hasty breath. "It's my ex." She sucked in a deeper breath. "That's…Stephanie."

Catherine could barely focus. Her breathing was shallow, her hands slick. Her pulse raced, fast and thudding, as adrenalin spiked through her. Her thighs twitched, as though ready to race somewhere. Anywhere but here. How odd that she'd somehow gone into flight or fight mode. Over *her*.

Lauren's head snapped back around to look at her ex—the infamous source who'd not only destroyed Catherine's life but sent her tumbling into an abyss of rage, bitterness, and self-pity.

No one had wanted to know her after her downfall. Her friends had deserted her, lest they catch political typhoid. Her new boss had tried to humiliate her, as if he could somehow actually worsen her misery. How little he understood. She'd been broken before he'd recalled her to LA and put her on the gossip beat. He just deepened her well of fury by making her the source of mockery. *Exhibit A—The fallen Caustic Queen. Stand clear of her sharp claws and teeth. She bites.*

All of it had happened because of one woman's web of lies.

The only thing Catherine didn't know was whether the lies were by design, intended to destroy her, or by accident. She had assumed she'd never find out. Her lover had disappeared the day her story ran, and she'd not seen her since.

But now here she was.

Catherine willed her gaze to cut through that impassive stare and produce the answer to the question that had plagued her for years. Had Stephanie been played, too? Fed lies to pass on to Catherine, believing they were true? Or had she known all along?

She could see no guilt, no fear. But Stephanie's expression was also not entirely neutral. Catherine was just too overwhelmed to decode what it meant. Once upon time, she'd known every twitch on her face. Or thought she had.

Catherine tried to think past her own immediate chaos. *What is Stephanie doing here, in Iowa? At the State Fair, of all places?* That couldn't possibly be a coincidence. Could it? Had she been following Catherine?

Her stomach lurched at that new thought. She remembered the prickle of being observed. Had Stephanie been watching her as she'd made a fool of herself, throwing balls at that idiotic game? Had she trailed her around the agriculture building, laughing at Catherine admiring a butter cow? The sick, helpless humiliation she'd felt after her downfall came racing back, filling her nose, her throat, and threatening to drown her.

"That bitch."

Lauren's hissed words cut through the roaring in her mind. Her face looked colder than Catherine had ever seen it. The hand on the small of her back had stopped its reassuring circles, and the tips of her fingers dug in for a moment. "What the hell does she want with you?"

The bile clawing at her throat rose higher. It was tempting to give into the confusion, to scramble away to safety. To be anywhere but here, exposed and vulnerable.

With effort, Catherine pushed the toxic emotions aside with the same cold detachment she'd long practiced as a journalist. The familiarity of the task calmed her. "I have no idea why she's here. I'll find out."

"I'm coming with you." Lauren straightened, arm falling to her side, and her pose shifted wider, increasing her height. Her body language, for the first time since Catherine had known her, actually screamed *danger*.

Catherine had never seen her looking imposing before. The fact she was still clutching a stuffed panda in a choke hold didn't even lessen her authority. It was silly, but Catherine felt safer. A wave of tenderness rushed over her at Lauren's instinct to protect her.

Stephanie was still just standing there. Watching. Waiting? The butterflies in her stomach intensified. "No," Catherine said in a tone more assured than she felt. "Wait here. Just…give me a few minutes to see what she wants."

Lauren's nod was grim. "I'll be right here."

As Catherine walked toward her former girlfriend, she started to see the subtle changes from four years ago. Stephanie's face seemed harder, and small lines were now around her mouth. Perhaps she'd taken up smoking again? She'd given it up when Catherine expressed her loathing for the habit. At the time, Catherine had thought it sweet that Stephanie had quit for her. Now she wondered if it had been a manipulation. Just another one, among many.

She drew to a stop in front of her. A wash of familiar perfume tickled her nose, and she hated the way her heart rate leaped, her body subconsciously acknowledging who this was. How much she'd once meant.

"Stephanie. In Iowa," Catherine said. "Did you get lost?"

The woman's smile was cool. "I could ask you the same thing. Sawdust, cow patties, and good ole boys is hardly your scene. The Cat I know is deathly allergic to flyover states."

"Don't call me that," she snapped.

"You used to love it when I did. *Cat.*"

"I got over it. I got over a lot of things. Like putting my trust in you."

"Well, that's unfortunate. Given I have information for you that you'll definitely want to hear. A story that's world changing."

Curiosity flared in Catherine, strong and sharp. She couldn't help that about herself—she lived for news. But just as fast, a flash of white-hot anger rose up at what had happened last time. With the greatest of effort, she kept her voice steady and light. "Not. Interested."

"Not even slightly curious?"

"You set me up once. Why would I trust a single word out of your mouth?"

"You think I set you up?" Her laugh was easy, friendly, familiar, which made it damned irritating. "You don't think we were both set up? Both played for fools?"

Catherine's mouth went dry. Time slowed to a crawl. She'd wanted to know this so badly. At first, she'd reasoned no one would fake months of a relationship just to bring her down. That was insane. She was a no one in the grand scheme of politics. On the other hand, Stephanie had a fierce intellect. It was partly what had drawn her to this alluring woman. And Catherine had a hard time believing anyone could ever trick her.

"Well, that's what you wanted to hear, isn't it? In fact, you've probably been dying to know the answer to that, haven't you?" Her gaze sharpened, and her voice was taunting.

Catherine swallowed back the desperate need to know. She refused to beg. She clenched her jaw and waited.

"Was I some pawn?" Stephanie suggested. "Or was I working you all along? I'm curious…" She edged forward. "Which way did you lean?"

Catherine stared at her closely. "I thought you knew the documents were fake." A complete lie. She had no idea.

"Of course I knew."

Horror flooded her. It had been a sting from start to finish.

"Ah." Stephanie gave her a knowing look. "So, you didn't guess the truth after all. Why, Cat, you're actually shocked."

Stephanie's face held no remorse. Nothing. Her tone was nonchalant when she flicked lint off her own sleeve and added, "I helped work out the plan, actually. Considered who you were in detail. The estranged parents, distant sister, and need to be seen as 'worthy' were thought to be your most obvious weaknesses.

"It was determined, however, that you were not likely to trust anyone new in the time frame required by my superiors. But perhaps you might trust a lover. That's where I came in." Her cool smile was wide. "We fit well together, didn't we?"

Horror rose up. She had been profiled. She was a target. Catherine's weaknesses had been laid bare and picked over by…who? Who had done this? A whole team, apparently. Stephanie wasn't just in on the scheme: she was the damned *mastermind*.

"Is your name even Stephanie?" she finally asked, her voice tight from holding back her anger. "Who do you work for?"

"Does it matter? It's in the past."

"It matters. The past matters."

Stephanie merely shrugged. "Not to me."

Not to me. Catherine cast around for something, anything to unsettle that cold mask of indifference. She recalled a shadowy figure who'd confronted them on their SmartPay story, a man they'd dubbed "Gabbana." He'd mocked Catherine for being played by this woman. And then he'd said one other unexpected thing…

"So you're not actually Michelle Hastings?"

Catherine took enormous satisfaction at the startled look on her face.

"Where did you hear that name?" Her voice was little more than a vicious hiss.

"So you *are* Michelle. And, apparently, I'm not entirely the fool you take me to be."

"I never said you were a fool. More like…blissfully unaware. Lacking suspicion where it would have served you well."

"Who suspects their lover of something like *this*?" Catherine glared at her.

"I suppose you have a point." She folded her arms. "Although what happened next I'd never have predicted." Her face twisted into disdain. "Hell, turning the great Catherine Ayers into some seedy LA gossip writer? My God, that must have dented your ego."

Dented my ego. That was one description for it. She shrugged and forced her words to sound even. "I bounced back."

"So you did. Good for you."

Catherine looked for the condescension in the words but couldn't find it. She actually sounded genuine. Well, that would be a first.

She glanced around. Senator Hickory had stopped droning on in the background and was shaking hands with his small crowd. Lauren had inched up right behind Catherine's shoulder. She could feel her body heat, like a strip of reassuring warmth at her side. She resisted the urge to lean into it, but just having her there provided her strength.

Catherine returned her gaze to her ex. "Why did you track me down? Have you been following me?"

"Ah, so much presumption. Never let arrogance stand in the way of facts."

Frowning, Catherine asked, "What does that mean?"

"Never mind. Look, what I can tell you is that your stories are connected. Yours and hers." She pointed at Lauren who stiffened.

Catherine warred with whether to just turn around and leave. Stephanie's story leads were nothing to trust.

"Are you listening?" Stephanie's tone became urgent. "This is serious. I've been completely honest with you—"

"This time," Catherine said, voice cutting. "Allegedly."

"Yes. *This* time. And your stories are too important." Her hand flashed out to grab Catherine's wrist. "You have to…"

"Hey!" Lauren cut in. "Hands off her!" She reached forward to wrench Stephanie's fingers off Catherine.

"Whoa there, cowgirl. I'm not touching your precious fiancée." Her hand immediately flew off Catherine's wrist, rising in surrender, and she took a step backwards.

Lauren eyeballed her. "Cowgirl? Okay, lady, you can cut the condescending crap about where I'm from. There's nothing wrong with Iowa. For instance, you get raised to stand by people and have some integrity." Her look was pointed.

Stephanie's gaze shifted to Catherine. Her eyebrow lifted. "Well, you picked a loyal one."

"I learned from my mistakes," Catherine looked at Lauren. "Let's go."

"Wait!" Stephanie said. "Look, I knew you probably wouldn't believe me this time. So I'll give you proof. A date. August 10." She pointed at Catherine. "Your story will be back in the news. You'll understand when you see it. Whatever happens, don't let it drop. Stay with it. That's all."

"Why tell us this?" Lauren demanded. "What's your angle?"

Stephanie ran her gaze over Lauren's outfit, from the shorts to her T-shirt to her cap, where she stopped and stared. "You really did pick a winner there, Cat."

"I agree," Catherine said. "Lauren has a great deal of integrity. You might want to look it up sometime."

"I have no interest in emulating your example. Although doubtlessly a roll in the hay with a cowgirl might be amusing for five minutes… Well, until the hay rash."

Lauren gave an incredulous snort. "You look down on me, but at least I'm not prostituting myself for my boss."

"You'd like to think that about me, wouldn't you, Ms. King?" Stephanie's voice turned into a purr. "That it was all business between Cat and me? Is that what consumes you at night?"

Catherine didn't know where to look. Nausea welled up and she flicked her glance at Lauren, who looked murderous.

Lauren's lack of answer gave way to Stephanie's mocking laugh. "Bullseye, huh? Oh dear. Enjoy the rest of the fair, you two. Have something deep-fried on a stick for me. Lovely seeing you again, *Cat*. I've missed your pretty claws. *Insatiable*. Oh, and Ms. King? Nice panda."

She smirked at Lauren, slid on a pair of designer sunglasses, spun around, and headed toward the exit. Her hips had a sway that screamed *screw you both*.

Catherine ground her jaw. She felt so...dirty. Her fingers were still shaking—from rage or disgust, she couldn't tell. She'd been so damned stupid to trust this woman. She knew that much.

Lauren drew in a deep breath and looked around. Her gaze lit on something and, in remarkably even voice, said. "It's okay. I got this." She placed the panda carefully on the ground and straightened.

Before Catherine could ask what she'd "got," Lauren raced off after Stephanie, caught up, and hissed something in her ear.

Stephanie stepped back in alarm. She regarded Lauren, who nodded and pointed at a local man lumbering toward them.

Stephanie pushed away from Lauren and took off with speed, arms pumping.

Catherine stared at her. She'd never seen anything spook Stephanie. She didn't even know the woman had a pace faster than indolent cat.

Lauren sauntered back to her, looking smug.

"What on earth did you say to her?"

"It was petty, okay, so don't judge me. But I explained that I have five beefy brothers built like linebackers who would use her for a piñata if they thought she'd upset their new sister. I might have suggested that Paul Bunyan over there—that man mountain with scowl face—was one of them." She gave Catherine a pensive look. "I know, I know, it's not very mature. And I played on her bias that Iowans are all a bunch of aggressive meatheads. I know you'll say it wasn't very evolved, but she brings out the megabitch in me. What a disgusting piece of..."

Her words were lost when Catherine pulled her into a tight hug. "Shut up," she murmured into her ear, then kissed it softly. "That was perfect."

"It was?"

"Yes. Now would you mind if we tracked down all your linebackers and headed home?"

Lauren reseated the panda firmly on her hip with the look of a woman set for a mission. "Let's go."

Chapter 12
Little by Little

THEY PULLED UP INTO THE drive, and Lauren virtually fell out. She was emotionally drained, beyond her usual physical flatline after a day trudging all over a fair in the hot sun. She could only imagine how wiped out Catherine was feeling. Her brothers all tumbled out and headed inside.

Catherine climbed out slowly and leaned against the truck. She made no move toward the house. She simply stared at it.

"Come on," Lauren said. "You look like you need some space away from the rabble. Let's go sit under the tree until dinner."

Catherine nodded, pushed off the truck, and started to walk in that direction. Flipping a folded blanket from the back of the truck over her shoulder, Lauren caught up with her.

After a few strides, Catherine glanced at her. "Would your brothers have really used Stephanie...*Michelle*... as a piñata if you asked?"

"Well, not literally, but sure, they'd have rattled her a little. And they'd do it if *you* asked, too. You do get some rights to go with the pains in your ass."

Catherine said nothing more, and they walked on in silence.

Sliding an arm around her waist, Lauren said, after a few minutes, "Want to talk about it?"

"No."

"Okay."

After a moment, Catherine suddenly exploded. "What is there to say? She was my worst-case scenario after all. I was a pawn. God, I should have known better. I'm a veteran journalist, and I trusted my source because I…" She stopped talking.

"Loved her?" Lauren wasn't too sure she wanted to know the answer.

"I… No. Well, it could have developed into that. She'd turned herself into what she'd determined was my perfect match. Hell! How easy must I have been to manipulate? How easy would it have been to make me love her?"

"You think she was your perfect match?" Lauren tried to push down the faint, curling tendril of jealousy.

"She certainly tried to be. I don't want to think about even liking her right now, though. Or what any of it means. I don't want to think about *any* of this."

"All right, topic change ahead." Lauren gave her a reassuring smile.

They reached the tree, but instead of stopping, Lauren took Catherine's hand and pulled her closer to the end of the property. She pointed to a favorite spot of grass. "If you sit just here and look between those two trees, you get a pretty spectacular view of the sunset."

She laid out the blanket. After dropping to the ground, Lauren patted a spot next to her. Catherine settled beside her.

"Going to be a beautiful one tonight. I can tell." Lauren slipped her hand back into Catherine's.

They sat in silence and watched as the skies changed from rich blue to red, then pink. Colors streaked across the horizon like an Impressionist artist's brush, bold and passionate.

Leaning against her fiancée, Lauren willed her to feel the warmth and love she felt for her.

Dusk shifted into night. Twilight stars had just come out. Lauren knew they should probably go in, but she didn't want to move when Catherine seemed so lost in thought. She had a lot to untangle, and Lauren would stay beside her for as long as it took.

Catherine finally shifted and said something soft and faint.

"I'm sorry, I couldn't hear." Lauren turned to her.

"I said you don't know what it's like to be me. You don't know what it's been like."

That was very true. She'd never been able to fully understand all the complexity that was Catherine Ayers. She'd tried many, many times to break through and see everything that lay beyond her walls. Occasionally, Lauren would get abbreviated accounts of Catherine's past, stripped of everything but facts. Never a word containing an emotional resonance. Then Catherine would immediately change topics. It was frustrating, but Lauren was always hopeful that one day she'd find out what made her complicated lover tick.

"No, I don't know," Lauren agreed quietly. "But I wish you'd tell me."

"You understand how difficult it is for me to share. That…that came from my childhood. I had only a few girlfriends after I left home, but I never let any of them in. I…couldn't. My family is powerful, controlling, and larger than life, and I didn't feel safe enough to explain myself or my parents. I learned well at their knee—vulnerability will get you shredded. It took a long time to feel safe with anyone. Stephanie would gently ask, and I'd put her off. And finally…" She made a pained sound. "I decided to trust her. I told her all about my family. My life. My childhood. Some of my secret fears. My hopes. My doubts. What it was like to be me."

Lauren inhaled sharply. The gift that the woman had been given was staggering. Lauren would have cherished such a gift to her dying breath. And now Michelle had ruined everything. The realization that because of that betrayal, Catherine might never share her whole self with Lauren felt like a kick in the gut. She had never hated someone quite so much as Michelle as she did at that minute.

"I trusted her with who I am," Catherine continued. "Do you grasp how hard that was for me?"

"Yeah. I do. I know."

Catherine pursed her lips. "Afterward, she took my hand and looked me in the eye. And she thanked me and said my secrets were safe with her." Her laugh was bitter. "That night, she made love to me like she really meant it. Like I was the most precious thing she knew. It was beautiful. Releasing. And the next day I woke up feeling loved. Special. Worthy. I was overjoyed. It felt like life had finally begun. Like I finally had what everyone else did. I felt whole. Free of my past at last."

Catherine turned, tears in her eyes as she met Lauren's gaze. "And it was all a disgusting lie. Every touch. Every look. Every promise. Was. A. Lie."

The tears spilled and slid down her cheeks. "I gave up everything… shared who I was, all of it…for nothing. I was *nothing* to her." Her hands balled into fists. "The day she left me, three weeks later, I learned a new lesson about trust—that it's an empty fantasy. Oh, I learned that lesson very well."

Her breath shuddered. "But even in the middle of my rage and hurt after she left me, every day I relived her expression when she thanked me." Catherine wiped her eyes. "She seemed so genuine. I believed her completely. Oh, she was a masterful actress. I tortured myself over the fact that I had not detected her true face. I was deeply ashamed I'd been so gullible. I...still am."

"Oh, Catherine."

"She broke me. I was so exposed and it was frightening." She glanced at Lauren. "The truth is, it still is." She lowered her eyes. "A part of me, larger than I care to admit, is terrified of having it happen to me again."

"I understand," Lauren whispered. "I really do. But it's just me here. Me. Nothing twisty about this kid from Iowa, I promise. But I know telling you that you're safe with me, that I don't ever want to hurt you, aren't things you trust anymore. So, let me say something else: you don't have to tell me anything about your past until you feel comfortable. Even then, maybe only tell me little by little. Or never. It's up to you. Only when you're ready. We have a lot of years ahead to discuss all this. I won't push if you don't want me to. Okay?" She reached over and wiped a tear from Catherine's cheek. "But for the record, there will never be anywhere safer for you than with me. Never doubt that."

Catherine's gaze held so much naked emotion—fear and hope warring—that it made Lauren's heart ache.

"And it's okay you didn't know the truth about your girlfriend," Lauren continued. "It doesn't mean you're gullible. It means she's extra tricky. That's on her. But also remember one thing: she's nothing to you anymore. Okay? You have all the facts now, and today you can draw a line under this and put her behind you. We're going to look forward. We're going to have a full and awesome life and not give that manipulative bitch another thought."

"What if...I can't?" Catherine asked softly.

"Can't what?"

Her expression filled with doubt. "Trust again?"

"But you already have. Look at us. We're getting married soon. I'm so grateful you let me in as much as you already have. I feel honored by the confidences you share just with me. Don't you know how special it feels that you chose me to share your life with?"

"Smartest thing I ever did."

Lauren smiled and lifted her eyebrows. "Let me guess—but if I quote you on that, you'll deny it?"

Instead of laughing, Catherine held her gaze with a solemn look. "No, Lauren. It *is* the smartest thing I ever did."

Something inside Lauren broke a little, in a sweet, soft way. A warmth welled up in her, and Lauren found her own tears leaking. "Now we're both crying. What a pair."

"A good pair, though," Catherine said quietly. "We might be faintly ridiculous right now, but generally we're the definition of everything that I think is good and solid and right."

"We are." Lauren hesitated. "Do you mind if I ask one last thing about…her? When we were in LA, you said she gave you hope. I just…I don't see it. She's so cynical. She's not a nice person."

"You met Michelle today. The woman I knew, Stephanie, had so much hope," she said after a few moments. "She was warm and interesting and had big dreams. It was all a fiction, of course. Michelle was the real woman." She grimaced. "It's hard for me to grasp even now that she was acting the whole time. I don't know what to think. It's so confusing."

Lauren wrapped her arm around her in a sideways embrace. "Well, here's what we do know about her: She's A) morally bankrupt. She's B) a complete idiot, 'cause anyone who'd give you up for any reason has rocks in their head. And C) for some reason, she wants us to follow up our stories."

"She does, doesn't she? Why?" Catherine frowned. "And who on earth does she work for?"

"Got me. But I can't work out her angle because I don't know her."

"I don't, either. I just thought I did, once upon a delusion." She glowered and scuffed the ground with the heel of her boot.

"Yeah. That really is the hard part, isn't it?" Lauren exhaled. "Feeling you don't know what's real anymore."

"Truly, I don't. It's…difficult to ground myself. Some days are harder than others. But it's been a lot better since I met you."

Lauren smiled. "Lauren King, life-sized anchor. You're welcome."

"Mmm. By the way, your defense of my honor today is duly noted. And most appreciated." She dusted a kiss against Lauren's cheek. "The look of her scuttling away like a twitchy squirrel… It went a long way to healing something inside. I'll have something different to remember when I think of her now."

"Good. And for the record, I plan to make it my mission that you don't remember her at all in the future. It'll just be thoughts of you and me filling your head. And then, in three months' time, we're gonna kick marriage's ass and people will say, 'There goes Lauren King, luckiest woman in the world.'"

Catherine laughed for a brief moment before her face crumpled. She turned away.

"Hey, don't," Lauren whispered. "Don't be embarrassed. It's just me. And I might be a tough Iowan kid, but you know how often *I* cry. Kitten videos, burnt toast, stubbed toes—you name it. Please never be afraid to be emotional around me."

"It's so muddled. I don't…" Catherine wiped her eyes and glanced at her. "I really don't understand why I am reacting like this. It happened four years ago. I didn't cry when my parents disowned me. I didn't cry when Phoebe didn't stand up for me to them. I was furious when I lost my job and my friends deserted me, but I didn't shed a single damned tear. And yet now, here, far from everything I've ever known, suddenly I can't stop." She lifted her hand to display the wetness glinting on her fingers.

"It's simple." Lauren grasped those trembling fingers. "Someone who meant a lot to you has dredged up a lot of painful old stuff, unresolved feelings and memories, and maybe right now, right here, is the first time you feel safe enough to let down your guard and really process it."

"Maybe so." Catherine's gaze drifted to the emerging stars. "You know, my parents always used to mock the Midwest as 'less than.' But I'm finding I appreciate its lack of artifice the longer I'm here. It's earthy, uncomplicated, decent, and honest." She glanced back at Lauren. "Much like you."

"Iowa grows on people." Lauren grinned. "You know, speaking of your parents—all this time I thought they were running some stuffy old company, the way you spoke of your family business. And you also said they'd be having vapors over the idea of you marrying me. Now I find out your dad's some sort of futuristic visionary? How does that fit?"

"My father is not a visionary. He's a good manager. *His* father was visionary. And the Ansom team they surround themselves with are spectacular. They're the stars."

"So why all the uptightness? The social conservatism?"

"To be fair, it's mainly from my mother's side. She married into a family that was wealthy and well-known. She was only nineteen, so she might have overcompensated in trying to do what she thought she should. Everything was all about appearances and trying to fit in with the elite."

"Well then, I can see why you marrying someone like me would give her hives."

"Absolutely. Her daughter marrying a female, a reporter, and an Iowan? *In* Iowa? I think it couldn't get much worse for her. Well…unless you were also a criminal." Catherine suddenly looked greatly amused by that thought. Her eyebrows lifted. "Do tell, are you?"

"Hey? Why assume that?" Lauren tossed her an askance look.

"I'm not hearing a denial. What was it, 'borrowing' sports cars and doing donuts behind the high school?"

"I did have a brief life of petty crime, it's true." Lauren hid her smile.

"Here it comes."

"When I was eight or nine, certain sweets found their way into my pocket at the local five-and-dime store."

"My hardened felon. So, what happened?"

"Mom was horrified and dragged me down to the local police station for a stern talking to. They had this junior officer lecture me about how if I kept this up I'd be on the road to ruin."

"Ahh. Did it work? Were your criminal inclinations curtailed?"

"And how." Lauren gave an amused hum. "I was in such awe of the cop. She was *beautiful*. My first crush. Not sure I heard much of what she said. But her in that uniform…wow."

"I don't think that talk went quite how your mother envisioned it."

"Nope, not even close. But it sure did clarify some things for me. I had a pretty clear idea after that as to why I never could see myself with a boyfriend." Lauren turned, suddenly filled with curiosity. "What about you? When did you get a clue? I know I've asked a few times. Don't think I haven't noticed you keep dodging the question." A tiny smile danced around her lips. "I mean, unless this is one of those things in your past you don't want to talk about?"

A wary look crossed Catherine's face, but she answered anyway. "I suppose my first inkling had to do with discovering that my boyfriend's sister was far more interesting to kiss than he was. We were fifteen. He was so outraged when he found out that he told everyone. Mom made a big fuss and the poor girl—"

"They blamed her?"

"Well, no Ayers could possibly be one of *those*, so who else was there to blame? My mother accused her of corrupting me." Sadness crossed her face. "In truth, I was the one who..." She pressed her lips together.

"What happened?"

"Her family suddenly had the funds to move to a different state. And my mother increased her vigilance on me. The rest of my teenage years became filled with homework, horse riding, and handpicked 'friends.'" Her face closed. "Those are not times I wish to relive."

"I'm sorry. But at least you're free of all that now."

"Yes. I thank the universe every day for that. I owe my parents nothing."

"Exactly. They're behind you; it's what's ahead that matters."

"Very true. And what's ahead is our wedding." Catherine nodded. "That's my focus now. Well, that and figuring out what Ansom's up to in Iowa. I'm far too curious not to dig about in our downtime a little."

"Well, I admit I am also a tiny bit curious about the August 10 date your ex gave us but, given she's about as trustworthy as a fox guarding a henhouse, I probably shouldn't be," Lauren said.

"No. You really shouldn't be." Catherine rose and dusted herself down.

Lauren also stood and gave the rug a shake. "Oh, hey, I meant to say earlier, thanks for being such a good sport this morning, indulging my brothers when they dragged us off to the tractor pull."

Catherine made a noncommittal noise and rubbed her temple. "It's nothing denial and a hearing specialist can't solve."

Laughing, Lauren leaned over and kissed her soundly. "God, you're funny."

"Who's joking?"

Chapter 13
Ansom Digital Dynamics

BREAKFAST THE NEXT DAY INVOLVED an enormous spread of toast, beans, bacon, and eggs. The sheer volume of artery-hardening edible matter the brothers were capable of mowing through was still hard to get used to for Catherine.

"So, what's everyone up to today?" Owen asked as he poured himself a black coffee.

"Doing that thing at John's work we talked about," Lucas said between bites. "Open house."

Everyone's eyes swung John's way. He blushed red from under his hairline, the hue burrowing under the shirt at his neck.

"Oh?" Lauren said. "Why are they doing that?"

"It's their first anniversary of the plant opening," Lucas said. "They invited everyone to bring along their families. Thought I'd check it out since work's light today. Show Johnny here some family support."

John slathered his toast with butter and did not look up.

"What time's it happening?" Lauren asked.

"Ten till noon," Lucas said. "But you don't have to go. It's just for anyone interested in where he works, a few speeches and all tha—"

"Excellent," Catherine cut in. "I, for one, would love a tour of Ansom Digital Dynamics International's Iowa division."

"You would?" Meemaw asked, brow furrowing.

"Oh, definitely." She glanced at Lauren. "Wouldn't you?"

Lauren caught her pointed look and nodded. "Yep. We'll be there with bells on. For John."

John gave them both perplexed glances before taking another hasty bite of toast.

"Do you know who's giving the speeches?" Lauren asked. "Any VIPs?"

Meemaw stopped laying out the food and gave them both a hard stare. "All right, what are you two up to?"

Catherine fixed her expression to neutral, deciding the truth that they were digging into a story probably wouldn't win them any allies at this table. "Learning more about Iowa's industry and where my brother-in-law-to-be works."

Lauren added, "Electric cars sound cool."

"Lauren Annabelle King," Meemaw said, "I've known you too long not to know when you're up to something. And you—" She gave Catherine a suspicious look, then pointed at her. "I can only guess at what your Trouble Face looks like, but I suspect I'm looking at it right now. Just don't start anything that'll cause a fuss. John loves that job."

"Best behavior. Check," Lauren said. "No problem." She turned to John. "Ten o'clock?"

He nodded but looked even more confused.

"Great." She shot him a smile, then poked her sausage with a fork.

After breakfast, Catherine was volunteering herself for dishwashing services—and being shooed out of the kitchen by an appalled Meemaw—when there was a tentative knock on the door.

"I'll get it!" Lauren's voice called, already halfway down the hall. A moment later, she stuck her head back in the kitchen and beckoned to Catherine. "Hey, c'mere. There's someone you have to meet."

Catherine followed her to the door, which revealed a thin young man with excited, bright brown eyes. He was adorned in a dapper blue suit. A perfect purple triangle of silk jutted from the breast pocket.

"Yes?" she asked.

"Hi, Ms. Ayers. It's such an honor to meet you." He blinked rapidly. "Both of you. I'm Zachary Branson. You maybe know my label? ZachB?"

Catherine gave him a baffled look. "Label?"

"Oh, so that's a no? Um, okay. Anyway, Josh—um, Joshua Bennett—said you have a wedding outfit emergency? He posted an SOS for Iowan designers who do wedding wear on this fashion designers' Facebook group we're in." He sucked in a huge breath and added in a rush. "Oh my God, I can't believe it's you."

"You know who I am?" Catherine found that hard to believe so far out of DC.

"Oh yes, ma'am." He bobbed his head up and down reverently.

Behind them, Lauren snickered.

"Joshua talks about you all the time," Zachary continued. "Quotes your snarkiest lines. He had us in hysterics over how you used to, ah, creatively threaten Ms. King at those LA events. Don't worry—it was just the public stuff when you were ice queening spectacularly. Anyway, our designers' group, Glad Rags and Fad Bags, have been fanboying over you for two years solid. You're a *goddess* among the stitches-and-bitches crowd. Oh, gosh, sorry. I'm rambling, aren't I?"

"Ice queening?" Catherine muttered. She felt like she was in an alternative reality. Perhaps in *some* world this made sense.

"Oh!" His expression fell and became stricken. "I'm making *such* a mess of this. Can we start again? Hi, I'm Zachary. I design wedding outfits. I'll do yours and Ms. King's for cost because it's totally an honor. I'd drop everything. I can have them back to you Friday. Also, Ms. Ayers, 'ice queen' is, like, legit the highest form of flattery that I know. Here. My designs." He thrust out a thick portfolio.

Catherine had a brief urge to bop him on the nose with it. She'd gone from a caustic queen to an ice queen? She glanced behind her at Lauren, who was no help given she looked about three seconds from bursting into laughter. Catherine tossed her an indignant glare.

"And Joshua recommends you?" Catherine turned back to him.

"Oh yes, ma'am. He picked me out of a short list of six others. He ran a contest in our Facebook group, and all two thousand three hundred and forty-two members voted to decide which of us had won the right to dress you both."

A contest. Trust Joshua to think that was a good idea. The man put scarlet tassels on handbags, for heaven's sake.

"Catherine, why don't we sit down and look through his portfolio?" Lauren suggested.

Zachary shot her a pathetically grateful look.

Catherine hated to admit it, but Zachary's portfolio was stunning. No wonder his peers had chosen him. She might have to retract her uncharitable thoughts about Joshua.

The dress selections, one of which she knew immediately she wanted to wear, all had an ethereal, floating quality. And the suit designs that Lauren was flicking through? Tailored beautifully at the hips and bust. These designs were made with flattering attention and focus on women. The female silhouette wasn't an afterthought, repurposed from a male line. Simply elegant. Catherine glanced at Lauren. Her relief was obvious as she studied the pages.

Yes, Zachary's designs would do perfectly.

"I do a lot of lesbian weddings," Zach said. "The market boomed when the marriage laws changed. Iowa was one of the first few states to allow it, you know. But most of the boutiques didn't change a thing about their range. I guess they didn't stop and think about why they should. Anyway, that just means I do really well. Business is so good that I took on a seamstress and a student designer to help me out. But I only sell online."

That explained why Mrs. Potts didn't know he existed. Catherine decided she'd remedy that.

"Do you see anything you like?" he asked, eyes hopeful.

"Many things," Catherine said. "You have a great deal of talent."

He brightened and turned to Lauren. "And you, Ms. King?"

"Oh yeah. I really love one suit in particular." She started flipping back a few pages. "It's the…"

"Wait! Um…sometimes the brides don't like to know what each other is wearing until the big day. So, if you want to keep it a secret from each other, I can do that. Just tell *me*, and I'll make sure the looks complement each other. It means you can still have a surprise reveal."

"Ooh, I like that." Lauren nodded.

"As do I," Catherine said.

"Okay, then." Zachary beamed. "Let me have fifteen minutes alone with each of you to do the measuring and work out your needs, and then we're done for today."

Zachary drew a cloth tape measure out of his suit and snapped it into a sharp line. "So, who's first?"

One glance around the foyer of Ansom Digital Dynamics International's Iowa Division, taking in the size and composition of the white front desk, and Catherine knew the plant's layout would be identical to every other factory her family ran.

They were greeted politely, signed in, and given an option of taking a map and seeing themselves around the green-coded areas at their own pace or following a tour guide.

"Tour," Lauren said. "I want to know what they think is a priority at this place."

Catherine could have answered that in one word. *Profit.*

They followed the signs and the small crowd of family members from room to room, listening to what each area specialized in, courtesy of the perkiest tour guide to ever exist outside of Disneyland.

They reached Electric Car Section 2-EV after fifteen minutes. It was as gleaming and futuristic as everything else.

"Our E-Vroom room," the guide said without a hint of amusement at the rhyme. "Ansom's still only at the experimental stage for its electric cars and is developing a longer-life battery. If it succeeds, it will roll out a full range in five years. This is the room that services all the test models."

Lauren let out a soft, embarrassed groan.

Curious, Catherine followed her gaze.

John King was in his blue overalls, working hard, servicing a car, which was on a hoist at head height. The work area had been roped off and Lucas was leaning forward across the rope and waving his arms to be more obvious in his brother's peripheral vision. He was also making "helpful" suggestions.

"Don't forget to kick the tires," he called. "That way you'll know how broke the car is. And twang that fan belt. Check it's extra-tensiony."

"Sir, please don't heckle our staff," the tour guide interrupted him. She added with a slight smile, "Even if they are clearly family."

John gave the woman a grateful nod and rolled his eyes at his brother.

"Damn," Lucas said. "That's a shame."

"'Extra-tensiony' is not a thing," Lauren called out to him across the room.

He spun around and caught sight of her. "Sis!"

She ambled over and gave his arm a light slap. "Stop bugging your brother."

"Where's the fun in that? Why'd you think I came?" He cocked his head. "That's my excuse, what's yours?"

Lauren shrugged.

"How 'bout this one then—why'd you wanna know about the speeches and the VIPs?" He eyed Catherine. "And how come you knew the company's whole name, Cat?"

She ground her teeth at the nickname that Stephanie—*Michelle*—had forever ruined for her. Instead of answering, she let her gaze trail around the room, as though random car parts held more interest than he did. Which was completely true.

The tour party started to walk en masse out the door to the next room. Lauren pointed at them. "Sorry, Lukey, our ride is leaving. Gotta go."

Catherine shot Lucas a thin smile. "We really don't want to miss a single scintillating minute."

The promised speeches were at the end of the tour, held in a glossy white room designed to dazzle visiting dignitaries. Catherine had to resist the urge to put her sunglasses on. Some things never changed.

"I'm going snow-blind," Lauren grumbled.

Catherine smiled. "White is clean. Clean is modern. Modern is futuristic. The future is Ansom. They paid a lot for marketers and psychologists to tell them that."

"I'd tell them for free not to daze their visitors."

A well-dressed group of dignitaries was assembling on a small raised platform as the tour group began seating themselves and talking in low tones.

Catherine's eyes roamed. She went rigid.

"Hey." Lauren nudged her. "Is Senator Hickory stalking us, or are we stalking him? Look—he's about to give a speech."

Catherine stared at the stage.

"Catherine?"

"My parents..." she whispered. She discreetly pointed to the couple being snapped by in-house photographers at one side of the stage. "...are right there."

"Oh." Lauren swallowed audibly.

Oh, indeed.

It had been twenty years since Catherine had last seen her parents. The spiteful, accusing words her father had flung at her the last time they saw each other still hurt. She could still remember the feel of her mother's gaze, watching her from the upstairs window as Catherine left.

She always did that. Watched. Never intervened when her husband laid down the law. Lionel Ayers ran the family like a company. Unsatisfactory, disloyal members were summarily terminated and shown the exit. And no one ever protested his decisions.

Her father's dark-brown hair was more salt than pepper now. He had retained his good looks, but he was thicker around the stomach and neck. His bespoke tailoring couldn't hide everything.

Her mother was still grace personified. She'd practiced far too long with a deportment tutor not to look the part now. She didn't walk anywhere; oh no, she swept or floated. Her peach skirt suit was impeccable. Pearl earrings twinned with her necklace.

Hickory's speech was almost over. Something about him helping Ansom to bring jobs to Iowans and the wonders of MediCache. The identical speech he'd given at the fair.

The applause was polite. Hickory then introduced Catherine's father as "Ansom's visionary."

The applause turned thunderous as Lionel Ayers took the microphone.

He cleared his voice. "I would have set up in Iowa years ago if I'd known this would be the response." He chuckled, as did the audience. "What is Ansom? It's a family business built into one of the greatest IT companies in the world. We stayed true to our American roots. We built on our successes. We valued our remarkable employees, and look at us now."

The applause started again. He soaked it up.

"But at its heart, we're still a family business. Family's what matters. Our business was started by my father, then was catapulted into the global market by me, and who knows what lies in the future when I pass the torch one day to my talented son-in-law?"

Talented? Phoebe's husband, Miles Sutherland, had all the initiative of a garden snail.

"I remember as a boy at my father's knee talking about how great things grow from little things, how you need an acorn to produce a giant oak tree, and that's what Ansom is now..."

She sighed, recognizing the words. It was her father's go-to speech about a supposedly tender moment between father and son. Given Grandpa Mason had never had a good word to say about his son—or anyone, for that matter—all her father's charming botanical homilies were pure fiction. She tuned him out and let her gaze drift to her mother's face. She seemed exactly the same. Older, beautiful, serene to the point of vacant possession. Her fixed smile hadn't changed. Her mouth was still hard.

Her father turned to look at his wife. "...and I couldn't have done it without my gorgeous wife." He beckoned to her. "Victoria?"

Oh, how her father liked to show his wife off—even though he'd screwed his way through most of the secretarial pool. He'd chosen her purely to further his image. Like a pretty trinket to be hammered to a wall.

Her mother stepped forward and took his outstretched hand.

"As a husband and a family man, I find it valuable to listen to my family's needs. And I am all about making technology accessible for everyone."

Listening to his family's needs? Catherine gave him an incredulous glare. Lauren's fingers found hers and gave a reassuring squeeze.

Perhaps her lethal look burned a spot in her father's head, because he suddenly caught sight of her. He paused, barely faltering, then continued. Her mother followed his gaze, and Catherine enjoyed her surprised reaction before her mask resettled.

His speech eventually wound up.

The crowd and its hubbub rose. Visitors now were heading for the exits.

Catherine remained seated, unsure exactly what to do next.

"I'm going to talk to your senator," Lauren said, standing, "because I'm thinking he probably won't want to see you after that story you ran on him last week."

"He should be flattered to be mentioned in the same story as Aldous Huxley." She folded her arms in defiance.

Lauren laughed. "Yeah, well, for some reason politicians don't like to be told they're helping usher in a dystopian *Brave New World* future to their nation. But nice try." She glanced at the stage. "You want to talk to your folks?"

Want to? No. Should she? Catherine contemplated her options. A thawing was only a remote possibility. It had been so long. What was left to say, really?

Lauren patted her arm before heading up to the stage as Catherine gathered her thoughts.

"You know," came a voice from behind her. "I didn't notice it at first."

She turned to find Lucas sitting behind her, regarding her with keen, cool eyes.

When had he come in?

"Notice what?"

"That John's big boss has the same last name as you."

Catherine stilled. "Oh?"

"And then I looked at the wife." He tilted his head toward Catherine's mother. "Did you know all you Ayers women look alike? Same...vibe." His nose wrinkled.

Glancing at her mother, Catherine studied the woman's hands-off, disdainful expression and felt only distaste. *That's* how Lucas saw her? She schooled her expression to bland. "I have a vibe?" she asked, tone pleasant.

Lucas just looked at her. "So," he said without inflection, "you're richer than God? That explains a lot."

Catherine gave him a dark look.

"And now I see your little speech about not being given any handouts and earning everything yourself was BS." He didn't sound pissed at her. He sounded... She couldn't put her finger on it. Disappointed? Maybe?

"No. I'm not rich. And the reasons why are none of your concern."

"Does Lauren know?" He leaned forward, brow drawn. "About them?" Lucas pointed at the stage.

"She knows."

He balled his hand into a fist and dropped it on top of the back of Catherine's chair in front of him. He lowered his chin on it and locked eyes with her. "Is this why you act like you're better than everyone else? Better than us? Better than Iowa?"

"Is that what you think?"

He looked at her intently. "Oh, I know it is. Shame Lauren can't see what's right in front of her. Even my brothers think you're okay 'cause they say you love Laur. Hell, Mark's been begging me to lay off you. But I'm not so easy to sucker. I'm looking out for her. I want to know: What's your game? Are you playing with my big sis?"

"How can I be playing with Lauren? I'm *marrying* her."

"I looked you up. I know you're the Caustic Queen. You aren't exactly famous for anything except being a bitch and bringing down corrupt politicians. The thing is, Cat, I know my sister way better than you, and for a lot longer. She loves you, I get that. But she doesn't always see what's right in front of her."

"And that is?"

"Someone who'll suck the goodness and decency right out of her and spit her out when they're done. I see you. You're dark. Dark and mean. She's not. So, what the hell are you doing with someone like her? Especially since you're rich as sin and could have anyone you want? Why Lauren?"

Catherine wanted to lash the obnoxious upstart. Remind him she knew Lauren far better than he did. She had been living with her, loving her, sharing her dreams for a year. She wanted to sneer at him for treating his sister like she was too stupid not to know who she was marrying.

But then he looked at her, unblinking, and she could see it in his eyes. *Fear.*

Fear she'd hurt Lauren?

She sighed. Just great. An overprotective brother to match the mother-bear grandmother. The worst of her anger seeped out.

Still, despite his poorly executed good intentions, it wasn't his place to demand anything of her. He hadn't earned her life story or the truth in her heart any more than Meemaw.

"You don't know me," Catherine said evenly. "You don't understand me, even though you're so sure you do. You base your concerns on a professional persona that has little bearing on who I really am. Your sister is beautiful, talented, kind, and amusing. So, if you don't understand what

137

I could possibly see in her, then I pity you. It means you don't know your own sister half as well as you think. And that's all I'm going to say to you."

Lucas's eyes narrowed.

Catherine rose, turned her back on him, and drilled her heels viciously into the floor as she strode toward the stage. Her lips compressed with the effort of not uttering all the things she'd dearly have loved to say to wipe that smug look off his face.

A moment later, she realized she had no plan as to where she was going. Just then her mother spotted her, turned fully to face her, and watched her approach with an expectant look.

Oh great.

Chapter 14
Ayers and Graces

"Hello, Mother." Catherine brushed her lips against the woman's ear in a barely there kiss. The familiarity of her La Vie Este Belle scent, with its hints of iris gourmand, filled her senses.

"Catherine." Her mother's plum-colored lips pressed together. Clear blue eyes looked Catherine up and down. "You're looking older."

Well, she supposed that was an improvement on her usual litany of Catherine's failings. At least this one wasn't her fault this time.

"As do you," she replied. "It has been twenty years." She allowed a faint edge of accusation in her tone.

"Your sister has kept me apprised of your movements. Back in DC again? Not humiliating yourself on gossip writing anymore? I suppose that's a marginal improvement. Maybe stick to the truth in your stories this time?"

Trust her mother to cut to the chase. "And how are things?" Catherine said, ignoring the dig.

"Much as I'd expect. Not a great deal has changed."

"Nothing? Is Dad still..." She paused, not sure exactly what she was asking.

Her mother gave her a sharp look, as if she'd just enquired whether her husband was still working his way through the company secretaries.

"...still Dad?" Catherine finished.

There was a flash of microaggression that Catherine knew all too well. The faintest lip clench. Then her mother's mask slammed down tighter than ever. "Your father is powering Ansom to ever greater heights. It's been in all the financial papers. Surely you've noticed, even while you're off having your midlife crisis."

"My what?"

"How old is she anyway?

Oh. Of course she'd see it that way. "Thirty-four."

"Astonishing. She looks twenty-five." She sighed. "You do know that's what people will remember—what things appear to be, not what's true. How could you forget all my lessons?" She made an exasperated noise. "Couldn't you have just bought the flashy sports car like men do?"

Catherine met her gaze wordlessly, although her heart started pounding. Her mother always did this. A few well-placed jibes and it was like being twelve again.

"I saw the undignified proposal video," her mother continued. "In front of the President, no less? He must have been appalled. And airing your dirty laundry before the nation's media, too?"

Dirty laundry? Her love was *dirty laundry* now? Catherine's jaw tightened.

"The only relief is that no one yet seems to have worked out who your parents are," her mother finished, darting her gaze around as if to make sure that wasn't going to change.

"Well, you did make sure of that, didn't you? Your overzealous lawyer always swoops in and 'corrects' anyone who might come close to drawing a link between us."

Her mother waved her hand. "I'd have thought that would make you happy. You're one step further removed from your parents."

"Ex-parents. Dad made that pretty clear. On Christmas Day, no less. I recall you didn't object."

Her mother merely smiled her fake smile that signaled this part of the discussion was now over. She adjusted her pearl necklace to perfectly straight.

The absent gesture hurled Catherine back in time. Her throat tightened.

Victoria Ayers had always been the most elegant woman she'd ever known. Aloof, beautiful, poised. Catherine remembered being schooled constantly in achieving that same level of perfection. Every lesson her mother ever imparted had been about erasing the parts of Catherine that weren't flawless. Collars yanked up, sleeves straightened, bows aligned.

That's all Catherine had ever been to her. A series of mistakes that needed correction. And yet they'd thought casting her out of the family would make her want to crawl back to have her flaws adjusted, fixed, and eradicated once more? The freest she'd ever felt was away from them. From her, especially. It was a startling reminder.

"I didn't expect to see you here," her mother was saying. "What brings you to Ansom Iowa?"

Catherine looked around, reminded of why she was really here. It certainly wasn't to try to mend bridges. Not possible, anyway. There was never any compromise from her parents' side.

Her mother stared at her with that same perfect mask of indifference after twenty long years apart. Not one thing had changed in her attitude toward her.

I'd think that would hurt more. How...unexpected.

Instead, all she could feel was that unsettling wash of familiarity from the scent of iris gourmand.

"Well?" her mother said, tone impatient. "I asked you why you are at Ansom Iowa?"

"Supporting family."

The flash of shock on her mother's normally guarded face was so profound that Catherine blinked in surprise. It was gone in an instant.

"I didn't think you cared about our business any longer," her mother said.

Catherine debated whether to correct the error. "I was in Iowa anyway," she said after a pause. "I heard about the first anniversary open house. Thought I'd do the rounds, see how things are going."

Her mother studied her face, seeking the lie. She always did that. Assumed her children were lying to her, although neither of them had been particularly deceitful children, beyond keeping the handful of secrets they didn't want taken from them—hobbies, beloved possessions, or friends.

Reaching over suddenly, her mother tugged the collar straight on Catherine's blouse.

Catherine felt it like a slap. Outrage welled up, and for a moment she had no words.

"Well," her mother said. "You'll have seen from the tour that business is fine. We have a new electric car project underway, and this MediCache idea is going to revolutionize things, or so your father tells me. Business is good."

"Why do MediCache in Iowa?" Catherine asked, jerking her collar back to unstraight. "It's not exactly Hsinchu Science Park around here."

"Your father likes something it has." Her mother's gaze fixated on the collar, eyes sharp.

"What?"

"It's not a what. More of a who." Her mother gave a triumphant smile. She always enjoyed knowing things Catherine didn't.

Years ago, Catherine had worked out it was because she felt stupid most of the time largely due to decades of being condescended to by her husband.

"Why so interested?" she continued. "In fact, why the interest in any of this? You never cared before."

"I cared," Catherine said. "But the family business has never been what I wanted from life."

"Ah yes, your wonderful life." Her mother's fixed smile became degrees cooler. "Let's go back to how you've decided to humiliate yourself by marrying that young woman. I hear she's from Iowa…" Her mother suddenly froze. "Oh. I see. Is *that* why you're in Iowa?"

"We're here to plan the wedding."

"It's not a real wedding. My God. If our friends or your father's associates knew, they'd…"

"Thanks for your input." Catherine turned to go. "If that's all?"

"Wait."

Catherine stopped.

"*Is* she here?"

Catherine's gaze drifted to where Lauren was in an animated conversation with Senator Hickory.

"Oh. I see she is." Her mother raked Lauren's body with her usual critical gaze. "I hope you've told her you've been disinherited."

"She didn't even know who I was until yesterday."

Her mother gave the most dignified of snorts. "Don't be so naïve."

"She didn't. Nor was she happy to find out. Not that I blame her. But if it puts your mind at rest, she knows I'm no longer part of this family."

"Good. We do not need some Iowan with a hay stalk hanging out of her mouth trying to lay claim to the family fortune. I did expect more taste from you in your romantic pursuits. You've been such a disappointment."

Ah yes. Disappointment and embarrassment were the two things guaranteed to bring down her mother's wrath. Her mother's disapproval still stung a little, Catherine was appalled to discover. Just a lot less now. Like finding a long-faded bruise.

She regarded her mother, debating how to reply. The last time they'd met, Catherine hadn't yet become the Caustic Queen. But that was then. Catherine straightened.

"What?" Her mother raised one impeccably arched eyebrow to condescending heights. "What's that look for?" Then, clearly no longer able to resist the frustrating imperfection, her hand flashed out, aiming for Catherine's collar again.

Catherine brushed it away with an irritated slap. "Stop that, I'm not a child. And that look's because I realized it doesn't matter anymore."

"What doesn't?"

"Your opinion. Or Dad's. I'm happy now. I just remembered how irrelevant you both are to me." Her words came out flat and plain. Saying it out loud, feeling the truth of it humming through her veins, felt powerful.

"I see," her mother said, voice low and warning. "You now feel it's acceptable to speak to me in that wa—"

Lauren suddenly appeared at Catherine's side. "Hi," she said, snaking a protective arm around her waist. Lauren darted a concerned look at her.

Her mother's expression froze at the intimate gesture.

"Mother, this is Lauren King, my fiancée. Lauren, this is Victoria." Her lip curled in mockery. "But she prefers everyone to call her Mrs. Ayers."

Lauren smiled and stuck her hand out. "Hi, Mrs. Ayers."

Her mother looked at the proffered hand and shifted her gaze to her face. Then she glanced between both women. "I pity you." It wasn't entirely clear who she meant.

She turned and floated off the stage, irritation in every line of her face.

Lauren took in Catherine's expression. "Was it that bad? You looked pretty annoyed."

"It's about what I expected. She will never change."

"Talked to your dad yet?"

"No. And I'm not sure I should now."

"Catherine, you know why we're really here."

Catherine drew in a deep breath and thought about what mattered. The story. Which always comes first. "Well, I suppose it is time we said hello to Lionel."

Lionel Ayers was a handsome man, Lauren decided, if you liked that rugged, tanned, older-man thing. It helped, she supposed, that he had a certain Catherine-esque quality to him. He was confident and strong, with alert eyes that seemed to weigh up everyone he spoke to.

His glance briefly scorched up and down Lauren's body, not even hiding his base interest, even though he was deep in conversation with a coterie of yes-men gathered around him.

"I'm sorry about that," Catherine murmured. "I don't even think he knows he does it to women. Which probably makes it worse."

Lauren winced. "Does your mother know?"

"She knows." Catherine leaned forward and tapped an executive on one shoulder, a man blocking her path to her father. "Excuse me."

He turned, glaring. "Yes?"

"I'd like to get through."

"You and everyone else. But Mr. Ayers isn't meeting the public today."

"Well, it's a good thing I'm not the public," she snapped. "I'm his daughter."

His face underwent a comical transformation, his gaze rapidly assessing her features. He suddenly swallowed.

Lauren wasn't surprised at the recognition she'd glimpsed in his eye. Catherine did look a lot like her elegant mother, once you knew the connection, and it was uncanny how similar their mannerisms were. But Catherine also had an inner warmth when you got to know her, whereas Victoria's chill seemed to go right to her core.

"Ma'am, I do apologize. I wasn't aware he had another... I mean... he's never said...um..." Folding almost double in obsequiousness, the man stepped back to allow Catherine and Lauren entry into the inner circle.

Lionel's eyes immediately fell on his daughter. For a brief second, they warmed before the softness leached from them. *Interesting.*

"Darling," he said, tone faintly mocking. "What a surprise." He turned. "Gentlemen, could you give me a few moments?"

The suited sycophants melted away until only Lauren, Catherine, and Lionel stood in an uncomfortable triangle on one corner of the stage, their eyes shifting from face to face.

"Dad, I'd like you to meet—"

"Yes, yes. Lauren King. The fiancée." He appeared amused.

"Hi," Lauren said, and stuck out her hand again.

The handshake was a crushing one, designed to intimidate. But she hadn't grown up with five brothers with fierce warrior grips for nothing. She gave as good as she got. His smirk fell away.

"So." Lionel turned back to Catherine. "What do you need?"

"Who says I need anything?"

"You're here. So? Business or personal? If it's the latter, don't bother inviting me to the wedding. I'll be busy that day. As will your mother and Phoebe."

Phoebe? Lauren glanced at her fiancée. She was sure Catherine's sister planned on coming.

Catherine's expression betrayed a flicker of surprise. "If Phoebe wants to come, she'll come. She's her own woman."

Lionel gave a bark of sarcastic laughter. "Sure she is." He looked her in the eye. "So, if it's not personal, then what do you want? Need a job?"

"I like the one I have too much." Catherine gave him a loaded look that Lauren couldn't decipher. "Tell me about MediCache. What are your plans for it? I know you won't be just stopping with sick veterans. Not your style. Too small."

His look was sharp. "So, you want an interview? You should have called the office. Set something up."

"I'm here now."

"So you are." He thought for a moment. "I'll grant you one, but the condition is I do not want one of those disclaimers at the bottom. You know what I mean."

Catherine tsked. "You know it would be unethical to interview you without revealing you're my father."

"Then I'm sorry. I find myself unavailable for comment."

"However," Catherine cut in, "Lauren is also a journalist, and obviously not related to you. She'd be happy to interview you in my place—and your inconvenient little secret about who your daughter is can stay safe." She gave a knowing smile, and it was clear this had been her plan all along.

Oh, crap. Lauren's heart began to race. She wasn't prepared. She'd done no research into the man. He was only the boss of one of the world's biggest technology companies and rarely gave interviews. Frantically, she thought through what little she knew about him. This would be a train wreck.

Lionel took Lauren's measure, then slid his gaze to his daughter. "Hmm." His smile widened. "That might be interesting." He cocked his head. "All right, Ms. King. Come with me. Let's see what you're made of."

As Catherine made to follow, Lionel turned. "No." He pointed at Lauren. "Just her." He continued walking.

A scowl crossed Catherine's features. She pulled Lauren aside and pressed her lips close to her ear. "Ask him why Ansom set up in Iowa."

Lauren nodded. She followed Lionel into what turned out to be a small side office not far from the stage area.

"Sit," Lionel ordered after closing the door.

Lauren did so, giving him a wary look, then took out her phone, flicking to the voice recorder app.

"No, no. No yet." He templed his fingers. "So, you want to marry my daughter?"

"Yes."

He regarded her. "I disowned her, you know."

"I know."

"She won't get a dime."

"I know what disowned means." Lauren offered a polite smile to lessen the bite. "It's fine. I get *her*, not the money. That's a far better end of the deal."

"Don't tell me you don't care about money?" He sounded curious more than anything.

"Not so much, no."

"Mm." He scrutinized her. "What do your parents do?"

"My dad runs his own car-repair business. My brothers are all mechanics, too. Mom's dead."

"Ahh, a mechanic. An engineer of sorts. There's no shame in that. I appreciate machines in all their forms. This whole company is about redefining technology. Making a smarter, faster, more perfect machine. We even have an electric car division here. Something new we're testing."

Lauren decided it'd be a bad idea to explain how she knew all about that particular division.

"So…Middle America won over my oldest girl?" His tone was taunting.

Lauren only just avoided rolling her eyes. "Why don't you want anyone knowing Catherine's your daughter? Aren't you proud of her?"

His laugh was thin. "Not especially. Half of DC hates her. Always poking her nose in the finances of various movers and shakers. These are all people I do business with or lobby. So, no, I don't like to advertise their Antichrist is my offspring. It'd make them uncomfortable. I prefer my partners very comfortable…and generous." He smiled.

"Is that the only reason?"

"There are a few family reasons. Not for public consumption." He eyed her for a moment, then pointed at her phone. "Go."

Lauren hit *Record.*

"MediCache," he said. "What do you want to know?"

"Why do it in the first place? You have to know any tech embedded in people is controversial."

He shrugged. "It's the logical next step. The next Everest. We do it because it's revolutionary. Oh, there are a few similar experimental products here and there around the world—hobbyists, companies, and scientists tinkering with the concept with trial schemes. But we're the first to mass-manufacture it. I'll give you a little scoop: there are some plans for it in the future that go far beyond its current application. Big plans."

"Such as?"

"We have all sorts of lifestyle options for the everyman and woman. You'll see."

"People will never freely line up to do this to themselves."

"Won't they? You might be surprised." He looked dead certain.

Lauren frowned. "Okay, what's the deal with Senator Hickory? You could have picked anyone to talk up your tech around DC. He's not exactly cutting edge. Why partner with him?"

"He's…enthusiastic. I like him."

"You *like* him?" Lauren bit back a sarcastic reply. "Why did you set up an Ansom manufacturing facility in Iowa?"

Lionel said nothing for a beat. "I believe I just answered that."

"Hickory? You really set up here because of him?"

"He made a good case for us having a plant out here."

"Which was what? Iowa isn't even a technology hub. Not like all your other divisions."

"I would have thought the people of Iowa would be delighted to have some of the wealth and jobs spread their way. Surely you're not opposed to that? Especially as an Iowan."

"I… No." Damn it, now she was conflicted. *Tricky little…*

He laughed at her expression.

"Are you paying Hickory?" Lauren tried again. "To be your advocate on Capitol Hill?"

"Why would we need to do that? We set up the plant in his state at his request. We gave him jobs to promote. He's happy as hell. He doesn't need money, too."

"So, you didn't donate to his campaign?"

"We donate to a lot of campaigns. Ansom believes in supporting anyone who invests their enthusiasm in the future of technology, regardless of which side of the aisle they're on."

"This isn't just *any* technology. Your company is making chips here that will get shoved inside people. You're merging the man and machine. It's sci-fi stuff. And it's about as controversial as it gets."

"No one's forced to use our chips. And you're not seeing the big picture. MediCache is just one of a variety of ways that we're *streamlining life*. That's our motto, by the way."

"What about the ethical considerations? Did you even think about what might happen if someone unscrupulous got their hands on your chips? What if some authority finds a way to make them no longer voluntary? Like in prisons? Or foster care? What if we started microchipping people like pets? There are so many ramifications—"

"Great ideas there," he said, looking thoughtful. "You know, that might be the next step. Turning them into tracking tools instead of storage devices. There might be some demand, with so many lost kiddies and so on. Imagine the market for rich parents with children at risk from kidnapping?"

She blinked. What an atrocious idea.

He laughed at her. "That's what you wanted me to say, isn't it? But the real point should be, if people want something, and I can provide it—and it's not harming anyone—tell me why that's unethical?"

"The prostitution argument." Lauren sighed. "And that rarely works out as perfectly in practice as it does in theory. There are always voiceless victims in these things. It's always an ethical minefield. That's true for vulnerable people in the sex trade, and vulnerable veterans needing healthcare."

"Well, that's your opinion. So tell me..." His voice lowered to conspiratorial. "Did you really get that SmartPay scoop with my daughter, or was it all her hard work?"

"Why would you—?"

"It must burn you up that everyone in DC assumes that you did nothing to earn your award. She's the star, and what are you? You know, I wanted to know the answer to that when she announced your engagement so... colorfully...so I looked up your career. Can you guess what I found?"

Lauren's heart sank. Not a whole lot beyond dry reports on root vegetables, grain yields, butter cows, and, later, LA celebrities behaving badly. "You wouldn't have found anything that revealed who I am as a person."

"No? Because I found you were a nobody until you met Catherine. But if I've misjudged you, do share."

"I..." Lauren's mind went blank. How had he homed in on the source of her insecurities so accurately? Was it a family trait?

"Eloquent, as well, I see. Does Catherine just let you use her for stories, is that it? Does she tolerate you for the perks of having someone so...well, perky?" Lionel's eyes shifted to her chest.

"This is inappropriate." Lauren's fingers tightened into balls.

"You're right." Lionel leaned forward and tapped the red button on her phone's screen, pausing the recording. He leaned back. "You *are* an inappropriate choice for Catherine. So, ever been with a man?"

"What? None of your damned business!" She glared at him, fury flooding her, and jumped to her feet. She didn't care who the hell he was; she didn't have to put up with—

He chuckled. "I take it by the fact you're standing now that this little interview is over?" He twirled his finger between the two of them.

Lauren stared. She promptly sat. "This was some sort of juvenile test?"

"And you've failed spectacularly. Not exactly big on the mental parry and thrust, are you? And a *softball* scholarship? I suppose that's one way to get into college."

"Are you finished?" Lauren ground her teeth. "Or do I have to show you my 3.7 GPA first?"

"That won't be necessary." He spread his hands out on the desk in front of him. "I believe I understand you now. So, Ms. King, it's like this: I don't care if my oldest marries a two-headed Hydra or a ball-playing dyke from corn country. It's my wife who gets hives about who Catherine slides into bed with. And unlike my business partners, I also don't care a great deal that Catherine's a journalist. That's just who she is. And it seems to make her happy."

Lauren stared at him in surprise. There was no hint of deception on his face.

"I'm a businessman, Ms. King, one of the best. I make money. *That's* my bottom line on all things. I have to stay focused. That's my measure of the man"—he waved his hand at her—"or woman. I was curious about you. Who are you? Are you focused? Do you fold at the first hint of pressure?"

Lauren met his gaze.

"What I see before me is a low-level reporter of average mental agility and limited career prospects who suspects she's a fraud and has hitched herself to someone far out of her league to get ahead." He smirked and lowered his voice conspiratorially. "Secretly, you probably also can't believe Catherine likes you, *Iowa girl.*"

The words felt like a stab to her throat. The sting of vulnerability warred with her rising anger.

Lionel leaned across the table into her space. He winked. "You must be a great lay if she keeps you around in spite of all that."

As instantly as her fury had arrived, it ebbed away. She could see it clearly now. Lionel was simply goading her to get a rise out of her. What a charming piece of work. She truly pitied his family. Lauren couldn't imagine growing up with a father as scheming and cold as this.

Lauren regarded him. "I think I understand you now, too. See, I'd wondered why you bothered to talk to me today, especially since you haven't spoken to Catherine in so long. You say you wanted answers, but it's all about ego, isn't it? You love control and being master of your domain.

Even now, you hate the way I'm talking to you, like I'm your equal, when you're probably thinking I'm some hick bug you'd love to squash. Are you working out how to put me in my place right now?"

His eyes became half-lidded, but not before she saw the glint of something dark in them. "You're hardly worth the effort."

"That wasn't a denial." She paused. "So, back to Catherine. She displeased you, I gather. Didn't take the family job she was supposed to? Maybe she also didn't take the shiny husband you'd picked out for her the way her sister did? Or was it something else?"

Lionel didn't reply.

"Whatever the reason, I'm guessing she didn't do exactly what you wanted, and you disowned her. Great parenting there, *Lionel*. Super job."

His eyes became darker.

"So, here's what *I* see. Despite all your bluster, I think you're secretly proud of Catherine. Maybe, in your head, you claim credit for how smart, talented, and independent she is. Chip off the old block, is she? Must be hell for you that you can't even boast she's yours to your cronies who fear her. And besides, you can't admit to admiring her when you're still too busy punishing her for her independence." She tossed him a friendly smile like a grenade. "Am I warm?"

There was a faint jaw clench. "You have no idea what you're talking about. All I'll say is what happened with my daughter is a family matter. A matter that's closed."

"Ah, family secrets. Well, everyone has those, I guess." She straightened. "So, let's talk business, then. You just told me making money is your goal. Top priority. Isn't that a bit shallow?"

"That's all my shareholders care about. It's the American way. And on that score, I am so *very* patriotic." He looked amused.

"Are you one of those people who'd cross any line to make more money?"

"What a dangerous question to ask someone. What about you? Are there lines you won't cross to get a big story?"

"Plenty."

"So you play it safe. Well then, you won't go far. You need a killer instinct to win. You need to shatter rules, not stick to them. That lesson's free." He glanced at his watch. "I have to get going. I'd say it's been illuminating, except it hasn't. You're exactly what I thought you'd be."

"And what's that?"

"My daughter is not hard to work out. She likes you because you're uncomplicated. Because you don't judge her the way her mother does. Anyone who checked those two boxes would have her undivided interest, so don't think you're special. But most of all she craves loyalty. She's desperately clinging to the idea you'll be by her side forever."

"Like her parents weren't."

If Lionel was offended, he didn't even flicker. "Like any cocker spaniel. And she deserved being terminated from the family because she was disloyal. You think you're so different. Yet your family would give you hell if you picked anything or anyone over them, wouldn't they?" He tapped the table with a forefinger. "And rightly so. And that's what happened with Catherine. She made the wrong choice."

Lionel thrust out his hand. "So, that's everything. I wish you well." His look was all warning. "You'll need it."

"Need it?" Lauren frowned. *Is he threatening me?*

His smile widened at her uncertainty. "Whatever you're thinking right now is probably right."

"You can't do anything to me." *Could he?*

"No? You'd be amazed who I know and what I can buy. Your unraveling would amuse me greatly. It'd take, oh, only one day. Goodbye, Ms. King. It *hasn't* been a pleasure."

Lauren shook his hand by rote—predictably, another crushing power play. She sighed inwardly and squeezed back, full force, until he softly grunted and let go. Her softball grip was still on point.

What an asshole. How could a man be so pragmatic about casting his daughter aside?

"Oh, don't look at me like that," Lionel snapped. "My God, you're really something. You're about as simple as my daughter's complicated. And you're also dead wrong about something…"

He bent over and jabbed the red button on her phone. It lit up and resumed recording. "There's not a single thing about my oldest daughter that I admire." He then stood and tapped the recording to *off*. His face was hard. "Feel free to quote me to her." Lionel produced a smile that was ice-cold. And with that, he was gone.

It was funny, Lauren thought as she pocketed her phone, for all his front and bravado, she could still see the lie in those words. It was in his eyes and had been from the moment she'd met him. Lionel Ayers might be a top-level scheming bastard, but he had a great deal of pride in his daughter.

Interesting.

Catherine waited anxiously for Lauren to reappear. She knew the drill. Lauren would be as thoroughly interviewed as she interviewed Catherine's father. If not more so. Whether he saw Lauren as a threat or not would determine how bad the outcome would be.

She spotted her father headed toward a side exit, with two lackeys rushing to join him on either side. Lauren appeared a few moments later, a deep crease between her eyebrows.

Catching up to her in the now-empty corridor, Catherine asked, "What did he say?"

"Not a lot. Well, not much on our story. A few riddles about the data-chipping tech being available for the everyman soon. I don't know his agenda. He seemed to want to figure me out more than give answers."

"He does that."

"I'm also pretty sure he threatened me."

Catherine sucked in a breath. "What did he say?"

"Something about the people he knows and what his money can buy. It'd only take him one day. *Blah blah blah.* So, is this where he sends the lackeys around to slash our car tires and torch Dad's house?" Her tone was light, but it contained an edge.

"He's usually all hot air, no follow-through." Catherine paused. *Usually, but not always.*

They started making their way back to the main area where the speeches had been.

"Well, he followed through with you, didn't he?" Lauren said. "Kicking you out of the family. What did you do?"

"I didn't back down on something and he took it as a declaration of war."

"Was it?"

"No. That's the stupidest part. I was pissed with him for telling me what I should be writing about instead of politics. I was trying to hurt him for being so vicious and insulting to my ambitions, so I lashed out and said whatever wild thought came to mind. It hurt him all right. Our relationship was severed in an instant that day."

She could still see the flash of white-hot fury that had lit up his eyes. She had never seen him that enraged. It had been terrifying and also strangely freeing. In that moment, they'd both known immediately it was the end. She could stop pretending his relationship with her was anything but dysfunctional, unhealthy, loveless, and little more than a power game.

"That's sort of a relief." Lauren bit her lip. "Not because of the hostility between you—I'm sorry about that. It's just that…" She inhaled. "If your relationship wasn't solid before, I might have just tanked it anyway. I lost my cool a little and said some smart-ass stuff that pissed him off. Although, to be fair, he started it. He was baiting me a lot."

"Oh, I have no doubt." Catherine's smile was reassuring. "It sounds like you held your own. He's a hard man to stand up to. I'm proud you were able to."

"Will you still be proud if he sets his goons on us?"

"He has far bigger ambitions than us—such as MediCache. Did he say anything useful about it?"

"Not really. I was getting the whole, smug 'You ain't seen nothing yet' vibe. Like he knows something we don't."

"Hmm. Did you ask why they set up in Iowa?"

"He claims it's because of Hickory. That the senator made some great pitch to get them here."

"That techno-illiterate idiot?"

"Yep. Lionel even sounded as though Hickory was valuable to him somehow."

"All right." Catherine straightened. "We need to do a much deeper backgrounding on the good senator from Iowa. We must have missed something. There has to be more to him than meets the eye."

Lauren's hand fell to Catherine's forearm. "Hey. I'm sorry, by the way."

"For what?"

"You losing the parent lottery. They're, well, so…lacking…in their own way."

Lacking. Well, that was a kind word for it. Catherine paused at what Lauren wasn't directly saying. "Did my father get to you? Upset you more than you're letting on?"

Lionel Ayers was a master at cutting to the heart of someone with a blunt knife, after all. He could flay her emotionally when she was young. She'd learned to develop a thick skin. It went with the sharp, anxious mind that filled with the biting comebacks she'd wished she'd had the courage to say.

"He has a rare talent," Lauren admitted. "I didn't let on he came closer to the mark than I'd like." She hesitated. "I'm not ready to talk about what he said, though, if that's okay."

Catherine nodded. "I know what he's like." She cast around for a new topic. "So, how did that meeting with Hickory go before you met my charming mother?"

"Short. All I learned was his involvement with Ansom goes back a few years. He's been talking them up since 2012."

"That far back? The plant wasn't even in Iowa then."

"I know. He didn't really say much more. Then he asked if you were here today, too. And when I said you were, he looked freaked out and left."

"Ah. He's still sore about that article I wrote after his press conference."

"Definitely."

Catherine glanced around. The tour members and dignitaries had all left. A few workers were stacking chairs against the wall. She took a sharp breath. "So, Lucas stopped by for a chat. He's worked out who my parents are. I didn't confirm his suspicions. But still. He knows."

Lauren winced. "Was he rude?"

"Not exactly. I'll go with *excessively blunt*."

"I should talk to him. His attitude's on the line."

"Don't bother. He'll just be more convinced he's right about me and that I've sent you in to fight my battles for me."

"Battles? What do you mean? What did he say?"

That I'm unsuitable. I'm too dark. Catherine gave a sharp head shake. "Nothing worthwhile. But I didn't tell him I'd been disinherited. It's none of his business."

"So now he thinks you're mega rich? That won't help his attitude."

"I told him I don't have money."

"Let me guess, he didn't believe you?"

"It's irrelevant. I don't care what he thinks."

"Ugh—family!" Lauren said in exasperation. "They're such hard work. Wanna elope?"

Catherine chuckled. "Not without Zach's gorgeous dress."

"Ahh." Lauren's eyes glazed over. "Yeah, I'm dying to see which one you chose."

"And I am looking forward to you dazzling us in your elegant suit. Besides, if I know Owen and Meemaw, you'd break their hearts if they didn't get to see you walk down the aisle."

"Also true. Okay, can we get out of here? All this white, futuristic, mind-game fuckery is giving me a headache. Not to mention the vibe of pure BS it gives off."

Catherine laughed. "Fine by me."

Chapter 15
North of the Border

THE MOMENT LAUREN'S SLEEPY EYES snapped open, she grabbed her phone and started trawling the news, curious as hell. It was August 10, exactly two days since Michelle's tip-off. Today was the day. Even though she hadn't told Catherine what she was up to, her fiancée had taken one look at her, rolled her eyes, and headed for the shower, muttering, "She's a paid pathological liar."

Michelle Hastings might be a paid pathological liar, but she wasn't lying this time. Lauren stared at the headline on her screen, itching for Catherine to hurry up and get out of the bathroom so she could show her what she'd found. Frankly, Lauren considered it the height of restraint that she hadn't burst in while the water was still running.

When Catherine finally reappeared, running a towel through her hair, Lauren bounced onto her knees on their bed and urged her to look at her phone.

"A group of fifty-two Mexican illegal immigrants have been caught trying to cross the Texas border, according to Immigration and Customs Enforcement."

"How exciting for ICE." Catherine began to dress. "Relevance? And why is that even national news? It's hardly a rare event."

"The men and women caught will be given the option to have data chips placed in their hands to streamline processing of their cases."

Catherine paused, midway through sliding on her bra, and, for a moment, Lauren's thoughts were utterly derailed. *Gorgeous.*

"They've been signed up to MediCache?" Catherine asked.

Lauren forced her eyes back to her phone. "It doesn't specifically say it's that. Just that it's part of a pilot program to reduce identity-fraud issues."

Catherine frowned. "They can't do that. Illegal immigrants still have human rights."

"Yes. And they get around that sticky issue by making it voluntary. Sound familiar?"

"Ah."

"Anyway, it says should the illegal immigrants say yes, they will each get speedy processing and any appeals listened to ASAP. If they say no, they get stuck in holding cells for an indeterminate period and put at the back of the line. Since usually it can take a couple of weeks to get the expedited deportation cases dealt with, it sounds like they'll make it much slower than normal for them. So, you know what this means?"

"Yes." Catherine sighed. "But even if Michelle *wasn't* lying, it doesn't mean she's not also manipulating us somehow. I could be getting played again. And this time, you'll get caught up in it with me."

"I know. But I'm a big girl. It is an important story, and I'm willing to take the risk. Look, it's already being picked up by all the major outlets." She scrolled down her news feed.

Catherine's finger flashed out. "Stop. Go back to that story above. The one with the photo of the ICE officers standing around."

Lauren scrolled up to the photo and zoomed in.

"May I?" Catherine took the phone and studied the screen closely. "Hmm." She frowned for a moment. "That woman at the back? I think I know her. I have a friend at the FBI—"

Lauren squinted at a Hispanic woman at the back wearing a sensible charcoal pantsuit. She was half turning away, so her features were partially obscured. "That's your FBI friend?"

"No, that's not Diane, but I've been to a few of Diane's parties and I've seen the woman in that photo there. She and Diane work together. She's not ICE at all—she's FBI."

"Wait a minute. What's the FBI doing involved in an immigration case?" Lauren took back her phone and scrolled to the end of the story.

The chip-implantation scheme has garnered the attention of at least one US security agency which says it will watch ICE's

*trial program closely to see whether it might be applicable for
deployment within its own programs.*

She scrolled down to another photo. A trio of Mexicans who had just
been data-chipped. They were pointing at their hands and smiling like stars
of a bad infomercial.

"Why does this reek so bad?" Lauren asked. "Who smiles over getting
bagged and tagged with some Frankenchip?"

"A better question is, what does the FBI want with MediCache? And
if the FBI's interested, you can bet the other security agencies want in,
too. You wondered why my father seemed cocky despite backing such a
controversial product? Maybe he already knew he had some high-level
clients in the wings who couldn't care less how unpopular the concept was?"
Catherine sat up. "I'll call Diane and see if there's anything she can tell us
about it."

"Hey? Aren't we missing the big question? How did your ex know about
any of this?"

Catherine paused. "Good point. Michelle's clearly well
placed. Somewhere."

"Doesn't it mean she either works for ICE or the FBI? Who else could
possibly be tracking a group of Mexicans two days out before they crossed
the border? I mean, I'm guessing she doesn't work for a sheriff's office
in Texas."

"Highly unlikely she's even been to a border town. She's allergic to
anything less than five-star luxury." Catherine frowned. "Or...she was.
Okay, so while I'm at it, I'll ask if Diane can find out whether Michelle
works at the FBI. You know, I always wondered if she might."

"Then why didn't you ask Diane to look into her before? When
Steph—Michelle—first disappeared?"

"I thought about it many times. But to what end? I refused to be
that pathetic person who chases after the one who left them. No matter
the circumstances."

"Oh. Makes sense. Sorry."

Catherine glared at the photo. "I'm tired of being lied to. I'd love to get
to the bottom of this, one way or another."

Lauren heard laughter coming from their bedroom after breakfast and headed in to find Catherine on a video call to Diane. She was a beautiful, curvy, dark-skinned woman with deep brown eyes, cropped hair, and an infectious, rich laugh. She talked to Catherine with a kind of shorthand, like two people used to finishing each other's sentences.

Catherine threw back her head and laughed again at one of Diane's jokes. Lauren hid her shock at the sight.

She had to admit the FBI agent was funny in a witty, layered-wordplay kind of way.

Lauren bit her nail. Lionel's words darted into her head like a snake. Anyone could turn Catherine's head if they met the basic criteria. Lauren wasn't special.

For the first time in a long, long time, as she stared at amusing, clever Diane, she stopped to wonder what Catherine actually saw in a simple girl from Iowa.

She was only too aware that she was nothing like Catherine's ex. For all the woman's nasty actions, Michelle was also gorgeous, polished, chic, classy, and intelligent. The outfit she had worn at the State Fair looked like it cost more than Lauren's entire wardrobe budget for the year. Lauren looked at her feet. She considered it a win if her socks matched.

There was more laughter. Lauren glanced back at the screen and realized why she was so unsettled. She'd become used to the fact her fiancée rarely laughed, and only ever with her. She sneaked a peek at Catherine. The happiness on her face was beautiful.

That's good, she reminded herself. This was very good for Catherine. Even if Lauren was feeling exposed, vulnerable, and a bit insecure thanks to Lionel and Michelle's tag-teamed taunting, this was her own issue. Catherine needed her friends. She didn't have many, and she'd been without for too long.

Lauren would let them catch up properly alone. Decided, she turned to sneak out when two words stopped her cold.

"Top secret."

Her backside promptly dropped to the bed.

Diane looked deadly serious. "You shouldn't poke your finger in that one, Catherine."

"Why not? It's one group of illegal immigrants among hundreds, right? What's with the top security?"

"I can't say."

"Can't or won't?"

"Both. I mean it. My boss is all over this, watching it like a hawk. I can't give you anything. There's literally nothing unclassified about this case except what has already been fed to the press."

"All right, then, let's not talk specific cases. How about the big picture? Off the record: since when is the FBI involved in an ICE case at all?"

"Since the director really wants to get in bed with that MediCache tech."

"That's why they're watching the data-chipping trial?"

"It's not a trial."

"It's not?"

"More like a foregone conclusion and everyone here knows it. If I were you, I'd have a closer look at the pictures in the paper regarding this case."

"Any photo in particular?" Catherine turned to Lauren, who promptly handed her the phone cued up to the last story they'd read.

"That's all I'm going to say on that."

Catherine scrolled through the photos. Lauren looked at the screen over her shoulder. They all looked fairly typical of an ICE arrest. Well, except for that one of the happy Mexicans holding up their hands...

After a pause, Catherine called it up and zoomed in. And then again. Her mouth fell open.

Lauren suddenly saw what Catherine had.

"Is this... I mean..." Catherine peered closer. "The screen's small, but either I'm going blind or those scars where they've been microchipped don't look real. Like...makeup?"

"What an interesting theory." Diane lifted her eyebrows.

"But if the scars are fake...are these even real illegal immigrants?"

"Oh, they're definitely Mexicans from south of the border. They were also definitely caught illegally crossing the border. Teams were waiting to detain them. Exactly as the news story said."

"*Waiting.*"

Diane said nothing.

"Why waiting?"

"Catherine." Her tone was warning.

"So, this whole thing is smoke and mirrors? It's faked for show? Wait, were these Mexicans just pretending to be illegal immigrants? Say, actors or something?"

Diane fidgeted. "I never said that."

"I noticed. Can you also 'not tell me' why anyone would go to the effort to set this all up?"

"I cannot comment on this specific case."

"Do you know, though?"

"*Know*? That's too strong a word. It's just speculation around the water cooler. But like I said, our director loves the possibilities of MediCache."

"And he needed a successful tryout to push for its use in security?" Catherine's eyebrow lifted. "Even if it's not even a trial but all faked for cameras."

"Interesting theory."

"So, what's the endgame? Is the FBI going to try and chip all private American citizens down the track or something?"

Diane shook her head. "The FBI can't do that, even if it'd probably love to. It would kick up a huge national stink, not to mention all the civil liberties laws it would breach. But the actual agenda? Your guess is as good as mine."

"Thanks, Diane. I guess we'll keep digging."

"Remember, I warned you. This one's a political hot potato." Her amused look said she knew Catherine would ignore her warning. "So, is that all you need from me today?"

"Just curious about that name I emailed you—"

"Oh, that's right. Hastings?" Diane shuffled through some papers and glanced up. "No, no one by that name works here."

"Oh." Catherine's features were cool, but her lips compressed.

"Anymore."

"What?"

"She did work here, years ago. But not now."

"How many years ago?"

"Recruited straight out of college. She got a better offer and left us."

"A better offer where?"

"I asked around," Diane said. "Only one old agent remembered her from back then. She was headhunted for some sort of consultancy work." She lifted her hand. "No, I don't know where. He didn't have a clue, either. Sorry. You'd have to find someone else who knows her."

"Thanks for trying."

"You're welcome."

Catherine smiled. "How's Pete?"

"Oh, same old. He's deciding whether to go back to college and finish his degree. We'll see." A baby's cry sounded in the background.

Diane glanced behind her. "Nathan's awake. I'd better go. It was great seeing you again. Please stay in touch." Her gaze shifted left to where Lauren was sitting. She smiled brightly. "Good meeting you, Lauren."

"You, too," she replied. She felt foolish at her passing insecurities. Lionel would probably laugh his ass off if he knew how successfully he'd messed with her head with just a few well-chosen sentences. She was an idiot.

The video screen closed.

Catherine turned with her smile still lingering. "And that was Diane."

"It was good to meet her at last. How did you two become friends?"

"On a story. Years ago, now. We were both starting out and found ourselves professionally useful to each other. But after a while, we found we enjoyed our social interactions more than the work ones."

"She seems nice. Makes you laugh."

"Yes." There was a sudden guardedness to Catherine's expression.

"What is it?"

"Diane was among the friends who stopped contacting me when my career was destroyed. Total radio silence."

"Oh." *Bitch.*

"She apologized repeatedly when I returned to DC. She explained that the day my disastrous story ran, word went out at her office that I was to be avoided by everyone. The memo had come from the director himself."

Lauren stared at her. "Why would the FBI involve itself in some journalist who was on the way out? Unless they…had a hand in it? Do you think they might have been involved in kicking you out the door? And, come on, is it just a coincidence that Michelle worked there once, too?"

Catherine blinked. "I have no idea. At the time I didn't care why Diane cut me off. All I remember was noticing she wouldn't take my calls. It took me a long time to forgive her. She's been trying so hard to make things right with me. Like this chat today. She was more forthcoming than she had to be."

"Well, lucky us," Lauren said, her tone cutting. "Your career and friendship sacrifices weren't in vain."

"She is a good person. I was too angry to remember that for a while. And she's excellent company."

"I noticed."

Catherine's lips curled. "Lauren King, are you…jealous?"

"So…where are we now?" Lauren suddenly found her notes fascinating. "We think the Mexican thing may be faked. And we know Michelle was once FBI. Of course, Diane's suggestion that we find someone who knows her is useless."

Catherine hesitated. "Actually, that's not entirely true. We do know someone who knows her. The man who told us her real name."

There was silence as it slowly dawned on Lauren who she meant. "Gabbana? But he's shady as hell! Not to mention kind of violent." Lauren scowled. "Also, he wouldn't tell us who he worked for back when he was following us. Oh, and I might have given his face a scar the size of Montana."

"Yes. You did." Catherine smirked. "So, can you imagine if we called him?"

Lauren's eyes went wide. "Um, can I remind you we don't know his name? I mean, we nicknamed him for his fancy suit."

"How many men who are now assigned to the US President's protection do you think wear expensive Italian outfits and sport a jagged scar down their left cheek?"

"Ooh. Good point."

Catherine nodded. "You know Charles Milton who runs White House security? He owes me a favor. He could look Gabbana up for us."

Catherine punched in a number and put the phone to her ear. "Hello, Charlie. Catherine Ayers. Yes, a long time. I know. Oh, I'm good. And you? Excellent. I was wondering how you'd you like to square that favor you owe me?"

"Okay, Alberto Baldoni is not a very Secret Servicey name." Lauren was chewing on a sandwich. Leftover meatloaf, slick with gravy, was wedged between the thick slices of Meemaw's homemade bread. The combo was to die for.

"I left a message with my email, phone, and Skype details," Catherine said. "He'll have no excuse not to get back to us."

"Well, if he does, I think he'll opt for the monologuing asshole option, like the last time I saw him. He seems to like to prove we didn't really beat him."

"It's still a long shot that he would ever want to cal—"

A Skype incoming call request lit up the iPad screen... An unknown user name.

"Don't tell me," Catherine said in disbelief as she opened it.

Sure enough, the lean, cold features of the man formerly known as Gabbana eyed them.

"I didn't believe it," he said. "Had to see for myself. *The* Catherine Ayers? Well, how the dead have risen." His head tilted. "And her trusty sidekick, the plucky pitcher from Iowa, Lauren King."

"Alberto," Catherine drawled.

His gaze scoured them. "I can only imagine what you two want from me."

"You must be dying of curiosity," Lauren said with a cocky lift of her eyebrows. "I assume that's why you waited all of two minutes to call. Miss us?"

"I *can* hang up." He leaned forward, holding up a finger over his phone's screen.

"Alberto? I have a question," Catherine cut in, reaching for a pen and note pad. "Michelle Hastings. Who does she work for?"

All amusement drained from his hard, scarred features. "So, you finally want to know where your little weasel fits in?"

"How do you know her?" Catherine asked.

"We were colleagues once upon a time."

"Before we got you fired," Lauren suggested cheerfully.

"I wasn't fired." His eyes flashed. "I had two masters back then. One was the organization where Michelle Hastings worked. When SmartPay USA went under, my expertise was no longer required there, and I was redeployed by my other employer. Either way, I was *not* fired."

"Who did you and Michelle work for?" Catherine asked.

"I decline to answer."

"Why?"

"I signed a nondisclosure agreement." He studied her for a moment, looking intrigued. "So, what are your intentions for her? You two planning on bringing her down?" He sounded gleeful.

"You hate her?" Catherine asked. "Why?"

"Oh my God, what a question." He laughed, and it was a cruel sound that grated along Lauren's nerves. "You'll be sorry you asked."

"Maybe. Tell me anyway."

"Do I hate Michelle Hastings? Yes, yes, I do. Why? Because my now-ex-wife enjoyed fucking you far too much back then for me to like her now."

There was a silence for a long beat.

"Oh shit." Lauren gasped.

"Ex-*wife*?" Catherine ground out at the same time.

"Yes and yes." He leaned forward. "Did you know that bitch got promoted for what she did to you? She wound up with a big fat pay raise and a corner office for a job well done when your career became an ash pile. I wound up with divorce papers. So, she fucked both of us over." He leered at Catherine. "Just you a little more literally than me."

Catherine's fingers curled into a white-knuckled grip around her pen.

"So, yes, I hope you bring her down," he said. "Do it nice and thorough, the way you cleaned house at SmartPay. A nice, flashy national scandal with her name attached to the stink. I think I'd enjoy that a whole lot."

"How can we do that?" Lauren flicked a concerned glance at Catherine, who was staring at the screen, face rigid. "If you want your ex-wife crushed, you have to give us something we can use to find her and her employer."

"Would love to help, but nondisclosure, remember? I will say this: where she works, they love political climate change." His expression became gloating as he regarded Catherine's shell-shocked face. "Well, this has been entertaining, it really has. But don't call again. I'll be deleting this account."

The screen shut down.

Catherine was chalk white. "They were *married*?"

"Catherine, we don't know. Maybe he was playing with you? He does enjoy twisting the knife and causing a shitstorm."

"That level of bitterness you only find in exes. He believed what he was saying. That hatred? That was real. And she got *promoted* for screwing with me...in every sense."

Lauren pushed her sandwich away, feeling sick. "I'm so sorry."

"She went home to *him*. Crawled into bed with him every night she wasn't with me. He's a cold piece of sadism if ever I saw it."

"I know."

"She could never have actually liked me. It's not possible if he was her type." Her face was ashen. "I'm sorry we ever contacted him." She slammed her iPad to the desk. "This was pointless."

"Actually, it wasn't pointless. He did give us a few clues."

"I fail to see what."

"Well, we know she works for a private company—a consultancy firm. And he mentioned political climate change. Is it their motto, maybe? That's something we can look up."

After exhaling slowly, Catherine said, "I suppose it's a start."

"Also, we know they worked together. So, it would be a company that employs a number of women, women at a senior level, since Michelle got some big corner-office promotion. This would rule out any male-dominant organizations, several military think tanks, and so on."

"Yes."

"And lastly, we now know Michelle really enjoyed being with you."

Catherine's eyes flashed to Lauren's with a look that was pure outrage. "Why would you go near that?"

"To stop you beating yourself up. Look, she didn't just *endure* her time with you. She liked being with you to the point it might have destroyed her marriage."

"That's supposed to make me feel better?"

"It means you shouldn't feel foolish for not knowing she was pulling a con. Because it wasn't *all* fake. Her ex-husband hated her for liking you. So, what you felt from her was at least in part genuine."

"Maybe. Or maybe Alberto's just the jealous type." Sighing, Catherine ran her hands over her face, rubbing her eyes. "In what universe is it a job to go to work and pretend to be someone's girlfriend? With everything that entails?"

"CIA?"

"Maybe, but that's not a consultancy company."

"No. Hell, I don't know." Lauren reached for the iPad. "But let's find out. Okay?" She entered "political climate change" into the search engine.

Over one hundred thousand results stared back at her. *Oh boy.* She glanced up at Catherine. "This is going to take a while."

"I see that. I'll go get us a coffee. If we're going to be up all night, I refuse to do so uncaffeinated."

Three hours later, Lauren had plowed through hundreds of search pages. She nudged Catherine in the foot. Her fiancée had curled up on the bed to "take stock" and appeared to have dozed off an hour ago.

"Hey."

Catherine's eyes flickered open. "Find something?" she asked, her voice thick with sleep.

"Sherlock Holmes comes to mind."

"Oh?"

"Once you eliminate the impossible, whatever remains, no matter how improbable, must be the truth." Lauren pointed at a page with a blank screen except for a tiny symbol at the top left and an input box with a blinking cursor. "All the other pages went somewhere, had links, or related to something specific with my search terms. This? This relates to nothing. And somehow it comes up in our search results even though I don't see *political climate change* anywhere."

Catherine leaned forward and read aloud: "Welcome, associates. Please enter password."

"So, any ideas?"

"Did you look up the logo?" She indicated the shape near the top of the page. It was like a black five-leaf clover, without the stem, sitting in a bronze circle.

"It doesn't seem to mean anything," Lauren said. "Although it does look vaguely familiar, but I can't think why."

"We could be fixating on a completely unrelated page."

"So then why's it in the search results?"

Catherine shrugged. Her gaze shifted back to the password box. "Try and enter Michelle's name?"

Lauren typed it in the box.

Access Denied.

"Baldoni's?"

Access Denied. You have been permanently locked out.

"That is some serious security." Lauren squinted at the screen. "That's okay." She flipped to the email program and wrote a quick note. "I'm asking Josh to show it to Snakepit and Duppy. Maybe his hacker bros can find a way in."

"Good idea. Ask about the logo while you're at it."

Lauren nodded and added a question. She glanced at Catherine. Well, at least her expression had lost its pinched look. She still looked washed out, though. "Hey, you doing okay?"

"She had a *husband*. The whole time. For all I know she's straight!"

"And maybe she's bi and thought you were the hottest lover she'd ever had. Who knows? It's confusing for me, too. I hate she had that time with you." Lauren stopped. "Sorry. This should be about you. Just ignore me."

"Both is possible. We could both hate her."

"True." Lauren grinned. "So, what's next? While we wait for our hackers?"

"I think it's time we ran Hickory's background and donors through the wringer and see what we can squeeze out."

"And we also have to figure out how our two stories are linked, right? Michelle said they were."

"Michelle said a lot of things," Catherine's eyes turned hard. "And not once did she mention a husband. She could even have two kids and a pet beagle. You know what? I'm done talking about her for the day."

"No problem. So, what shall we do instead?" Lauren's expression turned thoughtful. "Talk about which of the bakers we saw should do our wedding cake?"

"Well, that's one option. Although I'll be honest and admit I hated them all. Buttercream on everything? Must we?"

"It's popular out here."

"I gathered." Catherine sighed. "I was wondering how you felt about a bit of stargazing tonight. Under your dreaming tree. Because you're right about what you said the day we arrived: the skies are stunning out here."

"Catherine, how can we stargaze under that tree? It's too dense to see through."

"Foiled," Catherine whispered. "Perhaps we could do something else out there instead?"

There was a look in her eye, beyond the suggestiveness, that Lauren had rarely seen in her fiancée. Vulnerability. A need for reassurance.

It figured, after a day like today. Lauren understood. "I'll get the blankets."

Catherine kissed her, below her bottom lip. Then slid to her neck. Her kisses were hot and filled with need.

Lauren sighed. "And I'll get the p-pillows."

"You do that." Catherine's reply was husky. "I think we could use some attention tonight."

What she didn't say hung between them. *With someone I trust.*

Lauren met her eye. "We could." She trailed her fingers down her cheek. "Let me show you."

How much I love you. That didn't need saying, either.

Catherine's gaze darkened. "Yes" was all she said.

Chapter 16
Down the Rabbit Hole

THE NEXT DAY, DUPPY CHECKED in with Lauren. "That logo?" he said down the phone. "It's a pentalobe. It's the shape of a weird screw hole. Apple uses it on its devices. 'Cause of course they can't just use a regular star-tip shape or somethin'. That'd be too easy. I guess they don't want amateurs trying to take apart their gear."

"A pentalobe?" Lauren glanced at Catherine, who was bent over her suitcase looking for a lost shirt. Her jeans were in the God-help-me form-fitting category. Which reminded her of Catherine's shapely ass. Which reminded her of last night. Which had been heavenly and needy and all kinds of hot, as Lauren had showed Catherine how much she was desired and loved. Catherine had returned fire with a fierce, intense devotion to every part of Lauren's body. She had never felt so consumed.

Lauren forced herself to focus on Duppy's words. "Does a pentalobe have any hidden meaning?"

"Not really. Well, I guess you could infer ultrasecurity and protection, maybe? Or someone thinking outside the box? Shit, I don't know."

"Right. So, what about the password?"

"That's a bit harder. It's not often I'm beaten on crap like this. The encryption on that site is overkill. But I have some bros who can get us some brute power on a botnet that's for rent. Won't even charge me the going bitcoin rate, either. They're laying low after some big DDoS stunt they pulled last week, so they're happy to take on a small job like this today."

Lauren frowned. "Was any of that in English? Can you spell it out for me?"

"I don't have time to make the words small enough." He snickered. "Just trust me... Bot networks can do superfast, password-cracking shit in a few hours that'd normally take days or weeks to do with one computer."

"Okay then." She forced out a "Thanks, Duppy," despite his attitude. Of course, she had another longstanding reason to dislike him.

"You'll tell Catherine I did this?" His voice rose from its usual wheedling to hopeful. "'Cause it takes mad connections to do this. And hey, tell her if she ever wants to jump teams, I'm available. Anytime, day or night." His juvenile laugh set her nerves on edge.

"No," Lauren said through gritted teeth. "I absolutely won't be telling her that. Bye, Duppy."

He laughed at her outrage. "Later. Will text you the password when it lands." The phone went dead.

"Ugh, gross." Lauren's gaze returned to Catherine. She'd now pulled on a long-sleeved button-up with a starched, white high collar. *Popped-collar porn.* Lauren groaned internally. Catherine was killing her.

"I won't ask what Duppy's doing to wind you up this time," Catherine said, sounding amused. "But if it's about me, definitely don't share."

"His usual. And I won't. He says he's hiring some big guns to crack the password. Oh, and the logo is a pentalobe. Some screwdriver thing that's unique and helps secure Apple gadgets."

"Unique and secure," Catherine said. "Interesting."

"I guess?"

"So, what does 'political climate change' mean?" Catherine leaned against the sill, her legs crossed at the ankle.

With the light streaming in behind her and her auburn hair lit up, she looked stunning. Which reminded Lauren again of last night, under the tree, hands sliding against hot skin, strained gasps in her ear, and the heady rush she always felt whenever Catherine trembled against her.

It bothered her again how Lionel had gotten into her head so easily the day before. How had he ever made her question what Catherine saw in her? What the hell was wrong with her, doubting Catherine?

"What are you thinking?"

Lauren blinked and focused on her steady gaze. "About last night."

Catherine's smile curved into knowing. "Mmm. Delicious. And was that all?"

"Your father."

The smile disappeared. "I dread to think. Is this about how he tried to crawl under your skin?"

"He didn't just try." Lauren looked at her hands to avoid Catherine seeing her shame. "He succeeded."

"So...want to tell me what he said?"

Lauren swallowed. "Just that I wasn't special. That you'd be captivated by anyone who was not judgmental like your mother, and who'd be loyal and wouldn't leave you."

A beat passed. "That sounds like him. And what did you say?"

"I didn't."

Catherine glanced away, but the hurt she was trying to mask was clear. "And you believed that? Is that's what's been bothering you?"

"I..." Lauren hesitated. "A little."

"I see." A shadow crossed her face.

"I admit I've been driving myself a bit crazy since I met Michelle. She's the opposite of me. Not just looks, but in everything. And Lionel suddenly made me wonder why you chose me. I'm not much of a professional match, given you're at the peak of your career and I'm barely above worm food. And it feels weird, some days, that I even caught your eye. I worried that he has a point. I *am* way out of your league."

Catherine gave her a long, inscrutable look. "Is that so?"

Lauren looked at her hands. "Sometimes I wonder if we'd met before that story brought you down what you'd have made of me—back when you had a full life and lots of friends. Regardless of who Michelle turned out to be later, I look at who she was to you. A smart, stylish, beautiful blue blood. She's all class and prestige and old money. She's who you picked when you weren't at rock bottom. So, I've been torturing myself. I'm not sure *I'm* what you love about me, or even if I'm really your type. Or if it's just I was there when you needed someone the most, and that can be a very attractive thing."

Catherine gave a low strangled noise. She left the window and sat on the edge of the bed beside Lauren. "You think I loved you because you were just *there?*"

"Be honest with me: I know you love me but, Catherine, at any other time of your life, would you have looked twice at me? I'm a one-time college softball player from the Midwest. My family comprises a bunch of mechanics who think Homer Simpson's the funniest character ever written and that tractor pulls are the meaning of life. And then there's you." She pointed at Catherine's Fifth Avenue perfection. "Just look at you."

"Is this the money again? My God—"

"No, it's not the money. It's where I'm from and where you're from. It's who you are, culturally, socioeconomically, professionally, personally—all of it. I'm not being down on myself when I say this, but I just don't see what you, specifically, see in me. I don't think I ever really did. And I think... especially now, I really need to know."

"This is so typical of my father." Catherine folded her arms and glared. "Finding a person's insecurities and working them. Where do you think I learned it from? Not that I'm proud of it." Her lips thinned. "And as for you..." she said, looking exasperated, "for the love of my life, you can be quite ridiculous at times. You meet my father, who whispers all these doubts in your ear, and suddenly you need me to hold all my emotions up to the light for you to peer at."

Lauren knew Catherine was hiding her discomfort. She hated going to vulnerable places and rarely did it. But Lauren needed this; it was too important to be put off.

"Catherine, yes, I really need you to spell it out for me," she said softly. "Why choose me when you could be with someone..." *Awesome, cool, classy, like you.* "...else?"

"Why on earth would I want someone else?" Catherine's eyebrow shot up. "It's you I care for. I love you for the way you challenged me when no one else would. For your fierceness and dedication to those you love. And I love you for who you are, not because no one else was available." She looked deeply offended. "I am not so desperate that just anyone is allowed in my life. I am particular. I would rather be single than settle for less than what I need. You should *know* this. In a few months we will be married. Why don't you know this?"

"Um..." Lauren's voice was small. "Because you never told me."

There was a long silence punctuated only by the harsh intake of Catherine's breath.

"Couldn't you tell?" she asked. "The way I touch you? Hold you? Couldn't you see? Have I really been so cryptic?"

"Some days a girl needs to hear the words, too," Lauren said. "I'm a writer. I live for words." Her eyes implored her to understand. "I breathe them, swallow them, and worship them. Don't you understand? I memorize them for when I need them most. I need this."

"Words were memorized in my family, too." Catherine hesitated. Her face darkened. "They were misquoted, misdirected, used, and abused. The greatest protection I had was my silence. The day I finally unleashed my words was the day my father disowned me. The day I walked away, I never held back my words again.

"For that, they call me the Caustic Queen. What would people say if they found out the truth about those acerbic lines I peel off my tongue? That there's nothing regal at all about what happened to me? That I was little more than some tormented animal who found herself suddenly free, and lashed out to never feel oppressed in that way again."

"Catherine, I'm so sorry."

"It's in the past now." She gave Lauren a regretful look. "And I'm also sorry. It may take a long time for certain words...words that aren't weapons—the soft, unsafe, vulnerable words—to return to me. The hardest thing is to speak about things that lay me open. I always feel too exposed. I'm sorry for that. You deserve to be told how special you are to me, and often. But Lauren, know that even though I don't say the words, I think them. Every day."

Lauren pulled her down on the bed beside her, until they were touching forehead to forehead. "Thank you. That's...beautiful."

"It's just a fact." Catherine closed her eyes.

"No," Lauren whispered. "It makes me feel safer inside... Safer about us, knowing this." She felt the heat flood her cheeks from embarrassment. How needy she must sound.

Catherine stroked her from her temple down to her throat with her fingertips. "Lauren, trust me when I say this: I do love you. I'm not 'making do' until someone better comes along. I don't care where you're from, what your family does, how spectacular or otherwise your career is. These are not priorities for me. I want to be with the woman who loves me fiercely. I want the woman who thinks it's exciting finding out multiple uses of Nutella and thinks wearing battered tractor caps is funny. And I want the woman who looks at me the way you did last night. Who made me weak just from the way you said my name. That's who I'm in love with. Can you just…never doubt that again? Or I will have to question your intelligence." Her look was aggrieved.

Lauren laughed. "Thanks…um, I think."

"Better?" Catherine's expression morphed into amusement.

"Yes. And can I just say I'm also really glad you're not looking for a slick, elegant, elite, DC woman? I'd be in so much trouble."

"Superficiality is in ready supply in DC. I prefer the pride of Iowa just fine." Catherine pulled Lauren tightly into her arms and kissed her like she meant it.

The password arrived three hours later.

It made for a bit of good news after running Senator Hickory's donors list through the mill and coming up empty. It was almost suspicious how pristine his numbers were. Like someone had cleaned them with industrial-strength bleach. On paper, the man was a freaking saint.

The password was one long jumble of numbers and letters in a text. A call from Duppy a minute later to Lauren said only: "Use it fast; if their security is half as good as I think, they'll know they were cracked. You only get one shot. I'm not calling in favors again."

Lauren grabbed her cell phone, pasted the emailed password into the website box, and waited.

There was an anxious pause as the screen flickered. It suddenly refreshed, and a new web page appeared.

Welcome to The Fixers.

We are a top Washington DC consultancy team that can ensure the results you want. Our motto is political climate change.

Do you need to make contacts with top-tier Washington movers and shakers? Effect change? Boost your brand, image, or product in a daring and effective way that doesn't even look like marketing?

Diminish a competitor's image or products in a lasting way to ensure your success? The Fixers' expert team can advise you. We are security, discretion, and originality in a one-stop shop. We have specialists in the following areas who can brainstorm and consult with you:

Protection and security

Political connections

Business networking

Counterintelligence and espionage

Mass communication, message massaging, and trend development

Cybersecurity—improving safety and removing threats

"That's..." Lauren couldn't think of what to say. "Um..." She immediately took a screenshot of the page, in case they got kicked off the site. She emailed it to Catherine's and her own accounts for safekeeping.

Lauren glanced at a link at the top of the page. "Do we want to download a PDF with 'the most up-to-date list of the expert Fixers team'?"

Eyes practically gleaming, Catherine said, "We definitely do."

Lauren tapped on the *download* button. A moment later the PDF opened.

"Oh," Lauren whispered. "would you look at that?" She took a screenshot and sent that to their email accounts, too.

The list ran down the page:

Protection and Security

Consultants: M. Lee, D. Rowe, P. Carter, K. Richards, T. Howe, P. O'Brian. Our team features alumni from Blackwater, the US Marines, White House security, and the CIA. Overseas bodyguards also available to clients upon request.

Political and Business Networking

Consultant: M. Hastings. Six years with FBI; expertise in forging connections with all political parties and top business leaders. Full CV available upon request.

"Stop," Catherine said sharply. She pointed to *M. Hastings*. "The home page said they offer to diminish a competitor's image." She looked at Lauren. "That had to be her assignment on me."

Lauren re-read the words. "Yeah. It does fit with what happened to you."

"Who did this to me? Who paid for this career hit?"

"Michelle's field is listed as politics and business. Did you piss off some politician or businessman somewhere?"

"The list is as long as my arm. But I was never over the top. They all knew the game. I can't think of anything I've done that would have merited calling in a specialist consultancy firm to hurt my reputation."

"What about the FBI? Remember they ghosted you when you went down."

"They have no motive. I treated the FBI fairly in all stories. Although…"

"What?"

"It's probably nothing. Just a call I had from an irate FBI director about a column I wrote a few years back. But he went away." She shook her head. "This second-guessing is futile. I'll make myself paranoid." Catherine waved at the screen. "Keep scrolling."

Lauren returned to the page.

Counterintelligence
Consultants: R. Burns, P. Mason, D. Chin. Our experts have CIA, NSA, Homeland Security, and FBI experience. Full CVs available upon request.

Mass communication, message massaging, and trend development
Consultant: T. Brooker. Advertising, public relations, and marketing background and a former top-level media advisor to Government. Full CV available upon request.

Cybersecurity
Consultant: D. Lesser. Security software expert; IT consultant experience with the FBI. Full CV available upon request.

D. Lesser. "Oh." Lauren wanted to slap her head. "That's where I know the pentalobe thingy from. Douglas Lesser's office. That Evil Twin app guy? The logo was on some paperwork on his desk."

Frowning, Catherine said, "So they work together—Lesser and Michelle. That's how she knew our two stories were connected. We don't know how yet, but it's the first link."

Shaking her head, Lauren said, "Who runs this creepy Fixers show, anyway?" She hit the *Make Contact* page. It began to load slowly. An address appeared first—some office in DC. Then the word *Director* loaded, followed by what appeared to be the top of a photo.

Unauthorized access detected.

The website vanished.

"Oh, crap," Lauren said. "That's... Hell." She scrabbled for a pen and wrote the address down she'd glimpsed. She nudged what she'd written over to Catherine. "Is that what you remember?"

"I think so. We can't ask Duppy to get us back in?"

"He said not to ask. Besides, they'll be looking for another unauthorized attempt now. We've got everything we're going to get."

"Which is what? The name of Michelle's company. The fact Lesser does a bit of IT consultancy work for them. The same company that once recruited and later fired Baldoni."

"We also have the fact it's a super-secret organization that goes around upsetting everyone's apple carts for the right price," Lauren said. "Be they politics, business, or security. Advising them on dirty tricks, espionage, media, whatever it takes?"

"Seems like it."

"So how does Michelle fit in? Why is she talking to us?"

"I'm not sure." Catherine drummed her fingers on her thigh. "MediCache, Hickory, the missing food robot. What do all these things have in common?"

"Well, the first two have Ansom in common. Ansom makes MediCache and it uses Hickory to promote it. No clue where the robot comes in."

"That is odd." Catherine pursed her lips. "Ansom doesn't make that robot, does it?"

"No. Antonio said he imported his pair from a company in Estonia. They're not affiliated with any other company." She bit her lip as she thought. "So where does this leave us?"

Glancing at her watch, Catherine said, "It leaves us running late to interview wedding celebrants."

Huffing, Lauren said, "I bet Woodward and Bernstein didn't have to drop everything to work out which stranger will best encapsulate their love on their wedding day."

Catherine gave a small smirk. "I suspect not."

Chapter 17
Reign of Terror

THE REIGN OF TERROR, AS Lauren dubbed it, started exactly twenty-four hours after Lionel Ayers had vowed to screw over Lauren.

Well, he had promised it would only take a day.

One moment they'd been debating celebrants; the next, Lauren's phone began to light up with email after email. First came reminders of unpaid bills that she knew she'd paid. Next, an email came from her bank about her "stolen" credit card, informing her it had been canceled. Then things stepped up another notch.

"I thought you said your father wouldn't bother getting me back," Lauren complained as she worked her phone furiously, flinging off emails to correct the avalanche of mischief. "But he's sure as hell having his fun."

"We don't know it's him."

"Really? Have you seen my Facebook page lately? This stuff's really personal."

Catherine glanced at her screen, stopped, and bent closer. "Wait, you had three college-age DUIs, in between selling bongs and being a high-class escort to pay your college fees?" She shot her an incredulous look. "What is all this?"

Lauren shook her head numbly at the page that had been hacked about forty minutes ago. "I'm also interested in casual sex with strangers. I know this because it says so in that pinned post. With my head stuck on that naked model. It even has my cell number." She scowled. "No one could ever accuse your father of being subtle."

Her phone rang, and she glanced at it. *Unknown number.* The thirty-second call she'd gotten since that salacious ad had gone up. "Meanwhile, two of Dad's friends and one of Meemaw's have posted comments, apparently shocked that I'd 'do such a terrible thing,'" Lauren added, her fury rising. "God, *that* really gets me. Do they even have brains? As if any of this sounds like me! Oh, and don't start me on all these creeps filling my timeline with pictures of their junk."

"Can't you just delete that post?" Catherine pointed. Her gaze went down the screen. "And that one...well, all of them?"

"I've been locked out. I've complained to Facebook, but I'm still waiting for a reply."

Her phone rang again.

"Don't answer tha—" Lauren's objection died on her lips.

Catherine had already picked it up and answered. Her face quickly turned several different shades. "Oh really?" she snapped. "Well, listen to me, you perverted, festering pustule, I am a senior journalist with contacts at the FBI. I dare you to call again and see how well that works out for you." She ended the call and threw the phone on the bed beside Lauren.

In the second hour, twenty pizzas turned up at the house, all charged to Lauren's credit card, the same one she'd been told had been canceled. All the pizzas had only anchovies, double garlic, and pineapple on them. It would have been funny if it hadn't cost her four hundred bucks. The asshole who'd ordered them had asked for jumbo-sized. The King brothers shrugged, loaded up their plates, making short work of half the stack, while Catherine blasted the store owner for not checking such a suspicious order.

"He's useless," Catherine said in resignation, throwing her phone down. "He said there was no clue the order wasn't legitimate. No clue? Twenty pizzas, all with identically weird toppings? I give up. People used to be smarter. I'm certain of it."

"The Internet age has dumbed everyone down," Lauren agreed, picking the anchovy and pineapple off her pie, then taking a tentative bite.

With a moody look, Catherine asked: "How can you eat that? It'll still taste of the base ingredients."

"It beats starving while we find out what fresh hell Lionel's putting us through." She wiped her hands on a paper napkin. "I take it your credit cards are still good?"

"Yes. No change. I have alerted the bank to be aware though, just in case."

"Good." Lauren studied her. "You doing okay? You're not going to spiral into a catatonic state of despair on me, are you?" she teased. "I know the assholes in the human race can invoke that in you."

"Not right now." Catherine waved at the pizza. "The smell of garlic will keep me conscious."

Lauren was laughing when her phone rang yet again. She checked the name on her screen. "It's my boss, Theo," she said, hitting the *Accept* button.

"King? Some reason I have a large number of concerned members of the public up in my ear today suggesting you be fired? Something about you being a streetwalker, a dope dealer, and a corrupter of children?"

Corrupter of children? That was a new one. Lauren grimaced. "Someone's trying to harass me."

"I gathered. I know a call-in campaign when I see it," Theo said. "So, who are you pissing off?"

"It's connected to something I'm working on. A story sort of fell in my lap. Things have been going crazy ever since. My cards have been canceled. Bills that I've paid are being emailed to me again. My Facebook page has been hacked."

"Sorry, kid, you've obviously been doxed. Someone, somewhere, is getting people online to make your life hell." He paused, and then his voice lifted in obvious interest when he said, "Must be big if this is the response. Look, I'm gonna put you in contact with one of our in-house lawyers. She'll explain your options and will wave a few lawyer letters around to hurry up with content takedowns on social media. You can fill her in on the story, too. I'd ask for the details now, but my staff news briefing's about to start. Oh, and remember the best way to make this go away is to write your story. The spotlight shifting to the harasser usually results in them getting too busy with the fallout to continue a smear campaign."

"Thanks, Theo. But my story isn't nearly ready yet."

"Then make it ready. G'bye."

Lauren sighed and dropped her phone on the bed. What if there never was anything to file? They had nothing. A few screenshots about a secret business? So what? It wasn't exactly illegal to offer dodgy suggestions to companies wanting to screw over competitors.

Fake Mexican illegal immigrants? And?

How did that even fit anything?

The worst part was that Lauren could hear the hope leaking from Theo's voice, like his bet on hiring her was about to pay off.

Great. No pressure.

It took another hour, but the social media accounts were fixed, thanks to the *Washington Post*'s lawyer. But for every mess sorted, a new one took its place.

Raised voices were coming from the workshop. Catherine glanced around to see Lauren already bolting down the stairs. She headed to the window. An unfamiliar luxury car was parked in the driveway. Walking back to it from the workshop was a squat, balding man in an expensive suit.

She was sure she'd seen him on the news somewhere.

When Lauren burst outside, his step faltered, expression unreadable.

Catherine took off down the stairs at a fast clip. She reached Lauren's side just as the man drew level with her.

"So, the prodigal daughter returns," he said to Lauren, reaching his car. "I remember when you came up to my knee."

"And I remember when you and Dad were friends, Mayor Wilcox. And that was only a few days ago," Lauren countered. "What was all the shouting about?"

"Your boys seemed to take a poor view of a decision I made. I've just explained to Owen that I'll send someone around to pick up my other car that he's been fixing, ready or not. For... reasons."

Lauren gave him a hard look. "Political reasons?"

"It's all over the Internet this morning that your dad's running a drug den. And you..." His face darkened. "Well, I suppose you know what they're saying about you. It's unfair, I know, but I can't be seen to be supporting anything like that."

"Dad's serviced your car for years! Come on, you know the truth about us. You know this is all bull. Someone's smearing us."

He looked uncomfortable. "Lauren, it's not personal."

"I'd say it's pretty personal when you turn your back on Dad like this. Take the side of liars over him."

"I know it's baloney, but come on, you know the deal. Perception beats truth. That goes double for politicians. I don't make the rules, but they're a fact of life. With my approval ratings being what they are right now, I can't afford the risk the other side will use this against me." He looked pained as he opened his car door. "I really am sorry. I hope your father will see it from my side when things are all a bit calmer."

"That's so weak."

He spun around to face Catherine, the source of the cutting line.

"Excuse me?" He glared.

"Mayor Wilcox," she said, her voice deceptively soft. "Owen King is far too polite to do anything about this, so let me pass along a promise. If anyone in your team implies there's any truth to these lies, or does anything other than suggest that it's a smear campaign, then I know a lot of overcharging DC lawyers who'll hang you out to dry. And I'd make it happen on the national news."

He peered at her in disbelief. "And you are?"

"Catherine Ayers."

His face paled. "The Caustic...ah, White House reporter lady?"

Catherine folded her arms. "Yes. Are we clear? You'll stand by this family?"

The mayor scowled before gritting his teeth and giving a faint nod. He climbed into the car and slammed the door with the mutter of *bitch* under his breath. After starting the engine, he burned back up the drive with a squeal of tires.

"You know," Lauren said quietly, "I must have missed something in Journalism 101, but why would the national media give two hoots about some mayor in Iowa and a bunch of gossip about a mechanic?"

"They wouldn't." Catherine looked suddenly sheepish. "I was just banking on the fact the mayor wasn't aware of that."

"You were bluffing? You nearly had *me* convinced."

"That was the point."

Owen appeared at the door of the garage and ambled slowly over. He flicked his eyes up at Lauren. "Apparently, I'm running a drug ring," he said when he got within earshot. "And am of immoral fiber. I don't suppose you two know anything about that?"

Lauren sneaked a glimpse at Catherine.

"That's what I thought." He sighed. "Politics, huh?" He shook his head. "Don't bother explaining, I see what's going on." He turned and made his way back to the workshop, shoulders slumped.

Catherine eyed Lauren, who looked ill, watching him go. "It's not your fault," she said.

"Isn't it?" She gave Catherine a grim look. "I'm the one who tried to play with fire and pissed off your dad this much. He did *exactly* what he said he would."

"Then that makes this his fault, not yours."

Lauren bit her lip. "Seriously, I've never seen my father that mad. I think we should steer clear of him for a little bit." Her phone pinged. She pulled it from her pocket and scrolled through the new messages. "Oh, awesome. I've been signed up for the Scientologists' newsletter." She scrolled down her inbox and stopped dead. "Oh no!" She flipped the screen around to Catherine. "Shit, shit, shit!"

Catherine's eyes tightened as she read.

Dear Ms. King and Ms. Ayers,

Thank you for your email canceling your wedding at the Jumping Frog on November 18. We understand plans change, and we appreciate the notice. However, be advised, your deposit is non-refundable as per the paperwork you signed earlier this week. Thank you.

Evelyn Reid,
Manager
The Jumping Frog

"No!" Lauren said, stabbing out the number on her phone. "They can't do this!"

"Maybe it's not too late?" Catherine frowned. "When did she send the email?"

"A couple of hours ago!"

Lauren began talking to the manager, her wide eyes fixed on Catherine. She ended the call, expression dropping.

"Not good?" Catherine asked.

"They've already given our booking away to another couple. But, because this wasn't our choice and they've filled the slot already, she's agreed to give us our deposit back. She says she's sorry." Lauren frowned. "*How* is someone doing all this? How can anyone know who we booked with?"

Catherine studied Lauren, then glanced at her phone. Then back at her. "Lauren, it's your cell."

"What?"

"It all started after we went to the Fixers site, using your phone."

"Yes…but we didn't do anything there…" She stopped. "Oh. We downloaded a PDF."

"Mm. I'm thinking it wasn't *just* a PDF. Maybe it contains some sort of embedded hacking software?"

"Or spying software?" Lauren stared at her phone in dismay. "That means everything on this is compromised…every personal email." She swallowed. "My bank details… I've done banking on this since we hit the Fixers' site."

"I've heard of this… It's some sort of keylogger program? It records everything you type. That's how they learn passwords, gain access to email accounts, everything."

A note-writing app suddenly opened on Lauren's phone screen.

Slow clap. I was wondering how long it would take you, Lauren King.

They stared at the message. Hesitantly, Lauren bent over her phone and wrote a reply.

Who is this?

This level of cluelessness I suppose I should expect from the mainstream media. Heads well and truly up their asses. I had to laugh at you suspecting poor Lionel. I'm surprised you haven't figured it out by now. Rome is burning. Wake up.

Rome? Lauren typed back.

Nero fiddled while Rome burned. Try to learn a little history every now and then.

"You know, that's actually a myth about Nero," Catherine noted in the interest of accuracy. "It's impossible because the violin wasn't invented for another 1,500 years after the fire."

Lauren's exasperated look made Catherine clap her mouth shut. Lauren typed a reply.

What do you want?

You touch my things, I break your things. And not just your things. Give my regards to Cat. I know how much she loves that name.

Catherine's breath caught at that last line. Who knew that? A better question was: Who didn't? She told everyone not to call her that.

"What do we do now?" Lauren's voice rose.

Catherine grabbed Lauren's phone and whipped out the battery. For good measure, she removed the SIM card, too, and tossed it on the ground. They both stared at the phone parts, as though waiting for them to sprout wings.

"He had to have been listening in on our conversations," Catherine said. "We only ever spoke of suspecting Lionel, never wrote anything in an email. There's no other explanation."

"He's been spying using the phone's microphone?" Lauren blinked. "Or maybe even watching us. On the phone camera?"

"Yes." Distaste filled Catherine. "Our cyber stalker always seemed to know exactly what we were up to. That's how."

"Shit."

She said it with such venom that Catherine's head snapped up. "Lauren, we've found the source of our problems; they won't recur."

"Not that." Lauren's expression was bleak. "Where the hell are we going to get married now?"

Catherine headed out to the wooden bench facing the backyard, bearing the iPad as well as a notepad and pen—"old school," she joked when Lauren joined her.

Lauren brought out a pair of coffees, a frown, and a sinking feeling. "What do we know?" she asked after a sip. "I mean, we've pissed off someone who's accusing us of touching his things. So, he means when we hacked the Fixers' site, yes?"

"Most likely." Catherine opened the screenshot of the PDF on her phone of the Fixers staff list. "And only two people on the staff list know us. Michelle, a political expert, and Lesser, an IT expert." She tapped his entry.

"I feel a bit stupid. Lesser is right to mock us. Sorry I jumped to conclusions about your dad."

"He's only innocent this time. It's not unreasonable to assume he might show off his power."

"He does love to brag about breaking the rules." Lauren peered at her willow tree in the distance. "So why is Lesser warning us off? Or is it just about punishment because we trespassed?"

"The latter does seem to fit with what you've said about him."

"Yeah. So, what now?" Lauren asked.

"We ask ourselves, yet again, how does everyone link together? Hickory, Ansom, Lesser, Michelle, the FBI."

"Michelle and Lesser work together at the Fixers," Lauren said, ticking off a mental list. "Michelle knew ahead of time what was happening with the Mexican stunt—a stunt which clearly helps Ansom and its chip—so Ansom's probably a client. That fits with the fact its CEO loves to break rules. The Mexican thing, hell—now we've seen what the Fixers get up to, it was probably Michelle's idea all along to get publicity for the chip."

Catherine nodded. "Agreed. It's sneaky enough. And the FBI's connection?"

"No idea. Maybe they're really just interested observers like it said in that story."

"Diane thinks otherwise, though. But we can't just ask the director what he's really up to," Catherine said. "So that just leaves Senator Hickory, A low-tech politician who promotes Ansom's high-tech gear but isn't getting anything we can see for it. Why do I find that so hard to believe? Everyone else is up to their necks in this, all interconnected. What is the deal *he* made?"

"We could just up and ask him? 'Hey, Hicks, what's the dirt on you and Ansom? Oh, hey, are you in with the Fixers, too?'"

"Well, why don't we?" Catherine suddenly said. "The man's as transparent as a tapeworm and about as smart. One look at his face and we'll know the truth."

"Right. We do it in person, then." Lauren flicked through her notes. "His home address came up in the pecuniary interests search I did on him earlier. His place isn't even that far from here." She mentally flicked through which brother's truck they'd borrow. *Maybe Matty's. Good suspension. Or Kitten? She did love that old restored Chevy.*

Catherine gazed at her, an odd expression on her face.

"What?" Lauren asked, still distracted.

"It occurs to me that we're not doing a whole lot in the way of planning a wedding," she said quietly. "Or looking at any new venues."

"Oh. No, we're not." Lauren met her gaze, wondering if that meant something terrible. "Are you thinking it's a sign or something?"

A laugh slipped from Catherine. "It's a sign we're more excited about pursuing our story than figuring out the place settings, or whether to go with chicken or fish. That's not too terrible for a pair of news reporters, surely."

Lauren grinned. "No. And it's not like we're out of time to wedding plan—it's just, you know, this is happening *right now*. So maybe let's just procrastinate a little longer and see what Hickory has to say."

Catherine's smile widened. "I approve that plan."

"Maybe it'll go better now that Lesser's done messing with us. I mean, once the bad guy gloats, that's supposed to be the end of it, right?" Lauren's eyes were hopeful.

"True. In movies. I'm just grateful he hasn't found his way into my gadgets. Nonetheless, it can't get any worse than losing the only wedding venue we both really liked."

"Are you insane?" Lauren looked at her in horror. "Touch wood when you tempt the Fates like that!" She pointed at their wooden bench.

With a spectacular eye roll, Catherine dutifully knocked on wood. "I swear you have more eccentricities than a Vegas millionaire."

"I can't help it. All athletes are superstitious—it's how we win games. Besides, you love me anyway." She offered her a baleful stare.

With a tiny quirk of her lips, Catherine said, "That is true. And I trust you know why now."

Lauren leaned against her and smiled. "Yes. I do."

Chapter 18
The Woman at the Lake

"WHAT IF HICKORY'S ALREADY BACK in DC?" Catherine asked as they pulled up at the senator's property with a bounce and a squeak in Owen's inglorious death machine, Kitten.

"You only just thought to ask that now?" Lauren turned off the motor. She jumped out, slammed the door, and twirled the keys around her finger.

Catherine exited with a little less vigor. She supposed they could have called ahead first, but the odds of their prey scampering were a little too high. She couldn't entirely blame him.

The ranch house was grand, old, and weathered and situated on a sprawling piece of acreage, which included a sparkling lake at the end of a dusty path.

A dog barked. Some chickens squawked from somewhere behind the house, but everything seemed quiet otherwise.

An elderly woman came out, wiping her hands down her floral apron. "Well now, who might you all be? I wasn't expecting guests."

Lauren introduced them both. Mrs. Hickory's expression became immediately guarded and then her gaze flicked to Catherine.

"You're that DC journalist? Well, I certainly didn't expect you to be all the way out here."

"We had something important to discuss with your husband, Mrs. Hickory, so we thought it best to do so in person." Catherine smiled warmly. "I hope it's not an imposition."

"Oh no, not at all." The woman looked askance at the mere idea she was failing at being hospitable. "You girls can come inside and wait a bit. Fred's out and about with his adviser. But they're due back soon. I could make you a tea or coffee."

She bustled inside, and they followed, closing a wood-framed screen door after them. "Oh, and ignore Buddy," she said. "Despite his size, he's all bark."

A giant, lumbering black, white, and brown dog shuffled up to them, his heavy tail thumping on the floor.

"A Bernese mountain dog," Lauren identified, edging past. "I guess he looks tame enough."

"Mmm." Catherine eyed it. She lifted a finger. "Sit, Buddy!" She gave a sharp motion.

Buddy's rump dropped instantly to the floor like a sack of flour.

"Jesus," Lauren muttered. "One day you'll have to teach me that."

"Can't teach a gift."

Catherine told herself it was rude to preen.

The kitchen was a picture-perfect country postcard—bright, rustic, and filled with the aroma of the freshly baked date loaf sitting on the sill. Corn curtains adorned the unpainted window frame.

Mrs. Hickory was pouring them both coffees when the door banged at the front of the house. "Ah. He's home."

"Helena, honey, whose truck's that?" came a bellow down the hall.

Two sets of footsteps sounded. One heavy, one light.

Senator Hickory's smile fell as he caught sight of Lauren and Catherine.

Catherine's own polite smile in reply was washed away when his political adviser came into view. A cocktail of anger, humiliation, and pain clenched her stomach. Lauren's hand slid to her thigh under the table and gave a small squeeze.

Michelle Hastings.

Catherine recalled her at the State Fair. She had laughed in Catherine's face when she'd assumed the woman had been there to see her. She'd called Catherine arrogant. Catherine could see why. The answer had been right in front of them the whole time. She'd been there for Hickory, watching him give his speech.

"Well…" The senator's wild, white caterpillar eyebrows shot up. "You two. This is a surprise."

"Hi," Lauren said.

Catherine simply stared at Michelle, whose face was impenetrable as ever.

Mrs. Hickory took in the awkward circular standoff, then excused herself to let them "do your politics thing."

Hickory gestured to the woman behind him. "My political adviser, Michelle Hastings."

"We've met," Lauren said, her words clipped.

"Why, hello again, Cat," Michelle drawled. "Ms. King."

The old man's gaze slid from them to his adviser and back again. "Know what? I'm just gonna go wash up. I'll let you all get reacquainted." He slipped out, his footsteps receding into the distance.

"Together again," Michelle said as a door banged shut at the end of the hallway. She looked at Lauren. "Plan to threaten me again with being used as a piñata?"

"It was more a metaphor than a threat." Lauren ran her fingertips casually over the table. "But hey, if that's your kink, I could arrange it."

Michelle snorted. "So evolved. Class act, cowgirl."

"Better a cowgirl than a schemer who fucks someone to get ahead. *Real* class act there."

"You know," Catherine cut in, eying Michelle over her coffee cup, "I learned the hard way not to underestimate Lauren. I recommend you call a truce now before she stops playing nice."

"That's her playing nice?"

"Oh, it is." Catherine sipped her coffee, cupping it in her hands to hide the tremble in her fingers.

"Fine." Michelle pulled up a chair and sat opposite Catherine. "What do you two want?"

"I take it you were at the State Fair playing adviser to Hickory? And seeing me there was really was a coincidence?"

"Yes. I had no idea you were there until I saw you."

"So why talk to me?"

194

"Because your story matters more than our past or anything else."

"My story."

"Yes. You can't let it go. It's important."

"This is a tired old path we're treading." Catherine's laugh was dry and empty. "My God, why am I even listening to this?" She made to rise.

"I haven't lied to you even once over this."

"And what is 'this'? I can't even see the story. It's a jumbled mess. Give me something to work on."

"All right, Wave'N'Go."

"What's that?"

"The next big thing. Ansom's biotech data-chip product soon will be marketed at young people as a lifestyle option so they don't need to carry wallets. MediCache was phase one to get the government interested. Wave'N'Go is phase two, to get the masses on board and not fearing the tech. And to help it catch on, it'll be free initially."

"So, this is all creepy, vapid, but still voluntary. Where's the news story?"

"*Catherine.*" Michelle's tone sounded so disappointed, so mocking, that Catherine felt the censure down to her bones. "You know what this is as much as I do. I know you do. I read your Hickory story. Don't play some deeply uncurious member of the masses now."

Catherine inhaled. "All right. Whatever this is, it does feel like a slippery slope."

"You're right. It is the beginnings of a slow creep, a loss of citizens' rights, but it's so subtle no one's noticing. It has to be stopped, and I know you have the ability to do that." Her gaze flicked to Lauren's skeptical face. "Both of you."

Frowning, Catherine said, "If you believe all this, why are you Hickory's adviser? He's positioned himself as the go-to man for MediCache."

Michelle's voice dropped to barely audible. "Temporary adviser," she murmured. "I'm around Hickory for as long as he's selling MediCache. That doesn't mean I agree with him. We don't always get a say in our assignments, do we?" She leaned back in her chair. "I believe you know how that feels. How was it writing gossip in LA? Fulfilling?"

"Thanks for the reminder." Catherine thudded her coffee cup to the table. "It is insanity to listen to you again. Once burnt—"

"You did get my message, I assume?" Michelle interrupted. "The Mexicans on the border? Was I wrong?"

"How could you be wrong? Since your company most likely paid a group of Mexicans to agree to be fake arrested, pose for photos, and used for a political stunt to promote MediCache."

"Well, that *is* thinking outside the box, wouldn't you agree?"

"Your genius idea, I suppose?"

"All I can say is it was a win-win for several of my clients."

"Who are?"

"I can't say."

"Well, it's a simple process of elimination," Catherine said, "working out who benefited in all that publicity and posturing. Ansom, of course, and…" She paused. "The FBI, possibly? As for Hickory… How involved *is* the good senator in all this?"

"Not relevant." Michelle's face became a blank slate.

Lauren snorted. "I'd say it's plenty relevant if you want a story done. Like, you know what's really relevant? The fact you work for a sneaky little company called the Fixers."

Michelle's mask slipped a bit.

"Yeah, so much for a *top-secret* consultancy company."

"Who told you that name?"

"Not telling," Lauren said. "Answer Catherine's question. How deep in this is the senator?"

Hickory entered the room again and glanced at them all. "How deep am I in what?"

"Senator." Catherine spun to face him. "Have you heard of an organization called the Fixers?"

"No." He glanced at Michelle, eyes widening, and gave a mighty headshake. "Never heard of them."

"Really." Catherine dragged out the word.

"Yes. Now, thanks for stopping by. Ms. Hastings will show you out." Hickory waved toward the door. "And next time, call first and make an appointment." He fumbled through his wallet and slapped his business card on the table.

Lauren scooped it up, then climbed to her feet. Catherine followed suit.

Michelle smiled, and it was that same maddening smile Catherine had once thought was interesting. It wasn't interesting; it was all kinds of wrong.

They stepped outside, and Lauren shoved her hands in her pockets. "Can we just get to the pointy end of all this BS?" she asked, turning to Michelle. "Just tell us: why would you go against your own employer by directing us toward this story?"

Michelle sighed and peered at the cloudless blue sky. "Walk with me," she said, and headed off toward the lake at the edge of the property.

She came to a stop at a decaying boat ramp and glanced from Lauren to Catherine, who had followed. "Look, I get what you think of me. That's fair. But I have been careful on this to try and point you at the story without lying, but also without betraying anyone. It would be dangerous for me to come right out and leak to reporters. My clients are important people. You have no idea how powerful. I won't cross them—not directly. But I can certainly nudge someone capable of seeing the truth and hope that certain dots will be joined. That's all I've been doing." She gazed at Catherine. "The chip is a threat to everyone. Nothing else matters."

Catherine studied her. "Why didn't you just tell us all this at the fair?"

"Like you'd have believed a word I said if I'd gone in with a charm offensive. You'd have walked immediately. The only thing I could do was tell the truth and try to get your interest piqued in the story."

"And how involved is Hickory?" Catherine asked.

"Peripherally. But I still won't talk about him."

"You're his adviser. How can we not talk about him?"

"Only an adviser on paper. That's why he thinks I'm here. I'm actually undercover, keeping an eye on the bigger picture."

"Which is?"

"The chip. I'm shaping its rollout, watching progress, enhancing promotion, reporting market reception."

"For Ansom."

Michelle sighed. "I can't officially confirm clients' names, so you can stop asking."

"All right, forget clients. Let's talk colleagues. How does your IT guy Douglas Lesser fit in?"

"That knuckle dragger? He wrote the software the Ansom chip talks to whenever it's scanned."

"Knuckle dragger?" Lauren peered at her in surprise. "I've met him. He's got an overblown ego, sure, but he's educated, articulate. Why call him that?"

"Have you *seen* his app?" Michelle sounded incredulous.

"My Evil Twin? Yes. Why?" Lauren asked.

Michelle gave a mirthless laugh. "You really can't see it? Take another look." She glanced at Catherine. "Just stay on this story, okay? I'm not overselling how important it is. If anyone can get to the bottom of it, it's you. Or did I misunderstand how good you are at your job?"

"So good at my job you ruined my reputation in one simple sting," Catherine said with ice in her voice. "On that note, tell me who it was. Who paid to bring me down? Can you do that at least? It's ancient history."

"That'd also breach client confidentiality. I can't." She gave Catherine a half shrug.

Her lack of concern set Catherine's teeth on edge. *This is pointless.* Without another word, she turned on heel and retraced her steps toward the truck, snapping to Lauren as she passed her, "We're leaving. Our source is unhelpful to the point of useless. There's no story here."

They were halfway up the path when Michelle called after them. "Wait."

"Something to add?" Catherine said snidely but kept walking.

"Cat!"

Catherine didn't even pause in her stride.

"Catherine. Please!"

She stopped and turned.

Michelle caught up with her. "I'd like to help, but I just can't." She lowered her voice. "Our company works on *complete discretion.* Don't you get that? That's its selling point. If even one client found out there was a media leak, it'd be disastrous. That'd be it. End of the company."

"Tragedy. And you know damned well I never reveal my sources. I didn't last time, either, when everyone was baying for blood and demanding to know how I got my facts so horribly wrong. I could have hung you out to dry. I never said a word."

"I remember." Michelle's voice was soft.

For a brief second, Catherine thought she heard regret before she remembered the devious actress she was dealing with. "Then it's simple: give us what you have, or we don't write a word."

"This could end me."

"We've just established I don't break confidences. It's your turn to put your neck on the line. Prove to me how much you really care about this story."

"I could call your bluff." Michelle's chin lifted. "You always cared more about the story than yourself."

"True. Once. Now I have other priorities." She shifted her gaze to Lauren. "Actually, it might be a relief to get back to what we're supposed to be doing here. We do have a wedding to plan. You think this is fun for me? Dealing with you again, when I could be doing that instead?"

Michelle took her measure. She glanced at Lauren, who merely shrugged.

"What she said." Lauren folded her arms. "We've actually been dying to settle the whole chicken or fish debate. Oh, and what do you think, Catherine?" She sounded fascinated at the thought. "DJ or wedding singer?"

"DJ," Catherine said after a thoughtful pause. "Mrs. Potts did give us some interesting names. What do you think about DJ Oprah Spinfrey? Do you think Mrs. Potts is trolling us, or…?"

"Fine." Michelle raised her hands in surrender and glared at them. "You win. But you can't use a word I say, on the record or off it. You *can't*."

"We won't."

"What do you want to know?"

Catherine took in a deep breath. Moment of truth. "Let's start with that ancient history. Who brought me down?"

"I suppose the short answer is, *you* did."

"What?"

Michelle sighed. "It was something you wrote. Remember in late 2012, the FBI announced it was creating its Next Generation Identification database?" She glanced at Lauren. "The NGI's a national biometrics database which contains personal information about criminals and suspects—not just their names, but their identifying marks and features, palm prints, eye scans, voice, tattoos, scars, limps, piercings, eye color—you name it. All the things criminals can't hide or change. The FBI was very proud of its pet project. It was the jewel in its crown."

"I remember," Catherine said slowly. "It had issues, though. How do you know so much about it?"

"Because my now-colleague, Douglas Lesser, helped build it." Michelle gave Catherine a searching look. "Do you remember how many columns you wrote blasting the NGI just after it was announced it would be built?"

Catherine blinked. "I don't know. A couple. Are you saying *that's* why? The FBI wanted payback?"

"You didn't do a *few* columns. You wrote ten. Each more scathing than the last. Each arguing that gathering human biometric data into one national library was a terrible idea, an idea that breached an American's fundamental right to privacy, especially as some of those in the database were only suspects, not guilty of anything."

"Yes." She frowned. "I remember making that case."

"The line that was particularly effective, and that was starting to make some high-level senators wobble, was what happens if innocent, law-abiding people get swept up into the database? How would they ever get out? Would they be there forever? You also asked whether people in the database would be easy to track or even stalk. And what of identity theft?"

"Keep enough data about someone in a file, and sooner or later someone else might find it and use it against them." Catherine nodded. "That's identity theft on a worrying scale. You can't just cancel a credit card if that happens. You can't simply change your name. If someone misuses or alters the file holding all your physical identifiers, then what do you do? How do you even prove you're you, if someone changes what's listed as your unique characteristics?"

Michelle looked impressed. "I liked that column the best. It was an intellectual argument that had no counterargument. And I wasn't the only one to notice." Her look was hard and long.

"They were just columns," Catherine said, feeling faint. "I didn't dwell on them."

"You mightn't have, but a lot of people did. They were persuasive. You were starting to turn the tide of public opinion. Doubts were emerging. Senators were raising questions. You were becoming seriously inconvenient to some very powerful people."

Catherine sucked in a breath. "I wrote about protecting our privacy. A fundamental right. Are you saying my career got destroyed for that?"

"Ironic, isn't it? Know what else is ironic? Since the database has gone live, everything you warned about has happened. Non-criminals *are* in the database. One in five Americans is already in there, and it's growing constantly. More and more innocent people get swept in there every day. Personal privacy gone in the blink of an eye." She snapped her fingers. "But it doesn't matter that your concerns were all valid. You stepped on certain toes, so your destruction was necessary."

"Whose toes? The FBI's?"

"Well, you were making their lives hellishly difficult, but no. They didn't need to get their hands dirty, not when they had an ally to do it for them."

"Who?"

Michelle paused. "Lionel Ayers ordered your career's destruction."

"No." Catherine felt the air whoosh out of her lungs. It was ludicrous. Her father wouldn't do that.

Lauren scowled at Michelle. "You're lying."

"Not at all. Cat's father paid handsomely for her fall from grace. He visited me personally at the office to make sure I understood I was to use any means necessary."

"Any means," Lauren retorted. "I see you took him literally."

"I did what I had to." Michelle's gaze hardened. "I did my job."

"This makes no sense. I met Lionel. He doesn't hate Catherine, and he doesn't want her to suffer. I mean, I think he's secretly proud of her. He just wants…" She stopped.

"Yes?" Michelle probed. "What does he want?"

"Profit. Power. Control."

"Exactly. And although he didn't have a stake in the NGI database or what the FBI was up to, he was developing MediCache at the exact moment Catherine had begun telling everyone how terrible biometric storage is for our personal safety and security. The timing could not have been worse. He couldn't risk Catherine derailing his grand plans."

"This is insane," Catherine said. "He wouldn't—"

"I was there. I watched him write the check. Six figures, in case you're wondering."

"Six figures, huh?" Lauren glowered. "So that's how much it takes? Do you do this often? Bed your targets to seal deals?"

Michelle smiled. "Which answer would bother you more?"

"You don't even care about the lengths you went to for this?"

"This is just a body." She waved at herself. "It's an effective means to an end, and something your fiancée seemed to enjoy having a great deal. I use whatever assets I have that are most useful. But to me, my body's not really important. My mind is the sacrosanct thing. That, I am extremely careful about sharing."

Lauren's nostrils flared.

Catherine looked away, feeling sick. *Just a body.* Her thoughts hurtled back. How much had Michelle ever shared with her? Nothing much came to mind. Of course Michelle had kept her emotional distance. Why wouldn't she? She had a husband and another life to go home to.

"How do you sleep at night?" Disgust coated Lauren's words.

"Ordinarily quite well." Michelle looked unperturbed. "But not right now. Which is where you two come in. The story that has to be told. The dangers ahead."

"What's your interest in all this?" Catherine asked.

"I'm a student of history. Always have been."

"Oh, sure," Lauren said. "You expect us to believe this is all about the greater good?"

"Strange as it sounds, it's true. I was listening to Hickory give his speech at the fair. I was standing there, in the shadows, monitoring public response to it, thinking yet again how catastrophic the technology was, and what it might mean for society, ten, twenty, fifty years down the track when it's pervasive. And I suddenly see Cat."

Her gaze flicked to Catherine. "It was like I'd conjured you up out of thin air—the one reporter I know who's tenacious and clever, undaunted, and doesn't care if she writes an unpopular story. The same woman who grasps the big picture and had already condemned the data chip in her Hickory profile a week ago. If anyone could pursue this story to its bitter end, it was you."

"So, you're here to get me to do what you lack the courage to do?" Catherine asked. "You won't resign and walk away from this in protest, so you rope us in to doing your dirty work?"

"What good would me resigning do? I'd be easily replaced. The chip can't be stopped so readily. Not by me. But by you? I saw what you did with SmartPay."

"Oh yes, SmartPay. We met your charming husband on that job."

Michelle's mask slammed down so fast it was breathtaking. "He...is not relevant to any of this."

"Is it true your marriage ended after you took the hit job on Catherine?" Lauren asked.

Michelle's expression became tight. "I've said all there is to say on this. But if you plan to stop MediCache, you have three days."

"What happens then?" Catherine asked.

"The FBI will conclude it's reviewed the Mexicans' case and will recommend they support Ansom's new chip. They will suggest other security departments find uses for it, too. Any criticisms of the chip will be met with loud suggestions that the critic is 'soft on terror.'" Her fingers curled into air quotes. "You have three days, or there's no going back. Humanity will cross a line. You need to put aside your distaste for me and look at the facts. Stop this while we still can."

With that, she turned and strode back toward the house.

Catherine watched her go, wondering how much of any of this was even true. She sounded sincere. But then she always had.

"Hey," Lauren whispered, her hand settling on the small of Catherine's back. "You okay?"

"I suppose so." Catherine felt tired. It was too much. "What are your thoughts?"

"Is she playing us? She's manipulative. She clearly wants us to do this for her. Do you buy her greater good line?"

"I don't know. But even if she's manipulating us to get us involved, it doesn't make her wrong. This embedded chip scheme *is* a line that shouldn't be crossed."

Lauren nodded. "Right, then we need to research this. Go down the rabbit hole."

"Yes." Catherine straightened. "I believe I know where to start. The Grand Millennium."

"Oh?"

"It's the hotel chain my parents always stay at."

"Your parents...who tried to ruin you."

"I hadn't forgotten. We'll be having a little discussion about that, too." She steeled her shoulders.

"Oh." Lauren's eyes widened. "Oh, hell."

"Exactly."

Chapter 19
The One I Want

THE DRIVE HOME WAS SOBERING. Lauren wished she could say something to reassure Catherine. But how do you say *sorry your parents are total bastards who paid for your career to be blown to hell*? Or at least that was Lionel's excuse. Did Victoria even know the depths to which her husband had sunk? Lauren was pretty sure that was a question she shouldn't ask her brooding fiancée.

Catherine was chewing her bottom lip as she stared out the window.

With a worried glance at her, Lauren then turned into her dad's long driveway. "You know, maybe I should be the one to confront Lionel."

"No."

"Just no? If you're planning a frontal assault, we should be on the same page."

"There is no 'we' in this. It's time the Ayers family cleaned house. Witnesses not required."

"Catherine, it's not about me witnessing something messy. I thought you could use the support."

"No. I don't need it. And I'd like to get it over with as soon as possible."

"And I think maybe you need to take a breath and calm down before you do anything rash. If you rush blindly over there without thinking this through, things could blow up worse."

Catherine's expression was pure frost. "The more I think about it, the more enraged I get that my father did this to me. He tried to *ruin* me. He came close to succeeding. So, I'm adopting the scorched-earth policy as of right now."

"Uh...now?"

"No time like the present." She paused. "I'll call a cab to the Grand Millennium. I'm aware I'm in no condition to drive, even if I could manhandle this beast." She waved at the dash.

"It's not that. I mean, *now*... Ah, remember it's the bachelorette party in an hour or so? My brothers have been planning it for us all week. Can your scorched-earth option wait until the morning? Which might work out better, because you need to be rested and fresh for this." She shot her a hopeful smile as they finally pulled up.

Catherine slowly eyed her. "Are you serious?"

Turning off the engine, Lauren met her expression evenly. It had been a long time since she'd had to face this level of wrath from Catherine. She braced herself. "Yes."

"By all means, the ritualistic carousal of your infantile brothers should come ahead of my family's betrayal."

Sucking in a deep breath, Lauren said, "Catherine, I can see you're really angry, but I'm not your enemy. I'm the woman who loves you. We're on the same team."

"You would not understand."

"I know." Lauren lifted her hands. "I know. I get that I'm lucky with my family. And I know the timing is the pits. But how about this..." Her hand snaked out to Catherine's. "Maybe you could just put in a brief appearance at our party and try not to murder my infantile brothers, who I know probably deserve it, and you can wreak divine retribution on your parents tomorrow when you've slept on it." She swallowed. "But I will understand if you say no to the party. My brothers will just have to deal with it, okay? Besides, they might be having so much fun they won't even notice you're not there." She offered a reassuring grin.

Catherine regarded her. "And would you notice?"

Lauren looked down at their entangled fingers, unsure whether now was a good time to lie.

Sighing, Catherine said, "I'm fairly sure this engagement party wouldn't meet the minimum requirements with only half the couple there."

Lauren said nothing. She felt bad enough even asking.

"All right. I'll go for a little bit. But if your brothers ask me to do a *Grease* medley tonight, so help me I'll use a wrench on their softest parts."

"I hear you." Lauren exhaled in relief. "No Travolta medleys. Check. And I'm really sorry about all of this. Everything. Michelle, your parents, and the lousy timing of the party."

Opening the vehicle's door, Catherine turned back to her. "Unconditional family love is not something to take for granted. Never forget that."

"Yeah." Lauren hated the aching pain in Catherine's voice. "I know."

"Good."

Catherine was stalling. If she didn't hurry up and get dressed, Lauren *would* notice. But the thought of facing the music, the room full of strangers, the forced frivolity, when all she wanted to do was curl up in bed and stew, was crippling. She'd promised she'd go, but in truth she'd rather do anything else right now. She looked longingly at the bed as she slowly buttoned up a fresh shirt.

"I'll boycott."

Catherine's head snapped around. "What?"

"The party. You look so miserable. And you're taking twenty minutes to put a shirt on, for God's sake. So let's boycott. We'll stay here, and I'll keep you company."

Her eyes were so intense and filled with empathy that Catherine had to look away. "Don't be silly. I said I'd go."

"You look like you're prepping for your execution."

"This is how I dress for every party." Her attempt at humor fell flat.

"Oh, sure it is." Lauren ran her hand through her own hair. "I release you from your promise to attend, okay? I'm sorry I asked. It was wrong."

"No, it's not okay. Although, yes, I admit I'm going to have to work up to it a little." She forced a bright smile. "Tell you what, you go on ahead, meet and greet all your friends, and I'll be down in a little while, when I'm in the right headspace."

Lauren hesitated. Doubt streaked across her face.

"Go," Catherine insisted. "I mean it. Have fun. There's no point both of us sitting around moping. Just let me sort out my thoughts a bit. I'll be down later."

Lauren leaned over and dropped a kiss on her lips. "Think I can't see right through you? I know what you're doing. I really appreciate it. So much."

"Oh, please." Catherine gave an airy wave. "I've endured windbag senators pontificating on everything from toilet paper to Popeye. What's a little mechanics' mayhem for a few hours?"

"Thank you." Lauren's look was every kind of soft. "Love you."

It turned out getting in the mood was a lot harder than squaring up to blowhard politicians. Catherine finally pushed aside her hurt and fury, rolled over, and stood. *Now or never.*

She could hear the shouts of merriment from the workshop, along with thumping music which all sounded like it had a car theme. Catherine hated everything about this. But Lauren never asked much of her. She was generous, good, kind, and all the things Catherine probably wasn't, and certainly didn't deserve. So, she could do this small thing for Lauren. Put in an appearance for a few drinks and then crawl into bed and lick her wounds.

She made her way down the stairs, pausing in the living room. Flopped over a side table lay a pair of black garment bags. Oh, right. She'd heard they'd received a delivery. She approached the package marked with her name and zipped open the outfit's protective cover.

Oh. Oh yes.

Zachary had outdone himself. Her wedding dress was beautiful. Her fingers trailed across the flowing material. Stunning. She was tempted to take a peek at the other outfit, but the thought of seeing Lauren in it for the first time on her wedding day stopped her curiosity cold.

"It's beautiful."

Catherine started. She turned to see Meemaw on the sofa, watching her from the shadows.

"I think so, too."

"He was a lovely boy who came by. We sat him down and fed him coffee and pie 'til he had to go. Said if it didn't fit to call him, and he'd come back and adjust it. Left his card." She pointed to a white rectangle on the side table, with "ZachB" in purple lettering.

"Thank you."

"Where have you been all evening?"

"Work." If agonizing over how past story decisions had ruined her life counted as work.

Meemaw's face creased. "Is it important?"

"I suppose so."

"More important than Lauren?"

Zipping the dress back up inside its garment bag to buy her time, Catherine's hackles rose. "Why do you ask that? Do you not trust me to put Lauren first?"

"All I know is my granddaughter's upset about something. She's not talking about it. But if it's just work, then I'd say you've got your priorities all about-face. Wouldn't you?"

"It's not work she's bothered by." Catherine debated how much to say. "She's upset on my behalf. I discovered today I was betrayed."

"Who by?"

Pain throbbed. Her fingers slid to her temple, where her headache was starting. "My...parents." Saying that out loud made her feel so much worse. It felt like an admission of failure. It was humiliating. Enraging. And now she felt exposed along with it. It's not like Meemaw, surrounded by love, could possibly understand family betrayal.

"They'll not likely be at the wedding, then?"

Catherine felt the ache surge through her at the reminder. "No. Never." She regretted her honesty as she braced herself for Meemaw to begin her usual nosy cross-examination. Or perhaps she'd try to convince her that family was forever, and she had to forgive them. Or pray. She set her jaw.

"I'm sorry to hear that. That's a sadness that pains me in a way I have no words for."

Catherine regarded her with surprise.

"Parents are hard work, let me tell you." Meemaw's expression was grim. "They might be ours to respect and obey, but they aren't perfect and can be real disappointing. My own folks didn't approve of my marriage to Noah. They thought my man wasn't good enough for me, seeing he was only a farmhand. So, they punished me by not showing up. That one stung. It was a hurt I carried for years. No one knows about that, not even Lauren. Oh, we reconciled years later when their grandchild came along, but it was never the same. All I remembered each time I laid eyes on them was how they'd turned their backs on me during my most important day."

"I'm sorry." Catherine moved over to sit opposite her in the armchair.

"As was I. That pain sat with me for years and I clung to it like a precious thing. Then one day, I realized I was just hurting myself hanging on to it. It was my burden; my parents had long since moved on."

"Did you ever forgive them?"

"You'd think that, wouldn't you?" Meemaw gave an indignant huff. "I know I'm supposed to, but I never could. Not all the way down to my bones. Not that deep. When I needed them the most, they made their disapproval more important than me and my heart. That kind of thing just doesn't wash off easy."

"No. It doesn't."

"So I took a long, hard look at myself and realized the best I could do was enjoy what I had. Look at what *matters*. You can't focus on the folks who are never going to be on your side, no matter what you do or what they say. Some minds can't be changed. Focus on the people who are in your corner. They're *your* people."

"Lauren." Catherine cleared her throat. "Yes. She's been—"

Meemaw clucked her tongue. "Not just my granddaughter." She gave her a withering look. "You're thinking with your head stuck in a bunker like you're off to war. Think you've got your allies and your enemies all sorted. But haven't you seen what's right under your nose?"

Catherine didn't need to look. She appreciated the sentiment, of course. Oh, Meemaw meant well, but the Kings weren't the people she *needed*. The truth was she had nothing in common with them and everyone knew it but was far too polite to say. Not that it mattered, anyway, because aside from Lauren, Catherine didn't need anyone.

What a depressing little thought that was.

"I'll let you cogitate on that fur ball for a while." Meemaw leaned across and patted her hand with finality. "Now, how's about you go make that granddaughter of mine happy by putting in an appearance? And no protests. Because, honey, if I can tolerate that Travolta boy on repeat, you can, too. Come along." She grabbed Catherine's hand and tugged it.

"I should warn you," Catherine said as she rose, "I'm not really in the party mood."

"I know, honey. Neither am I. When you get to my age, parties feel like the Battle of Normandy, with all those flashing lights and loud noises. But don't let anyone ruin your fun. You can torture yourself over that unworthy family of yours anytime but, see, tonight's about celebrating getting to spend your life with Lauren. Don't you let anyone take that away from you."

Catherine plastered on what she hoped counted as a convincing smile and stepped inside the workshop. All the cars were gone, the benches gleaming, and giant photocopies of posters from *Grease* were stuck up all over the wall. A booming soundtrack from the movie was on full blast.

Right now, there was a lot of hip thrusting going on as the brothers, wearing matching leather jackets, belted out *Greased Lighting*. Suze was beside them, in badly fitting mechanic overalls rolled up halfway to her knees, windmilling an old yellow leather tool belt. She seemed to be swaying arrhythmically. And doing the lyrics for an entirely different song.

Catherine had to give her props for staying standing while that plastered. She glanced up. Oh good. Mirror balls. Hanging from the fluorescent light fittings. Because that's what truly adds class to a party.

The song ended with a foot stomp, a hip swish, and a flourish, and Catherine almost slumped in relief for a break from the thudding.

"Catherine!" Lauren bounded over. Her breath reeked of beer, and her eyes were too bright. "You came!" she added loudly. "And look who else did!" She waved her arm, and a tall, good-looking young man ambled over, his arm around the waist of a young blonde woman with candy-colored lipstick.

"'Lo," he said with a grin. "I'm Tommy, Laur's youngest brother."

"Ah. I was starting to think you were a myth." Catherine smiled.

"This here's Candice." He gestured to his date.

The girl offered her a toothy smile, her gaze dismissive as she turned back to coo at her boyfriend.

"Hello," Catherine managed.

"Nick, her brother, is around here, too." Tommy waved in the direction of a laughing, upside-down blond boy doing a handstand against the wall as his friends cheered.

How very...flexible, Catherine thought.

"Right then," Tommy added, "we better go top up!" Tommy waved an empty, foam-dripping glass at her and wheeled away, Candice in his adoring slipstream.

On his way to the bar, he slapped Nick on the stomach and laughed hard when the man's shaky handstand crumpled into a heap amidst a bawdy roar of masculine cheers.

Well. Tommy was obviously worth the wait.

Catherine glanced at her fiancée. "Having fun?"

"This is the *best*. And I'm so glad you came. So glad." Lauren offered a happy sigh. "Hey, let me get you a drink. If anyone's earned some hard liquor, it's you."

She headed off to the bar before Catherine could answer. There was a crowd gathered around Owen who was playing bartender.

"*So you're the one that she wants, ooh, ooh, oooh.*" Suze sidled up, singing. She did a little thrust from the dance number as she finished.

Catherine gave the faintest nod, acknowledging the butchered song lyric. "I am indeed."

"Well, that's Lauren for you. She always did march to her own drum," Suze said. "First walking away from softball... She had a national team tryout. But nope, not interested, 'cause journalism was calling. And now there's you."

"Me?" Catherine folded her arms.

"Mm. We all kind of assumed she'd wind up with an athlete. Some cool chick called Frankie with a crew cut and a mean fastball. Not someone..." She waved her hand over Catherine. "Elegant. Classy. From *Boston*." She looked frankly astonished at that last one.

"Boston's what you're most shocked by?" Catherine's eyebrow tilted up.

"Actually, yeah. Ha. You're so..." She waggled her finger at her, then ran out of words. Or forgot them. She shrugged. "Can you tell me one thing? Why Lauren?"

Catherine suppressed a sigh. Was she to be plagued with this question for the rest of her life? Between Lucas and Lauren questioning her choices, and now Suze, did she really seem such a poor match to the population of Iowa?

"Why not Lauren?" She narrowed her eyes.

That seemed to confound Suze. "Because you like her? You *do* like her, right? For who she is under that banging body? 'Cause, see, Lucas has been telling me this whole other theory."

"Oh?" Catherine lowered her voice to a notch just above dangerous.

"He says you're using her to feel young again. Then you're gonna get bored, ditch her, and move on to the next hot thing. You're, like, having a midlife crisis and only *think* you love her." She tried to straighten up but only ended up wobbling. "I told him you're too young for a crisis. Sorry, I'm a little buzzed. But just in case he's not full of it, I have to say, as Laur's best friend who has known her since grade school…" Her face turned to pleading. "Please don't hurt her. She's my favorite person on earth. She wouldn't hurt a fly. You have to treat my girl right."

"I will." Catherine's dark thoughts shifted to Lucas. "It's not Lauren I'd ever want to hurt."

A new song started, which perked up Suze. "*Beauty School Dropout!* Oooh. Gotta dance!" She gave Catherine a hearty slap on the shoulder and took off, adjusting the knot on the bright-blue handkerchief around her neck.

Catherine's gaze sought out Lucas, who was arm wrestling with one of his brothers. Her anger at the day she'd had was beginning to get the better of her. The awful music didn't help. She was thoroughly out of sorts, enraged by her parents, and Lucas badmouthing her now was too much. She squared her shoulders, cutting through the crowd on a mission. People instinctively gave way at the sight of her.

Whichever brother was arm wrestling Lucas slammed his arm onto the workbench.

"You got lucky! Best of three!" Lucas shouted, rubbing his abused arm.

"No, actually, I think he's busy right now," Catherine said, her voice like honey. She glanced at the other brother—John, she identified—and gave him a pointed look.

He took the hint and scuttled into the crowd behind them.

Lucas's smug expression didn't improve Catherine's mood. He reminded her of her father—so damned superior.

"You look about to take my head off," he said, leaning an elbow on the high bench. "So, what've I done to piss off the millionaire?"

"Not a millionaire."

"No? You know, I asked Lauren to show me a picture of your home. She showed me the one in LA first. That place in the Hollywood hills? You're up to your eyeballs in money."

Sighing, Catherine decided she couldn't be bothered explaining the perfect storm of a tanking property market, a bankrupt film executive panic selling, and her generous new employment contract. "Are you one of those people who hate people with more money than you?"

"Nah. I'm just not fond of liars or hypocrites. You act so superior and pretend you've had it hard, too. But all I see is some rich lady slumming it."

Catherine's eyebrow slid up. "You think I'm slumming it with your family?"

"Aren't you? Come on, you look at our place like it's Mars or something. You are so out of place. You know it. I know it." He leaned forward. "You think my sister will ever be happy in that political swamp of DC long-term? This is where her roots are. Sooner or later, she'll remember that, too. And when that day comes, you'll toss her away. No way you'd ever move to Iowa for her."

"Lucas, your sister really enjoys her life in DC. She has no interest in returning to Iowa."

"You don't know that."

"I do," she said with certainty.

Lucas straightened to his full height and glared. "Then it's your fault. You've been filling her head with such crap. I heard some of the shit you said about Iowa at the fair. You were a real bitch about it."

The prickling sensation. So, she *had* been watched. Her pulse quickened at the thought that her private comments intended only for Lauren's entertainment had been overheard. "Well, aren't you the charming little stalker."

"I went to get some food. I was only behind you for a minute, but hell, it was long enough."

"Ah, my secret's out." Catherine rolled her eyes. "So now you know the shocking truth. I have a sarcastic tongue and like to amuse my fiancée with it."

"It was more than that." Confusion and hurt streaked across his face. "You made her laugh *at* us."

"Lucas, she wasn't serious any more than I was."

"She wasn't like this before she met you."

Catherine gave a mocking laugh. "Seriously? Lauren's one of the most stubborn people I've ever met. If you think I could change her mind on anything she cares about—including who she loves and where she wants to live—then you really don't know her."

Fear and fury warred in his eyes as his stare became hard. "You're saying she's never coming back here?"

"Lucas." She sighed. "What were her dreams as a girl? Do you remember? Did she talk about where she wanted to go, what she wanted to do? Deep down, you already know she's where she wants to be. That's why you're so angry at me—because you can't get angry at her."

Lucas's eyes narrowed.

"Lauren loves being in DC. With me," Catherine continued. "And we're a package deal. So what are you going to do with that knowledge? What's your plan here? Because if you keep carrying on like I'm the enemy, it'll only drive a wedge between you and your sister."

"I'm not the bad guy here," he said. "I'm just protecting Lauren."

"Then prove it. Starting now. A truce." She offered him her hand.

He stared at it, the uncertainty clear in his eyes. Then his lips twisted. "I'm right about you. Sooner or later, she'll see it, too."

Catherine had had enough. She dropped her hand in disdain. "Grow up, Lucas."

"Get fucked, Ayers."

"Hey!"

They turned to see the widening eyes of Lauren, approaching from one side, holding two drinks.

"What the hell is going on here?" Lauren glared at her brother, then slammed the glasses on the shelf next to him. "You did *not* just tell Catherine to get fucked."

His face fell at being caught.

"Apologize! Shit, I mean it, Bro. What the hell!?"

"She's taking you for a ride." Lucas's eyes turned pleading. "I'm looking out for you."

"You're looking out for me so much you just told my fiancée to get fucked." Lauren's gaze was hard, and she seemed instantly sober. She turned to Catherine and said in a low voice, "Please go back to the house. Consider this a reprieve from a party you hate. I'm truly sorry you had to put up with any of it."

Lucas looked triumphant at her dismissal, as though she'd picked sides. He was a fool.

"And you," Lauren said through gritted teeth, whacking her brother's arm hard with the back of her hand, "will come with me. *Now.*"

Chapter 20
A Jar Full of Fireflies

LAUREN WALKED BESIDE LUCAS IN silence toward her dreaming tree. Where else would she go to shake the chaos in her head? Someone in the background had turned the music up as the party kicked on, still in full swing.

"Lauren—"

"No." Her voice was hard and low. She glanced up. It was another cloudless night, with the stars creating a bright canvas. It was so peaceful and beautiful, yet her gut was churning.

They reached the tree, and Lauren turned on him. "That was the rudest thing you've ever done."

"You heard it out of context."

"There's no good context to explain that. Did I see her offer you her hand to shake? Before you said that?"

Lucas was silent.

"That's what I thought. How long's this been going on? Have you been pissing her off since we got here? Attacking her every time my back's turned?"

"What the hell do you see in her?" Lucas exploded. "She's cold, mean, and bitchy. You need someone who—"

"No! You don't get to tell me who's right for me." Lauren stabbed her finger in his chest. "Not now. Not ever. Look, can we just cut the crap and put it all out in the open?"

That clearly stymied him. He peered at her. "Whaddya mean?"

"It's not about Catherine at all. It's about Mom."

Lucas's headshake was so adamant, it was a blur. "No fucking way. Look, I know you half raised me when she died, but that just makes me more protective of you now. I just—"

"Don't bother." She glared. "Who I choose to spend my life with has nothing to do with you. *Nothing.*"

"I'm not trying to hurt you, I swear." His tone was beseeching. "It's just no one else can see it. I don't want you to get hurt, but Ayers isn't good or kind or decent. God, she's nothing like the woman I figured you'd end up with."

"The woman *you'll* end up with, you mean." Lauren gave him a considering look. "In other words, she's not some idealized version of Mom." She shook her head. "I know you can't see it, but Catherine *is* decent, good, and kind, too, even if she doesn't wear her softer side on her sleeve. But that's irrelevant right now. Your attitude stinks. I won't have you wading in, acting like you're saving me from myself. You're not the hero in this scenario. I promise you, Lucas, do not make me choose between you two. It'd end badly."

His face creased into shock.

"Come on, you had to know that. I love you, but Catherine's my life." Lauren's face turned grim. "And don't think for a moment I'm ready to forgive you trying to mess that up for me. You crossed a big line tonight."

He stared out over the dark-grassed area.

Lauren gazed out along with him. She followed a firefly dancing at the edge of the lawn.

"Remember when we were kids, and I used to collect those?" Lucas murmured. "Put them in jars, hang them from trees? Well, only when I was apologizing for something stupid I'd done. A 'sorry' note stuck to it. I'd go and hide until you saw it and forgave me."

"And I always did." Lauren remembered those days. Simpler times. The worst thing he'd ever done was sneak out with her old bike, then accidentally pile drive it into the creek. Trying to ruin her relationship was a lot harder to forgive. "You were lucky you were so hard to stay mad at as a kid." She hardened her expression. "But we're not kids anymore."

Lucas turned to her. "Sometimes I wish we were." He spread out his hands. "All together like before. I miss that. Those were good times. The best."

"I don't miss them at all."

He stared at her. His mouth fell open. "Why not?"

"Because I didn't have the childhood you did. I was the eldest. I had to step up and look out for you boys. I was barely hanging in there some days. I was trying to grieve but also be strong. Some days it was so damn hard keeping it all together. It got better when Meemaw moved in after Grandpa died, but even then it was still so damned hard."

"I remember you playing with us all the time and teaching us stuff." He looked shocked. "Were you really just sad every day?"

"Of course not. But there were many days I didn't want to get out of bed. You were so young, you only saw what you wanted to. Problem is, Lucas, I think you've been spoiled. We've all protected you because of how hard you especially took Mom dying. But now you seem to still expect the world to revolve around your feelings. Tonight I've never been so disappointed in you. Truth is, I'm not sure I even want you at my wedding."

"What?" He gasped.

"A wedding's for people who want the best for the couple. And Catherine's what's best for me. So if you can't get behind me and her one hundred percent, don't bother showing up. I don't want you there."

"Laur!" Hurt lanced across his face.

"Come on," she snapped. "Don't act like the victim." Lauren pointed at him. "*You* did this. It's one thing to screw up with me, but you deliberately hurt someone I love. That'll never sit right with me."

"Never?" He blinked at her. "You don't mean that."

"I said it, didn't I? Look, just…stay out of my way for the rest of the week, okay? And leave Catherine the hell alone for good, or we're done forever. I mean it. Got it?"

He nodded, looking shell-shocked.

She turned and left him in the dark and headed back to the house.

It sounded like wildebeest were rampaging down the hall when the party broke up. Catherine had kept her ear out while reading her latest book, a biography on Elena Bartell, a powerful US media mogul who had married her female former assistant. The pearl-clutchers were still recovering from that one.

The bangs of doors as Kings, one by one, went to bed resounded down the hall. But there was no sign of her fiancée. An hour or so later, Lauren slipped into the bedroom and slumped against the back of the door she closed. "Hey."

"Hello. I dread to ask where you've been. The stampeding hordes turned in hours ago."

"I wanted to get a head start cleaning up so Dad can use his workshop tomorrow. Also, Meemaw's too old to tackle all that mess herself, and I just know she'd get up early and try."

"You should have called me to help."

"Nah, you needed some space. And I wanted to think some more."

"Oh? About Lucas?"

"Yeah. It brought up a lot of stuff. Mom dying, raising my brothers, that sort of thing. We cleared the air a bit, but he's still in my bad books. I think he thought I'd forgive him like I always did when we were kids. He could commit blue murder and then hang a jar of fireflies up on my tree with an apology note and I couldn't stay angry. I was probably too easy on him. We all were." She huffed out a breath. "I suppose I should have seen this coming. When Mom died, he clung to me like a second mother. He's grown up too protective of me now. And because of Mom, he really gets upset at the idea of me..."

"Dating."

"Leaving."

"Ah."

"He hates change. Never goes anywhere. It's why he still works with Dad when he really should go off and see the world, get some perspective, and do his own thing. It'd do him a lot of good."

"He should. He's far too old to have that chip on his shoulder."

"He really is. I'm so mad with him. And I'm really sorry he's been such an asshole to you."

"I've dealt with worse."

"Yes, but this is different. He's..."

Catherine lifted her eyebrow. "Family? As I said, I've dealt with worse."

Lauren bit her lip. "Shit. I'm sorry to go near that topic. But since it's raised, how are you doing? I hope you haven't been lying up here brooding all night?"

"What do you think? Knowing me as you do?"

"Oh. You *have*. And you're working out, to the word, probably, exactly how you'll take your father apart tomorrow. Assuming he hasn't gone back to Boston yet." Lauren paused. "Hell, what if he has?"

"He hasn't. I rang the Grand Millennium. He's still there. Penthouse suite."

"You sure you don't want me to confront him for you? Or with you?"

"No, it's my family. Some things I have to do myself—as you found with Lucas."

"Yeah." Lauren wandered over to the window and leaned against the frame, staring out. After a moment she whispered, "Wait...what?"

"What is it?"

"Be right back."

She returned in a few moments holding a pair of binoculars.

"What's out there?" Catherine sat up.

"There's something in my dreaming tree." She adjusted the zoom. "Oh."

Catherine slid out of bed and padded over to the window, gently taking the binoculars. A glowing jar swayed gently in the breeze. "It must have taken some time for Lucas to collect that many fireflies."

"I guess my threat to uninvite him to the wedding hit him between the eyes."

"You don't have to do that on my account."

"I didn't do it for you, but for me. Us. It's about respect." She leaned against the window's frame, warming Catherine's side. She waved at the tree. "Well, it's a start at least. But I'm less forgiving than I was as a teenager."

"They're very beautiful," Catherine mused, still studying the bright jar. "Striking how the fireflies light up the branches like that. They shimmer when the branches move. It's almost ethereal." Catherine lowered the binoculars and turned to give Lauren a thoughtful look. "I wonder..." Her mind exploded with the possibilities. "*Oh*."

"You're either having a genius idea or an orgasm."

"The former." She smirked. "And while I'm visiting my parents tomorrow, I think there are some calls you should make."

"Calls?"

"To get our guests here for Sunday. For our wedding."

"W-what? You do know that only gives us a day to prepare? And we don't even know where we're holding it!"

"Sure we do." Catherine had never felt so right about anything. She pointed. "Right in front of the tree that means so much to you. The dreaming tree will be our backdrop. We could do it at dusk, with jars full of fireflies and other tree lights threaded throughout it. As the sun sets they will light up your golden willow like stars. It will be gorgeous."

"That sounds amazing."

"And here's the best part: We get the people we want there. Joshua and Tad. I already know they're free this weekend."

"Oh my God!" Lauren slipped an arm around Catherine's waist. "That's brilliant! And the reception? I know where to have it. At the tiki bar." She pointed at the ramshackle structure, barely visible in the darkness. "We'd get the whole thing catered so Meemaw doesn't try to kill herself in the kitchen. But yeah, we could have the reception here, too?"

Catherine saw the soft plea in her eyes. "Well," she said, trying to think of something positive to say about the weathered construct. *It has that lived-in look? If we're lucky it will still be standing before the toasts end?* "As tiki bars go…it's…conveniently located."

"Not the most ringing endorsement." Lauren snickered.

"Okay, why the tiki bar?"

"It's got form. See, if there's one thing I know, it's how awesome the King backyard is for holding a party around that bar. You'll see. We've had so many classic blowouts there. It'll go off like a cat-four tornado party. Trust me, that's big."

Catherine blinked. Her imagination failed to supply the necessary source material to convince her. It didn't matter, though. Lauren's joyful face was everything. "I'll take your word for it. Well then, the tiki bar it is. And who should cater?"

"What do you want to eat?"

"Not the best question. The French tasting plates I love would likely make your family want to hurl them against the wall. So a better question is: What would make an eclectic bunch of LA, DC, and Iowan guests happiest?"

"Hmm, when you put it like that…"

"Yes?"

220

A wicked grin split Lauren's face. "Rube's! They cater weddings. They come out, drop off the meat and these big grills, and leave the guests to it."

Catherine lifted a skeptical eyebrow. "You propose our guests should cook their own food?"

"Yep. See, here's why it's a winner: For the LA and DC crowd, it'll be a novelty. Something fun and unusual to do at a wedding, and they love a surprise. And for the Iowan guests, it'll be like a tradition and honoring the local thing."

Catherine considered that. This now went so far beyond her realms of comfort on what a wedding reception should look like. It had always been expected in her family that when she got married—to a man, of course—it would involve five-star elegance. However, she couldn't exactly picture the Kings sipping cocktails at the Cedar Rapids Hilton and chatting in hushed tones. It sounded like something she'd endured for her sister's big day.

"Hey, if it's too awful for you, the whole DIY-barbecue reception, we can go for something less scary. Respectable, even." Lauren threw her a hesitant smile.

Catherine shook her head. "I was actually thinking about my sister's wedding. It was elegant, refined, and entirely respectable. And it was miserable. No sense of family or connection, and certainly little love. The reception was like a perfect *Vogue* spread, with about as much warmth. I never want to have something like that. So, yes. Fine." She waved her hand. "Guests can turn up and cook their own cow."

"Really?" Lauren's eyes lit up.

"Yes. Really." She smiled at Lauren's enthusiasm. So maybe this would work out after all. Even if Catherine did have to eat more Iowan specialties.

"Wow. We're all set. It's going to be brilliant."

"It is." Funnily enough, the moment Catherine said it, she believed her words. It probably wasn't a coincidence that the least Ayers-sounding wedding she could imagine would be the one she'd end up having. And it was one she was so looking forward to.

"Of course, the irony is that most of the credit for the idea should go to Lucas and his jar of 'sorry' fireflies," Catherine noted with amusement.

Lauren's eyes narrowed. "Do not *ever* tell him that."

"Duly noted." She smiled.

Chapter 21
Showdown

SEATED IN THE LIVING ROOM the next morning, Catherine watched the whirlwind of activity around her. Meemaw was figuring out some sort of wedding logistics, with a phone at her ear, looking thrilled. Her voice was bright, her crooked smile wide, and she kept smoothing down her apron as though trying to channel all her excited energy.

Mrs. Potts was on a cell phone beside her, trying to drum up seventy chairs, looking exasperated.

Owen had a pencil in his teeth and was frowning over the father-of-the-bride speech he was writing. "How do you spell *incorrigible*?" Owen asked no one in particular. "And does it mean what I think it does?"

Catherine turned to the other side of the room. Matthew was on his phone, cajoling Rube's to make an exception and cater on a Sunday with only a day's notice. "Free car servicing for a year for you and all your staff," he said, sweetening his deal. "You will? Excellent! Come by at four."

Lauren dropped to the sofa beside Catherine, beaming from ear to ear. "Everyone's coming. Mariella's free, and Tad and Josh are booking flights as we speak. So it's officially happening!"

"What about a celebrant, though?" Catherine asked. "We never really clicked with any of the ones we've met so far—"

"We have Josh. He's offered."

"Joshua can do it?"

"He did some online course last year. He wanted to marry all his friends, and he joked it guaranteed him an invite to their weddings."

"Can a best man marry someone? Isn't that, I don't know, a conflict of interest? Or will he be too busy?"

"Oh." Lauren frowned, then brightened. "What about co-best men? Like Mark and Josh? Josh does the ceremony, Mark does the other stuff?"

With obvious delight, Mark called out from the other side of the room, "I can work with that." He turned back and pointed at Owen's writing pad. "*Mischievous* has a *C*, Dad."

Catherine shrugged. "No objections."

"I have a cake!" Meemaw slapped down the phone in the kitchen and rounded the corner into the living room. "Frances will do that fancy French thing you wanted. She runs the bakery on 16th Ave."

"Croquembouche isn't fancy." Lauren laughed. "And it's so delicious. Balls of toffee and custard and…" Her eyes glazed over.

Catherine smiled at her dreamy look.

Lucas ambled in, with loops and loops of fairy lights over one shoulder. "For the willow tree," he said, sounding subdued. A kicked puppy came to mind. "Jace's crew along with Suze had some more lights lying about. They also brought extra ladders and spare hands." He threw a thumb over his shoulder to John. "We're gonna hang them now. They're solar, so we need them to get as much sun as possible to charge right for tomorrow."

Lauren nodded, lips pressed together.

He shuffled outside, his expression drooping, trailed by his brother. Owen watched them both and then shot Lauren a questioning look.

"Don't ask, Dad." Lauren turned back to Catherine. "Hey, I have something to show you." She grabbed the iPad on the coffee table. "This ad's all over social media today." She cued it up and hit *Play*.

A group of smiling young people were cavorting on a beach before traipsing up to a beachside bar, towels slung over their shoulders. They ordered drinks, and comically patted their swimwear for wallets they obviously did not have.

"No cash? No problem!" said the voiceover. "Introducing Wave'N'Go— the new lifestyle chip that lets you carry cash wherever you are."

Everyone in the group took turns waving their hands under a scanner and then got back to drinking, laughing, and looking symmetrically perfect.

"Dear God," Catherine said. "That is ridiculous."

"I know." Lauren dropped the iPad back to the table. "You should ask your dad about it this morning."

Catherine nodded, her stomach tightening at the reminder. She glanced at her watch and rose. She'd wait outside for the taxi. Maybe the fresh air would do her good.

Lauren silently joined her in walking to the door. The cab pulled up as they reached it.

"Good luck with the chaos in there." Catherine glanced back at the house.

"I keep telling you, it's only chaos if you stop and look at it. Rest of the time it's just fun. We'll be fine. You look after *you*. Call us if you need us. The Kings can be a formidable force, just with a whole lot less diplomacy than your parents would be used to."

"Thanks," she said with a tight smile even as warmth spread inside her at the suggestion she had reinforcements in her corner. "Good to know."

Climbing into the taxi, Catherine told the driver, "The Grand Millennium." She turned to gaze at Lauren. Her butterflies only intensified when she caught her fiancée's worried look as they pulled away.

Catherine knocked on the door of the Grand Millennium's penthouse suite. She glanced at her watch. Her father would be on his third coffee and halfway through the *Wall Street Journal* by now.

The door sprang open. "I didn't order any—" Lionel Ayers straightened. "Oh. I should talk to management. They'll let anyone bribe their way to this floor."

"May I come in?"

He stepped back and held his arm wide, allowing it.

Catherine glanced around. "Mom here?"

"Shower." He closed the door behind her.

Catherine made her way to a cluster of three leather chairs with a low table between them in the middle of the room. She sat in one.

Her father detoured past a breakfast nook, collected a steaming coffee, and then followed. He sat opposite her. "I'd offer you one, but I sense you're not staying long."

"Wishful thinking?"

His eyes glinted with a matching hint of amusement. "Humor?" He stretched out his legs. "That's new. Your Iowan girl making you soft? That one will do it to you."

Catherine didn't respond but turned his words over, trying to unpick his meaning.

"You'll sprain something trying to figure it out." He looked pleased.

Of course. He was up to his old tricks. "Why do you think I'm here?"

"Well, if it's about your return to the fold, we both know my position hasn't changed."

"Neither has mine. I'm never agreeing to a lifetime ban on going after your favorite cronies in Congress, so no. If they're up to their necks in corruption, they're fair game."

"A shame." He eyed her over his coffee cup. "You know they're not all that bad. Some are halfway good." He smiled.

"They're compromised. Let's face it, that's why you do business with them in the first place."

He waved his hand. "We're not going to plow over old ground, are we? What's left to say that we haven't already said?" He suddenly laughed. "Oh, tell me you're not after my approval for your marriage to the plucky Ms. King? She's a sweet thing, isn't she? Got a dash of salt, too. But you always liked them a little salty."

Catherine inhaled. "You're baiting me."

"Tell me, does your girl next door know what you're really like? How contrary? What happens when she tires of your eternal bad mood? When your sharp tongue seems less clever and just plain bitter?"

She counted to ten. Even though he always did this, his arrows slammed home with their usual unerring accuracy. "Thanks for the pep talk. Excellent as ever," she said, brushing lint from her pants. "By the way, I saw the ads. Wave'N'Go. That's your chip, I presume?"

"Phase two. And what did you think?" he asked, looking curious.

"Catchy tune. Dreadful concept. But you knew that, too."

"Like I care. The kids will love it. It's free. At least for the first few years. A rapper we have lined up to front it has ten million followers. It'll be the hottest thing since My Evil Twin."

"You know about that app?"

"Of course. Number one in the USA right now. It's my job to know what's at the forefront of technology. Oh hell, you should see who it matches your mother with." He leaned forward, eyes sparkling. "*Martha Stewart*. She wasn't sure whether to be flattered or appalled."

"Knowing her, she'd go with both. So—Wave'N'Go. Why do it?"

"It's cutting-edge."

"So's a six-blade razor. You don't make those."

"We're pushing technology to the limits. We do it because we can, and we'll be first to go mass scale with it."

"Or perhaps you're really just trying to make a controversial technology acceptable—or popular. But why go there, really? Who wants to be first to an Orwellian future?"

"The tech has more uses than you can possibly imagine."

"Such as?"

"Security enhancement."

"You mean the FBI's interest in it?" She snorted. "*That* plan?"

His eyes became guarded. "You don't know what the plan is."

"Is that so?" She injected every bit of smugness into her tone and hoped like hell she was convincing. "You know that I'm a good journalist. What makes you so sure I don't already know all about it?"

He wagged his finger at her. "I do believe my girl's lying."

"Am I? I know the Fixers paid some Mexicans to cross the border to get fake-arrested, fake-data-chipped for the benefit of the media and your company. All so the FBI can tap its chin and announce in a few days' time it should get into bed with Ansom's revolutionary data chips."

His startled face confirmed every word Michelle had said.

"Look, I know what's happening," Catherine said, leaning forward, "so show me a little respect and don't bother with all the fake surprise and denials. I am a little disappointed you'd get involved with a man like Douglas Lesser, though. Do you even know what he's up to?"

It was a bluff, something Michelle had said in passing about him being a knuckle dragger, but she prayed it would pay off. She'd learned early in her career that suggesting she already knew something yielded a surprising number of people who coughed up more information.

"Of course I know exactly what Lesser is. We all do. But this is business. It's always business."

"You knew and hired him anyway?" Catherine wished she could just ask straight out what Lesser's secrets were. But that would end the conversation abruptly.

"Yes, I hired that prick anyway. Despite his noxious little hobby, it doesn't change the fact he's still the leading expert in his field, and that's why we hired him. Anyone who could help build the FBI's biometric database could handle our far smaller biometric software needs."

Catherine waited, a curious expression affixed to her face, hoping, as always, her father would fill the silence with his usual self-aggrandizement.

"Lesser proved he *was* worth it," he said. "In so many ways. And my God, the idea he came up with? I'd be a fool not to go with it. It's a case of mutual back-scratching. Everyone wins."

"Why keep giving Lesser the kudos? It's not your style."

He gave her a slow-curling smile. "I'm playing it smart. They say success has many fathers, and failure's an orphan. Not for me. Failure will have two fathers."

"Fall guys," Catherine deduced. "In case it blows up in your face."

"You know how much I like to look long-term. I don't mind kicking a bastard and a fool to the curb if I need to later. Not like Lesser and Hickory don't deserve it, let's face it." His laugh was mocking. "They'll be first ones I nuke if this project self-destructs."

"You laid down all that money to build a factory in Iowa just to keep Hickory in reserve as a fall guy? Just in case? For insurance? That's…"

"Audacious? Visionary? Smart? Yes." He looked pleased with himself. "But, to be fair, Iowa did pass the cost-benefit analysis anyway. Cheap land and labor, an at-will state? A few malleable politicians? I might have invested here sooner anyway if I'd known."

"I suppose I can see why you're so proud of the plan," she suggested, waiting for him to resume gloating. He was nothing if not predictable.

But judging from his sudden head snap, she knew she'd overplayed her hand.

Suspicion coated his features. "A minute ago, you thought I was bringing in an Orwellian future. Now this scheme is something to be proud of. Which is it?"

Oh, damn. "I can disapprove and admire a thing at the same time."

"No, you can't. Not you." He tilted his head. "My devious daughter is playing me." His voice had a dangerous tone to it. "Tell me, Catherine, what *is* Douglas Lesser up to? Share in detail his genius idea that you claim to know all about."

The temperature in the room cooled. Catherine sifted through and discarded several answers.

The door opened from the bathroom, and Catherine turned to see her mother emerge in a white hotel robe. In an instant she forgot about her story, about trying to pry details from her father, and just saw a woman who'd made her childhood hell. A woman who had also stood by her husband when he'd kicked Catherine out. Suddenly, all she wanted to find out was how complicit she'd been in everything since.

"Did you know?" she croaked out. The words fell out of her mouth, surprising her.

"Catherine?" Her mother turned and floated over with her usual grace. "Know what? And it's early. You might have called first. Did we raise you to ignore decorum?"

"Did you know?" Catherine's voice was stronger. "What Dad did to me?"

"What am I supposed to have done?" her father asked, tilting his head.

"Destroyed my career." Catherine swallowed. "Paid someone at the Fixers to ruin it." She looked at her mother. "I'm curious. When Dad paid for me to be ruined, did you know how they'd go about it? Did you know the Fixers sent an employee to start a relationship with me? She got me to lower my guard until I trusted her. And then she crippled my career by planting a fake story for me to run."

Her mother's face turned an interesting shade of gray. "They were only supposed to befriend you to carry out their assignment. Not... Nothing more!"

So she'd known. Catherine felt ill. "Oh, she befriended me all right. About three or four times a week."

"Disgusting."

"You paid for it, not me. I suppose that makes you both johns by proxy. Or my pimps? What *is* the right word? Won't that be a fun one to debate with the ladies at bridge club. Christ, you barely even admit you have a second daughter, let alone a lesbian—"

"Don't use that word, I swear—"

"—and now you admit paying a woman to bed me."

"Stop it!" Shock was etched on her face. "She was supposed to harm your image professionally until you quit or were fired. She wasn't supposed to—"

"Victoria," her father said, tone warning.

"Lionel, this is not what we paid for. Tell her! You said—"

"Victoria." His tone was a bark.

"Great. You both admit it." Catherine threw her hands up. "My parents paid strangers to destroy their daughter." Her laugh was bitter. "I deserve an explanation."

"We told you, asked, pleaded, and finally demanded you stop," her mother said. "But you wouldn't! You deserved it."

"Stop what? Did you destroy me because I wouldn't stop being a lesbian? Is that it? How does that even make sense in your head?"

"Enough." Her father shot them both dark looks. "The conversation is being sidetracked. The deal had nothing to do with your mother's…issue."

"So it *was* money." Catherine gave a soft snort. "Money trumps family. Fantastic."

"You brought this on yourself," he said. "You wrote so many columns attacking stored biometrics data. People were listening. In certain quarters, there was panic that this had to be taken care of. There was a fear laws could get passed outlawing what we were doing if we didn't act quickly."

Catherine couldn't believe it. "I wrote a handful of columns and you had your own daughter ruined."

"You're talking to me about disloyalty?" His expression darkened. "Remember what you said that day you walked out of our family? You looked me dead in the eye and said 'I don't care how long it takes me. Every senator you've ever had around for Sunday lunch to grease their palms is now on my list. I'll take them all down, one by one.' That was personal. Your little vendetta against me? *That's* what cost you your family. That's what made it so easy to put in a request with the Fixers to end you. I just reminded myself how little you cared about your own family and then it was easy."

Catherine started laughing at the absurdity.

He stared at her in confusion.

"God, the worst thing is, the dumb thing is, I didn't actually mean it." She threw her hands up. "I was lashing out because you'd been such a bastard about my job."

"Bull," he snapped. "You went after two of my senators immediately. You not only meant it, you followed up."

"No." Catherine shook her head. "I didn't. I'd been assigned both stories by my editor. I hadn't singled your allies out, I just did my job. I never chose any of your special interest senators then or later. I followed through if any got caught, like every other reporter, but there was no agenda. You saw what you were expecting to see. God. You have no idea what you cost me."

"Well, what were we supposed to think? We responded in kind."

"In kind?" Catherine gritted her teeth. "Haven't you even noticed? If I wanted to betray or hurt you, I'd have dragged Ansom through the mud years ago. I didn't even touch your precious business. And yet you talk to me about loyalty."

Her father eyed her and then flicked a gaze at his wife. The air seemed to go out of him.

Catherine hadn't expected an apology. But even an acknowledgement of the pain he'd inflicted on her would be something.

Instead, he rose without a word, heading for the kitchen at the far end of the room. She could see him in the corner, pouring his coffee into the sink and starting a new one, clanging plates, cups, and spoons as he did so. She'd seen this tactic before. It was his way of telling someone they were less important than some menial task he'd seen fit to do. Silence was a dismissal.

Catherine glanced at her mother who sat still, subdued. "Have you got nothing to say, either?" She kept her voice low, out of her father's hearing.

"What did you expect?" she replied. "You spend your life laying down with dogs, I'd expect a few fleas. In business or…" Her lips twisted. "Otherwise. And even if your father misunderstood your intentions, he was right to act. Family and business must be protected at all costs."

"I used to wonder why you always sided with him, even when he did terrible things," Catherine said slowly. "Even as a girl."

Her mother didn't reply. Her lips pressed together.

"But I understand now. Your motives. Your weaknesses."

"Really?" Her tone was extra snippy. "Unlikely." Her mother's lips thinned. "You always were such a willful child. So frustrating. Disobedient. Headstrong."

"You forgot 'lesbian,'" Catherine added helpfully. "So willfully *lesbian*."

"Stop it."

"You couldn't cure me, though." Her voice was so soft. "No matter how hard you tried."

"Is that why you're doing all this?" she asked with an icy glare. "You're bitter? Flinging all this nonsense in our faces? For what, revenge? Yet you're the one doing disgraceful things. Where is your shame?"

"Where's yours?" Catherine leveled a stony gaze at her.

"What are you talking about?"

"I looked at you in Ansom Iowa, and suddenly I saw you as you really are. Inside you're still just an anxious nineteen-year-old girl, desperate to be accepted by the rich man's family. You've always had imposter's syndrome. You're terrified someone will point out that you don't belong. That you're just the poor girl from Connecticut who married her groping boss instead of reporting him."

The color washed from her mother's cheeks. Her eyes became hard. She flicked her gaze to Lionel and back, as though to make sure he hadn't heard. "I'm your mother." The menace in her tone was undermined by the tiniest quiver in her voice. "How can you say such—"

"I just meant that I feel sorry for you."

"*You* feel sorry for—"

"I'm sorry that you felt you had to put your girls through hell to turn us into proper ladies, just so you'd feel good enough to sit at his table. I'm sorry that your husband cheats on you and everyone knows it. I'm sorriest of all that you're so jealous of me."

"Jealous?" Her mother's blue eyes flashed. "How could you ever—"

"You're jealous that I escaped the cage. I have freedom to be myself and you don't. You hate me for it in a way you never could hate Phoebe, who's so damn compliant. You hate your suffocating life that's all about maintaining the perfect illusion while enduring a manipulative husband who trots you out like some collectible doll. So I'm sorry. I forgive you. I mean it. It can't have been easy."

Her mother's eyes, laser sharp, fixed on hers. Catherine picked out the surprise mixed with rage—easy given she'd spent a lifetime attuned to watching out for her mother's moods. To Catherine's shock, though, she also detected a glimmer of tears at the edge of her eyes. She used to wonder if her mother was incapable of crying. Until this moment, she'd never witnessed it.

Catherine told herself she wouldn't feel bad about it.

That didn't help.

Gentling her tone, Catherine said, "It would be nice if you could just admit what he did to me with the Fixers woman was wrong. This is important to me. If you don't acknowledge even that, I don't see how we can ever be family again. It will be the end for us." She hesitated. "Please, Mother."

They took each other's measure. For a moment, Catherine wondered if her mother might indeed admit to something that wasn't in lockstep with her husband's views.

"We did not approve any whore's seduction," her mother said. "Understand that. So your father should not be judged for it. He didn't know they were going to do that."

"But the rest? He set out to crush me just to keep his data-chip plan going. My career's everything to me, and you knew it. It sounds like you're fine with what he did."

"The response was appropriate for what we believed to be true at the time."

"I *was* loyal." She raised her voice so her father could hear. "I could have hurt Ansom a dozen times. I never did. So how can it have been appropriate?"

Her mother's eyes glazed over and she looked away. Discussion over.

Her father slowly sauntered back into the room with a new coffee. He probably thought he'd won some unseen point, controlling things. It was pointless.

All of this was.

"I never hurt Ansom," Catherine repeated. She drew in a breath and shared a decision she'd made last night, lying in bed. "Past tense."

Her father's eyebrows shot up. His tone was mocking. "Is that a threat? If you expect me to beg forgiveness, don't bother. I don't care about the Fixers' methods. They worked and I needed them to work. I'd change

232

nothing. Well, I might ensure they did a more long-term job. You appear more adept at a rebound than most."

Catherine glanced at her mother. Predictably, she said nothing. *Well. That's that, then.* "I see." She met her father's eye. "Consider this your warning. I'm taking the gloves off. If Ansom does a single corrupt deal, I will be on it in an instant and make sure the world knows about it."

He seemed amused. "I have teams of lawyers who'd swat you like a fly. They'd bankrupt you."

"Only after I've put the truth out. And you know very well I don't care about money."

"You'd have to tell everyone who you're related to," Lionel retorted. "And we all know how much you hate admitting the family connection."

"I hate it only slightly less than you do. But if I have to, I'll do it. Big fat disclaimer at the bottom of every damned Ansom story. So, tell me, how many business deals will dry up on the spot when they see who I really am and that I'm gunning for you? Because we both know they'll assume your daughter knows where all the bodies are buried."

"You have no proof of anything."

"You're so used to me ignoring Ansom in my stories that you took risks. Today you made some interesting admissions to the Washington bureau chief of the *Daily Sentinel*. Taped admissions."

For a moment, the only sound was the hum of the air conditioner.

"You recorded this?" He looked incredulous. "Without my permission?"

"Your permission's irrelevant under Iowa law, as long as one party being recorded was present and gave consent."

"You still have nothing. You don't even know what Lesser's scheme is."

"Give me time."

He stalked over to her, leaning over her in her chair, dropping a hand on each arm rest.

"Seriously?" Catherine affected a bored look. "Is this where you try to find and destroy the recorder? I suppose that'll add color to the story. *Ansom's CEO tries to stop story by roughing up reporter daughter.* How interesting that'll look in the headline."

He straightened. "Fine." He stalked back to the chair and sat. Then he smiled triumphantly. "If you do this, I'll fire him."

Catherine felt her blood chill. "Who?"

"If you don't care about your own family, I know you care about hers. You think I'm an idiot? You expect me to believe you just wandered into Ansom's open house on a whim? I called up the security footage. You and your fiancée had a conversation with an employee in the electric car room. I looked up the man's employment records. John *King*. A mechanic—the same career your fiancée told me her whole family is in. I don't believe in coincidences. So let me be clear: I will fire his hick ass if you or Lauren King write any story that says one negative word about Ansom. Also, as I fire that young man—in person—I will make it very clear that you are the sole reason why he is losing his job."

"You can't fire someone for that."

"Iowa's an at-will state. I can fire him for virtually any reason I say. See how much the new in-laws like you then. Think of how much sweet Lauren's heart will break at you hurting her family. But that's what you do, isn't it? Hurt families?"

"Well." Her mother cleared her throat. "I think that concludes the family business." She gave Catherine a measured look. "For all time."

Catherine's gaze slid between her parents, the finality of it all hitting her. There was no coming back from this.

Her father smiled. Smug and wide. Like a man who's won. "I'll let you see yourself out."

She left without another word.

Chapter 22
Deal with the Devil

CATHERINE RETURNED HOME TO FIND Lauren bent over a cell phone in the living room, typing furiously, legs stretched out along the sofa. "What's happening?" she asked her.

Lauren looked up. "Oh, hey, how'd it go?" She dropped her feet to the floor to make room beside her.

"About what you'd expect." Catherine lowered herself to the sofa. "My parents confirmed they paid for my career's destruction."

"Ah, hell." Lauren's eyes filled with sympathy. "Damn."

"With a small twist: my mother was adamant Michelle was supposed to befriend me, not romance me."

"So Michelle overstepped?"

"I'd say that's the understatement."

Lauren bit her lip. "Jesus." She shook her head. "I'm really sorry. And hey, your parents... I mean...where is that at?"

"Our relationship is over." She lifted her recorder from her pocket. "There are a few bits on here we can use for our story. Stuff about Lesser being the key and he and Hickory being set up as fall guys if Ansom's data chip blows up in their faces. But the rest is just..." She took in a breath. "It's humiliating. They don't have any regrets about what they did to me."

Lauren leaned into her. "I'm so sorry; I really am."

Catherine waved dismissively. "I don't think I really expected otherwise. But it would have been nice, just once, to have been pleasantly surprised."

"Yeah. It sure would."

Catherine decided a change of topic would do her depressed mood good. "So what's happening? You looked pretty industrious when I came in."

Lauren straightened. "Well, we've squared away all the wedding prep… mostly. The stuff we couldn't figure out, Mrs. Potts is fixing. We're definitely in her bad books. Apparently, weddings thrown together in a day is "crazy talk." Still, she's doing a great job. So that's all good. But what's better is this…"

She waggled an unfamiliar phone at her. "It's Matthew's—I'm not risking mine to do anything anymore, of course. So I was telling my family this morning there might be something weird with My Evil Twin but that we just can't see it. My brothers tried to figure it out. They couldn't, so they suggested we crowd source the answer with our friends. We offered a Meemaw pork sandwich to the first person to spot it."

Was second prize two sandwiches? Catherine hid her smile at her inner joke. "And?"

"We owe Zachary a pork sandwich. He spotted it in ten seconds, *bam*. I guess that makes sense. A designer would have an eye for detail." Lauren opened the app. "There are forty faces on this phone of random people of every shape, size, and background. We've put them all into My Evil Twin. Now watch."

One by one, each face was matched to a supposed criminal.

"See anything unusual?" Lauren asked as she went through them.

Catherine looked. She frowned. They were close matches, by color, face, and hair. People with facial tattoos were even matched to others with them, too. So what was she supposed to notice?

"Do it again, Catherine," Lauren instructed. "And this time focus on the crimes."

A pudgy white man's face. Matched to a pudgy white bicycle thief. A tall African American paired with a tall African American rapist. A teenaged white woman paired with a teenaged white shoplifter. An elderly Asian man paired with an elderly Asian drug runner. A black woman with tattoos, paired with a black female killer with tattoos.

Catherine's breath caught. "Oh."

"Yep. White folks' shit don't smell on this app. Lesser's just a smooth-talking racist piece of crap."

Catherine settled cross-legged on the bed, placing her iPad in front of her. The moment she'd understood Lesser's game, a plan had struck her. It was a simple one: given she now had the upper hand, she'd simply squeeze him until he popped.

She took in a deep breath and hit the button to establish the Skype interview Lesser had agreed to by phone earlier. His eagerness fit what Lauren said about him. He was smart and cocky. He liked outwitting people, testing himself with them. She'd grown up with a man exactly like this. You just had to know how to tackle them.

She hit *Record* on an iPad app and waited for Lesser to respond.

Lauren came in, quietly closed the door, put a cup of coffee on the bedside table for her, and assessed Catherine's posture. "He agreed?"

"A little too quickly."

"Hmm. Not shocked." Lauren sat beside her. "Careful with him. He's so damn slippery."

The screen shifted as Lesser's face suddenly appeared. "Catherine Ayers, what an honor." He beamed at her. "When my secretary told me you wanted to Skype me, I thought it was a hoax. Because what could a woman busy planning her wedding in Iowa possibly want with me?"

"We could start with where to send the bill for the cost to remove the spyware in Lauren's phone."

"I have no idea what you're talking about." He looked amused.

"Hell of a business model you have there," Catherine continued. "So, how does it work? Any Fixers client who downloads your staff list gets spied on? I didn't think you were derivative."

"Derivative?"

"Stole the idea from SmartPay?"

He laughed. "You have no idea why that's so funny."

"What do you mean?"

"A conversation for another day." He glanced to Catherine's side. "Ahh, I see Lauren King has joined us. How *is* Iowa?"

"Awesome," Lauren said. "You should visit sometime."

"I'll pass. So, what do you two want?"

"It's about MediCache," Catherine said. "The software you wrote to go with Ansom's data chip?"

"And by Ansom, you mean your father's company." He lifted his eyebrows.

"You think I should be impressed you know that? I'm not. But this is about you. And what my father thinks of you."

She hit *Play* on the recording she'd cued up.

I like to look long term. I don't mind kicking a bastard and a fool to the curb if I need to later. Not like Lesser and Hickory don't deserve it, let's face it. They'll be first ones I nuke if this project destructs.

Lesser's expression was thoughtful. "Ooh, shocking."

"That's all you have to say?"

"If you had any actual dirt, you'd have played me a far juicier quote." Catherine's lips thinned.

"Is that really all you have?" His tone was pure boredom. "Because I have important things to do."

"I know you've come up with a plan that the FBI wants that's going to affect national security. I have sources who—"

"Oh, come on, Catherine, what plan? You don't even know. Let me save you some work. Next, you'll tell me you have high-level sources willing to speak out. Then you say if I tell you my side of the story, you'll spin it so I come off sounding not so bad. Right?"

Catherine's jaw worked.

Lesser leaned forward. "I know you're bluffing."

"That's a bit of a risk to take. What if you're wrong?"

"Call me crazy, but I'm going to take the bet that your father—a man who paid to have you fucked over in so many ways—did not tell *you* the plan."

For a moment, there was silence. There was only the hiss of Lauren's breath, the tick of the old wooden clock on the wall, and the thud of her own racing heart.

"And besides"—he smirked—"you're too late. Dear old Dad's already called to warn me you know jack."

Damn it.

Catherine stared at the screen, and her eyes drifted past Lesser to the office wall behind him. "Nice pit bull," she said, after a moment.

He turned, looked at the framed photo, and turned back. "So?"

"I see you're a man who appreciates signs and symbols. That one"—her finger shifted—"is a Klan symbol. "And all the twelves? Why so many?"

He looked unsettled now. "It's my favorite number."

"Not surprised. One and two in the alphabet is A and B. So twelves represent AB, or the Aryan Brotherhood. The dog? Pit bulls have, of late, been adopted as a white-supremacist mascot." She pointed to the wall to the right of his head. "That is an Othala rune, which white supremacists also love. Are you going to tell me all of this is a coincidence? Or do you want me to scour the Charlottesville neo-Nazi parade footage to see if you're waving a tiki torch, too?"

Lesser scowled. "Let me guess. Your gambit now is to tell everyone I believe in white rights if I don't spill about the plan for Ansom's data chips?"

"Well, I wouldn't write that because, it wouldn't be true."

He blinked.

"I would tell everyone that you are a fully-fledged white supremacist trying to poison the world with your racist agenda. Far more accurate."

"How am I doing that?"

"Are you really going to pretend My Evil Twin isn't just pure racism?"

He shifted in his seat.

"Oh, it is devious," Catherine continued. "And subversive. White people matched with whites who've done minor misdeeds. The crimes increase in severity the darker the skin of the people using the app. The darkest-skinned people are matched with only rapists, pedophiles, and murderers. Your app subliminally tells users that black people equal violence and the worst crimes."

"Or it's just a computer algorithm."

"An algorithm that you told Lauren you designed yourself. And I notice you don't deny My Evil Twin does what I said it does."

He peered at her. "No comment."

"Well, if you won't talk about what you do at Lesser Security, let's talk about Ansom. What's the big, bad plan? The one my father is willing to tell the world you masterminded if it goes sour."

"Not biting."

"Okay, then… Let me lay it out for you. If you refuse to help with my story, I will tell everyone that you built America's most popular and most racist app because you're a neo-Nazi. I will plaster your name everywhere. If you think the Charlottesville protesters couldn't even get a job in fast food after a tiki-torch hate march, what will America make of an unrepentant, hardcore neo-Nazi, with the white-supremacy app to prove it? An app that aims to corrupt their sweet little children."

Catherine leaned in close to the screen. "How long will the FBI and any of your future clients want to work with you then?"

"They already know my position on things," Lesser said. "They don't care. I'm too valuable to them."

"Really? So far only the insiders know. But when the *whole world* knows, that's when it stings."

He cocked his head. "And if I do cooperate?"

"Then my story on your racist app will merely explain what it does, and will not call you out by name, only your company."

"Except the people who know me, know that's my app. It'd be the same as outing me anyway. Why would I agree to that?"

"Let me tell you something as a woman who has been nationally vilified—keeping the number of people who know your failings small is preferable. Anything is better than being mocked in the street or being the nightly butt of jokes by talk-show hosts. It's better than being unable to leave your house without jackals thrusting microphones under your nose. Only a small number knowing? That would have been a dream. So tell me, Mr. Lesser, do I sound like someone who doesn't know *exactly* what she's talking about?"

The condescending smile he'd worn from the outset fell away. "So you're a blackmailer. How…unexpected."

"I prefer 'someone who knows other people's weaknesses.' The choice is yours."

He tilted his head. "All right. I'll do it only if you name me as a whistleblower in your Ansom story."

"Name you? With your real name?"

"In full."

Catherine stared at him in confusion. That had no benefits to him at all. Quite the opposite. What on earth was he up to? "I'll consider that if you take Fiona Fisher out of your app database now. As an act of good faith."

Lesser leaned forward and made a flurry of tapping noises. "Done. Feel free to check."

Lauren pulled up the Evil Twin app on Catherine's phone, tapped a few buttons, then looked up and nodded.

"That it?" Lesser asked.

"And you call off the dogs," Catherine said. "No more doxing us or hacking us or spying or anything in between. Now or ever again. Or our families. Leave us alone for good."

"Fine. Dogs off." His eyes glinted. "That wasn't an admission of guilt, either."

Lauren cut in. "Hey, how did you know about me going to Iowa when we first met? You hadn't cracked my phone then." She blinked. "Had you?"

"Have I made you paranoid?" Lesser looked proud of himself. "Well, if you really must know, you two are popular topics on the Hill. DC's a fishbowl, and you can learn just as much about people from watercooler gossip as any other way."

Catherine narrowed her eyes. Great. As she'd suspected.

He cracked his knuckles. "Now, I believe we have a deal? Douglas Lesser, whistleblower in your Ansom story. But you're not to mention me in connection with My Evil Twin."

"We have a deal," Catherine said.

"So," he said, "we're now on the record with this interview." His voice became mockingly polite. "What would you like to know?"

Catherine sized him up and her smile was feline. "Everything."

"It's like this," Lesser said. "MediCache's data chips are all well and good, but then what? The bio-info on you just sits in your body and does nothing till the next medical person scans you. How is that useful? Especially given how valuable data is these days. It shouldn't go to waste."

"Let me guess," Catherine said. "You found a way to value-add."

He nodded. "It's not dead data anymore. It gets a second life."

"How?"

"My solution was data scooping. We scoop the valuable data out of one pot that does nothing, MediCache's clients—the military veterans—and tip it into another, the FBI's database, where it gets to live again. It makes sense. Biometric details were being gathered anyway, so why not poke them in the biggest biometrics database?"

"Except the biggest database isn't medical, too. It's for criminals."

He shrugged. "Like I care. Anyway, at a think-tank security meeting, I was asked whether I had the ability to take data from MediCache and copy it into the NGI. The FBI director loved the idea. I said sure I could do it—quite easily, in fact."

"I suppose the veterans have no clue this is being done with their data?"

"It's in the fine print when they agreed to the MediCache trial that any data may be shared with government agencies. None of this is illegal."

"It's unethical and creepy," Lauren said. "And now innocent people who aren't even criminals are in the NGI."

"There were always non-criminals in that database. I know; I helped build it. There are a lot of errors that get people stuck in there."

"How did Fiona Fisher get pulled into it?" Lauren asked.

"I don't suppose you noticed her hand when you met her? She have a little scar just here?" He pointed to the soft skin between his thumb and forefinger.

"No way," Lauren whispered.

"Oh, yes, she's a MediCache trial participant. Served in Iraq, discharged after an injury. So later, when that food-bot photo of her was entered into the computer system by local DC police, the photo was also automatically uploaded to the FBI computers. That was a neat little bit of coding from the FBI end. What local police don't know, won't hurt." He grinned. "Anyway, Fiona Fisher's NGI file, which exists thanks to her using MediCache, was updated with the new photo and the fact she was a suspect in a theft. I was pretty happy when you told me about her complaint. It meant my data-sharing system is working to perfection."

"How do you get away with taking people's information from an FBI database for use in your Evil Twin app?" Catherine asked.

"The FBI allows a few security companies to use its database contents if they are for legitimate security reasons."

"My Evil Twin is *not* legitimate."

"My other security apps are, and I have clearance for those. So I simply share the NGI's database with all my apps. And even if the FBI knows I'm data-sharing between my apps, they'd turn a blind eye. I'm too useful to them."

"But what's the point of all this?" Lauren said. "I don't get it. Why poke average citizens like Fiona, or even beach-loving teenagers, into a criminal database? Where's the advantage in it?"

"You really don't get it?" Lesser asked. "The secret is the FBI wants *everyone* in their database eventually. That's their dream. They think crimes would be a cinch to solve if everyone's identifying features were in one big nationally shared program."

"Abuses would be a cinch, too," Catherine said. "Data could be leaked, stolen, sold. Well, it's already being sold, if security companies like yours have access. But some operators could on-sell our information to criminals. The dangers are endless."

"Oh, endless," Lesser drawled.

Catherine glared at his flippancy. "This is awful. It could result in anything from sophisticated identity theft to crude blackmail. What if a person in the database took an unpopular view on politics? Could someone leak their most personal medical or physical details to the world? I also imagine that some people who had, say, Caesarian scars from secret pregnancies, or hidden deformities, or fatal allergies wouldn't want that recorded in some database file that can be easily bought or shared."

Lesser's look became wry. "The truth is ninety-nine percent of the population won't care about this, even if they knew about it. It doesn't matter how unethical or sneaky or *awful* it all is." He put mocking air quote marks around the word. "They'll just say 'Well, *I'm* not doing anything illegal so why should I care which department has my data?'"

"That's naïve. When any government controls our private information, it controls us. The biometric and medical histories of innocent citizens are *none* of the FBI's damn business. This is Big Brother stuff. It should be fought at the highest level. But instead you're sitting here, smirking, and telling us you've just made it happen and you don't even seem to care."

"Why should I?" Lesser said.

"You don't care you will be in there one day, too?"

"I won't. I'm too smart for that. I can get my name out of any database."

"What does Ansom get out of any of this?"

"It wants their chips to be everywhere. And with every security agency in the country soon to be demanding them, Ansom has a smash hit on their hands. Profits will be spectacular. I'd sure as hell be investing in Ansom shares if I were you."

"Profit." Catherine felt sick. "Great motive."

"It is to your father. Lionel's smart, though. He's been hedging his bets. If all of this stuff sounds too unpalatable to the public, Wave'N'Go will be there. It'll get the skittish masses used to the idea. By the time they're all paying for their public transport or cab drivers or McDonalds with a wave of a hand, these chips will be seen as so convenient, the people will have forgotten why they even thought to object. And by then, the FBI and its alphabet soup of security friends will have what they've always wanted. Everyone chipped, collated, and, eventually, monitored and traceable."

Lauren stared at him. "You really don't care, do you?"

He shrugged. "Why would I? I have offshore retirement plans. Somewhere warm and laid-back. In the southern hemisphere, I think. Not a fan of DC's winters. Not good for my chest."

Catherine exhaled. "You mentioned a think tank? People who met to discuss this idea. Who was in on it?"

"The FBI director and Lionel Ayers and a few of their other security agency chiefs."

"Hickory?" Lauren asked.

"Hell no. He's not too bright. He's for patsy purposes only."

"So who was keenest on the data scooping idea?" Catherine asked.

"Lionel… Number-one ticketholder and cheerleader."

"It's not like him to be so bold. He rarely leads from the front."

"Really?" Lesser's gaze slid upwards and to the left. "'The profit always comes first, gentlemen. I'll supply the method for you to get every American in that database, but you have to supply the motive to make people demand it.' Does that sound like him?"

It did. "What does he mean by motive?"

"First, the Mexicans at the border. So ICE could make a showy arrest and introduce data-chipping as a concept for security purposes. Then the FBI will announce they've looked at it and worked out how much data chipping people would streamline criminal investigations having illegal immigrants' biometric data in their system. Which makes no sense, but it plays to people's fears of the unknown. They feel safer thinking those *sneaky illegals* are more closely monitored.

"Down the track, some foreign-looking crisis actor will be 'caught' by the FBI before a nonexistent terrorist attack is committed. Most crucially, he'll somehow be traced and arrested in the nick of time, thanks to the illegal-immigrant data chip in his hand.

"Then the good senator for Iowa is scheduled, in an impassioned speech, to declare this arrest to be proof of the success of these chips. Hickory will demand that the program gets expanded to include all criminals, miscreants, and even legal immigrants, and pretty much any other groups that get people whipped into a lather of fear. By that time, with those measures passed, half of America will be in the database."

"How is the FBI fine with this insanity?" Catherine couldn't believe it. All the FBI people she'd ever dealt with, such as Diane, were good-intentioned and law-abiding, and would be horrified by such a scheme. "Didn't they object to any of this?"

"Gotta understand we're talking about those at the very top. And they're not just fine with it, they're driving it. Never get in the way of a security agency chief within sight of a power grab. They're enthusiastic as hell. Power *and* control? They're hot for it."

"If we ran this story, everyone will deny all this," Catherine said. "It sounds utterly implausible. They'll say you're some conspiracy nut."

He shrugged. "Not my problem. I've told the truth and it's up to you to prove it. Now, I've fulfilled my end of the deal, so we're done here. Remember, I'm the whistleblower. Make sure you say that. Oh, and try to and make me sound heroic the way you did that guy in your SmartPay story."

Lauren peered at him. "Why?"

He smiled. "For reasons."

"You'll be pissing off powerful people when this story comes out," Lauren said. "You know that, right?"

"Of course I'll annoy some people, including powerful people who'll threaten me with never working again or much worse. But two things—I know where the bodies are buried, and they know I'll have insurance if they try to hurt me, so they won't want to do much more than bluster. And I'm also uniquely skilled. So they'll get pissed at me for a bit and come crawling back when they want their next job done. I've been through this many times. I'm bulletproof."

"The dirt just slides right off you, doesn't it?" Lauren said.

His laugh was pleased. "Always. Now, if we're finished, I have a new app to work on. It's just come to me. Something honoring the world's bravest people. Our Heroic Voices? What do you think? I'll put myself top of the list, of course, as the whistleblower who saved the US from sweeping privacy violations. Oh, and I'll leave any colored folk out of it. That wouldn't fit the special narrative I have in mind." He laughed and stabbed a button with a flourish. He waved.

The Skype call ended.

"What a thoroughly noxious man," Catherine grumbled. "Probably the only thing I agree with my father on."

Lauren merely nodded. She was staring at the phone screen. "Uh…"

"What is it?"

"Lesser just deleted My Evil Twin."

"He what?"

"So, basically, we'll be blowing the lid off an app that longer exists. What a screw-you parting shot."

Catherine scowled. "That man is really starting to annoy me."

Lauren closely regarded Catherine, who was scribbling up her notes from the Lesser interview, and then drained her coffee. *Ugh*. Cold. "Tell me something," she said. "How'd you know all that stuff about racist signs and symbols on his wall?"

"I did a story on the rise of white supremacy a few years back." Catherine didn't look up, her pen scratching the page. "It's worse now, though."

Lauren hesitated. "You know, I wasn't a fan of that deal you made with Lesser. He deserves to be hung out to dry by his toenails for creating that racist app."

"He would have been." Catherine sighed and glanced up. "I had planned to get someone else at the *Sentinel* to do a follow-up on the Evil Twin story in a day or so, naming and shaming him anyway. I only promised Lesser that *we* wouldn't write about him." She slapped her notebook closed. "But I doubt there'll be two stories now. Neil might not even be interested in one.

Dead news isn't good news. I'll write it anyway—*The App America Loved, and its Secret Racist Core.*"

Lauren regarded her, impressed she'd thought of the second story to get around the deal. "You're sneaky. You have this level of smart I'll never have."

"It's not being smart. It's manipulative. I learned young to keep my brain sharp for weaknesses and loopholes."

"And that's why you're ten steps ahead of everyone else. Turns out your dad was good for something. In a weird way."

Catherine gave Lauren a long look. "On that topic, I need to talk to you. It's about John."

"My brother?" She smiled. "The man who still hasn't said a single word to you?"

"The very same. But before that, I have a job for you. Do you still have Fiona's cell number?"

"Sure."

"Call her; confirm she has the chip in her. If she does, explain to her how she wound up in the app, and make sure she knows that even though My Evil Twin is dead she's still in the FBI's criminals' biometric database. Ask her if I can interview her in an hour."

"An hour? Why not now?"

"She should be fully outraged by the time I call her back. And do you have Hickory's business card?"

"Still got it."

"Call him, too." She tapped a few buttons. "I've just emailed you the secret recording from this morning with my father. Play back his worst quotes about Hickory and get him to talk. *Really* talk. It's time Lionel Ayers and Frederick T. Hickory headed for an acrimonious divorce."

Lauren bit her lip. "What makes you think he'll open up to me on all this?"

"Well, he won't talk to me anymore. And he's a white, entitled, middle-aged male who is being mocked as an imbecile and a fall guy, a puppet to be tossed aside. His ego won't stand for it, and he'll be furious. Use it. This could be the lynch pin of our main story. Everything will hang off what you manage to get out of Hickory. Okay?"

Lauren swallowed. "Okay."

"I know you can do this, Lauren. You already know what we need. Lay it all out for him. Tell him everything that we know. I get the feeling he's completely clueless on most of it. But that fake-terrorism event he has a speech ready for means he's at least up to his knees in the dirt. Find a way to get through to him."

"Okay, I'll do my best. And what will you be doing while I'm interviewing Hickory?"

Catherine's smile became rigid. "I want to catch up with your family for a bit. Explain why we've been so unfocused on the wedding."

"Is that all?"

"Why?"

"It's just that…well, you look about ready to throw up."

Catherine didn't answer. She rose. "Good luck with Hickory. You'll do great."

Chapter 23
The Vote

CATHERINE THREADED HER WAY SLOWLY down the stairs to the living room to find most of the King clan lounging, working on a wedding checklist. She could hear the clatter from the kitchen nearby, indicating Meemaw wasn't far away, either.

It was time. She breathed deeply and came to stand in front of them.

"Excuse me, everyone... Could I have a minute?"

Everyone in the living room sat up, expressions curious. Meemaw poked her head around the corner, then bustled fully out of the kitchen, wiping her hands on a dish towel.

Catherine hesitated. "I...I met with my parents today. They're in Iowa at the moment. There's no easy way to drop this on you, so I'll just say it. My father is the President and CEO of Ansom Digital Dynamics International."

There was a complete lack of reaction. She studied them in confusion. Did they not understand what she'd just said?

"Was that all?" Meemaw peered at her. "Thank goodness. I thought it was something serious. Lucas told us already. We looked up your family on the Google thing. What's a man need with so many yachts, anyway?"

"I have no idea." Catherine frowned. "Anyway, in case you're now all thinking Lauren's marrying a multimillionaire, I've been disowned for two decades now."

Owen recoiled. "What on earth for?"

"I have a habit of running stories that affect my father's business associates. He thinks it's disloyal. And my mother has certain other issues with me that I can't change." She gave them a wry look, making it clear exactly what the issue was.

One by one, their faces went taut as they each got it.

"So I guess you also know John works for my father?" Catherine asked. Nods all round.

"Didn't seem polite to make a thing of it," Owen said. "We figured you'd get to mentioning it if it became important."

"It just became important. We have a story that will be devastating for Ansom. But my father has warned me he'll fire John if we run any negative story about his company."

John's look of shock made her stomach even queasier.

"John loves his job," Lucas said. "Like, freaking loves it."

"This is not right," Matthew said. "Could we fight it?"

"You'd lose," Catherine said with certainty. "Or possibly win after a very long, drawn-out battle designed to bankrupt you."

"How important is your story?" Owen asked. "I mean, is it a little thing?"

"It's very big. Not running the story would threaten the privacy of every American. In fact, it could go global, too."

For a moment, no one spoke.

"So we need to resist now, while we still can," Catherine added.

"And you'd take John's job away to run this story?" Lucas asked.

"It might not just be your brother's job." *Here it comes.* "The last time we ran a story where a company was making a compromised product, the entire company went bankrupt. Ansom is a lot bigger and more well-established, so I wouldn't expect that outcome. But worst-case scenario is they might shut a plant or two in regional areas if the share price plummets on the back of bad publicity."

"You've got the power to do all that?" Meemaw looked at her as if she'd never seen her before. "But there's just one of you."

"Lauren has that power, too." She spread her hands. "*This* is what our jobs are. Digging up uncomfortable things. What we write can affect the whole country."

"Well," Owen said. "That's…more than I ever expected you could do."

"Same," Mark whispered.

"The whole country?" Lucas repeated, his tone even. "That's some flamethrower you're threatening to unpack. You must really want to piss off your old man."

"No. I don't enjoy this." Catherine held his gaze. "It's not about my pride or a vendetta; it's about what's right. No matter what happens next, someone suffers. John, definitely, and possibly many of his workmates. Or the privacy of everyone in the US. I'm not saying it's not personal, I can't help that there is that element, but I didn't make this about family. My father did. We can complain for hours about how unfair all this is, but the facts won't change."

"I'm hearing a lot of speculating here," Lucas said. *"Maybe* they'll close a plant. *Maybe* there'll be big job losses. You're just guessing. So, am I right that about the only thing that is guaranteed is the choice involves throwing John under a bus?"

Catherine paused. Well, not exactly how she'd put it, but... "Yes, I suppose. And it's because of that guaranteed outcome that I'm even here, standing before you, asking... What do you feel should be done?"

Shock flashed across their faces.

"You haven't decided to run it?" Lucas said.

"It's not going to be up to me at all, actually." Catherine drew in a deep breath. "I originally thought I'd do a deal for my paper and Lauren's to jointly run the exclusive. But I've rethought that. It's going to be Lauren's call. I've decided to give her our story."

"Wait," Lucas said. "You're going to get Lauren to do a number on her own brother? Is that it? So *you* don't have to?" Suspicion flickered across his eyes.

"No, that's not why. I think it's important that, because a family member is affected, it's family who should be consulted and who should decide the outcome. And if it's a yes, then family should write it. And we all know the truth here. For all the warm welcome I've received, which I appreciate, the thing is..." She turned and met Meemaw's eyes. "I'm not family."

The to-and-fro-ing over what should be done went on for fifteen minutes.

"John adores that job," Meemaw kept saying. "Ain't an easy one to come by, all that futuristic carry-on. But John..."

"Stop it!" The voice was low and irritated. "Everyone's speaking for me like I'm not here. Ask me."

Ah. John speaks. Catherine eyed him curiously.

"Lucas is right," John continued. "That job's my whole life. That's a fact. It's like a dream come true."

Catherine's heart sank. "So, John, you're saying you want to keep your job, then?"

"I don't just want it. I *need* this job. It's everything." His whole face was a picture of dismay.

There was silence. Catherine exhaled. And there it was.

"I see." She nodded once, her disappointment in John—in all of them really—washing through her. "Well." She'd thought it would have gone differently, that these down-to-earth people would live up to who she thought they were. Maybe all families were self-absorbed after all.

No one was meeting her eye except Meemaw, whose look was sharp to the point of brittle. "I'd say we've voted no, dear," she said.

"Thank you for your time." Catherine left the room. She paused outside and considered her next move. She'd leave Lauren in peace to do her Hickory interview. In the meantime, she needed to clear her head.

Catherine headed for the dreaming tree, which was now festooned with swirls of tiny lights reflecting in the sun. The boys had done a great job. It looked covered from tip to roots. It would be stunning at night.

Reaching the tree, she lowered herself to the ground and leaned against the smooth trunk, facing away from the house. She tried to make sense of how everything had gone so badly wrong. Not just her misjudgment of the King family, but the loss of her own.

Maybe the truth was that she was terrible at dealing with all families. She couldn't read them, understand them, or get on with them. Maybe *she* was the problem.

Catherine closed her eyes.

An hour or so later, she heard footsteps approaching. She glanced around the tree to see Lauren, with a face like thunder, storming up to her.

"When were you going to tell me?" she demanded. "Giving me our story. Putting it to the vote? John's job being at risk?"

"After your interview. I didn't want it on your mind."

"Well, it's on my damned mind now. What were you thinking, doing it this way? What were you thinking at all? The story comes first!" Lauren paced under the tree. "Did you or did you not spend weeks drilling that into me as we crisscrossed fucking Nevada! Is it that you didn't want to be the bad guy here?"

"That's not it at all." She grew alarmed at the rising rage on her fiancée's face. "Please, can you calm—"

"Oh, do *not* tell me to calm down. I'm so mad right now. And you're going to have to explain it to me, because it looks a hell of a lot like you just took the gutless option in there. Catherine, we saw thousands and thousands of people fired by SmartPay, and you didn't even bat an eyelid. Explain!"

"It's just... The story *doesn't* always come first."

"What?" Lauren staggered backwards. "What the hell?"

"I'm not destroying your family for a story. I refuse to."

Lauren gaped at her. "Millions will be affected. *Millions.*"

"Yes."

"And yet you're fine with that because the King family of Cedar Rapids, Iowa, said no?"

"It's how they feel."

Lauren dropped to her haunches. "I still don't understand why you did this."

Catherine gazed at her. "You mean more to me than a story. How hard is that to understand?"

"*Me?* How does this become about me? And it's *our* story."

"*Your* story. I won't write it either way. I'm not budging on that, so don't ask."

Lauren appeared truly baffled. "Look, I know it's awful that John will lose his job. It sucks, I know. But he's a really talented mechanic; there will be other jobs. We have *one shot* at destroying these assholes before they commit wholesale privacy theft. How can we ever rein it in after the FBI announces Ansom's chip is crucial for national security? By then, it's too late. And yet you just walk away? Leave me to it? On my own?"

"That's not what I'm doing."

"Then tell me what you are doing, because I'm lost."

"Do you remember, before we left DC, how anxious you were about coming here? You recall why?"

"I was worried you and my family wouldn't get along."

"Yes. But specifically you were worried your family wouldn't like me. Wouldn't understand me. And I think you were afraid you'd have to choose. You had nightmares about that."

"So?"

"How many times have you told me your family looks after its own? And you're right, it does. I see that. Well, I'm still an outsider here, Lauren. Maybe they'll accept me as time goes by, but right now, the truth is, I'm not one of you."

Lauren said nothing.

"So think about it," Catherine pressed her. "When it comes down to it, having some outsider imposing her will on your family, costing John his job without even talking about it—how do you think, deep down, they'd react to that? If you don't want your family to resent me for years over this—"

"That's what this is about? You're afraid they won't like you?"

"No. I don't care whether your family likes me or not," Catherine said quietly. "I never have."

Lauren's eyes widened. "What?"

"I'm used to being disliked. I told Meemaw that on day one, and it's true. But I do know *you* need them to like me. You need us to not be on opposing sides. It'll eat away at you. Even the thought of us being at war was giving you cold sweats. So this was the only way I could think to not be that Boston bitch who swept in and ruined John's life. I made the decision *theirs* and the story *yours* so it could never be something about the Kings versus an outsider. It would all be family."

Lauren glared. "I hate that you've put me in this position. You have no idea."

Catherine looked down. "I was thinking of you. Of us."

"You're doing what you always do," Lauren said with an aggrieved sigh. "Deciding for us both. Did it never occur to you to discuss this with me first?"

No. It didn't. She'd seen the obvious path and took it.

"Yeah, didn't think so. Damn it, Catherine, I don't want John to lose his job, but this was supposed to be obvious. The story comes first. End of. And now you've made it as complicated as hell."

"Family comes first," Catherine said weakly.

The incredulous look on Lauren's face reminded Catherine of her own hypocrisy. "The way it does with yours?"

Low blow. Catherine felt the sting of it in her gut. She had no witty words to rebut that. Actually, she had plenty of words for it—barbed, stinging words. She said none of them, though, as stared at her fiancée. "Well, thank you for making my already terrible day worse," she muttered.

"Don't you get it?" Lauren said, eyes dark. "Don't you see what you've done? My family voted *against* this. But I'm fully committed to running it. Because I put what's right ahead of family loyalty. But now it means that when I write this, I'll be a bigger asshole to my family than if I'd just told them about it after the fact, as a *fait accompli*. What you did made it a hundred times worse. Do you get that?"

Catherine stared at her hands. "They were supposed to vote yes. I had assumed—"

"That you knew my family? Salt of the earth? Do the right thing? You were dead on about their loyalty, but sometimes they're so blinded by it, they don't always put their priorities in order. They're only human and I'd have been happy going to my grave never knowing how insular they can be. But great, now I know they'd put one family member, one man's job, ahead of millions of people they don't know, and I'm ashamed of them. And I *still* have to do what's right. This is a nightmare. We're screwed."

Her gaze met Catherine's. "Oh right, I forgot. Not we, *me*. I'm screwed. You abandoned ship on me."

"I never abandoned you. I was thinking of you. Of them. I did what I thought was for the best."

"Yeah? Well next time try asking first." She stood and thumped nonexistent dirt off her jeans in angry swipes. "I'm gonna write up the story. Because the damned story *does* always come first no matter how you've twisted it in your head otherwise."

Lauren gave her a hard look. "Oh, and my interview with Hickory was fantastic, thanks for asking. He eventually rolled over on everything. Now he knows Ansom's going down and that Lionel sees him as a patsy, he refuses to go down with them. So he confirmed everything—on the record. And Fiona Fisher has agreed to your interview. She wants to scream blue bloody murder about her privacy being invaded. This story is golden. It's a freaking triumph." She threw her hands up. "And you've made it taste like ashes. Thanks for that."

She turned and strode back to the house.

As Catherine watched her go, bile rose up her throat.

Chapter 24
The Power of One

FIVE HOURS LATER, LAUREN EMAILED Catherine a copy of the story with no note.

Didn't even deliver it in person. Emailed it from their bedroom where she'd secreted herself in order to write it. Catherine had stayed out of her way, wondering how the hell she'd messed things up so badly.

She'd been so sure when she'd come up with her perfect solution that the Kings would do the right thing. They were those kinds of people. Decent. Meant well. They'd give Lauren permission, and it would be a little less hard on John to lose his job because he'd had a say in it. And Lauren would have been immune from fallout for the same reason.

She'd been blindsided by the family's selfishness. Well, maybe that was too strong a word. It turned out they were just people. People who loved one of their own and wanted whatever made him happy.

Catherine ignored Lauren's email alert and focused on giving a final read over the My Evil Twin story she'd been working on from the living room.

As promised, she'd left Lesser's name out of it. It was a cool, cutting dissection of what had been the most popular and secretly racist app going. Her own dry tone was deliberate to make Fiona's powerful comments reach out and grab readers by the collar. She scrolled down her story to read over the woman's words one last time.

"I been betrayed twice," Mrs. Fisher said. *"Once by my government, who sent me to Iraq and then sent me home on a*

stretcher but didn't help me as much as I needed. That made me go to desperate measures, to let them put this tech in my hand. Then they betrayed me again. The FBI and this...thing under my skin. Those soulless people at the FBI, they been stealing the essence of who I am. They been takin' bits of me, private pieces and chunks, my scars and my tattoos, my health business, all the things I am, all the things that make me me, and they been poking it inside some computer for anyone to look at. Worse... they poked it in the place that's supposed to be just for criminals. Now, that feels like a violation to me. And I don't take it well when my own government, who I fought for, turns on me. I'm spitting mad. And if they don't take me outta their criminal NGI thing, well, I'll just go get me a lawyer and start a class action. Then see how much the government likes their own people poking back at them."

Fiona was not taking it lying down. With her words, she'd make everyone forget they'd ever laughed at her in that meme of her peering at the robot's camera. Fiona Fisher was blunt, smart, and magnificent.

The best part of it was that everything had come to light because of her. She'd demanded to know why she was being humiliated in Lesser's app. Now Fiona could end up tearing it all apart. Now Ansom and its associates would be exposed. The FBI director would most likely be investigated. And the app which hurt Fiona so much was already dead.

The power of one.

Catherine smiled and hit *Send* on her phone. Even her picky editor would love it, she was sure. She opened her inbox and scrolled down to Lauren's story and opened it.

For five minutes she devoured the words, eyes widening at everything Lauren had managed to unearth.

It was brilliant. Probably the best thing Lauren had ever written. She'd used a few quotes of Catherine's father from the recording. She wondered what Lauren made of the rest of that conversation. Embarrassment flooded her at the thought of anyone else hearing it. Lauren now knew exactly what her parents were like. And she'd heard Catherine shredding her mother to pieces.

She forced herself not to dwell on that and keep reading. Because Lauren had some incredible quotes from Hickory. He even admitted he'd been rehearsing a speech given to him by the FBI for when the crisis actor got "caught" about to commit terrorism. How on earth had she gotten that out of him?

Pride swelled in her. A day ago, if she'd told Lauren how incredible this story was, Lauren would have been bouncing out of her skin with delight. Now she probably wouldn't even acknowledge her reply.

Catherine typed out her two-word answer.

It's brilliant.

She hit *Send*. And waited. And waited some more.

No reply.

She pocketed her phone, then rose from the sofa, deciding a coffee couldn't hurt. Catherine almost backed out of the kitchen when she saw John talking to Meemaw. He stopped immediately when he saw her, his head doing what it usually did, dropping, eyes examining his boots.

Christ. Things were turning to water because of this one shy man who loved his job more than his country.

She was probably being uncharitable again.

"John?" Catherine said.

He looked up.

"I'd like you to read something." She fished her phone out of her pocket and scrolled through it. "It's Lauren's story."

Meemaw frowned. "I thought there wasn't going to be a story. John voted no. And we backed him."

"Lauren has written it in case John changes his mind." Catherine decided the lie was better than the truth—that his sister was going to run it regardless. "But I thought you should know exactly what it is you're saying no to."

John shook his head and took a step away.

Anger flared within her. "I didn't take you for a coward, John."

Meemaw's head snapped around. "Manipulating my grandson, Catherine? I thought it wasn't your story anyhow. So what's it to you?"

"Lauren's tearing herself apart over this. And she's angry with me for putting her in that position." She looked at John, who was now his usual stoplight-red color. "So I think the least you can do is own the decision you made, not stick your head in the sand. If you read this and still say no, I promise I won't say another word about it."

John's head slowly lifted, and she met his gaze for the first time. His eyes were startlingly blue, more so than his brothers. He held out his hand. Catherine placed the phone in it and watched as he read.

Meemaw made Catherine a coffee, gaze sliding between John and her as she did so, then pushed the mug across the table. "Here."

Catherine thanked her, sipped silently, and waited.

Meemaw peered over John's shoulder, reading. "What does a 'crisis actor' mean?"

"It means they play the part of victims or perpetrators at a crisis scene. The scene is set up by someone, usually a government agency, to test out a scenario of, say, responding to a bomb or a terrorist attack. It's used in training exercises. This one was meant to have tricked everyone into believing it's real."

Meemaw's frown deepened. "That is not right."

"No." Catherine glanced at John, who hadn't said a word.

After five more minutes, he put the phone on the countertop and pushed it back to Catherine.

"I love my job." His words were barely a whisper. Finally, he met her gaze. "Do you get how much?"

"I do."

"But this"—he pointed at the phone—"is seriously messed-up stuff. I couldn't keep on going to work like nothing had happened, knowing all that. It'd make me sick every day. How could I enjoy my work there after that?"

Catherine tried to tamp down the surge of hope. "So what are you saying?"

"Do it. Run it. Whatever you need to. It's okay. That's all I'm saying."

There was a silence.

Finally, Catherine spoke. "Thank you, John."

He shook his head. "I'm sorry."

"What for?"

"I should have said yes first time. I was…afraid."

"You said yes now," Catherine said, her tone kind.

He looked down again and focused hard on his boots. That, she supposed, was as much eye contact and social interaction as he had in him. He left the room.

Catherine turned to Meemaw. "Did you agree with him about not running it? Earlier, when John made his decision."

"It wasn't up to me." She looked at her cautiously.

"Did you agree, though?"

"No."

"Did the others? I know you'd know what they were thinking."

She regarded her. "No, I don't think so. Owen definitely disagreed. Not even Lucas, and he's closest to John."

Her gaze hardened. "You were all prepared to let millions suffer because of one man's view?"

"I don't think you understand how family works, Catherine."

"I'm disappointed you don't see your whole country as family."

Meemaw snorted. "Don't play naïve; it doesn't suit you. You know that's not how things work. This whole country's a patchwork quilt of divides, this group and that, them and us. So you pick your tribe, and that's who your loyalty's with, and that's it. Those are your people. My people are my family, my friends, my neighborhood, and my church."

Catherine exhaled at that.

Meemaw's eyes became narrow. "Are you judging us? Even though every single person, everywhere else, does the same as us?"

"On this? Yes. That insular view is why nothing ever gets done. It's why our political system is a gridlocked, useless, partisan joke."

"Well." She straightened. "I'm not gonna disagree on that. Yes, I'm glad John did the right thing in the end. But I'd have stood with him either way."

Catherine gave a hollow laugh. "My family stands by only the things my father decides. Everyone and everything else can go to hell."

"Then I correct my earlier statement. I don't think *your family* understands how family works."

"No. I'm fairly sure they don't." Catherine finished off her coffee and put the mug in the sink, running water into it.

After a long look, Meemaw cleared her throat. "Okay. You got what you needed. I hope that story's worth it if you're warring with my granddaughter over it."

"You know the answer to that."

"Then what are you standing around yapping to me for?"

Catherine settled on the bed beside Lauren, who was typing furiously. "That first draft? Your story's good."

"So you said."

"Hickory's quotes are astonishing."

"Yes."

"John says you can run it."

Lauren froze and turned. "What?"

"You can run it. I showed him your story, and he changed his mind."

"Just like that?"

She nodded.

Lauren exhaled. "I'm still mad at you."

"I see that. Why?"

"Because I've spent most of the day worst-case scenario-ing everything and imagining my life ahead without my family's love. That was a terrifying thing to have in my head while I'm trying to write a story."

"Ah."

Lauren glared at her screen. "It's what you have in your head all the time, isn't it?"

Catherine's lips thinned. "I prefer not to dwell on them. Not worth it."

"So that's a yes?"

Rising and walking to the window, Catherine leaned against the frame, staring out. "How long do you plan to stay angry at me for?"

"I don't have a timeline." There was a hard stab on the iPad. "You put me in a terrible position." *Stab.* "You didn't discuss our story; you just made a decision for both of us." *Stab.* "I thought we were supposed to be equal partners, but no..." *Stab.* "Catherine Ayers decides everything." *Stab.* She looked up. "Is that how it goes?"

"I thought it would go quite a bit differently, actually."

"Oh, yeah, I know. Well, that's another humiliation for me, isn't it? It's what you always assumed about Iowans. We are insular and only care about our own issues. Now you have absolute proof."

"Except John just refuted that."

"Probably only after you held his feet to the fire." Lauren gave a pained huff. "It's been a thoroughly sucky day—you showing me my family's failings while throwing me to the wolves for my own good, apparently, while also—and here's the really fun part—not considering me important enough to talk this over with first."

"Lauren—"

"No, don't bother. So… help me with work or leave."

Sighing, Catherine turned. "How can I help?"

"I need to figure something out. Michelle Hastings." Lauren reached for her notepad. "What was her motive in all this? Everything she's done suggests she really did want us to pursue the story. But what was her agenda? If I didn't know her, I'd say she actually was trying to be a whistleblower— well, in her own oblique, useless way that didn't tell us much. So what was really in it for her? Have you wondered?"

"I have."

"And? Any conclusions?"

After a moment, Catherine said, "Michelle's Jewish."

"How do you know?"

"She told me she was, back…then. She had no reason to lie about it."

"Fine. Relevance?" Lauren flipped her notepad to the next page.

"She told me her grandmother used to say 'never again' to her. A lot."

"Right…" Lauren scribbled a note to herself.

"A data chip under everyone's skin. A number tattooed on everyone's wrist. Do these things not sound a *little* similar?"

Lauren froze and looked up. "She really did want us to stop this? She wasn't just playing with us?"

"Not this time. I am starting to believe she really was appalled when she found out about Lesser's scheme. Maybe it's just as she claimed. She was at the State Fair, saw an opportunity when she recognized me, and decided to make sure…*never again*?"

"Maybe." Lauren bit her lip and puzzled over that. "That's a pity. I so wanted to screw her over somewhere in all this."

"I know the feeling. That would have been poetic justice. She screws me over, I screw her over." She gestured at Lauren's story. "Well, by proxy."

"About that, I'm still mad at you."

"I know."

"Although, having now listened to the recording of you and your parents, I know how shitty your day was, too. And you might have more than a small case for being pissed at me for the mean thing I said about your family. How yours doesn't come first." Her eyes were softer, and there was regret in them.

"Ah. That."

"I'm a little surprised you didn't wipe the floor with me for my cheap shot."

Catherine gave her an intense look. "I love you, Lauren. Why would I do that?"

Lauren's composure crumpled. Tears pricked her eyes. "Oh hell. You…"

Pulling her into a hug, Catherine murmured, "I'm sorry, Lauren."

"Ugh. Damn you. Me, too. But you left me," Lauren said, muffled against Catherine's chest, which was feeling wetter by the second. "Right when I needed you. Whatever happened to solidarity? You just tossed me the story like a grenade, left me to face a nightmare with my family, and disappeared."

"I did no such thing. I never left." Catherine strengthened her grip. "But I'm very sorry you saw it that way."

"I do love you, by the way," Lauren said. "But I'm still so mad."

"I know."

"And you have got to stop doing this." She arched her head back to meet Catherine's gaze with watery eyes. "Deciding my fate for me. You did this in LA, too. Deciding we had no future, because you were off to DC and you'd just assumed I was staying behind. What will it take?"

"I am sorry. I'll try. I know we've been living together for a year, but I'm still so used to making decisions on my own, it's hard to remember sometimes that I don't have to solve everything myself."

"Well, you're on notice," Lauren said with a fierce look. "That excuse only flies until the wedding."

"So you still want to get married tomorrow?" The faintest hint of uncertainty in Catherine's voice came as a surprise.

Lauren's eyes widened. "Catherine, we are gonna fight sometimes. Come on, we fell in love while fighting. But even when you're being extra impossible, like today"—she poked Catherine's chest—"it's always been you for me. My love for you isn't just painted on. Even if I'm still mad with you."

She sounded so adamant that Catherine laughed. It was also a release over how relieved she felt at hearing the unmistakable humor in Lauren's voice.

Her laugh earned a light slap to her chest, and then Lauren slid out of her arms, twisted, and hit a few buttons on the iPad.

"Okay, enough of you distracting me with those big, impossible-to-hate eyes. I'm sending my story."

"Would you like me to have one last look at it first?"

"No. You said it was my story, right? So I'm taking ownership of it. For good and for bad." She glanced up. "I think it's time I stepped out of your shadow anyway. Journalistically speaking..." She tapped the *Send* button and slid back into Catherine's arms. "Physically speaking, however, for some reason, my shadow's extremely fond of yours."

"Is that so?" Catherine took a chance at feathering kisses along her jaw.

Lauren's breath hitched. "Mmm...yes. It is."

Catherine lost track of the time she spent reacquainting herself with the softest of skin along Lauren's neck.

A soft ping sounded.

Lauren twisted away again, reached for the tablet, and tapped a few buttons. "It's from my boss." She tilted the screen Catherine's way and they read it together.

Are you kidding me, King? I turn my back for five mins and you give me the story of the year. Well done! JESUS. Knew I was right about you. Running this when the lawyers OK it. Probably Monday – Theo

PS Since you've obviously been working all week, you can take next week as your vacation. I've cleared it. Once again—great job.

"Well," Catherine said. "I see he appreciates talent."

Lauren grinned. "Yep. Even better, I'm now a lady of leisure. If only I had someone to be leisurely with."

After pulling out her phone, Catherine tapped out a message and sent it. "I believe that makes two of us."

"Just like that?"

Catherine smiled. "Neil will approve it. He owes me, and he's been on me to take some more of my overdue vacation time for ages. Besides, he loved the My Evil Twin story, so he'll be in a good mood. Now, where were we?" Her fingers slid along Lauren's sleeve. "I can't help but think there's something we could be doing instead of fighting."

"You're right," Lauren said with a firm nod. "Planning a wedding."

"If it's not planned by now, we're in a great deal of trouble."

"Oh my God." Lauren's eyes widened.

Catherine leaned back to eye her. "You forgot we're getting married tomorrow?"

"No. I just remembered all the people coming in for it. The whole 'worlds collide' concept." Lauren's expression turned dubious. "I wonder what Tad will make of Iowa."

"What will Cynthia? Or Phoebe? If she's coming." She frowned. "She never replied to my texts."

"Has it occurred to you how many high-strung people we know?" Lauren asked. "And how will they all get along? Cynthia Redwell versus Meemaw? My God, think about that match up. Your acidic, snobby oldest friend versus my sharp-tongued, proudly Iowan grandmother."

"My money's on Meemaw," Catherine said with a soft snicker.

"This is serious! You know, I think I preferred things when I was focused on a national conspiracy to end privacy in the US and put us all in a mammoth government database. Maybe I should start planning the follow-up now."

Catherine rolled her eyes. "Lauren, you might have to just accept that you can't always get the end-times story you want, whenever you want it."

"Spoilsport. But seriously…" Lauren considered her for a beat. "Your money's on Meemaw?"

Chapter 25
Kith and Tell

CATHERINE STARED INTO THE FULL-LENGTH oval mirror in Meemaw's bedroom, where she'd been isolated for her preparation. Her goddess-style ivory wedding dress flowed to her ankles. It had intricate embroidered silver brocade at the waist. She spread her hands down her stomach, not that there was a wrinkle in sight. It was a perfect fit. She turned, catching a look at herself. *What will Lauren think of it?*

"Well?" she asked her silent observer.

"Gorgeous," Tad said, admiration warming his tone. "I'm just sorry Mom's not here. She'd love to be in on the zhuzhing and fluffing up. All the girly stuff."

"Zhuzhing is not a word."

"It is when Carson Kressley says it."

Catherine looked at him blankly.

"From that really old cable show they remade? *Queer Eye for the Straight Guy*? Bravo had a marathon of it a few months back."

"You know, it is mystifying to me how you've stayed in the closet for as long as you have."

Tad laughed and then glanced at his phone. "Ooh, gotta go. I'm on guest pickup duty with that dishy King brother. We're helping all the older family members get here who don't have transport."

"The dishy brother? They all look the same to me."

"Oh, fine—the gay one."

Catherine turned in astonishment. "Lauren has a gay brother? Who?"

"Pfft. Like I can keep track of names. Anyway, he legit checked me out. He's *so* on our team. I'll point him out later. Okay, see you at the ceremony."

"All right." She paused. "Tad? I'm glad you could come."

He smiled and it was pure warmth. "Me, too. Us pink sheep of the family have to stick together." He hesitated, biting his lip, then opened his arms.

My family does not do hugs, her brain protested, even as he pulled her into a hug, warm and fierce, like the ones she'd become accustomed to seeing the Kings offer each other.

We should have, her brain murmured a moment later, as love for her good-natured nephew welled up in her.

He held her for a few moments until she relaxed and her hands came up to his back. "If you think this means a rent discount…" she whispered in his ear.

Tad gave a hearty laugh and stepped back. "Not sure how you can discount zero. Ooh, unless you plan on *paying* me to live in your LA digs?"

"Thadeus." She gave his back a playful slap. "Now go, be useful."

"Yes, Aunty C." He chuckled.

As his long legs whisked him from her sight, another shape passed him at the door.

Catherine's gaze returned to the mirror. She still felt a little emotional; as a general rule, she did not do emotional displays any more than she did hugs.

The new arrival came to stand behind her and watched with appraising elderly eyes.

"Just beautiful. She'll love that dress," Meemaw said.

"I hope so."

"She will. But I've yet to see you step a foot wrong when it comes to this fashion business. Is it all just effortless to you?"

"Grooming and deportment classes—four years." She turned to Meemaw, lips tugging upwards. "My mother ensured from a young age that I would never embarrass her."

"Well, that's ridiculous, isn't it? What parent hopes for that?"

"I'd have thought most."

"Nonsense. Children need to make mistakes and satisfy their curiosity. Insisting on them doing nothing embarrassing is just raising a robot. And yet…" Meemaw tilted her head. "You're not like that, are you?"

"No." She gave a rueful sigh. "My sister, though, didn't have quite the level of defiance I had."

"A pity. Where is she?"

Catherine wished she knew. But given Phoebe's track record on never defying their father, she would probably call in a few days and claim she'd only just found the wedding invitation text.

"I had thought she'd be here, but she's probably been ordered to make herself scarce."

"Well, at least that splendid nephew of yours is here," Meemaw replied. "An actor, you said? Good heavens, he's handsome. Could be a model. What's he been in? I'm sure I've seen him in something."

This time Catherine's smile was full. "Infomercials."

Meemaw nodded earnestly. "That'd be it, then. You look lovely, by the way. Any mother would be proud to see her daughter looking so fine." She brushed some lint off Catherine's sleeve, then patted her, looking pleased. "All set. You're perfect."

It was such a familiar gesture, one her own mother did often. But it felt so different. She didn't feel like a flaw to be corrected. Catherine had never been declared "perfect", either.

Meemaw's expression changed to affection.

How do the Kings do this so easily? How do they offer acceptance to people like it's nothing at all? She remembered Meemaw once suggesting she look at who her allies really were. But it was easier said than done.

"What are you thinking in that wiry brain of yours?" Meemaw's eyebrows lifted. "Because your face is shifting like the sands. To places not so pleasant, I'm guessing."

"I am considering your family. It's so at odds to mine. I'm also weighing up what you said earlier. About noticing what's right in front of me."

"I'm pleased to hear it."

"It may take me a while." Catherine stepped back from the mirror and turned to slip her heels on. "It's not you or your family. I'm just not good at…trusting."

"Lauren loves you, and that's one thing you can trust with your life. I know you said at the vote that you're not one of us. I suppose that's true."

Catherine felt her stomach twist. It felt surprisingly unpleasant, given while she believed it, she'd never expected the stark admission from Meemaw.

"We *are* from different worlds," the other woman continued. "I suspect on many things we won't understand each other."

Nodding, Catherine looked away, unwilling to show her dismay. Had Meemaw suddenly changed her mind on embracing her into the family?

"But that doesn't matter. Look at me, dear."

Glancing back, Catherine was caught in the other woman's intense warm gaze.

"You love Lauren, and we love her, so this"—Meemaw waved her finger between the two of them—"is a done deal. You're stuck with us now. I mean it. You're ours."

Catherine's stomach unknotted itself. Relief flowed through her, the strength of which was almost shocking. It was a surreal sensation being claimed by this imposing woman. After a lifetime of feeling not good enough, not worthy enough to love, she didn't know quite what to feel now.

"Plus..." Meemaw lowered her tone to conspiratorial, "I caught Miss Chesterfield cheating on me with you."

Surprise shot through her. She'd been circumspect around the fickle cat, careful not to be too obvious in giving it attention within Meemaw's sight.

The other woman's eyes crinkled. "She's a bit like me and you, I suspect. Doesn't give her affections lightly. If Miss Chesterfield thinks you're worthy, that's more than enough for me. I can tell you this: that fussy madam never liked any of Lauren's other girlfriends."

Catherine felt absurdly pleased at that tidbit. She regarded Meemaw under her lashes. When she'd first met her, she'd assumed that at best they'd have a cool truce forever more. That would have been fine with her. But this was far out of her wheelhouse.

Just because Catherine didn't care if she was disliked, that didn't mean she didn't appreciate it when she wasn't. But now...to not only be liked and approved of, but claimed as family, too? It was almost confusing, picking that apart. She had no context for processing any of this. She felt both lost and lighter. Struggling to answer, all she could manage was a murmured "thank you."

Meemaw nodded, like it was nothing at all, this offer of real friendship, and began patting her pockets. "Ah. Now, I came to see you, to give you this to wear. It's a tradition. I wore it at mine."

Catherine was wary, a little afraid of what she might produce.

A fine golden bracelet lay in Meemaw's palm. "It's been in our family for generations. It matches a necklace I'm giving Lauren to wear. I hope you'll both find as much happiness as the women in our family have found over the years." She slid it around Catherine's wrist and did up the clasp. Then she straightened. "Oh, Margaret would have loved this."

"I'm sorry she can't be here." Catherine's fingertips toyed with the beautiful bracelet. "I would have greatly liked to have met Lauren's mom."

"You'd have made her so pleased, putting such happiness on Lauren's face. She would have had a few words about being good to her girl, mind." Her expression became knowing. "But I don't need to do that, do I?"

"No." Catherine straightened. "Never."

"Good. Now I'm going to find out how that bride of yours is doing. I'll send one of the boys in to fetch you when it's time."

"Thank you," Catherine said. "For everything."

Meemaw met her gaze and squeezed her hand. She blinked rapidly, turned, and abruptly left.

A few minutes later the door opened and shut again. Catherine didn't have to look up. She'd recognize the soft, slinky footfall of her oldest friend anywhere.

"So you did it," Cynthia said. "Got the girl."

"I did. Jealous?"

"Oh, madly."

At Catherine's startled look, Cynthia laughed. "I'm not pining after your Iowan princess, fear not."

"Smart move. I've inherited some family members who'll apparently take up the cudgels for me. They'd snap you like a toothpick, which is fair since you resemble one."

"Miaow, Catherine." Cynthia smirked. "I've missed you. Missed us. Remember, in our twenties, how we used to terrorize those intellectual midgets in the newsroom? The ones who thought glass ceilings were designed to keep the natural order?"

"I remember you doing the terrorizing. And I remember me wondering how you did it."

"I was the brave one, then. But look at you now. You took a risk. And see where it's landed you."

Catherine searched for the usual sarcastic bite. "Where?" she asked cautiously.

"With what we both so desperately wanted in our twenties and never had." She looked uncharacteristically sincere.

"In love?"

"Please. I've been in and out of love so many times, I can't remember all their names. Not love, Catherine." Her expression was intense. "Family. A home in the best sense of the word."

"Ah. Not that my gilded cage ever matched what you went through in foster care."

Cynthia's hands came to rest on her shoulders and she met her eye in the mirror. "It's not a contest. Our childhoods were both atrocious in different ways. I'm glad you struck gold now. Even if she is from this backwater."

"Cynthia, can you do me one favor? Try not to antagonize the Kings too much? I don't think they'll see scalpel-sharp incisions into their way of life as a form of affection."

Her lips twitched. "I make no promises."

"*Cynthia.*"

"But the Midwest crowd is so easy to bait."

Catherine glared. "I like these people. They're decent, hardworking, and good. I don't want them hurt."

"Fine. I'll try." She rolled her eyes and smiled. "For you, since it matters so much."

"So what about you?" Catherine asked quietly. "I've found who I'm meant to be with. Do you think you'll ever come out? Might actually make you happy for once to be honest about who you love."

Cynthia's lip curled into mockery, even though her expression became wistful. "You're getting married to an ex-softballer from Iowa. *In Iowa.* Let's deal with one moment of madness at a time. Now, shift a little." She gave Catherine's head a tiny adjustment and reached for a brush on the dresser. "Let's see if we can get all traces of flyover state out of your hair."

Josh looked very handsome. Lauren told him so more than once while babbling like a crazy woman. He beamed, straightening the collar on her outfit, and put away his make-up kit.

"So do you, dearheart. Like Hepburn meets Dietrich, but even gayer."

She chuckled. "High praise."

"I'll say. So how are you doing?"

"Nervous."

"That's to be expected. You're marrying a goddess. I should know—I worship them all, from Garland to Gaga."

"That doesn't make me feel less nervous."

"Well, maybe this will help." He led her over to a tall mirror and showed her the result of all his primping.

"Oh." She stared at herself. She did look so…well, elegant. Different. Sleeker. Her ivory satin blouse's sleeves folded at the cuffs over the navy jacket's sleeves for dramatic contrast. The top four shirt buttons were undone, allowing a peek of lacy bra underneath. The pants were tailored to highlight her long, lean legs.

"You have the blue," Joshua tapped her sleeve, "and Meemaw will be here soon with the borrowed. So kick off those sad heels, girl—I bring you the new." He pulled out of a bag a pair of exquisite low-cut designer boots with part of the back stylishly cut out. They matched her pants. "Zach sent me the color. I already knew your size after all our shopping sprees together. Best of all, I knew Via Spiga's newest line would be a dream match."

"I love them," Lauren said after she slipped them on. Josh was right—they were perfect for the outfit. Edgy and chic. "Just beautiful. Thanks, Josh." She gave him a kiss on the cheek.

He grinned. "Pleasure, treasure."

There was a brisk knock, and Meemaw bustled in, then paused and beamed. "And here's the other bride."

Lauren perked up. "How's Catherine?"

"Oh, same as every other bride in history. Like a long-tailed cat in a room full of rocking chairs. She hides it better than most, but I can tell. She does look gorgeous in her dress."

Josh stepped back to give her space. Meemaw reached into her pocket and lifted out the thinnest gold necklace. "This was your mother's. She wore it on her special day. It's yours now. Matches the bracelet Catherine's wearing." She leaned forward and slid it around Lauren's neck. It settled into the vee of her shirt as though made for it.

Meemaw gave a slight huff as she fussed over the chain. "Lord, how many buttons are undone here? You're not for sale." She did up the bottom button. "There now, much better."

A knock sounded, and Mark stuck his head in. "Hey, Laur, we're all ready and waiting. And the bagpiper's getting antsy."

Lauren froze. "Bagpiper?"

Meemaw glared at him. "Mark, you're the best man…" She slid a look at Josh. "Well, one of them. So start acting it. Don't rile up a bride on her big day with nonsense. Now get out there. We'll be down soon."

"There's not really a bagpiper, is there?" Lauren asked.

"Course not. What a notion." She glanced at Josh. "Young man, could you give my granddaughter and me a few minutes?"

"Sure thing." He left the room, closing the door.

"I'm not one for speeches," Meemaw began, meeting her gaze in the mirror.

Lauren snickered. "Unaccustomed as you are…"

"Hush, you." Meemaw waggled a finger, then smiled. "Lauren, dear, I'm so very proud of you. For the young girl you were, who took on so much responsibility, helping raise her brothers. For the woman you are today. I love you, my dear. All my blessings." She dropped a kiss against her temple.

"Thanks, Meemaw. I love you, too."

"And as for that Catherine of yours, I wasn't too sure about her when we first met. But I've watched the way she talks about you. The way she looks at you. She loves you. You can see that from outer space. You've chosen well."

"Thanks." Lauren grinned. "I think so."

A wailing sound from below started, that sort of resembled wedding music.

"Shit!" Meemaw's head whipped around. "There *are* bagpipes."

Lauren's eyes widened in astonishment at her cursing. She'd never heard a swear word from her grandmother in her entire life.

Meemaw flew out of the room, her fleshy arms flapping as she hollered, "Mark Elijah King, what in the blessed Lord's name is going on down there! What is with that damned racket?"

Lauren doubled over and laughed hard.

Chapter 26
Tree of Dreams

THE DREAMING TREE WAS GLOWING with the strings of hundreds of golden fairy lights, and the flickers of jars and jars of fireflies. Two sections of white chairs had been placed in front of the enormous tree, with a grassy aisle between them.

The smell of spicy sauces and the grill heating up wafted from the tiki bar area behind them.

Lauren's father led her down the aisle as a classic tune began its mournful wail.

"Dad," she hissed under her breath. "Why's there a bagpiper? And why's he playing *Amazing Grace* at my wedding? It's the saddest song ever. Plus...hello...*bagpipes!*"

"I don't know, sweetheart." He gave her a helpless look. "I figured you requested him."

Lauren flicked her eyes to the stout, kilt-wearing musician. His red bearded, puffed-out cheeks were round from his exertions. In the distance, from where they were locked up safely in the living room, Boomer and Daisy began a wailing howl to match the maudlin music.

Snorts of laughter sounded from the crowd. The bagpiper's ear-splitting wails grew louder, his elbow pumping the bellows harder.

Right. Lauren was going to kill whichever brother had thought this was a genius idea. Assuming Meemaw hadn't caught up to Mark when she'd sprinted out after him earlier, looking a lot like a farmer's wife chasing a chicken with an ax.

They passed Catherine's friend, Cynthia, who had lost her customary aloof stare and was laughing so hard that a pair of mascara trails were running from her eyes. On the other side of the aisle, Suze had her fingers shoved in her ears and was wearing an apologetic look. An apologetic *guilty* look.

Lauren narrowed her eyes. Suze ducked her head at the sight of her.

Culprit identified.

Her brothers were lined up at the front in matching rented suits. Lauren realized they had never gotten around to figuring out which groomsmen would stand where. Mariella was on Lauren's side, of course, as her matron of honor. But to Lauren's surprise, she realized Lucas was standing on Catherine's side.

He caught her gaze and gave a hesitant smile.

"He volunteered," her father whispered in her ear. "Something about doing right by you."

Lauren digested that, her ball of anger at her little brother's actions loosening a little. Well. It was a start. A good one.

They reached the front, and Josh beamed at her from the middle of the group, where he stood resplendent in his mustard tuxedo jacket, starched eggplant shirt with a black bowtie, and sleek black pants. Somehow, he managed to make the look work. He grinned from ear to ear and then hurriedly signaled to the bagpiper.

The musician changed to *Here Comes the Bride.*

Well, better late than never. Unfortunately, on bagpipes, it sounded like the desperate wail of a funeral dirge dedicated to ten thousand dead Scotsmen. They reached the front, and Lauren twisted her head around to glare at Suze again, who mimed *sorry.*

Oh, Lauren was so getting to the bottom of this story.

Suddenly Lauren didn't care. Because there, behind her, was Catherine. Backlit by the setting sun, her flowing ivory sheath dress was made of the same silken material and color as Lauren's shirt. Wow. Zachary was a goddamn superstar.

Catherine's auburn hair, radiant under the setting sun, made her look like a fire queen. Lauren's heart thudded painfully, and she teared up. *Gorgeous.*

Her gaze flicked to Tad, leading his aunt up the aisle, looking handsome and proud in his tux.

Lauren held back the tears until Catherine reached her side.

"You look beautiful," Catherine whispered, her eyes soft.

"God, you, too." Her smile was watery. "So much."

"Dearly beloved," Josh began. "We gather together in the sight of beautiful family, friends, a glorious dreaming tree, and an unexpected bagpipe…"

The crowd snickered. The Scotsman huffed.

Lauren couldn't wipe the smile off her face. It felt like warmth was filling her from inside out, like sunlight wrapping itself around her heart.

She was going to marry Catherine Ayers.

The ceremony flashed by in a blur. Lauren caught only snippets of it. Her dad's loving look. Her brothers laughing at Josh's occasional jokes. And Catherine, whose face filled with an expression Lauren had never seen on it before.

Uneasiness?

Nervousness?

She reached for her hand, and found it trembling.

Josh paused, smiled, and asked them to exchange their vows.

The trembling intensified.

At Josh's expectant nod, Lauren began.

"Catherine," she said, facing her. "When I think of the woman I met back in LA, I had no idea who you were. I made a whole bunch of assumptions. And they were all wrong. Piece by piece, you let me really see you. You showed me the things you hide from the world. And I found an intelligent, warm, clever, beautiful woman. I'm honored to be your wife. I vow I will love you in good times and bad, in sickness and in health, and until we're old and gray and you're still making me laugh with your perfectly wicked wit."

Catherine's smile was fixed, her hands now a constant tremble.

Joshua turned to her. "Catherine?"

Lauren clasped her hands tighter, willing her to draw strength from her.

"Lauren, I know I don't share myself with anyone except you. I accept I will never be the warmest, most relaxed, or nicest person in any room. But I *will* be the one who loves you deepest, with all that I am.

"I remember how it felt when…" Her breath hitched. "I was at my lowest ebb. When I was in such a dark place and I was comfortable there, because there's nothing left to risk at rock bottom. I had no interest in looking out at the world, at the light." She stopped, and Lauren soothed her hands with her thumb.

"But you forced your way in, Lauren, and I'm still not sure how you did that. And one day I looked around and realized it wasn't the light I could see. It was you. You were the brightness I could see, the warmth I could feel. You were the reason I could face my day. You were more than I deserved. I thank you for being you. I thank your family for giving you to the world."

Her gaze slipped from Owen to Meemaw and the brothers. Lauren glanced at them, too.

Mark was beaming as though about to burst with pride and love. Matthew, John, and Tommy were blinking back tears and pretending hard they weren't. Lucas looked stunned, as though he'd never seen Catherine before in his life. In a way, he hadn't. He'd never met the woman Lauren loved, and he'd never believed that this Catherine even existed. But now he knew. That pleased her in a way she had no words for.

"Lauren," Catherine continued. "I am humbled that you love me as I love you. I vow to do so for as long as I draw breath. For as long as you will have me. I simply can't imagine my life without you in it. You are everything to me. Now and always."

Tears flowed down Lauren's cheeks. She didn't care. Catherine was all she could think about. She wanted to hold her now and kiss her senseless for making such a vulnerable speech that had clearly been difficult for her. She recalled Catherine's words from a few days ago. "The hardest thing is to speak about things that lay me open. I always feel too exposed." Lauren's heart swelled at the fact Catherine had laid herself bare for her.

The rings they'd pointed out to Mrs. Potts materialized somehow on their hands as Lauren was lost in soft eyes.

"So, by the power invested in me by the Church of the Latter-Day Dude—"

A gasp rippled through the guests, followed by sniggers.

"—which is *totally real* and legally recognized in Iowa, don't worry, I checked twice—"

The laughter spread.

"I hereby declare that you are now married. You may both kiss your bride."

Lauren immediately pulled Catherine into a heartfelt kiss, as applause and good-natured hooting and whistles started from her brothers.

"Get a room!" Suze called with a bawdy shout and a hearty laugh.

"Get an original line!" Cynthia's distinctive mocking voice called back.

Suze's outraged snort was enough to make Lauren break the kiss and laugh. She smiled up at Catherine. "Hey. We're married," she whispered.

"Yes. I noticed that, too."

"I loved your vows. I know that was hard for you. Witnesses and all."

Catherine exhaled, and a trace of nervousness reappeared in her eyes. "It was…not easy for me. It was also the best gift I could think to give you."

Lauren hugged her tight, kissed her temple, then took her wife's hand to lead her down the aisle.

There were more shouts and applause, the bagpiper's wail starting up in a ridiculous song choice, the dogs howling again, plus a few more amusing insults hurled between Cynthia and Suze.

"Lauren?" Catherine bent to her ear. "Why is there a bagpiper? And why's he playing the *Star Wars Imperial March*?"

Chapter 27
Friends and Frenemies

CATHERINE'S GAZE ROAMED THE RECEPTION. She was unsure whether it was "going off like a cat-four tornado party", as Lauren had predicted, having no frame of reference for celebrating a potentially deadly weather event. But the gathered throngs were laughing and chatting, drinking and sounding generally happy.

Now dressed in a more comfortable outfit of black pants and a starched, cream-colored linen shirt, Catherine stood at the bar, waiting for the attendant to pour drinks for her and Lauren. Her new wife was somewhere, doing the rounds of family and friends. And she had a lot of them. She'd be awhile.

Tommy's wallflower girlfriend had turned out to be a surprisingly adept DJ, Catherine thought as she gazed around the gathering.

Suze, looking contrite, suddenly dashed over.

"Panpipes," she'd whispered, grasping her arm, an imploring look on her face. "It was meant to be *panpipes*. They gave me the job to book the music, and I tried this online musician booking service. I put in the wrong musician code, and I was in a hurry and didn't read the email they sent back too closely. Please tell Laur I'm *so* sorry. I'd tell her myself, but I'm avoiding her right now on account of the fact she definitely wants to murder me. Trust me. I'm dead woman walking."

Panpipes? That might have been nice. "I understand," Catherine replied. "But why *The Imperial March*?"

"Um, that one's on him." Suze looked mournful. "God, Hamish said he only knew three American tunes, so I said, 'Well, just play whatever's the most appropriate wherever, without doubling up'…and…" She threw her hands up. "Gah. Don't hate me."

"It did make the ceremony unique," Catherine noted, biting back a smile. But truly, Lauren's best friend was impossible to hate.

"I guess." Suze rolled her eyes. "By the way, what's the deal with your catty friend? Has she got something against me or just the whole Midwest?"

"Only the fact it exists." Catherine smirked. "Why don't you talk to her? Be sure to mention all the Iowan regional delicacies you can think of. Especially fried things on sticks. She'll love that a great deal. I sense she is dying to learn more about your state."

Suze looked her up and down, seeming impressed. "You're totally evil. So"—she leaned in, —"wanna tell me what else will rile her up?" Her grin was pure mischief.

Oh, Catherine liked her a lot. She added a few of her best pointers, knowing that Cynthia's idea of fun was being challenged. Her oldest friend could thank her later.

Suze thanked her, waved, and disappeared.

Catherine reached the front of the bar line when Lucas sauntered up.

"Yes?" she asked, not bothering to hide her irritation.

He said nothing for a moment, then sucked in a deep breath. "You offered me something a few days ago. I should have taken it." He held out his hand.

She took his measure—doubt, embarrassment, and shame seemed to be competing for dominance.

With a sigh, she shook his hand. Life was too short. "Is this an end to it?"

"You won't be hearing any more crap out of me. When you said your vows, I saw how much you meant them. It was, I don't know, the most honest thing I've ever heard. And I think maybe…I get you now. I made some wrong assumptions. Catherine…um…just… Sorry. Okay?"

Catherine could see his regret. And he *had* finally said her name right. "Thank you."

She didn't forgive him. It was too soon to forgive a man for trying to destroy the most important thing in her life. But maybe one day, if he proved his words weren't empty.

Lauren looked around in relief. Everyone seemed to be having a good time, eating, grilling, drinking, and dancing around the fire pit. Her voice was sore from greeting so many old relatives she hadn't seen for a year or more.

"Lauren, sweetie!" Mariella swished into view in a cloud of perfume and a bright, breezy muumuu, waving a bottle of beer.

Beer. She squinted at her in disbelief. Then her eye fell to the label. Her upscale LA publicist friend was swigging from a bottle of Tip the Cow beer. Before this, the most basic drink she'd ever seen Mariella holding was a cocktail with three French names.

"It's wonderful to see you again, darling." Mariella air kissed her deftly and then offered a rueful chuckle. "Sorry, dear. Force of habit. Harold complains I forget with him, too." She planted a proper kiss on Lauren's cheek and hugged her tight.

"Great to see you, too." Lauren gave her a hearty squeeze back. "Thanks for flying in on zero notice."

"As if I'd miss such a momentous occasion." She smiled and stood back. "Let me look at you. My goodness, you seem so happy. And you're not the only one." Mariella winked. "Well, aside from Catherine. It's Harold. I swear he's having the most fun he's had in years. I've dragged him to thousands of weddings and parties over the years. This is the first time he actually looks like he's enjoying himself."

Lauren's gaze swung over to Mariella's portly, balding husband in the grill line, debating hot sauces with her brothers as he waved about his tongs. "Great." She looked back at her friend. "So you guys don't mind having to cook your own meal?"

"Mind? Harold couldn't wait. Now he keeps telling me all weddings should be like this. So, where is your lovely bride?"

"She's getting us drinks and being sociable."

"The Caustic Queen sociable? How things change." Mariella chuckled. "You're a civilizing influence on her."

"Actually, I think it's Iowa that's getting to her. I'll have her checking out the American Gothic Barn in no time. Yes, that is exactly how it sounds."

"I'd pay to see that."

"Pay to see what?" Catherine asked, arriving with a wine glass and a beer. She handed the latter to Lauren. "Hello, Mariella, good to see you again."

"You, taking in Iowa's earthier sights," Mariella replied. "We're debating whether Lauren's home state is mellowing you."

"I'm an extremely mellow person," Catherine deadpanned. "I have no idea where people get any other idea."

Lauren laughed.

"In truth, it's hard to muster much energy for evisceration out here," Catherine continued. She took a sip of her wine. "In fact, I suspect the air is doing funny things to a lot of people. For instance, I just saw Suze challenge Cynthia to beer pong."

"What?" Lauren peered at her. Then she spun around trying to spot her friend. "I've been trying to talk to Suze all evening. I swear she's ducking me."

Catherine tilted an eyebrow. "Not surprising. She was put in charge of getting some music for the ceremony. She wanted panpipes, but there was a slight booking mishap."

"Ah." Well, that almost made sense. "So did Cynthia shred her on the spot for daring to suggest an economics expert turned TV executive would be into some frat party game?"

"No." Catherine looked amused. "Cynthia, competitive woman that she is, immediately accepted. And she is crushing the competition. Although, given how excellent we know Suze's hand-eye coordination is, I suspect she's tanking on purpose. See for yourself." She angled her head in the direction of the ping-pong-ball carnage.

Lauren blinked at the scene of the forbidding, angular Cynthia Redwell tossing plastic balls into cups at the end of a table with pinpoint accuracy, celebrating each direct hit with a cackle of delight. "Okay, I'm in the *Twilight Zone*." She waved her hand helplessly at the scene. "'Cause that's ridiculous."

"I agree," Mariella mused. "Flirting is not how I remember it."

"What makes you think they're flirting?" Catherine asked. "Cynthia could be just being friendly."

Lauren coughed into her beer.

"*Ex-actly*." Mariella eyed Catherine. "Plus, I do have decades of experience as an LA publicist trained to hide this sort of thing. Cynthia's not as discreet as she thinks she is. Not the way you were, Catherine. Oh, and some people can't hide it at all, let me tell you. Like that brother of yours, Lauren. He's such a sweetheart, but he really isn't fooling anyone."

"Wait, what?" She looked around frantically.

"You didn't know?" Mariella blinked. "Oh, well. I do apologize. When I was chatting with Mrs. Haverson earlier, she seemed more than aware."

"*Meemaw* knows?" Lauren squeaked.

"And your father. Delightful man, by the way. So charming."

"Dad knows? Wait! Which brother?"

"Oh no. I'll let him talk to you in his own time." She tapped her nose. "Publicist's code. No outing out of turn. No telling people who don't know already. And on that note, they're playing our song. I think I'll whip Harold out for a nice dance around the fire pit."

She put down her drink and went off to find her husband.

"Um, did you know I apparently have a gay brother?" Lauren demanded.

Before Catherine could answer, Lauren's father appeared, looking handsome in his black suit, hair slicked back. He smiled warmly at Catherine. "Hello. If it isn't my new daughter-in-law."

She smiled back.

Owen turned and pecked Lauren's cheek, giving her a fond look. "So, sweetheart, are you both having a good time?"

"The best." Lauren grinned. "Despite the bagpipes stuck in my head."

"And you?" Owen asked Catherine.

"It's the nicest wedding I've ever attended," Catherine said. "So I'm particularly glad it's my own."

Owen chuckled. "Good, that's good." He reached into his pocket. "I thought long and hard about what to get you two as a wedding present. And then it came to me." He opened his hand and a key ring with a car key sat on his palm. "I know Lauren loves her Beast to bits. And, see, Kitten is like that car's sister. So, Catherine, it seems only fair you get her; you'll have Hers and Hers 1970 Chevrolet Chevelle SS's in your garage. And I figured, what with your nickname and all, it feels like fate." He beamed proudly.

Catherine didn't speak. A smile seemed to squeeze itself onto her frozen lips.

"Oh, uh, you're not sure which one it is?" Owen guessed at her silence. "It's the blue car you drove to Rube's in that time. Sure, the, suspension's still a little rough, but I've fixed it near perfect now."

Catherine's expression became strangely fixed.

Lauren couldn't believe how huge this was. "We're getting Kitten? Dad, that's awesome. Love it!" She flung her arms around him and squeezed, breathing in the familiar smell of him, wishing she could take him home with her along with the classic car. She finally stepped back.

Owen dropped the keys into Catherine's left hand and closed her fingers around them. "I'll have one of the boys get her sent over your way by the end of the month. I know you'll take good care of her. I worked on her for about a year. Be sorry to see her go, but I'm glad she's staying in the family."

Catherine's smile softened. "Thank you. I'll think of all the effort you put into it every time I look at it."

His face reddened, and he looked pleased. "Well now." He rubbed the back of his neck. "I also just want to say, it's been so good you both chose to have the shindig right here. It really warmed me that you went and did that." Owen suddenly took Catherine's hand and shook it. "I also wanted to say, welcome to the family. And thanks for putting that look on Lauren's face."

"I have a look?" Lauren asked.

"Oh, you sure do, sweetheart." He nodded vigorously.

"My pleasure." Catherine smiled.

"Well, I'll leave you two youngsters to it," Owen said, dropping her hand. "Enjoy the rest of the party." He ambled off.

Lauren shot her wife a knowing look. "You know, you won't actually be able to make tank jokes about the Beast anymore if you're driving Kitten."

"Oh, I won't be driving Kitten."

"Wanna bet? She grows on you. A bit like me." Lauren offered her cheekiest grin. "And you know how well we worked out."

"You know, I think Mariella is right," Catherine said with a smile. "A dance is an excellent idea. I've seen what's on the playlist, and the songs won't stay this good. That catfish man hollering about his big black pickup truck is coming up. So, darling wife, may I have the pleasure?"

Lauren melted into the warmth of Catherine's arms sliding around her. They swayed in the dancing shadows from the fire pit, the lights of the willow tree twinkling behind them, the swell of music enfolding them. Half a dozen more couples joined in, and beyond their flowing forms were happy voices, roars of laughter, clinks of bottles, and a feeling of abundant good will.

"You were right," Catherine murmured. "The tiki bar is an excellent area for a party."

"I know, right?"

"And don't look now, but your gay brother's trying to secretly take his love for a spin."

Lauren almost gave herself whiplash trying to see who it was. And there was Tommy, in the darkest shadows, under the edge of the willow tree where he presumably thought he was out of sight, arms wrapped around his girlfriend's brother, Nick. Or not-girlfriend, she corrected herself, given the way Candice was smiling at them both from behind her mixer deck.

"Oh. Wow."

"So now you're not the only one," Catherine said quietly.

"You know, I had my money on John. But good for Tommy. It doesn't matter anyway. Not in my family."

"Our family," Catherine whispered. Her eyes were dark and soft.

Lauren's throat tightened. "Oh," she said, overcome with emotions. She kissed her gently on the cheek. "Yeah. Like 'em or not, they're both of ours now."

The music shifted. And suddenly there were masculine whoops of delight. The crowd gleefully took up the tune. Voices raised to the heavens, bottles clinked, and feet stomped, as they shared lyrics about jacked-up trucks, rows of corn, and catfish dinners.

"Oh yes." Catherine's voice was dry as gin. The affection in her eyes undid her tone. "All ours."

Chapter 28
Pillow Talk

LAUREN TOOK IN THEIR BED-AND-BREAKFAST and sighed happily. Their room was perfect. Huge, beautiful, and above all else, quiet. She dropped their bags by the bed and led Catherine on a tour.

"Mrs. Potts wasn't kidding about the shower," Lauren said as she stuck her head in the bathroom. "I've never seen one bigger."

"Well, you did specifically ask her for a 'sweet place with a huge shower.'"

"True. She must have thought I thoroughly valued cleanliness."

"Oh, I'm quite certain that's *not* what she thought."

Lauren laughed. "Well, either way, I'm a big fan of showers. In fact, the one at your place in LA left me some very…lasting…memories."

"I know the feeling. On that note, you must be dying to give this one a try. Do you want to go first? I'd like to unpack."

Lauren understood even though she felt a stir of disappointment. Catherine always liked having things squared away before she could really relax. Some A-type personality thing.

She grabbed her essentials and disappeared into the bathroom. Within five minutes, the room was full of steam, and all her muscles started to sing in relief.

Scenes flashed through her head of the wedding highlights. It had been a perfect day. The croquembouche cake? Food of the gods. Her dad's speech had been as affectionate as Josh's and Mark's were risqué and hilarious in turn. But it was Mariella's words, as matron of honor, that Lauren still turned over in her head. She closed her eyes.

"I watched Lauren fall in love before my eyes," Mariella told the hushed crowd. "More than that, I watched her stride up to the most intimidating reporter that ever was, without a moment's hesitation or fear. It's as if she looked into Catherine's eyes and saw what was always there. What no one else had noticed. And those two have been fighting love, finding love, and everything in between from the day they met. It was life affirming, entertaining, and so beautiful. Witnessing it was like drifting near a fire. Powerful, intense, and heated."

Lauren's thoughts then drifted to Catherine. Her gift to Lauren—exposing her heart in front of everyone. She had no words for how much it meant.

There was a small noise and she looked around. The fogged-up shower door opened.

Catherine stood before her, sleek, beautiful…and very naked. "I thought we should re-create our first time," she said, her voice a purr. "Only with fewer clothes on my part."

Desire shot through Lauren. Her breath hitched as her gaze swept Catherine's nude form. She stepped aside to make room. "Yes. Great idea. Best ever."

Catherine stepped under the shower stream, closed her eyes, and tilted her head back, allowing the rivulets of water to streak across her skin. She carded her fingers through her hair, thoroughly wetting it. Angling her head to one side, Catherine's fingers then roamed across her neck, and down to her breasts.

Lauren dropped the soap.

A low chuckle sounded. Catherine's soft, amused gaze locked with Lauren's. "Focus, King," she said, her tone promising all sorts of naughty deeds, "Or you might miss something." She stepped forward and slid her hands to Lauren's shoulders, before pulling her into her arms.

Breast to breast, stomach to stomach, Lauren felt her mind empty of coherent thoughts.

Catherine's mouth dropped to Lauren's neck and her lips began a leisurely exploration.

The sensation of heat, from the soft lips, fingers, and coursing water, was sensory overload. Catherine's fingers danced down to Lauren's ass, sliding across and kneading the skin.

"Remember our first night?" Catherine asked in a husky voice. "You offered yourself to me after we'd had our brush with death."

"Well, I remember you said no," Lauren teased her with a pout, "and then sent me to my room. All alone."

"Yes, well, my resolve lasted all of five minutes before I stormed your shower."

"Now *that* was unexpected."

Pleasure curled from Lauren's center as Catherine slid a hand to her stomach and performed a taunting swirl.

"It was…shocking…how badly I wanted you that night," Catherine admitted. "I was so tired of fighting my need for you. It was unsettling enough that you'd been featuring in my dreams." Her fingers pushed lower, sliding through swollen flesh.

"That feels so good." Lauren sighed. She rocked against her hand. "I dreamt about you, too."

Catherine's teeth nibbled Lauren's ear lobe. The slippery sounds of fingers entering soaked flesh rose above the stream of falling water. "Tell me everything," she urged Lauren.

"We were in Nevada." Lauren swallowed hard as her pleasure rose. "I'd had a bad dream. You rushed into my room and leaned over me, and, um… well, there was a lot of cleavage."

"Lauren," Catherine whispered, "that actually happened."

"Not the part where I reached inside your shirt and touched you. Not the part where my mouth tasted your breasts. And not the part where I pushed you down on the bed, ran my hands up your thighs, and found you weren't wearing anything at all under that shirt. You looked into my eyes and told me I could touch you anywhere. I'm sure I'd remember that actually happening."

"As would I." Her voice was tight.

"In my dreams, you came silently." Lauren slid her fingers toward Catherine's center. "You're always hiding what you feel, even in my dreams. But then you gasped out my name." She slipped inside her, welcomed by the heat and wetness she found.

"You like that, don't you?" Catherine's breath hot against her ear. "Watching me unravel."

"You already know it's the hottest thing for me. I love watching you come undone." She plunged inside her, over and over. The tremble told her Catherine was close. "Like now." Lauren slipped her fingers up to her most sensitive spot.

Catherine gasped.

"Look at you trying so hard not to come." Lauren pressed hard, just where Catherine loved it. "But I'm going to make you anyway." She swiped her clit lightly, then pressed against it.

Catherine's whole body went taut, she gave a small cry, then slumped toward the shower wall, taking Lauren with her. Catherine's arm shot out to brace herself against the wall. Water crashed over them, and Lauren kept stroking her, waiting for the waves to pass, overcome as always that she had the power to pull apart this beautiful, intriguing woman.

Catherine's eyes fluttered opened, glazed with desire. She raked a gaze over Lauren—her confident and commanding self once more—the look that ruined Lauren every single time.

"We need to get out of the shower," Catherine murmured. "Because I have an idea. One I think you'll like very much."

"Get onto the bed," Catherine demanded, voice low and daring, "and close your eyes."

Lauren eagerly did as she was instructed, ears straining to work out what Catherine was up to. She heard the zip of a suitcase. A faint rustling and nothing more.

The bed dipped on the edge, and Catherine's hot breath was suddenly across her face.

"King?" she said.

The timbre of her voice hurtled Lauren back to a different time—when they didn't have affection for each other and it was more like molten heat, barbs, and prickles.

Her eyes flashed open. Catherine was leaning over her, wearing the same white button-up shirt she'd had on in Nevada, the night she'd woken Lauren from her nightmare.

"Cath…" She paused at her lover's half-lidded look. "*Ayers.*" Because that's most definitely who was now crouched over her. Arousal slithered through her. Delicious.

"Who else?" Catherine drawled. "That perky Carson City concierge downstairs?" She leaned forward, and Lauren had a most deliberate, unimpeded view down her shirt.

Bare, beautiful breasts tipped by deep red nipples bobbed into view. Lauren swallowed. She slid her hand up, into the shirt, cupping the nearest breast.

Catherine's breath hitched. "That's bold," she hissed. "How do you know I even like wome—"

Lauren sat up, scooping the breast out from the shirt, and latched onto the erect nipple and began to suck. Hard.

"*Oh.*" The pained word was dragged from Catherine's throat.

"You like this," Lauren murmured into the soft flesh. "Don't you, Ayers? More than you'll ever admit. Doesn't fly with your icy image, though, does it? Desperately wanting some hayseed from Iowa."

Catherine's eyes had darkened. "You have no idea what I want."

"No?" Lauren's hand slowly meandered up Catherine's inner thigh, tickling and teasing. When she neared the junction of her legs, she paused.

Catherine's breathing stopped.

Pulling away from her breast, Lauren gave her a knowing look. "I wonder how icy you really are? Or does your maddening colleague with ugly tractor caps secretly do it for you?" She rolled them over and crouched over her.

Catherine's nostrils flared as Lauren's fingertips slid up until they brushed against her trimmed thatch of dark hair, already slick.

"Naughty," Lauren whispered. "So is it true you weren't wearing anything at all under this shirt that night?"

"It was too hot to," Catherine murmured. "I threw this on when you cried out in your sleep."

Lauren's breath hitched at the thought of Catherine sleeping nude the whole time they were in Nevada. Her stomach clenched.

"You're so wet." Lauren ran her fingers through the proof. Her tone turned to a purr. "Dripping even."

Catherine's eyes took on a wicked gleam, and in a flash she was back to the imperious woman Lauren had first met. "Of course you would assume that's about you, King."

Lauren's own eyes narrowed as she plotted her revenge for that line. Her expression earned her an amused twist of lips.

She rubbed her thumb over Catherine's clit, admiring how slippery the flesh was. "So me touching you like this doesn't do anything to you?" She thumbed over it, then slid up one side, winning a small, tight huff. "Nothing?"

Catherine said through gritted teeth, "*Ah*. No. Of course, I don't—"

Lauren plunged her fingers inside her, curling them up, until she felt a telltale shudder ripple through her lover. As she removed them, her thumb flicked her clit. She repeated it over and over until Catherine's groan wrenched from her chest. "Oh!"

Lauren pulled out her fingers and grabbed at Catherine's shirt. With feverish fingers, she wrenched the buttons apart until she could see all of her. She needed her naked and spread out before her.

Stormy eyes stared up at her, burning with need.

Lauren pushed Catherine's thighs apart and feasted on the sight in front of her. "Not indifferent to me after all, then." She leaned forward and blew softly on her sensitive skin. She darted her tongue out just to flick her. Barely touching.

"Ah," Catherine whispered. Her chest rose and fell quickly. "Ki—" She sucked in a breath and tried again. "*King.*"

"You want me," Lauren goaded her. *Flick*. "You always have. Even when you fought with me and pretended you didn't want me, you did." *Flick*.

Catherine actually whimpered.

"Didn't you?"

"God," Catherine gasped, her breathing quickening. "Even when you made me furious, I thought you were so damned attractive."

"Good." Lauren slid her body on top of her, relishing the heat Catherine's body was throwing off. She pressed her thigh between Catherine's legs and leaned up to kiss her.

The kiss was like the first time, passionate and desperate, tongues and teeth clashing, fighting for air and with an untamed, primal neediness. It was wanton and hot, and it took everything Lauren had not to come from the intensity of it.

Catherine's exquisite fingers sought out her nipples, pulling and squeezing, as Lauren began to push and grind herself against Catherine's thigh.

"Fuck, oh, I think... I'm going to..." Lauren groaned as she came. She hadn't even realized how close she was. "Oh my God." The quivers ricocheted around her body.

Catherine's throaty chuckle was silenced when Lauren's fingers fell between her lover's thighs and took her in rough, fierce strokes. "No gloating. Not when you're on the edge, too."

A rush of warmth coated Lauren's fingers. Catherine's sensuous neck arched back, and her groan was long and deep. She gave a soft, satisfied sigh, as she relaxed slowly back down onto the sheets.

"Oh, Lauren," she said, reverting to the familiar tone that oozed affection.

"Catherine," Lauren murmured, unable to believe how aroused her wife could get her. "Making love to you is gonna kill me one of these days."

"Probably." Catherine huffed out a breath and sat up. "That was intense. And exceedingly fun."

"Oh yeah."

"But just so you know, you were never just some hayseed from Iowa to me." She eyed her. "You were always much more, even when we were barely friends."

Lauren chuckled. "Oh, I know."

"Just for that smugness, I'll tell you something else. That night in Nevada?" She cocked her eyebrow. "I knew you peeked down my shirt."

Despite the heat that suddenly rushed to her cheeks, Lauren couldn't help but grin. "There's a coincidence. Because I know I peeked, too."

Chapter 29
Out of the Rabbit Hole

CATHERINE AWOKE TO THE SENSATION of Lauren's tongue slowly sliding up her leg. She cracked an eyelid.

Well, this wasn't unpleasant in the least. Her body twitched in awareness of the ascent of Lauren's tongue. "What's the occasion?" she murmured.

"We got married yesterday. Oh, and our stories should be out today. I wanted to properly celebrate."

"Ah. You wanted the first full day of our honeymoon to go off with a bang *and* a whimper." Catherine smiled.

"Word puns during sex? I must not be distracting you enough." With that, Lauren's tongue found its goal.

Warm heat coursed through her as Lauren's mouth thoroughly claimed her center. A finger slid inside her, followed by a second. Lauren's eyes were bright as she licked Catherine harder.

"You love making me squirm," Catherine whispered. "But wasn't yesterday enough of me doing that?"

"Never enough. Never tiring of you. Or this. What can I say? You're just so unflappable, so I like making you...flappable."

Catherine widened her legs, loving how warm and languid she felt. "No objections." How right this felt. She sank into Lauren.

Her gasp turned to moans as Lauren began curling her fingers up and slipping her teeth across her most sensitive spots. "There," Catherine gasped. "Don't stop. *Oh.*"

Lauren smiled against her and sped up her dance across her slippery flesh.

Catherine's pleasure peaked. It wasn't hard and explosive like some orgasms. It was a swelling of bliss, gentle and enveloping. It curled her toes and tightened her thighs and her back to form a perfect, taut arch. The rush of warmth was intoxicating, as was the sensation of Lauren's lips all over her.

She slumped back, the flooding endorphins making her boneless and happy. "Marry me," she ordered. "This instant."

"Sorry, sweetheart, I'm spoken for." Lauren slithered up her body. "But I wouldn't be opposed to a bit of hanky panky with you. You're sexy as hell."

"Ah," Catherine said. "By all means, then." She slipped her fingers down Lauren's body and found the heat between her legs.

"You won't have to do much," Lauren confessed. "I almost came when I was trying to wake you up. God, you're so beautiful."

"As are you." Catherine slipped her fingers between Lauren's thighs and buried them inside her. "I love that I turn you on so much."

"You do. God, yeah." She wriggled impatiently.

Her sigh was strained as Catherine began to work faster. There was little resistance. The heel of Catherine's hand pressed against her clit.

"You look so delicious. Maybe I'll taste you next," Catherine teased. "How will that feel? My mouth all over you? Tongue inside you? Is that what you thought about on those long nights in Nevada alone in your hotel room? Did you touch yourself and think of me?"

Lauren stiffened, her body clenching around Catherine's fingers, as she gave a tight cry.

After Catherine withdrew her fingers, she slowly licked them. "So you did?" Her eyebrow lifted.

"No. But it seems I really enjoyed the idea." Lauren exhaled. "God, I want to go again, but I'm still a bit wiped. After all, I had two lovers keeping me on my toes yesterday. You *and* Ayers."

Catherine smiled and drew her close, loving the feel of her body next to hers. They stayed that way for a lazy half hour.

"I suppose we'll have to get up soon," Lauren eventually muttered. "But I don't want to."

"On the other hand, it's our honeymoon," Catherine reasoned. "We don't need to be anywhere."

"But the stories..."

"Mmm. Yes, I can definitely see the appeal of another big scoop. Or you can play with my breasts again." She shifted Lauren's hand to her body part in question. "You decide."

After a shower came lunch, which comprised croissants and more idle playing with breasts. Lauren finally couldn't take not knowing. She grabbed the iPad and logged on to the *Post*'s website. Catherine, with a resigned huff, did the same at the *Daily Sentinel* with her phone.

"Good God," Catherine said.

"Holy…" Lauren whispered. Her heart started pounding. "Did we just melt down the interwebs?"

"Looks like it. The *Sentinel*'s running an AP recap of your story," Catherine said. "'Privacy Uproar as FBI Steals Veterans' Data for its Criminal Database.'"

"It's everywhere." Lauren's fingers swiped through the headlines quickly. "Hey, so's Fiona. All the TV networks have interviewed her after your story."

"Good—she's an exceptional witness. Her outrage should be everyone's."

"Ooh, she's found a lawyer who's threatening a class action for all the veterans. Looks like Lesser would have lost his bet. He told me she'd never sue."

"Did you see the Reuters story? Ansom's announced it's shutting down MediCache, subject to a review of its software." Catherine tapped the screen and stared at it for a long moment. She slowly slid her gaze to Lauren. "Lauren, it's also closing its Iowa plant. Looks like my father thinks tossing Iowa out as a scapegoat will contain the damage to Ansom's share price."

"Damn it!" Lauren scowled. "Hell. John and his colleagues don't deserve this."

"No, they don't. Ansom Iowa makes a hell of a lot more than those chips." Catherine sighed.

"I have to call home."

Catherine passed over her phone. "Here."

Lauren bit her lip and dialed. The phone answered on the second ring, with a familiar voice. "Meemaw," she replied. "I just heard the news. I'm so sorry."

"Lauren, dear, why are you calling us on your honeymoon?"

"I heard about John. And the plant, I..."

"Your brother is fine. He was expecting it, after all, thanks to Catherine giving him the head's up. We all were. And your father's offered him a job for as long or short as he wants it, so he won't be moping about long."

"Oh. That's good. Can I talk to John?"

"Not unless you call the Whiskey River. His friends from work decided to drown their sorrows there."

"Ah. No, I won't get in the way of that."

"I'll tell him you called when he gets home. But he doesn't blame you—either of you."

"Okay." Lauren sucked in a breath. "But he *is* fine?"

"He is. Now go, act like a newlywed and disappear off the face of the Earth for the rest of the week."

Meemaw ended the call.

Lauren stared at the phone for a moment, then passed it back to Catherine. "She says he's fine. Out getting drunk with his work buddies by the sound of it."

"Ah."

"I still feel terrible. Even though I know we had to run the story."

"That's natural. But try not to feel guilty. This one's entirely on my father."

Lauren returned to refreshing her news screen. She clicked the next story, a local one which had interviewed the Iowan senator. "Hickory's furious about the plant closing. He's calling it revenge for him going on the record against Ansom." Her eyes widened. "And they've responded by saying he loved the chip until a day ago. They're suggesting he knew all along about the data scooping." Lauren shook her head. "He didn't, though. He almost swallowed his tongue when I told him the secret behind what he'd been talking up."

"Well, it's war," Catherine said. "Ansom will throw everyone at it they can to avoid scrutiny closer to their own HQ. And my father did say Hickory was going to be a scapegoat."

"Oh!" Lauren sat up. "Breaking news. 'FBI Director on Leave Pending Investigation.'"

"That explains the three missed calls from Diane." Catherine paused, looking guilty. "Neil's emailed, asking how much I knew about the story and why his paper doesn't have a piece of it." She began tapping out a reply to her editor. "I'm going to say that I knew you were writing it, but it's entirely your story."

"Will he believe that? I mean, everyone just assumes…" She trailed off.

Catherine stopped typing. She studied Lauren. "I'm not totally oblivious, you know."

"What do you mean?"

"I'm sorry I didn't think of it when I originally outed us both, but later I realized what it would mean for you. That your colleagues would assume I'd done most of the work on the SmartPay scoop, not you. Even though you never said anything about it, I figured…"

Lauren swallowed. "You knew?"

"I know newsrooms. So with this story, you got to show them how good you are."

"Is that why you gave me the story?" Confusion lit her eyes.

"No. I was honest about my reasons. But this is a nice side effect, don't you think? Your story is brilliant, Lauren."

"Catherine, *you* got the Lionel quotes. *You* got Lesser to spill by figuring out what would get him to turn on his associates."

"Both sources were not strong enough without someone official giving it credibility. Lauren, somehow you got a sitting US senator to admit to being part of a planned FBI operation to fake a terrorism arrest in order to prove the worth of a data chip they want to exploit. Do you understand how big that is?" Her expression became suddenly curious. "How *did* you do that, anyway?"

"I learned from you with Lesser and figured out what mattered to Hickory. I appealed to him, one Iowan to another. Explained how bad the whole state would look if those slick big-city weasels pinned this on him. We know how you DC types look down on us." She poked Catherine in the ribs. "We're always the butt of elitist jokes. He knew exactly what I was talking about. Eventually, he agreed he should get ahead of the story, put his version out first before he got thrown to the wolves by Lionel. It helped that Hickory was so damned outraged at being used. And he decided he wanted to be on the same side as you this time, since last time you did such a thorough job of shredding him."

"He deserved that. Quantitative easing for Iowa? *Please.*" Catherine's phone beeped. "Ah. Diane's telling me the stood-down FBI director's just told staff he's resigning. He's doing it rather than be investigated and is refusing to comment on anything."

"Confirmation in itself," Lauren said. "I'd say all the cockroaches are trying to scuttle into the dark corners now."

"On that note, did you see Ansom's media release? They have outed Lesser as a racist right-winger responsible for My Evil Twin. Ansom asks how can anyone trust anything a racist says, let alone believe a word he says against Ansom? Oh...unbelievable...the company's including a link at the bottom of the statement to my Evil Twin piece!"

"Who said your dad never appreciated your writing?" Lauren joked.

"Lesser won't like that one bit. He was fine with being a racist. Not fine with all of America knowing and judging him."

"Why do I suspect a doxing is in your dad's future?" Lauren asked.

"I'd say the odds are high."

"And somehow, I don't think Lionel will appreciate a ton of garlic, pineapple, and anchovy pizzas landing on his doorstep as much as my brothers did."

"I think it might get a lot worse for him than just pizza. Let's just say my father has a lot of secrets he'll want to stay buried. And Lesser has the ability to dig them up."

"Couldn't happen to a nicer guy. Oh, sorry. I know he's still your dad."

Catherine eyed her. "You heard the tape. He's done with me. It's mutual." She shifted closer. "Now, let's put our devices away. Toss work on the back burner. We've done our duty. Saved the world." Her lips curled. "How about we congratulate ourselves a bit more?"

A few hours later, there was a soft knock at the door. Lauren was snoozing on the bed. Catherine, wearing a robe and nothing else, was amusing herself, finishing off reading the media mogul's biography. She padded to the door. "Who is it?"

"Phoebe."

Lauren rolled over and cracked an eyelid. "Tell her it's damned rude to crash someone's honeymoon," she grumbled.

Catherine couldn't disagree. Her eyes fell to the expanse of skin along Lauren's back and decided the view was almost too attractive to open the door. A sheet barely covered the swell of her ass. The play of muscles was calling for Catherine to trace them.

"Want me to take the meeting in the hall? Spare your blushes?"

"Why should you be put out? She's interrupting a honeymoon—she deserves whatever she gets." Lauren's eyes had a mischievous gleam. She stretched, the sheet dropping lower. She pulled it up, but only a little.

Catherine cracked the door.

"Phoebe." She tilted her head. "I'm on my honeymoon."

"I know. I'm sorry. That crazy grandmother, Mrs. Haverson, told me that about fifty times when I turned up and asked where you were. I need to talk to you." She eyed the door pointedly.

"We're not exactly set up for guests." Catherine gestured at her robe.

"But it's urgent. Please can I come in? Just for a minute."

Catherine sighed. She stepped back, letting in the younger woman who, in many ways, looked a lot like her—except for her constant nervous energy. She was always moving. Her dyed blonde hair was impeccably curled into a style Catherine always thought of as "primetime newsreader." Earrings, pearl. Dress, designer. Heels, ridiculously high, ridiculously expensive. She was more their mother's clone with every passing day.

Phoebe entered, shoulders rigid, her gaze darting about.

Catherine stepped quickly past her, blocking most of Lauren's sprawled body from her sister. Lauren rolled over and sat up, shifting the sheet to fully cover everything but her bare shoulders. She ran a hand through her chaotic bed hair.

"Oh!" Phoebe caught a glimpse of her and blushed.

Well, what was she expecting? Catherine rolled her eyes.

"I am so sorry to intrude," Phoebe babbled. "Hi, you're obviously Lauren. It's nice to meet you at last."

Lauren rubbed sleep out of her eyes and her natural politeness seemed to return, because she said, "Hey, Phoebe. Same here."

Catherine closed the door and leaned against it. "So. You missed the wedding."

"I know. I'm sorry. Miles needed me at work. I do some secretarial stuff there now."

"You didn't call or text."

A silence fell. The tension felt thick as a fog.

"I'm sorry. I was really busy."

"So you took the job? The one Dad's always been trying to foist on me for decades?"

"Only part time." She folded her arms. "I go in when things get busy. Like now."

"Mm. Coffee?" Catherine led her into the kitchenette, in a nook out of sight of the bed area. From behind her, she could hear the rustle of sheets as Lauren doubtlessly got up to dress.

"How are things?" Phoebe asked.

"Seriously, Phoebe? Things?"

"All right, how was your wedding?"

Catherine spooned granules into two cups, knowing Lauren wouldn't want any at this time of day. She put the coffee pot on. "It was beautiful. It would have been better if your son wasn't the only member of my entire family in attendance."

"I know." Phoebe's voice took on a pleading quality. "I'm sorry."

"So Dad suggested you not come?"

Phoebe licked her lips.

Catherine glared. "Since when does filing paperwork take precedence over your only sister's wedding?"

"I feel really bad about that, truly. But it was a crisis situation. You have no idea. Dad said you were maybe about to run a big story on us, and it'd be bad. Miles is so stressed. He's starting to suspect that..." She ran a shaky hand down her dress. "He thinks Dad might shift the blame on him for MediCache's software. Because Miles was on the committee that approved Douglas Lesser being chosen to design it. But Miles had no idea what it really did. None. And Dad's suddenly saying he must have. Dad's starting to... I mean, he's as bad as I've ever seen him."

"I'm sorry about your husband. But our father deserves whatever's coming to him."

"I know."

"What?" Catherine thought she must be hearing things. Phoebe's Stockholm syndrome had been tedious for years. Their parents could never do any wrong in her eyes.

"Better late than never, right?" Phoebe said, giving her a wry look. "This chip business has gone too far. I'm now expected to choose Dad over my own husband? That's… It's too much. So for once in my life, I've picked a side."

"Which side is that, exactly?" Catherine passed a coffee to Phoebe and gathered her own.

They made their way back to the open-plan living/bedroom area.

Lauren was dressed in a long-sleeved T-shirt and shorts, sitting cross-legged on the bed, facing the living area. Catherine sighed inwardly that she was being kept from her beautiful wife right now by this invidious topic.

On the other hand, it was earth-shattering news if Phoebe had actually grown a backbone for once in her life. A faint seed of hope blossomed inside her. She directed her sister to the pair of armchairs facing each other, a coffee table between them.

"Well, I'm on Miles's side, of course," Phoebe said. "But yours, too. I've brought something for you."

Phoebe reached into her shoulder bag and then slid a manila folder onto the table. "This is what Dad's so afraid of. It's the minutes of the meeting between Dad, Lesser, the FBI director, and a few others in various security agencies, about the data-sharing idea."

"Data stealing, you mean." Catherine eyed the folder. "It's not some friendly information exchange. It's taking personal, private, health, and biometric information from people without their permission and putting it in a criminal database. A database that's so unsecure, even Lesser was cavalierly milking its contents for his racist little app."

"I know."

"How did you get this?" She pointed at the unopened folder.

"Miles. He took it as an insurance policy."

"And your husband—who is one of the most risk-averse men in existence—has suddenly decided his house is on fire?'

"Actually, it was my idea. I told him he had to use it now. I was afraid Miles would just sit back and allow Dad to use him as a sacrificial lamb. He always sees the good in people, and he hoped Dad would do the right thing and protect those loyal to him."

Catherine gave a faint snort.

"I know what you think of Miles, Catherine. That he's dull and safe and a bit too trusting. But he's a good man. He's decent, he's been kind to me, and he doesn't deserve to be blamed for this."

"Did he take much convincing?"

Phoebe shook her head. "He can see the writing on the wall. And you and I both know when Dad decides you're not on his side, you're gone. Look, this wasn't easy for him to get, but here. Take it. Do what you have to." Phoebe pushed the folder closer to her. "Use it."

Catherine regarded the folder for a moment as she sipped her coffee. Her gaze flicked back to her sister. Phoebe tilted her head to one side, looking pensive. The familiarity of the movement struck her. It really was odd, sometimes, how similar they both were most of the time.

Except for now.

"Do you remember when we were young," Catherine said, "and you sneaked into Nanny Michaels' bedroom and took her ring? The opal one you loved. You liked to look at it in the light outside. And she found it missing and was going to go to Mom."

"I remember."

"And I was the one who convinced her not to. I explained it's just how you are, drawn to colorful things, and you don't think things through. You never meant any harm. You weren't stealing it."

Phoebe looked at her in confusion and nodded.

"Do you remember your first boyfriend? Rick something? I passed along those notes for you and kept them hidden from Mom."

"You did."

"Who protected you when she found one? Who asked her why it wasn't all right for you to have a boyfriend? Who got a hard slap across the face in response?"

Phoebe swallowed. "You were always so brave. I always felt useless next to you."

Catherine studied her hands then balled them. She looked up. "Do you remember when that scandal brought me down? I thought my career was over. Remember how humiliated I was? How shell-shocked? How...broken, given I'd been betrayed personally as well as professionally?"

For a moment, Phoebe didn't reply. And then her voice was a harsh whisper. "Yes."

Catherine's anger rose. "You know what I went through with that. You know how I protected you when we were children. And *this* is how you pay me back? This is what you do to me?"

"What?" Phoebe blinked, horror spreading across her face.

"You think I'd be so stupid as to trust another document from anyone without corroborating evidence?"

"*Catherine.*" Phoebe's face was pure shock. "You think this is faked?"

"Oh, I know it is!"

"If you'd just open it…"

"I don't have to. I've known when you were lying since you were four years old. Tell Dad, thanks for the setup, but I never make the same mistake twice."

"Cather—"

"No. I don't want to hear it." She regarded her. "You know, your son has a hell of a lot more spine than you do."

"Leave Thadeus out of this."

"I have a simpler solution. I'll leave you out of it. Out of everything. What you've done today is so low that we're done. You can go. Tell Dad you failed."

"Catherine!" The plea was heartbreaking.

"What?" She tilted her head. "Catherine, *what?*"

"I'm *so* sorry."

"Sorry you got caught, you mean? Leave."

Phoebe rose and without another word, snatched up her bag. At the door she turned. "By the way, you're wrong about him. About Dad."

"What?"

"The reasons he hired the Fixers on you. I heard him talking to Mom. Something about stopping you before someone else stopped you in a worse way." She shook her head. "You know who his allies are. How high up they go. And if they wanted to, they could have really messed you up. Physically, not just professionally. It just means… Well, Dad's not as bad as you think. He must care if…you know…"

Catherine gaped at her. "Not as bad? You're saying he ruined me back then *in case* someone got it into their head to hurt me? And I should feel grateful that all I got was nationally humiliated and played for a fool? Should I send him a thank-you card?"

"Catherine, he does care about you, underneath everything."

"Really? Is that why he's using one daughter to set up the other? You know what? I don't care how he spins the things he does just so he can sleep at night. I do care about the fact that you—after everything we went through together—went along with this plot." She slammed her hand on the folder. *My own sister.*

"I..."

"Get out of my sight."

Phoebe hesitated, then finally left, closing the door quietly.

Rage, frustration, and nausea flooded Catherine. She felt Lauren's presence as Catherine tried to control her breathing. Warm fingers slid around her shoulders, offering comfort.

"Oh, Catherine. I'm really sorry."

The voice was soft and sad, and Catherine didn't want to hear it. Not right now. She had no wish to start unraveling, like some ball of string without end. Over what, anyway? Her scheming family that always put her last?

"Did you believe her?" Lauren asked. "About his reasons for betraying you the first time?"

"I know my sister believes it, but that doesn't mean much. She always believes him. I no longer care. They've shown what I am to them—something to be used and discarded. The reasons why are irrelevant." Catherine flipped open the manila folder and scanned its contents. "Juicy. Just the way he knew I'd like it. Do you know what's pathetic? This time, my ex-girlfriend was telling the truth, and it was my own sister who was setting me up."

She glanced up at Lauren's paling features. Catherine handed her the folder. "Do me a favor? Take some photos of this on the iPad, then email a copy to Lesser. Explain where we got it and how. Since he was at this meeting he'll know which parts have been messed with. And, somehow, I have no doubt he'll know exactly what to do with it. Let him." She was surprised how calm her voice sounded. The nausea threatened to rise again.

"Lesser? But he's...."

"Right now, he's the enemy of our enemy."

"Your father's officially the enemy now?"

Catherine exhaled. "Not just him." The horror of what had just happened hit her again. "Now it's my... It's all of them. Phoebe, too."

"*Catherine.*" Lauren wrapped her in a sideways hug. "I wish I could make this better."

"So do I. Phoebe never did have much of a backbone, but I never thought she'd stoop to this." Her jaw clenched. "Well, if I was on the fence before about my father's fate, I have no pity for whatever happens to him now."

"How did you know? About Phoebe lying? You sounded so certain."

"She'd never defy anyone. Her story was ludicrous. The moment she talked about convincing that stubborn husband of hers he *had* to do things, I knew. Saddest thing is, she knew that I'd know. She tried it anyway. That is the weakest sort of human there is. I cannot believe we're related."

"I'm really sorry. But at least you still have Tad in your corner. And me. And, oh, a million Kings."

"Yes." Catherine dearly wished that that alone could will away the hurt still churning in her stomach.

Chapter 30
Farewell, Iowa

HONEYMOONS WERE NOT LONG ENOUGH, Catherine decided, as a cab drove them back to the Kings' place to farewell the family.

She had drawn into herself these past few days. Catherine had spent longer in bed, making love to Lauren, showing how much she meant to her, and Lauren had responded in kind.

They both knew what it meant. Catherine wanted to show the person in her life who appreciated her most how much she mattered. That Catherine was now investing all her energies and focus only on those who cared about her in return. That list was presently standing at two—Lauren and Tad.

Not quite true, a voice whispered in her head. *And you know it.*

She gazed out the window, unwilling to give that thought voice. She might have been overcome on her wedding day and had claimed Lauren's family as her own. But it was still hard for her. She'd spent so long protecting herself. Ironic, really, since the betrayer who'd hurt her just as much as Michelle had been inside her walls all along. Phoebe had probably hurt her more.

Her thoughts shifted to the documents. Lauren had sent them to Lesser. He had called them fake and spread them to the whole world. It was a clever gambit, because a guilty man would never spread around incriminating evidence. Somehow, that cunning little eel kept sounding like the honest one in this entire mess. Every single official at that think-tank meeting was now squirming and slithering like a worm on a hook.

Ansom had hit back with its now standard "racists can't be trusted" line. And that's when Lesser had pulled out his ace card. He'd called a news conference.

"It's well known from Lauren King's story that I'm a whistleblower," he'd said, injecting every bit of emotion into his outraged voice, "and this racism claim is all part of a terrible and cruel campaign to discredit me by a dishonest corporation."

Catherine had to hand it to the slippery piece of work. It was genius. The moment he'd done the deal to be named as their informant, he'd clearly worked out where all this was heading. He was always intending to spin himself as a martyr, even if his white-supremacist secret caught up with him. He simply supplied a motive, suggesting anyone who attacked him or called him a racist had an agenda to bring him down.

Shares had been dropping steadily at Ansom all morning.

Hickory was having mixed fortunes among his constituents, with opinions divided. His rage at Ansom closing the Iowa factory had prevented his approval ratings from going through the floor.

Only Lesser had somehow emerged smelling sweet. My Evil Twin was yesterday's calamity, virtually forgotten, especially with much bigger fish to fry. He was setting the agenda and pointing fingers away from himself with his usual smug prowess.

And in the middle of it all, my own family tried to ruin me.

Catherine exhaled. She turned. Lauren's expression was wistful as she studied the flashes of fields passing by. "How are you doing?" she asked.

Lauren shrugged. "I'll miss us having this quality time together. I'll also miss being home. I know you like to make fun of it, but it really... It makes my heart lighter being here."

The green of the farms whizzing past caught Catherine's gaze. It all screamed solidness. Sustenance. Basic needs and comfort. All the things Lauren was, too. Everywhere, there were people with dust on their jeans, comfortable boots, easy grins. Catherine was in a land of big, black pickup trucks, horizons of endless stars, and proud growers of prized legumes.

She had been born into obscene wealth and had wanted for nothing, materially. She'd also been surrounded by cynicism, cunning, and elitist condescension.

The divides between her and Lauren's worlds were enormous. She tried to work out what it meant. How to resolve who she had been and who she was now. Who she loved.

They pulled up into Lauren's driveway and deposited their bags by the front door. They'd be leaving soon enough for the airport. Not much point hauling them in.

There was a slap and bang of the screen door flinging open as Meemaw came flying out, wiping her hands on a dish towel.

"Ah! I thought I heard you." She rushed over to Lauren and enveloped her in one of those trademark hugs—all squeezes and butt wiggles and feet off the ground.

Then, before Catherine could object, she was swept up in one, too.

Two weeks ago, she'd have endured it with a grimace, her mind supplying an acerbic commentary about personal boundary issues. Instead, she allowed it. Her hands slid around Meemaw's broad back and squeezed her thoroughly in return. It was like soul food, a hug from this woman. Encompassing, soft, and warm.

And it actually felt...good.

She was deposited back on her patch of dirt. Meemaw sized her up, then produced a broad, knowing smile. "Family now." She pointed to the glitter of her wedding ring. "So you get the hugs that come with it."

A smile tugged at Catherine's lips. "Ah."

"Come in, come in. The boys are having an early lunch before they take you to the airport. There's pork sandwiches if you'd like them." She glanced at Catherine. "Also made you a salad. In case my signature dish isn't to your tastes."

Catherine's felt warmth flood her at the gesture. "Thank you."

"Lauren, can you go on in, turn the pot off on the stove? I think I left it on. And my legs aren't what they used to be."

With a nod, Lauren headed through door. The moment she was gone, Meemaw rounded on Catherine.

"Well?"

"What?"

"What's going on? Are you two okay?" she asked. "I've seen happier cattle in the slaughterhouse."

"A lot's happened. Not between us. We're fine. In the wider world, I mean."

"That it has. Your sister came by here to find you. Did you sort things out with her?"

"Yes." Catherine's fingers clenched into fists. She offered a tight smile. "I believe I did."

"Good. That's good."

Not really.

Meemaw's smile was encouraging. "Come inside. There's someone who misses you. Well…someone *else*."

Catherine eyed her. "Who?"

"You'll see."

She followed Meemaw past the wooden screened door, which shut behind them with a satisfying slap. Immediately, Miss Chesterfield leapt from a stand near the entry and began to wrap herself around Catherine's ankles.

"Been sitting there every day since you've been gone, sulking, waiting for you. I was highly offended, I don't mind telling you." Meemaw's eyes crinkled.

Catherine bent down and gave the white-haired feline a thorough scratch behind the ears. "I've missed her, too. Turns out I'm a cat person." Rising again, Catherine glanced at her. "Is John okay?"

"He'll be fine. Better question is, will you? And whatever's going on with you?"

"I'll be fine. Eventually." Catherine half convinced herself it was true. She looked around the living room, taking in the care-worn furniture and timber floors. Simple but homey. She could smell the pork on the stove, could hear Lauren's laugh, followed by louder masculine ones.

"You know, I think I'd like to come back sometime, if it's okay with you." Catherine paused. That was not what she'd meant to say at all. She wondered if her confusion showed. Her words felt right, though. No taking it back now, anyway.

"Good. Christmas?" Meemaw suggested.

Catherine had an astonishing moment of realizing just how much she was looking forward to it. She nodded. "Assuming Lauren can get time off work, too, then yes."

"That's settled, then. Come on in and join us for lunch. You must have worked up an appetite."

Surely Meemaw wasn't alluding to their honeymoon? Catherine peered at her. For the first time since the nineties, she blushed. "Yes, quite an appetite. It was a long drive."

"Oh, yes. Ten whole minutes." Meemaw sounded amused.

Catherine cleared her throat and glanced behind her. "Come on then, Miss Chesterfield, food's up."

Miss Chesterfield mewed, stuck her tail in the air, gave it a dramatic swish, and trotted after them.

Chapter 31
Clean-up on Aisle 12

LAUREN STARED AT THE REAR wall of the CEO's office at Lesser Security. It was now stripped of all the signs and symbols she'd seen the first time she'd been here.

"Lauren King," Lesser said, as smarmy as ever. "Back in DC so soon? Congratulations on the wedding."

She fidgeted and tried not to be freaked out that he knew they'd gotten married early. DC really was a fishbowl. She hoped that's how he knew, at least. "Redecorating, I see?"

"I've decided I like the *less* personal touch."

"You mean if Catherine could spot your little racist shrine, others might, too?"

His smile didn't even falter. "Actually, I have new plans afoot. Enough about my décor, what do you want?"

"I saw the profile on you today in the *Wall Street Journal*. It made for interesting reading."

"Ah yes, 'America's Rogue Privacy Hero.' Great headline. Even better kicker line—'The man who brought down Ansom and the FBI's chief.' I did like that piece. They captured the essence of my renegade streak."

"Brought down Ansom? Not quite."

"No, not yet. Give it time. Rumor has it there's a secret treasure trove of complaints against Lionel Ayers from the secretarial pool. Not that I'd know anything about where that is or whether a dossier on those outrages will make its way to police soon." He coughed. "Busy boy, your father-in-law. He'll be forced out before too long."

"I see."

"Your lack of surprise is interesting."

Lauren ignored that and folded her arms. "What's next for you?"

"Am I being interviewed? Is this a cozy off-the-record background chat?"

"Sure, we can do that. Look, the *Wall Street Journal* article was vague, and, really, I'm here because I'm curious. The story implied you were let go from your consultancy firm, if 'at a loose end' is a correct interpretation."

He shrugged. "The Fixers don't take betrayal well for some reason. When I became a heroic whistleblower and tipped the dirt on a few of their clients, I got my marching orders. I expected it, but frankly, they're lucky to have had me as long as they did. I have many prospects."

"Which clients?"

"You know I did actually sign a nondisclosure agreement." His eyes narrowed as he seemed to weigh up his options. "But then they fired me. So payback is only fair. They don't scare me."

"They might not, but aren't you afraid of payback from some of the security agencies you've upset?"

"They wouldn't dare. I can tip dirt on everyone and have made provisions that all my files be released if my death is untimely. So I'm untouchable. So...the Fixers' clients that were involved? Ansom, the FBI, and Senator Hickory."

"The FBI was a client?" Lauren was staggered. "Why? Couldn't they do whatever they want themselves?"

"Well, to be specific, it was only the director who used the Fixers, and even then it was mainly for making business connections. Although he did love that they could meddle in gray areas where the FBI was legally hamstrung. So the Fixers did a few small things off the books, here and there, that the FBI had deniability on."

"And Hickory? How'd he end up on their client list?"

"He dragged himself in to see the Fixers in 2012 after your lovely wife had trashed his reputation the first time. He asked the Fixers to find a way to give him more credibility and to kick start his career. Michelle Hastings was assigned as his advisor and told him he had to hitch his star to someone or something on the rise. Around about then, Ansom approached the Fixers for the first time, saying it had some controversial new tech in the works and they needed someone on the Hill to champion it for them. Someone loyal but not too bright. It was a match made in heaven."

"But how—" There was a mechanical whirring sound, and Lauren turned. "What the..."

A white, squat robot was rolling its way toward them. It was identical to Antonio's delivery bot.

Lesser beamed proudly. "Ah, my secretary's sending in lunch. I know, I know, it's a silly gimmick, but I am fond of it. I do like to show off. So sue me."

Lauren blinked. "That's the... I mean, ah...where did you get that?"

"A pizzeria owner sold it to me. I'm fairly sure you can guess which one." His eyes were positively gleaming now. "Said it had done what he needed it to, but he didn't need two of them anymore. One's plenty."

"Um, what did he need it to do?"

"A publicity stunt. He'd reported one stolen and then stashed it away."

"It wasn't even stolen?" Antonio had played her? *Why, that little...*

Lesser laughed at her. "I thought the media were a special kind of stupid the moment you told me that Fiona Fisher story. How could an autonomous delivery unit that *live-streams* its whereabouts be stolen in the first place? That didn't set off alarm bells?"

Uh. *Shit.*

He shook his head. "I knew immediately what Antonio had done. I've always wanted one of these things, so I visited the clever Italian and explained how obvious his con was. I said if I could figure out what he'd done, the cops would, too. I had Antonio half-convinced they were going to raid at any moment, find he still had both his delivery units, one hidden, then arrest him for making a false statement. So he sold his second one to me. Win-win for both of us. I got it for a song." He waved happily at the device at his feet.

Lauren felt a headache coming on. "All this...*all* of it...resulted from a publicity stunt just so Antonio could spread the word that he delivers using a robot?"

He folded his fingers across his stomach and chuckled. "Mm-hmm." Lesser smirked. "So, we're digressing. You asked me what's next. Well, after I finish helping officials with their inquiries into Ansom, I think I'll run for office. I know some folks who'd appreciate a man with my particular...leanings."

A chill flooded her. "Politics? You?"

"I'm well connected. You have no idea how well."

"You'd lose."

"Would I?" He leaned over the robot and unpacked a sandwich. He slapped the lid closed and it did a one-eighty-degree turn and trundled out of the room. "How do you figure that?"

"You're a neo-Nazi who—"

"I prefer *alt-right.*"

"—designs apps that push a white-supremacy subtext."

"Interesting theory. But I see no apps of mine up and running that do what you say." He peeled back the top bread slice on his sandwich, inspecting the ham on it. "And even if true, what part of that would disqualify me from office?"

She stared at him as he bit into on his lunch, robbed of any retort.

He swallowed and smiled. "Even if my winning personality doesn't get me over the line, let's just say you weren't the only one who downloaded my surprise-package PDF from the Fixers. And unlike your vanilla emails— really, King, country music mailing lists? *Star Trek* fan clubs?—I have enough dirt on certain people to get me far up the ladder. Who's going to stop me?"

Lauren's eyes widened. He wasn't wrong.

"See yourself out, Ms. King. It's been fun. Oh, and mind your step around my robot. I'd hate it to get hurt."

Catherine was curled up in bed with a new book when Lauren came home. Her wife trudged into the bedroom and leaned against the door, exhaling heavily. "Hey."

"Hello." Catherine eyed her. "Something wrong?" She slid a bookmark between the pages. "And what can I do to make it right?" She added a little throatiness to the question, to expand the list of options. A girl could hope.

Lauren held up takeout bags. "Chinese—that always makes everything all right. Even hearing about douches who are running for office." She disappeared in the direction of the kitchen.

"*Douches* does not narrow it down," Catherine called out, rising to follow her. After extracting a bottle of wine from the fridge, she plucked two glasses from the shelf. "Who are you railing against now?"

"Douglas *Bastard* Lesser. He's gotten off scot-free. He's everywhere in the news, playing up the hero whistleblower saving America from privacy breaches that he was somehow *forced* to create. And any hint of his racist, creepy side he wipes away under 'Oh, poor me! It's an Ansom smear campaign!' And if that's not all, he told me today he's going to get into politics. He has a big dirt file, so everyone will get the hell out of his way. Catherine, I think he could do it. He has to be stopped, but I don't know how. He's too damned smart and well connected."

She pushed a container of food toward Catherine. "Don't wait for me, or it'll get cold. I just need a quick shower." Lauren trudged from the room.

Catherine laid out two sets of cutlery, poured the wine, and considered the conundrum of the man at the center of the story who was, indeed, far too cunning. A man who had so far outwitted them, and everyone else, at every turn.

A few minutes later, the hiss of water stopped, and Lauren reappeared in yoga pants and a T-shirt. She slid into a chair. "By the way, Lesser hinted he's going to be exposing Lionel Ayers soon over his secretary groping. Between that and the official MediCache investigations, one way or another, your father's about to have all his shit blow up in his face."

Wincing, Catherine reached for her wine glass. Her mother would be horrified. The loss of face alone would torment her for months. For a brief moment, she wondered whether she should warn her.

Why would I, though? I'm not even family anymore to them. Her parents had made that clear.

"So it seems a bit one-sided, Ansom copping all the blame for MediCache," Lauren continued. She began forking through her food. "They *all* did it. But especially Lesser. It was his damned idea, for God's sake."

"I know." Catherine nodded. "I know it's hard, but sometimes you don't get everyone." She speared some noodles on her fork. "Unfortunately."

"And are you okay with that?"

"No. But I'm practical. This isn't over. If Lesser runs for politics, I will make it my life's mission to get him then. Aside from everything else, his racism alone is disgusting. I will make sure he doesn't get away with anything."

"But I really wanted to nail his ass to the wall now," Lauren said with a growl. "With his IT skills, who he knows, who he can blackmail, his dirt files—imagine what he'd be like teamed up with real power."

"He's clever, it's true. He was always two steps ahead of us. He anticipates every move like a chess master. It is annoying."

Lauren looked thoughtful, then took a sip of wine. "Maybe we need to do something basic, then. Think like a pawn."

"Oh?"

"I have an idea. Leave it with me," Lauren said slowly.

"Sure." Catherine wiped her fingers with a paper napkin. Her gaze followed the flow of Lauren's neck as she continued eating.

Lauren finished off her plate and put the dishes in the sink.

"You really are very beautiful," Catherine said as she watched. Her tone must have had the desired effect, because Lauren's head snapped around, one eyebrow sliding up.

"Catherine Ayers, are you flirting with me?"

"It's highly possible. We are still in the honeymoon phase, after all."

Lauren smiled, running water over the dishes. "No argument from me."

"Excellent. I happen to have a bed that's missing you."

"Not just the bed, I hope."

"Oh, definitely not." Catherine was rather proud of just how smoky her voice sounded.

A fork clattered into the sink. "God, woman, you're impossible to resist."

Catherine's fingers toyed with the top button on her shirt. "The dishes can wait. Wouldn't you say?"

Chapter 32
Fixed

LAUREN SAT IN THE FOYER of a spacious, luxurious office twenty-nine floors up that had no displayed name. It did, however, have a big logo on the gleaming chrome wall. A pentalobe.

"Our CEO will see you now," a middle-aged woman said, ushering her down the end of a long, bright hallway.

Lauren rose from the sofa. Her plan was so stupidly simple. The Fixers had fired Lesser. They had to be furious with him for turning informant on their clients. So, she'd simply ask the CEO for something on their traitorous ex-employee. The dirt didn't have to be on the record. It could be background information for her to tease out elsewhere. And maybe they'd be more than happy to hurt him by proxy, keeping their own hands clean. Actually, it sounded exactly like the sort of plan these political schemers would appreciate. Right up their alley.

Lauren glanced around. Whatever she'd expected from this shady seller of corporate and political advice and favors, this was not it. It was an airy, expensive office with lots of glass and impressive views. She came to a wooden door, which the assistant, walking ahead of Lauren, swung open in front of her.

"Ms. Lauren King's here," she announced. She turned and left, closing the door behind after Lauren stepped through.

A black leather executive chair faced the window. An odd, faint hiss filled the air. The desk was frosted glass with shiny steel legs. Perfectly neat piles of paperwork were stacked at one end.

"I suppose I'm not surprised you found us," a voice from the chair said. "But I'd half expected it would be Cat doing the visit." Spinning around, the chair came to face her. "Hello, again, Ms. King."

Lauren promptly sank into the visitor's seat opposite. "Michelle? You're the...you?"

"Who did you expect ran this organization?"

Lauren shook her head. "But aren't you the political contacts person?"

"I can be both."

"Oh."

"How did you find us?"

"Your address is on your secret website."

"Ah, I see. That security intrusion that had our former security head frothing a little while back. So that was you? Well, I suppose Lesser stitched you up in the usual manner? He always took any unauthorized access to the site he created as some sort of personal slight."

Lauren didn't bother agreeing to the obvious.

They regarded each other.

"I assume this is to be an off-the-record conversation?" Michelle asked. "Yes."

"This room has a white-noise dampening field in it, as well as some cutting-edge technology that will prevent any recording devices from working."

"I don't have any."

"How interesting." She cocked her head. "So why are you here?"

Lauren flattened her hands on the desk. "Before I get to that, I don't get it. Why have any role involving MediCache if you hated the idea of what it really does? You're in charge, so you could have ordered Lesser to shut his mouth and decline any request to create that software for Ansom."

"It was out of my hands from the start. Lesser independently came up with the idea of copying MediCache's veterans' data, after working with two organizations at separate times which used biosecurity tech—"

"Ansom and the FBI."

"I won't be confirming that. Anyway, my overambitious employee suggested to the bosses of each company that he'd had this great idea of how they could use each other. They did the deal between themselves. They were so enthusiastic when they saw its potential, and Lesser knew very well that I couldn't kick over their precious anthill. All I could do was ensure we continued in the role we were hired for."

"Which was what?"

"To assist in supporting MediCache being popularized. I had to sit on my hands and pretend I didn't know there was any more to it." She pursed her lips. "So no, *I* couldn't destroy that project, and in so doing, alienate a few major clients, but a reporter could expose it for the danger it was. Congratulations, by the way. Your story stopped a nightmare and also gave me grounds to fire Lesser."

"Couldn't you have fired him before then?"

"In the past, our directors, who are the only ones with the power to fire employees, have decided Lesser was too talented to lose, despite his unsavory leanings. But after your story, they decided he might be clever, but he was disloyal, and discretion is the number-one thing we promise our clients. So he was axed." Her smile was wide.

Suspicion filled Lauren. "Were you really bothered by MediCache? Or were you were just using it as a way to get rid of an employee you hated?"

"Really, Ms. King? You'd love that to be all there was to this, wouldn't you? You like the black hat, white hat thing, no pesky shades of gray. But I can hate a project for more than one reason."

Lauren tilted her head. "What other reasons did you have?"

Michelle waved her hand. "Irrelevant."

"Really? Can I guess?" She leaned forward. "I think you find it personally repugnant because you weren't lying when you said you're a student of history. You're Jewish. *Never again*, right?"

Surprise filtered across her face. "I am a little impressed Cat remembered that conversation, especially given neither of us were particularly sober that night. I shared a little more than I intended. But yes, you're right. Some lines should never be crossed. That one's mine." She laced her fingers again in front of her. "Now then, enough of me. Your turn. Why are you here?"

"I want Lesser."

"He's no longer in our employ. I fail to see—"

"He wants to run for office. Congress, probably. It's where the power is."

Michelle's lips thinned and surprised lanced her features. "I...see."

"He has dirt on powerful people, and he could get there."

"He not only could, he would." Her face became grim, and she drummed her fingers on the desk. "That cannot be allowed to happen."

"No, it can't. And honestly? We don't know how to stop him. I'm hoping maybe you have something we can use against him."

Michelle considered that for a moment. She leaned forward and hit an intercom button. "Tilly, can you bring me Lesser's package?"

As they waited, Michelle studied her. "You look good. Marriage suits you."

Lauren kept her face neutral. Did everyone know? Was it on some DC insiders' newsletter she should have subscribed to? "Thanks. You should try it sometime. Or…you know…again." She couldn't resist the dig.

Michelle's eyes narrowed to slits. "No thanks. Once was more than enough."

"Your ex-husband wanted us to ruin you, you know. Alberto was very hopeful we would succeed."

"I'll bet. And yet…you haven't." She shot her a curious look.

"We're catching sharks this week, not small-fry."

Michelle laughed. "How interesting you see us that way." She was surprisingly beautiful with her face relaxed like that.

Lauren felt the pang she usually did when she thought of all the ways this woman had used her charms to take advantage of Catherine. Her jaw went hard.

The assistant reappeared with a folder and an orange USB drive on top. "Thank you, Tilly."

The woman bustled out again.

Michelle looked at Lauren. "You had some hackers expose SmartPay, if I recall. Give them this." She pushed the thumb drive across the desk.

"What's on it?"

"Evidence Douglas Lesser created the SmartPay virus and was the one to release it."

"*He* did it?" That bastard.

"He did."

"Wasn't that virus created by order of the Fixers? Won't this get you into trouble?"

"Our only role in SmartPay was to bring together certain parties after the fact who were interested in whatever data the virus would net, and to provide security during the rollout to prevent certain other individuals getting in the way." She looked pointedly at Lauren. "Lesser built that virus before we'd ever heard of him. Although he did get subcontracted to be our IT expert based on his exceptional abilities in creating it."

"You took him on knowing he was a virus creator? How could you—"

"I wasn't CEO then. I wouldn't have said yes to that."

"I see." Lauren looked at the USB thumb drive.

"This is full circle for you, isn't it?" Michelle said after a moment. "Your first big break was the SmartPay story, and now you know the architect of the virus. You can put him away for decades with this information."

"Yes." Lauren turned the drive over in her hands, debating whether to ask what she most wanted to know. "Regarding Catherine…" She hesitated and looked up. "I realize you weren't the boss then, but what would have happened if you said no to the assignment on her?"

"Actually, I could have said no. I chose not to."

"Why?"

"She intrigued me. She was a very impressive figure in DC. A bold, passionate journalist, totally unafraid, who took no prisoners in her news stories. Her opinion pieces, too, were setting the place on fire. She was all anyone was talking about. Her fearlessness was such a breath of fresh air. She was someone I very much wanted to meet."

"You did a lot more than meet her."

"Yes." Michelle smirked, eyes becoming half-lidded. "I certainly did."

"So you just decided to mix business and pleasure? Because you were attracted to her? That it?"

"Attracted to her? I don't know if that's what it was exactly. But power is a draw in itself. She had so much power, and she didn't even realize it. She wasn't even aware of her greatness. It was heady being that close to her back then, at the peak of her fame. You wouldn't understand. You never met the Catherine I did—so pure in purpose and ambition, at the height of her glory. The Catherine you know isn't much like her. She's just…less radiant. Less powerful. *Less.*"

It was such a cruel barb. Uncertainty flooded Lauren—as Michelle no doubt intended. For a moment, she tensed, as doubts tap danced all around the edges of her mind. Her brain wanted to whisper that she'd never known the *real* Catherine.

But what was real?

Real was now. Real was the woman she married. The woman who loved her back. She was as real as whomever the woman was Michelle had dated.

She regarded the Fixers' CEO. It was odd, now that she thought of it—Michelle's occasionally belligerent, goading tone that she sometimes adopted. It was deliberately combative. Designed to hurt and mock.

Lauren considered it further. In fact, each time they met, Michelle went out of her way to upset them and try to make Lauren angry or jealous. She just kept pricking at her, teasing, slicing into her insecurities. She'd been especially rude the first time they'd met, at the State Fair.

But why? Why be needlessly rude? Maybe that was just who she was?

She turned that over and eyed Michelle, whose expression was more watchful than smug. No, she seemed too calculating and shrewd for that. It had to be deliberate. But why?

What does anger ever do for anyone?

Lauren thought hard. Angry people are off-balance. Angry people never see what's right in front of them. And they never ask the right questions or think of the obvious answers, because they're distracted by emotions. Blinded.

Oh.

Did she dare? Ask those questions and not get distracted? Lauren swallowed, drew in a deep breath, and asked the thing she most dreaded discussing. "Tell me how it happened. You getting involved with Catherine. Everything."

"You want all the gory details? Are you a voyeur? Is that your kink? My, my, I'm surprised at you." There was that goading tone again, but those still, wary eyes contained nothing playful in the least.

Lauren waited her out in silence, willing her hands not to curl into telltale balls of anxiety. "The details," she finally said, her voice as even as she could manage. "Tell me. I need to know."

Her lips curved, but Michelle's eyes were now darker. "You wouldn't want to know."

"I agree. Tell me anyway."

Michelle sighed and leaned back in her chair. "I suppose it doesn't matter anymore. Especially now." She rubbed her temple. "Catherine Ayers was delicious to study. The most impressive target I'd ever had to get to know. I admired her strut. Her confidence. I bumped into her, on purpose, of course, at a media Christmas drinks event in 2012. One thing led to another."

"So the seduction was deliberate?"

Michelle hesitated. "Quite the opposite, actually."

"Ah. You tripped and landed in her bed?" Lauren drawled.

"I…I had absolutely no idea she was gay." Michelle's eyes lifted to the ceiling. "Well, not until she kissed me on our third meeting. I didn't expect it, but suddenly…new possibilities presented themselves. I realized I could take advantage of that side of her. Accelerate things."

"You lead her to believe that you'd profiled her weaknesses in advance and worked out some big mastermind scheme and decided that seducing her was the best way to get her. Now you say it was an accident even finding out she was gay. So which was it? Why did you say any of that crap to her at the fair? You enjoy being heartless? Twisting the knife?" Lauren's tone turned cold. "Is that *your* kink?"

Michelle's nostrils flared.

For the first time, Lauren saw real anger in her eyes.

"I told Cat what she needed to hear," Michelle snapped. "Actually, I did her a favor. She could move on with her life, shoving me into a box marked 'pure bitch.' It's cleaner for her. Better." Her anger faded, and an odd look crossed her eyes.

Lauren stared. Why did Michelle care how Catherine felt? Why give her a moment's thought at all? A job was a job. In fact, she'd destroyed Catherine so well, she'd even been promoted. Was this guilt? But surely she'd done jobs like this before and not…

It took a moment before Lauren could finally identify that strange expression. "Oh." Lauren murmured. "I get it."

Michelle gave her a sharp look. "No, I doubt you do."

"Really? See from where I sit, it looks like you were some rising-star political consultant, with the good life, a husband at your side, ambition—everything's great until the day the new mark you admired so much suddenly kissed you." Lauren paused. "You felt something, didn't you?"

Michelle's face was awash in disbelief.

"And you couldn't stay away. Catherine Ayers was powerful and intriguing. You were supposed to just befriend her, but you wanted a taste of more. So you dated her and told yourself you were getting close *for the job*. And she was fascinating. Then the day came that you had to destroy her. But you're a professional, right? You went ahead and did your job. You ruined her. And it was utterly devastating." She paused. "But not just for Catherine."

Michelle had gone pale, perfectly still, her breathing shallow.

"You probably never meant to get involved," Lauren said softly. "Did you? You didn't even realize how deep in you were. It was some messy, awful mistake. One that you got so caught up in that it cost you your husband. You probably hated yourself for how unprofessional it all was. I mean, hell, what a lapse. There you were—paid to professionally assassinate the woman you'd accidentally just fallen in love with."

Loss flitted into Michelle's eyes. There was no denial.

"Know what I think?" Lauren said, even softer now. "You saw Catherine at the State Fair, and it reminded you of the awful thing you'd done. But you suddenly saw a way to kill two birds with one stone. You pushed Catherine toward the MediCache story to fix things. After all, that's what you do, isn't it? You're a fixer? It was a perfect solution—you'd blow up the data chip scheme, which you hated, and you could give Catherine a national exclusive that was actually true this time—which is what you'd promised her last time. You'd get absolution. All that guilt you endure every day, gone." Lauren's laugh was dry. "And the irony is, she turned around and gave that story away to me. Bet you didn't see that coming."

Michelle's eyes narrowed. "Such wild speculation. You can't possibly know anything I feel."

"Oh, but that's where you're wrong." Lauren leaned forward. "Because I've kissed her, too. It's not something you soon forget. That passion she has for her job? She shares with her lovers, doesn't she? She puts everything she has into someone she cares for. So, yes, I think you fell in love with your target, then you broke her in the worst possible way. And it's probably eaten you alive ever since."

Michelle's face became stony. "So, who are you going to tell your interesting theory to?"

Lauren's eyebrow lifted. "You're afraid I might tell Catherine?"

"If you truly love her, sharing this ridiculous tale could only harm her more. Wouldn't you agree that it's cleanest if she simply hates me?" Michelle's look was intense.

It wasn't a bad point. Lauren thought about that as she glanced around the room. No framed photos. No knickknacks or signs of family or loved ones. Her gaze settled on Michelle's bare ring finger. She looked back at the closed features across from her. The woman was clearly unsettled.

"Is there no one else?" Lauren asked quietly.

Michelle said nothing.

"Has there even been anyone else since her?"

"That is *none* of your business." There was heat behind it. Her eyes flashed, telling her the answer.

"I could expose you, you know." Lauren waved at the room. "Sleeping with a woman just to destroy her is terrible. I could expose what your company does in general. It might not be illegal, the guidance you give your clients, but it's highly immoral. That'd be nice revenge, wouldn't it? Me splashing your secrets everywhere as payback for what you did to Catherine. You'd lose everything."

Her face grew even paler.

"But you know what? I don't have to ruin you. When I look at you, I see a sad woman who already has lost everything but her pathetic job. Tell me something: was it worth it?"

Michelle scowled at her, eyes flashing. It was the most emotion Lauren had ever seen from her.

"Mmm, that's what I thought. Sucks to be you." Lauren shook her head. "My God, you had *Catherine Ayers* and you threw her away. For what? A CEO job and a nice view? That's nuts. So I can answer your question for you. It wasn't worth it. And the worst part is I can see you know it, too."

The pain in Michelle's eyes was bordering on uncomfortable to witness. Lauren didn't want to look at it anymore. She stood and made her exit, hearing Michelle pivot her chair back to face the window to gaze out of her soulless glass tower.

An empty person in an empty office. What a fitting pair.

326

Chapter 33
What Goes Around

Eight Months Later

CATHERINE CHECKED HER WATCH AS she made her way to the White House briefing room. She nodded at the familiar face of the security guard, who didn't bother to check the laminated credentials that she held up.

"Good to see you again, Ms. Ayers," he said. "I think you're a bit late, though. They're wrapping up."

"It's fine, Robert. I'm not here on business today," she said before slipping into the room.

"And finally," the White House chief of staff's voice was droning on, "we want to highlight the arrest of US fugitive Douglas Malcolm Lesser. Mr. Lesser was believed to be hiding out in Saigon, Vietnam, since news broke about him being wanted in connection with creating the SmartPay virus. We'd like to confirm earlier reports that he was arrested in Australia, at 02:30 local time. He is fighting the extradition, claiming he is innocent and targeted for being a whistleblower. We expect him stateside to face charges within the week."

A sea of hands began to shoot up.

In the second row, third from the right, Lauren raised her hand, too.

The chief of staff scanned the room. "It seems only fair we hear from the reporter whose story sparked Mr. Lesser's arrest warrant and subsequent manhunt." He pointed at Lauren.

Catherine smiled from her spot against the wall.

"Lauren King, *The Washington Post*. Is there any truth to the rumor Lesser was found hiding out in a trailer park in Broome, Western Australia?"

"That is correct."

"So a spyware scam man on the lam in Vietnam was caught in a trailer in Australia?" Lauren suggested, humor filling her tone. Her eyebrow arched.

The room broke into laughter at the unexpected rhyme. Even the chief of staff's fixed expression wobbled slightly.

Catherine snorted. The man hadn't cracked a smile for years.

"Something like that," he said. "And I can see our newest member of the White House Press Corps intends to be an entertaining presence for us." He cleared his throat. "All right, that's it for today. Check your inboxes later. We'll be sending President Taylor's schedule for his Asia-Pacific tour by two. See Sue about seat allocations."

The room broke up. A few reporters turned to Lauren and introduced themselves on the way out, laughing about her unorthodox question.

Catherine made her way over to her. "Quite the icebreaker," she said, as they dispersed. "My first question in here was some earnest dross about a possible error in the budget. It was important, but no one remembers it."

"That was my intention," Lauren said. "Getting noticed. I know I'm only filling in while Max is on leave, and even then it's only because Lesser story's getting White House attention, but maybe one day this will be my beat."

"And you're off to a good start. Which is why I'm here. Come on, I'm taking you to lunch to celebrate your debut press corps briefing. Hope you don't mind a little walk."

"Sure. Lead on."

They made their way out of the building.

Lauren's eyes widened when she realized where they were going. "So we're re-creating history?" she asked. "How romantic."

"Perish the thought. I just liked the symmetry of it," Catherine countered, as they entered the gardens and found their old seat in Bartholdi Park. "Huge nymph fountains and all. This is where your story began. Us sitting right here when that ridiculous robot rolled up."

"Ooh." Lauren looked around. "Is Antonio's delivering something tasty today?"

"No." Catherine reached into her bag and pulled out two sandwiches from bags stamped with Lauren's favorite eatery. "I thought we'd go back to basics."

"Leaf Long and Prosper? I love their BLT sandwiches. Plus, hello, *Star Trek* joke. Thanks."

Catherine smiled and pushed one over, made to Lauren's specifications. It contained a lot more B than LT.

Naturally, Lauren dug in happily.

"So tell me," Catherine asked, as she reached for her own sandwich, "why would Lesser leave Vietnam, which has no extradition treaty, and go somewhere unsafe for him? He had to know the US would demand his return if he bobbed up somewhere like Australia?"

Lauren shrugged. "I guess even smart bastards like him get bored in exile and need a vacation. But you know what this means? We did it! They're all facing justice now."

"Except for Michelle. She never paid for anything."

Lauren looked at her wife and felt a stab of shame. Damn. She really should have talked to her about this before now. She'd kept putting it off, thinking Michelle had been right all along—consigning herself to the role of clean-cut villain was less messy and would make it easier for Catherine to put the memory behind her.

"All right, what is it?" Catherine asked. "You suddenly look guilty as hell."

"Would it help if you thought Michelle felt bad about what she did to you?" Lauren asked, trying to sound light. "Would it improve your life, if, for instance, you'd found out she had cared about you?"

"She didn't. She made that very clear."

"Her ex-husband thought she did."

"Alberto wanted reasons to hate her."

"Sure, but let's just say you knew for a fact that you mattered to her and it wasn't all a scam. Would that improve your life?"

Catherine thought about that. "Yes. I think a little bit."

Lauren took a deep breath. She could see the rapidly fluttering pulse at Catherine's neck. Oh hell. She really shouldn't have kept this secret. She'd given Catherine such a hard time for deciding things for Lauren. How was what she'd done any better these past months?

"You know how I told you I went to the Fixers for dirt on Lesser, and Michelle turned out to be the CEO?" Lauren said.

"Yes."

"We didn't just discuss Lesser."

Catherine stared at her and then put down her sandwich. "Oh." Her voice turned chilly.

"I worked out she has feelings for you. Both then and now."

Skepticism filled Catherine's eyes. "Unlikely."

"She admitted that seducing you wasn't some scheme to get to you. It was an accident. She didn't even know you were gay until you kissed her."

Catherine's gaze bored into her.

"And you're wrong—she didn't get off scot-free," Lauren continued. "She lost her husband. She lost you. I don't think she has anyone in her life, now or since. She's...sad. Empty. And yes, that's all on her, her bad choices. And I also believe, in part, she gave you that story to try and make amends. So, do you get how amazing you have to be to make someone doing a hit on you fall for you so hard that she forgets herself? Don't you see? You weren't the fool. If anything, she was."

"You forget how she was to me in Iowa." Catherine's words were rasped out. "She didn't hide her disdain. Her words were cruel."

"Yes, they were. Exactly as she intended. She thought if she was hurtful, you'd hate her and move on. But Catherine, Michelle was *never* indifferent to you. When she betrayed you, she broke inside, too. But the karmic kick of it all is, I think she's still broken, while you've gone on to have an awesome life."

The anger in Catherine's eyes that was always there whenever her past came up seemed to fade. She nudged her sandwich around on its flattened paper bag.

"I'm sorry I didn't tell you sooner," Lauren said. "I thought it'd help not having her messing up your head again. It was wrong. I should have."

Looking up, Catherine said quietly, "Yes, you should have. But I also know why you didn't. I'm...glad you told me now. This will take a bit of processing, I think."

Her shoulders eased a little. Then a little more.

"You know," Lauren said, "for the first time since I've known you, you look completely relaxed."

"That's not true. I think I've been slowly relaxing ever since I met you. There's just something about you that lowers all my defenses. I think you may have me under some sort of spell so I'll put up with your awful tractor cap, that beast of a car that you drive way too fast, and your crazy Iowan family."

"Oh, please, you love all of that stuff. I know you had fun at Christmas, no matter how much you protest otherwise. You got that huffy cat all over you again, Meemaw let you help her cook, and John and Lucas were off driving around Route 66, finding themselves or whatever the hell they're up to, so you didn't have to put up with my most annoying brother."

Catherine's lips curled. "That was a decided plus."

"You also got to watch the hilarious spectacle of Tad attempting softball—badly. And the excitement of dodging Josh while he was trying to take photos of you for his Facebook page. What'd he tag those pics of you? 'Hashtag unironicallyinIowa?'"

"Pure defamation. Especially the 'cornfedchic' hashtag. I have no idea what Thadeus sees in that boy." The softness in her tone gave her away, though.

"The same thing you see in me." Lauren elbowed her. "We remind you you're alive. And besides, we're far more fun than an Ayers family gathering."

"That you are. I'm grateful you offered Tad somewhere to escape to so he could avoid a toxic family Christmas."

"Is it still bad?"

"I don't even know where to start. Tad's father's having some sort of midlife crisis. And my father's trying to settle out of court over the harassment claims, and he's got the DA tied up in legal knots over MediCache. Meanwhile, Phoebe is running around with her hair on fire, trying to claim everything is a setup and no one is guilty. Of anything. At all."

"Oh, hell. Well, maybe don't focus on that. Just focus on you. On how everything is working out for you these days."

Catherine smiled. "It's working out for you, too. At least for a month, you're finally where you've always wanted to be."

"In the White House press corps." Lauren beamed. "Which makes me your direct rival." She slid her an impish look. "Do you love it that we're in the trenches together again? Or is it the rivals bit you like most?"

"What an interesting question." Eyes bright with amusement, Catherine added, "I'm sure that's where we came in."

"Yeah, we're back where it all began—circling each other. Only with more politics now."

"And fewer goats." Catherine smirked.

"Hey! Come on, your goat story on me was such crap. Stop milking it."

"Goat puns, King?" Catherine teased. "Whatever do you do for an encore?" She leaned over and curled a loose hair around Lauren's ear. "Truthfully? I love that we're on the same beat again. I can't imagine anything better than taking you on again."

"Me, either." Lauren quirked her eyebrows. "But remember, I won't go so easy on you this time."

Catherine's eyes lit up. "I expect nothing less. In fact"—she lowered her voice to a pleased murmur—"I really can't wait. Ayers and King, matching wits again."

"*King* and Ayers." Lauren gave her a playful look. "Watch out, world."

About Lee Winter

Lee Winter is an award-winning veteran newspaper journalist who has lived in almost every Australian state, covering courts, crime, news, features and humour writing. Now a full-time author and part-time editor, Lee is also a 2015 and 2016 Lambda Literary Award finalist and has won two Golden Crown Literary Awards. She lives in Western Australia with her long-time girlfriend, where she spends much time ruminating on her garden, US politics, and shiny, new gadgets.

CONNECT WITH LEE
Website: www.leewinterauthor.com

Other Books from Ylva Publishing

www.ylva-publishing.com

The Red Files

(*On The Record series – Book 1*)

Lee Winter

ISBN: 978-3-95533-330-0
Length: 365 pages (103,000 words)

Ambitious journalist Lauren King is stuck reporting on the vapid LA social scene's gala events while sparring with her rival—icy ex-Washington correspondent Catherine Ayers. Then a curious story unfolds before their eyes, involving a business launch, thirty-four prostitutes, and a pallet of missing pink champagne. Can the warring pair join together to unravel an incredible story?

The Music and the Mirror

Lola Keeley

ISBN: 978-3-96324-014-0
Length: 311 pages (120,000 words)

Anna is the newest member of an elite ballet company. Her first class almost ruins her career before it begins. She must face down jealousy, sabotage, and injury to pour everything into opening night and prove she has what it takes. In the process, Anna discovers that she and the daring, beautiful Victoria have a lot more than ballet in common.

Chasing Stars
(*The Superheroine Collection*)

Alex K. Thorne

ISBN: 978-3-95533-992-0
Length: 205 pages (70,000 words)

For superhero Swiftwing, crime fighting isn't her biggest battle. Nor is it having to meet the whims of Hollywood star Gwen Knight as her mild-mannered assistant, Ava. It's doing all that, while tracking a giant alien bug, being asked to fake date her famous boss, and realizing that she might be coming down with a pesky case of feelings.

A fun, sweet, sexy lesbian romance about the masks we wear.

The Lily and the Crown

Roslyn Sinclair

ISBN: 978-3-95533-942-5
Length: 263 pages (87,000 words)

Young botanist Ari lives an isolated life on a space station, tending a lush garden in her quarters. When an imperious woman is captured from a pirate ship and given to her as a slave, Ari's ordered life shatters. Her slave is watchful, smart, and sexy, and seems to know an awful lot about tactics, star charts, and the dread pirate queen, Mir.

A lesbian romance about daring to risk your heart.

Under Your Skin
© 2018 by Lee Winter

ISBN: 978-3-96324-026-3

Also available as e-book.

Published by Ylva Publishing, legal entity of Ylva Verlag, e.Kfr.

Ylva Verlag, e.Kfr.
Owner: Astrid Ohletz
Am Kirschgarten 2
65830 Kriftel
Germany

www.ylva-publishing.com

First edition: 2018

This is a work of fiction. Names, characters, places, and incidents either are a product of the author's imagination or are used fictitiously, and any resemblance to locales, events, business establishments, or actual persons—living or dead—is entirely coincidental.

Credits
Edited by Michelle Aguilar and Amanda Jean
Proofread by Paulette Callen
Cover Design and Print Layout by Streetlight Graphics

Made in the USA
Lexington, KY
18 June 2018